Convict Shadows

OF THE

Past

Sara Powter

Bible Quotes from King James Version

ISBN: 9780645783315
Paperback

Pacific Wanderland Publications
ABN 99 768 734 831

Kincumber NSW 2251

saragpowter@gmail.com
www.sarapowter.com.au

1st edition 2023 printed by Kindle, an Amazon Company;
available on Kindle Unlimited & KDP

Acknowledgement of Country:
In the spirit of reconciliation, I acknowledge the Traditional Custodians of
country throughout Australia and their connections to land, sea and
community. We pay our respect to their Elders, past and present and extend
that respect to all Aboriginal and Torres Strait Islander peoples today.

Australian Historical Novels

A First Fleet Story (1788)
Gentle Annie Soames *(2024)*

The Hunter to Macquarie Trilogy (1795-1820)
When Upon Life's Billows *(2025)*
Saddler's Song *(2025)*
Tuppence to Pass *(2025)*

Unlikely Convict Ladies Trilogy (1790s - 1840s)
Dancing to her Own Tune
(co-authored by Sheila Hunter & Sara Powter)
Amelia's Tears
A Lady in Irons

The Lockleys of Parramatta (1800-1900)
Hands Upon the Anvil
Out Where the Brolgas Dance
Diamonds in the Dirt
The Earl's Shadow
Once a Jolly Swagman
Jonty's Journey

The Convict Stain Collection (1830s -1840s)
(All stand-alone books)
No More, My Love
The Vine Weaver
Scotch at The Rocks {*Sequel to The Vine Weaver*}
Waiting at the Sliprails
Convict Shadows of the Past
(The following are coming soon)
In Defence of Her Honour *(2024)*
I Can't Stop Tomorrow *(2024)*
Madeline's Boy *(2024)*
Jam or Marmalade for Tea *(2025)*

Shelia Hunter's
Australian Colonial Trilogy (1840s- 1850s)
Mattie
Ricky {*Jonty's Journey is a sequel*}
The Heather to the Hawkesbury

Between 1788 and 1868,
one hundred and sixty-two thousand
convicts were transported to Australia.

Seven of these were direct ancestors of ours.
More convicts married their siblings or children.
This story closely follows my history about the discovery of our
convicts and the struggles they faced as they managed to survive.
Much of their history is gruesome (which I try to avoid),
but they survived, if not thrived.

In 1820, the dairy industry really started in earnest in Australia. The quality of
the cheeses improved almost overnight. Dr Harris had the first commercial
dairy in Ultimo Sydney, followed by settlement on the NSW South Coast, but
the milk was shipped to Sydney. Bathurst also had a growing dairy industry,
and Captain and Mrs Piper and a Scottish couple, Mr and Mrs Rankin,
made cheeses of renown from the 1820s onwards.
But it got me thinking: who taught them?
By 1840, the South Coast of NSW dairy industry had taken off
and never looked back.

As I wrote this book, I spent part of the week next to one of these early dairies.
It is still a functional business that supplies milk
to the cheese factory at Bega NSW.

Thank you!
To Stephen, my wonderful husband, who is always so supportive.
Thank you from the bottom of my heart.

Thanks, too, to Roby Aiken
who patiently corrects my punctuation errors,
and Noreen Robertson and Linda Upcroft,
my Beta readers and Street Team.

This book was written in November 2022 as part of the NaNoWriMo competition.
(NaNoWriMo = National Novel Writers Month)
The first 50k words were completed in a mere two weeks.
The story just flowed.

However…
A visit to the Parramatta Female Factory inspired it,
where I saw two crosses carved into stone blocks in the airing yard.

I wondered about how many fingers had worn these smooth
over the past two hundred years?

Author's Note

W hen I was eight, in 1968, my grandfather came to live with us. He had recently sold the family home and farm (an orchard, not a dairy), and now in his eighties and somewhat ill, he was bored.

My parents had always loved his stories about his childhood, but I had not heard them. Now that he was to live with us, I knew I could not escape the boring talks.

However, the morning after he arrived, things changed. I finally listened to him chat and was astounded at what I heard. Now, I would sit quietly, wide-eyed with anticipation knowing more stories would be told. Bushrangers, convicts, floods, fires and danger all were discussed, and over the months he was with us, a passion for my family history unfolded into a lifelong obsession.

My mother suggested that he write these down to while away his days while he lived with us. She purchased a dozen exercise books and a small box of lead pencils, enabling him to capture his stories. Each day, over morning tea, we would sit and discuss how his writing was going. The stories drew me closer to him and planted a seed for learning more about our convict history. Unfortunately, he died later that year, but the seed was sown. We joined the Society of Australian Genealogists in Kent Street, Sydney.

A visit to two of my father's maiden aunts followed, and it was there we discovered the existence of four convicts. These two aged ladies had all the convict paperwork but refused to show it to us. They were horrified that we might discover our criminal past. So, sadly, after our visit, they burned everything. *(I still cry over this!)*

A few years later, Old Sydney Town at Somersby NSW opened (1975), and my school and many others in our area went to the official opening in costume. To step back in time to those early colonial days was amazing. As everyone was in costume, we all looked the part of waifs, convicts and strays. There were soldiers in red coats and blasts of cannon fire. A convict was strapped to a whipping post and flogged. Blood and gore splattered the audience (only red ink). But I wept! I felt like I was there, living through what my ancestors lived through. When it closed in 2003, many Central Coast locals were upset. In 2012, a Facebook group started, and I ended up as President of the "Bring Back Old Sydney Town" group. I am still working to see it re-open.

One of the Piper family descendants has given me a few bits of info and that Mrs Piper did most of the cheesemaking. I was also informed that they took their skill to Bathurst.

After visiting the Parramatta Female Factory in October 2022, I touched crosses on the wall and saw the blocks my ancestors touched and walked where they walked, and those feelings returned.

The echoes of the past were still tangible, and the story of the two Jennifers was born.

Sara Powter

Table of Contents

The grammar and language in this book are
Australian English spelling.

KEY
~ - Time passing in the same locality

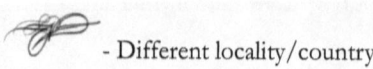 - Different locality/country

Chapter 1   Jenny Kellow 1968

*E*ight-year-old Jenny Kellow wasn't so sure about the old man coming to live with them. He was grumpy and always told her to be quiet when he was around. His arrival in the big car saw her slink into her room and quietly close the door. She would rather disappear into a book rather than face him and be yelled at again to quieten down. She loved stories; her mother would sit and read to her each night before sleeping. Jenny knew she would need to appear for dinner, but that was some time away; in the meantime, the words of another adventure awaited. She was reading the *Muddleheaded Wombat* and wondered what he would get up to next. She loved Mouse and Tabby Cat and identified with the poor Wombat quite a lot, as he often thought that no one was ever as silly as he was. Jenny felt the same; even her teachers told her mother she "doesn't try hard enough" or "needs help with her reading." They never said anything good or nice about her. They never complimented her when she helped others or if she tried her best. No, all they did was pick on her. Pick, pick, pick! So she withdrew further inside herself. She wanted to make herself invisible and rarely spoke in class unless forced. Jenny hated school. She hated being picked on and unable to keep up with the other kids in class.

She heard noises and realised it was the arrival of her grandfather, aunt and uncle. Ignoring them, she returned to her book. The sounds faded away as the words of the story turned into pictures in her mind.

Dinner that night came far too quickly.

Jenny had finished that story and two more. She had just picked up *Snuggle Pot and Cuddle Pie* when her mother called her to help prepare the dinner.

For once, dinner passed without any derogatory comments, and she knew that she would get used to her grandfather's presence, but hopefully, it wasn't always her who did the backing down about something.

After dinner, Jenny politely said goodnight to her parents, aunt, uncle and even her grandfather, then snuck off. With a huff, she went to bed without her mother having time to read to her.

~

Morning tea was a time for everyone to gather upstairs. It was at ten every day, and visitors knew it was a good time to call in for a visit. Today, there was just the family.

Jenny's job was to put the biscuits out in a little wooden bowl and make sure everyone had enough to eat. The biscuits today were some of her favourites. Mum had made cornflake cookies and also Anzac biscuits. Hopefully, they would not eat them all.

It was Saturday morning, and there was no school. Jenny completed her chores before ten. She always helped her mother with the wringer washing machine, and it took two of them to wash the couple of loads and hang it on the old wire clothesline. Gramps was left to her aunt and uncle. Dad was due home at lunchtime, but Jenny had to be good and help in the meantime.

Celia placed the tray on the coffee table, and Jenny handed out the mugs. Trying to be invisible, she took a chair to the side and sat to listen to the ordinarily dull conversation. However, two words caught her attention: bushrangers and convicts.

She couldn't help asking, "Gramps, what do bushrangers and convicts have to do with our family?"

Gramps smiled at me. "Jenny dearest, our family has some amazing stories about bushrangers. We even have convicts in the family. Grandma Sylvia has four in her bloodline, but there are stories of floods, fires, and the early days of settlement in the colony. And, of course, there is the dairy and cheeses. Have you not heard about the convicts? Do you know you are named after one?"

She shook her head; her eyes were nearly popping out of her sockets. He now had her full attention. She didn't even notice that everyone else was looking at her. For once, she didn't care. She wanted to know who the person was; she wanted to know everything.

What followed changed her attitude towards the old man. It also changed her life.

The old man sat reminiscing for a while, then said, "I believe the first Jennifer had a flair for making cheese; however, more than that, or how she got here is a mystery to me. I don't even know where she came from or her crime. I remember my Uncle Chris used to say there was some shadow of a conviction hanging over her, but I have no idea what he meant."

Chapter 2   Jennifer Kellow 1799

October 1799 in Newlyn, Cornwall, saw the birth of a long-awaited daughter for a tin mining family. Jennifer was the seventh child of the Kellows and their first daughter. Her six older brothers were all destined to work in the tin mine in Madron near Penwith with their father. This was near Newlyn and Penzance on the southern tip of the Cornish coast. These mines were reportedly the oldest working tin mines in Cornwall. Three mines were close to each other: *Good Fortune, Wheal Malkin,* and *Hard Shafts Bounds.* Tradition said the merchant, Joseph of Arimathea, once visited this area with Jesus. Jennifer, of course, knew nothing of this. Other mines dug copper and lead, but Jennifer's family had chosen to work the closest one, and that was for tin. The lead mines were known to be far too dangerous to one's health. Jacob would not permit his family to work in them.

As the first girl after six boys, Jennifer was adored by her family and their neighbours. Her parents, Phoebe and Jacob, loved the bubbly baby. She was one of those children who cooed and giggled when any other child would cry or demand attention. Her brothers adored playing with her, and the youngest one, Alfie, delighted in keeping her occupied.

~

By the time she was three, Jennifer's four eldest brothers, Logan, Oscar, Samuel, and Leo, were walking the four miles to the tin mine each morning, and they would come home at the end of a tough day, coughing and covered in filth. Jennifer hugged them and gave them some milk from the dairy next door. Often, they were so tired they didn't even wash before falling asleep, soot-faced, and in their work clothing.

Jennifer's life in the small, overcrowded cottage was as idyllic as a toddler of the time could expect. A very expectant Phoebe would watch five-year-old Alfie and three-year-old Jennifer as she spun yarn with her spindle. The little girl already knew how to tease out the fibres of the fleece and comb it for her mother to use. She had become Phoebe's helper.

~

By six, Jennifer had a little sister, Isla, who was nearly four and another brother, Kitto, the latest newborn infant. Jennifer loved helping cook and, with help, could whip up a meal for all eleven family members. Her mama would make the pastry and filling, then leave the assembling of the vegetable pasties to her. Seven of these needed to be made daily for the boys' work lunches. She did a lovely job of rolling and making the beautifully crafted pasties. Her fingers deftly twisted the edges together and curled the ends into handles. Occasionally, they would have some meat, like a rabbit, to add to the filling, but mostly, it was just a potato-rich stuffing. The pastry was glazed with a beaten egg before placing in the oven. She had burned them a few times when she started helping; now, she knew to ensure the heat was just right before putting them in to bake. She loved it when they came out perfectly golden brown all over.

Her father, Jacob, had managed to source some canvas water bags so the boys could have water to drink down in the hot but wet mines. The frigid conditions above ground were often reversed five hundred feet down the shaft. Someone had once mentioned to Jennifer that the temperature was over one hundred degrees underground. She did not understand how hot that was, but she realised the work was backbreaking because the boys always came home filthy and exhausted.

When Alfie turned seven, he had to go and work in the tin mines with Papa and the other boys. Jennifer missed him. He and Oliver had to push the big trolleys along the tracks in the tin mine. It was better than digging the hard granite, but this could also be dangerous. The older boys and men dug at the mine wall. Granite was hard, and they often sent rock chips flying into the eyes or cutting them as the shards flew past. In some mines, ponies hauled the heavy carts, but in their mine, it was children who did this hard labour. A rope was also attached to each trolley, and a pulley tugged the carts up the hills; however, the ropes were often old and frayed. And all the men would come home with new cuts and scrapes.

Jennifer learned how to doctor these with homemade gin. Alfie had nearly lost some fingers last week when a trolley had rolled back onto him. He had managed to pull his arms in, but the side of his hand had been grazed. Jennifer treated him, and the wound didn't infect. Thankfully, there was now a wagon that collected the miners from their village, and the trip was now only twenty minutes, so the boys no longer needed to walk to and from the mine.

~

With another sibling due soon, Jennifer, now ten, knew that the bulk of the work would fall on her shoulders. For some reason, her Mama wasn't well this time. Jennifer knew she should have been sent out to work long ago, but Mama could not cope alone. The dairy down the road had offered her a job, and she had accepted a morning shift. Mr Bryn Williams was a nice man and understood that she had responsibilities at home. She loved the big cows, and their warmth on a cold morning was nice. Isla was old enough to come but had to help Mama until the new baby arrived.

Jennifer always had Papa and the boys' lunches ready for them, and it was her job to be up to stoke the fire and make them breakfast. She would leave the porridge and cream prepared for them and do an hour's milking before the little ones were awake. Usually, she would be back before the wagon collected the men.

Phoebe was tired. Tired of being so big, tired of trying to make ends meet, and tired of the squabbling small children. Isla was helpful, but she missed Jennifer in the mornings. Some days, her feet were so swollen that they hurt when she first put them on the ground. Ten confinements were telling on her body, and she wished there was some way to stop her from falling with child, but she adored Jacob, and her body cried out for his loving touch. He was the best of men, and she craved the closeness of their intimate times together. He was normally so tired when he came home in the evening that he would wash, eat, and sleep. However, the mine was closed on Sundays, and the family would all attend church. This meant they would all have a bath on Saturday night. Once their children were in bed, they finally had some privacy and could sate their desires.

By the time Pascoe was born on Easter Day in 1807, Jennifer had taken over the cooking at dinnertime as well as breakfast preparation. Isla was now helping with the afternoon milking at Mr Williams's farm. Two-year-old Kitto was helping Mama with the fleece preparation and spinning. Papa had been able to buy Mama a proper spinning wheel instead of her using a spindle, and she could now turn the fluffy rolags of fibre into spun single-strand thread much faster. Papa had also made her a stand that took three full bobbins so she could make thick balls of yarn and then knit pullovers for all the family. With so many in the house, it was a never-ending job.

The daily grind of work never seemed to get the family further ahead.

With more children arriving every few years, the eldest ones would soon need to leave and start their own homes.

~

By 1810, Polly was the latest arrival, and Jennifer, now eleven, had handed her household chores to Isla. At Mr Williams's request, Jennifer was currently employed full-time at the dairy and was a dab hand at making cheeses. This job was a delight, and it certainly beat pushing full mine carts half-naked in the semi-darkness of the tin mines. Jennifer loved the dairy work. She loved the cows and the earthy smells.

After the dawn milking, she would set it aside for the cream to rise, then skim off the set flakes of the thick yellowy substance from the previous milking. The remaining fluid still had plenty of cream, so it was ladled into milk cans for sale. The skimmed milk would be filled from the large vat, and the cans loaded onto the milk cart. Mr Williams would drive his small cart around the village selling the milk to the households in the area.

~

1814

Four years later, Mr Williams now employed Leo Kellow to do the milk run. Jennifer often found that Mr William's son Billy arrived in time to walk her home each evening, especially if she worked late.

After ten hours, the milk was skimmed and poured into the big urns. With Jennifer's help in cheese making, they produced more. Mr Williams had been able to buy two Channel Islands cows. They were big, honey-coloured, gentle beasts called Guernseys. Their extra creamy milk significantly improved the cheese they made.

The afternoon milking would be turned into cheese as they had more time to work on it. The fresh milk would be heated to the correct temperature, and then the culture would be added. The milk would set into a giant jelly-like block, which would then need to be diced with the special wire cutter paddles and then set to strain in the cheesecloth lined moulds. As the dairy made a hard cheese, the dicing of the curd needed to be very small. So, it was time-consuming as she needed to make sure it was even.

Now fourteen, Jennifer was strong enough to do this process by herself. Once it was all cut, she had to scoop up the curds and place them in their cheesecloth-lined moulds. Then, she had to wait for the excess whey to drain away. Doing this was a pleasant job. She took pride in ensuring all the wheels were a uniform weight. Each batch of curd made about three big wheels of cheese. Each of these cheese moulds was then placed on a rack to drain. When the initial draining was done, the first full mould would be placed in the cheese press. The wooden press was set over a dish to catch the whey. This process took about twenty minutes before it was ready to turn out and set aside.

The time between milking was spent sorting and preparing the previous days' cheeses. Each press needed to be scrubbed clean before using for the next day's work. Then, she needed to start all over again. The timber presses were cleaned, dried and set aside, ready for use the following day. Once the new cheese was removed from the mould, the top of the cheesecloth needed to be trimmed, folded over, and made neat. The cheeses were then placed inside the cave to mature. Each one would be hand-covered in a thin film of lard, and this process needed to be repeated over every cheese in the storeroom.

The task of cheese rubbing was time-consuming, and unless they sold a lot of wheels quickly, more of the family would be needed to assist in the rubbing. Jennifer had already been teaching Isla to assist her. Rubbing with their hands made the fat spread evenly over the rind. It was to protect them from contamination. They were then set aside to ripen. This occurred in an enormous cellar that was lined floor to ceiling with shelves.

The cellar, or cheese cave, stayed the same temperature all year round. It had hundreds of wheels of cheese in it already. Each needed rubbing to keep the blooms of mould at bay. On Saturdays and Sundays, the milking was done but sold as full cream. On these days, an Italian lady gave grooming and deportment lessons to the girls on Saturdays. Sunday mornings were spent at church, followed by Sunday school. Jennifer loved these sessions so much that she forfeited her free time to learn more from the minister. He was teaching her languages.

Every week, Mr Williams would check his product and choose a batch of cheese to send off to the local market. Once a month, some were sent to London for sale at the markets there.

Mr Williams found that selling his big cheese wheels was almost a saturated market. As they now had a bit of a glut of product, he permitted Jennifer to use some of the now excess morning's milk to experiment with some flavourings.

After discussions with her Italian friend, Jennifer made a mixture of various herbs and made brine flavourings and then added them after the initial curd stage. Making sure she labelled them carefully, she made small batches of cheeses and set them aside from the bulk of the storeroom so as not to taint the main stock. One had a caramelised onion flavour; another was a butter sautéed garlic, and the third used stinging nettles. As she had some of each brine left over, she combined them and made a fourth cheese. This had a mixture of the three flavours. Small moulds were used, and she made sure that she rubbed these after she had done all the other cheeses, ensuring no cross-contamination of cultures or flavours.

They needed to mature for a year to ripen properly as they were to be hard cheeses. The flavour would need to be tested at about six months. Like the regular cheese, they still needed to be handled by turning them and rubbing them regularly.

~

The year passed with the stock in the cave growing, but the sales had plateaued. It was still a worthwhile venture as the £9 a month well and truly covered the costs of Jennifer and Isla's wages and still made some profit.

Towards the end of summer, Jennifer's first flavoured cheeses were ready for tasting. She was keen for Mr Williams to tell her what her products tasted like, but she was afraid to ask. She knew he would try them soon but had not told her when.

One morning, towards the end of August, Mr Williams came into the dairy and called her to follow him. She liked him, but this morning his voice was gruff. She followed with some trepidation, wondering what she had done wrong. Had her cheeses gone off or contaminated the stock? She tripped along behind him, following the cobbled pathway to the farm. He led them into the cheese cave. However, he stopped in front of her cheeses. She noted that each had a core sample taken from them and wondered if today was the day she would find out if her experiment had worked.

Mr Williams abruptly stopped and turned to face her with a beaming smile. "Jennifer Kellow, do you have any idea what you have done?"

Jennifer shook her head somewhat timidly. "Did you try them? Are they mature now?"

Mr Williams was holding out his hand for her to shake. "Jennifer, they are superb. They are as good as any imported Gouda cheese I have eaten, but these have a unique flavour. Can you make more? Big ones this time?"

She nodded. She was feeling giddy with relief. She had not done anything wrong. And no stock was ruined.

He stood looking around the immense storeroom. "I'll have to add a partition, like a waxed curtain, to keep the flavoured cheeses from the plain ones, but I think you have a winner here. Your first three kinds of cheese have a mellow taste when they first touch your tongue, but then the hint of the seasoning hits with an incredible explosion of what I describe as pure luxury. The nettle one has a bit of a bite to it, too, but I would like to add a bit of pepper to that one. I think the two would work well together. As an after-dinner cheese, they are incredible." His smile was reassuring.

She swallowed nervously. "And the other one?"

He turned to the triple-flavoured wheel. He had obviously not tasted this one yet. "I haven't tried it yet. If this is as good as I expect it to be, my dear, I shall give you a percentage of all the sales on all four flavours. You have done all the work, and this could well turn the business around." He turned and picked up the cheese corer. He wiped it clean with a brined cloth. "Ready?"

She nodded. Her cheeks were sucked in as she nervously bit them. The anticipation of a long wait hung on this moment. Her eyes focused on his as he stabbed the probe into the centre of the cheese wheel. With a deft twist, he pulled out the plug and sniffed it. His eyes flew open, but he remained silent.

Jennifer watched. Did that sniff mean it was off? She almost reached out and grabbed the core to taste it for herself. She fidgeted while she waited.

Mr Williams broke off about an inch of the sample, sniffed it again, and then popped it into his mouth. He closed his eyes, and his head lifted.

Jennifer was unsure if he groaned with pain or a moan of delight. Whatever it was, he was totally absorbed in savouring it.

Rather than say anything, he broke off another inch-long section and added it to his mouth. The almost wicked grin that he had on his face when he finally spoke to Jennifer made her gasp. He leant over and broke off a third section of the sample. "Oh, my, my! You must try this for yourself and tell me what you think." He popped it into her mouth.

The flavour explosion hit her palate like fireworks. The caramelised onion was the first thing she tasted, followed by the hint of garlic, then a flash and bite of the nettle. Her furrowed brow vanished. She liked it, but did he? She met his gaze, and although wishing to scream with excitement, she needed the verdict from Mr Williams. The cheeses would be sold under his name, which was at stake.

Mr Williams stretched out his hand for her to shake it again. "Congratulations, Jennifer! Wipe the worry from your brow. Let me assure you that I have never tasted an English cheese this good. This could easily have come from one of the top merchants in Europe."

Mr Williams was grinning so broadly that she had never realised how perfect his teeth were. Jennifer's jaw dropped. "You mean they are that good?"

His smile was encouraging. "Not just good, Jennifer, they are excellent. Yes, I would say it is the best I have ever tasted. You will be given the freedom to use that milk as you wish. If we can double our production using the excess milk, then I'll double your pay. It's all money in the bank for me, as well as you and your family will certainly benefit. Actually, my dear girl, I really will give you a cut of all the profits."

Jennifer gave a jig of elation. "Really? It was just an experiment, but I'm glad it worked."

Mr Williams had one more surprise for her. "Jennifer, I'm naming these three flavoured ones *Kellow Specials*. But the triple, I think we'll call it…" He was obviously thinking deeply. "Um… how about *Southern Belle*? What do you think? We are on the Southern tip of England. They will be a new range of gourmet cheeses and will, therefore, fetch more than twice as much as a standard cheese. Actually, please don't make them the same size. Use the half-size moulds, and I'll get some different coloured waxes for the various flavours. Red for nettle, green for onion, orange for garlic and for the mixed one, which I think is the best, we'll use a royal blue coating. It will be priced even higher than the others. Get cracking, girlie; you have work to do. I hope your mama will be pleased; she needs a break. This should help a bit with finances at home, too." She was about to leave when he said, "Jennifer, it will still be a year before we have any to sell, but until then, tell Isla that she will now be full-time, too."

Jennifer gave her boss a curtsy. She wished she could throw her arms around him and hug him, but that would have been wildly inappropriate. To say she was excited was an understatement. The first thing she needed to do was to source some onion and garlic and then make the brine solutions. There were nettles aplenty around the dairy, but she needed some gloves to pick them. She gave a skip of happiness as she followed her boss from the storeroom and stood waiting as he locked the door. Once done, he put the key above the lintel and told her to follow him again. They turned the corner of the stone entrance to the underground room, and a wooden box sat on the small dairy wall.

He stopped beside a box. "I thought you couldn't make the cheeses without the flavourings. Here are some onions and garlic, and the brown paper packet is a pair of long leather gloves for you to collect the nettles. I have also told our cook to permit you to use our stove to make your lethal soups from these. Four new stock pans with lids are awaiting you in the kitchen."

This time, Jennifer was so overwhelmed that she did hug him. "Mr Williams, you are so kind. Thank you so much!" Happy tears clouded her eyes.

The big man chuckled. "Send your papa to see me, Jennifer; I'll discuss the arrangement with him."

Bryn liked the Kellow family *en masse*, but Jacob was his best friend. He admired that they never complained and were nearly always the first family to step up and help some other struggling person. Phoebe had befriended his wife at church when he was new to the area. Delen was a local girl, but he had come from Wales. They had met at the market where she was selling her homemade cheese. That had been over twenty years ago now. Phoebe had been expecting their first child, as had his wife, Delen. Both boys were currently working at the tin mine. Phoebe and Jacob's boy, Logan, at twenty-two, was a rock wall miner who had taken a course in explosives. Bryn's son, Billy, was only weeks younger and was a foreman of the next-door mine. The two boys were friends and worked well together. Delen and Phoebe Kellow remained friends, and it was how the two Kellow girls came to be asked if they would like to work in the dairy. The girls were rarely late, and only a dire incident at home would cause that to occur. Usually, that would be the birth of a child, and he was usually well-forewarned about this happenstance.

After saying farewell at the kitchen door, Jennifer began preparing some onions and garlic for the flavouring solution. Once the first two pans were set to simmer, she donned the gloves and took the now empty box to gather nettles. The stinging plants grew thickly around the milking shed, and she would be pleased to remove many of them. The gloves made stripping the stalks easy; however, once she did that, she pulled the stripped stems up from the edges of the pathway. There were plenty around the back of the milking shed that she could use later. At least the pathway would be traversed with less pain now. The nettles often stung Isla's bare legs. Her skirts were not yet long enough to cover her tattered boots. Jennifer was pleased that Mrs Williams had given her a serviceable long skirt for work. At nearly fourteen, her girlish figure vastly differed from the stick she had been as a small child. Her well-endowed curves had needed a modest covering. Isla was beginning to change, too, and Jennifer knew that she would need to share her long skirts with her little sister soon. The short skirts would be handed to another family until her baby sister Polly needed such clothes.

Jennifer went to work making the briny solutions. The onions had nearly caramelised. The garlic also needed peeling, sautéing and browning before making it into the required consistency. The four pots could be boiled and sealed. The salty brine mixes could be reheated and kept sterile for some time. The ingredients were plentiful, and the smell of the process drew Billy into the kitchen. He sat and chatted with her while she worked.

Even though he was six feet tall and as strong as an ox, Billy's lungs gave him some problems when he was young. The cold or dusty air would make him cough. However, he was now mine foreman and often worked the afternoon shift. Working the afternoon shift meant that the cold morning air could be kept to a minimum, and his chest had improved.

Jennifer really liked him. She didn't like the other village boys as they tried to paw her, and once, one even tried to kiss her. She felt safe with Billy, and after a word from him, the boys never came near her again.

When younger, the two families sat together in the church, and as space was limited, the younger children sat on the laps of the older ones. Jennifer noticed that Billy often manoeuvred himself to sit next to her. Now, the younger ones had to sit on the floor in front of the first pew. But Billy often claimed his usual spot. They shared a hymn book and an occasional shy smile.

On weekdays, Billy never left for work without sticking his head into wherever Jenifer was working. He acknowledged Isla but never missed out on seeing Jennifer. As time passed, Billy's visits increased. Day in and day out, Billy always made some excuse to see her, even if only to say hello or farewell. In winter, they were often still in the dairy, working under the light of candles in the sconces on the dairy workroom walls. Billy would walk the girls home before heading down for an evening swim to clean up.

One morning, about a month after tasting her first cheeses and after the milking, Jennifer asked Mr Williams if she could make a batch of special rich cheese as a test. "Sir, if we use only the Channel Island milk to make the triple-flavoured one, it would be even creamier. It could even be sold as a soft or medium firm cheese. I only need two gallons to make a one-pound test cheese." Her four flavours were ready to make the next batch of cheese, but she wished to try something even more special. The cream from the rest of the milk was already in the vat, but she had milked the Guernsey cows last and kept it aside. She wanted to use this milk unskimmed.

Mr Williams smiled. "I don't see why not, lassie. I think you are correct about a really creamy cheese."

One of the milk customers had purchased their own cow, and this was the first time anyone else had decreased their order. It meant they now had excess milk from the morning session. If Jennifer could use some excess creamy morning milk, that would reduce the waste. She took the two-gallon pitcher and was tempted to dip it in the vat to fill. However, knowing that it had been sitting on the ground, it would contaminate the entire batch if she did.

She picked up the bucket of milk and was about to carry it to the dairy processing room when she heard footsteps approaching.

Billy was heading off to work and saw her struggling with the heavy coopered pail. He came to her rescue and relieved her of the heavy wooden bucket. "Jen, call me if you need something lifted. I'm always willing to help."

Jennifer adored him abbreviating her name. She so wished she was older as she admired the handsome young man. Billy was eleven years older than her, but she was half in love with him already. He always seemed to be at hand when required. She wondered if he was watching her. She certainly hoped so. She gave him a beaming smile. "Thanks, Billy," she said shyly.

Billy waited until she moved a large pan onto the heat. "Jen, I mean it; never hesitate to ask me." He saw he had splashed her face with a drop or two of the milk. He thumbed it away and nearly bent to kiss her. "I'd do anything for you, Jen. I hope you know that. Anything!" Without waiting for a reply, he turned and left.

At twenty-six, he was fully grown. At over six feet tall, he towered over Logan. As boys, they had often come to fisticuffs, but with Jennifer, he was always gentle.

He had almost kissed her. She was sure of that. She so wished that he had; she would have liked that. At his comments, Jennifer's jaw dropped open. Her eyes followed his dark-headed figure departing. Had he really just declared himself to her? Is that what he meant? She was far too young to be courted. As he reached the end of the path to his home, he turned and looked back at her. She had not moved an inch; her mouth was still agape. Next year, she would be old enough to marry.

He lifted a hand to wave, then vanished from her view.

Jennifer's heart was thumping twenty to the dozen. If he meant his words, she would be delighted.

Chapter 3   Discoveries 1968+

*T*he stories Gramps told inspired many conversations. He had also spoken about his grandfather, who was the son of a convict. That tiny comment had elicited gasps from all listening. Jenny watched the shock blanch her aunt's face.

Aunty Bev gazed at her father, unbelieving at what he had just said. "Convicts! Is there a criminal in our family? Are you kidding?" She was obviously hoping he was joking.

Gramps slowly took in the astonishment on each face. "Ah, yes, well, more than one if the truth be told. You see, both of my great-grandfather's parents were convicts on the maternal side. But I won't go as far as calling them criminals. Most were sent here for thefts of food valued at a few shillings. I think there are more on different branches; however, I'm not sure where they fit in. Father would not discuss it with us."

Jenny was almost bouncing with excitement.

Gramps nose screwed up as though there was a bad smell. He flicked his eyes over to his daughter-in-law and then to his granddaughter. "Jenny, one of them was named Jennifer, and you were named after her. It's not the most popular topic of conversation, you know. Bev, your reaction is minor compared to some. I don't think there is any way we could find out much more, but I do confess I wish I had listened to Father when he told me. It's always why I loved the name Jennifer. I went and lived with my grandparents when I was just five. They were getting older, and our house didn't fit all the children. I only saw Mother and Father on Sundays for the next seven years. Popa and Nana never spoke about their family, so back beyond them, I know nothing except the name of Jennifer belonged to my great grandfather's grandmother." He counted on his fingers to see if he had got the generation correct. He nodded, then shrugged and put his hands raised in resignation.

Jenny's eyes were as big as saucers. "Gramps, can Mum and I try? I'm sure there are records somewhere. I know I have a birth certificate. I'm sure that back then, there was some way people were recorded."

Everyone in the room remained silent. Eyes were flicking from one to another. No one wished to answer Jenny's question. Gramps would have the final say. Eventually, all eyes rested on him.

Jenny was not going to let this rest. "Please, Gramps, please." Jenny waited, watching the emotions roll across his face.

With a sigh and a huff, he finally said, "Fine, you can try, but I have no idea where this wild goose chase will take you. I have heard rumours about that it's the Kellows line, but there was nothing concrete. Names have remained in the family. Unusual ones like Logan, Christopher, Phoebe and, as I said, Jennifer. William, too, but it's not unusual. Each generation has a smattering of each. I have cousins my Popa liked, but I do not know where they are now. Phoebe was one of them"

Jenny was so excited that she ran across the room and threw her arms around his neck. "Thank you, Gramps, so much. I'm sure we'll find something. Won't we, Mum?"

Celia's expression was of surprise, yet she knew she was just as interested. A chuckle escaped her lips. "Fine, Jenny. We'll give it a go. I have no idea where to start." She sat back in her chair and wondered how they could access any data.

The conversation turned from family history to what Gramps would do to keep occupied. Celia had given this some thought already, and as he asked, she reached down beside her chair. Moments later, a parcel wrapped in brown paper sat on her lap. "Gramps, I wondered how you were going to stay occupied, and I have bought something for you. As you have just seen, Jenny loves your stories, and I know I do too. But as we age, we forget things. Once our older generation goes, most of the history will be lost. What you said proves that."

Gramps raised his hand to stop her. "Celia dear, you may use the word die or death. It will happen to us all sometime." He nodded, then waved her on to continue.

Celia smiled at his words. "Fine then, when you die, so will your stories. I don't want that to happen." Celia motioned for Jenny to take the package and give it to her grandfather. "This is a dual-purpose gift."

Gramps tugged at the string with his gnarled and twisted fingers.

Jenny watched him as he rolled up the string and pocketed it before opening the wrapping. She would have loved to rip off the paper and see what was inside. She released a sigh in annoyance. He reused everything.

Gramps saw her frustration and said, "Jen dear, half the excitement of a gift is the suspense. If I simply ripped off the wrapping, then there would be no anticipation." He smiled before slowly pulling the flap of paper up so only he could see the contents. Teasingly, he flicked his eyes to watch Jenny's expression. She was bouncing in her seat. To put her out of her misery, he folded back the wrapping to reveal a dozen new exercise books, a box of pencils, a sharpener and an eraser.

Horrified, Jenny was unable to hold in her sadness. "Mum, why does Gramps need a stack of school books?"

Celia chuckled. "Not school books, poppet. These are for Gramps to write his stories. If he writes a little bit each day, we will have a first-hand record. I might even write as he tells them to us. These will also give us a place to start hunting, but I've had another thought."

Aunt Bev turned to her and said, "What, Celia?"

Celia said, "Newspapers!"

Uncle Hilton had remained silent until she had said that. "Ahh, yes, newspapers; I believe that the Mitchell Library has a vast collection of every newspaper printed in our land. I think you're right there, Celia, but do you know how to find the information? Also, Church records. As Jenny said, Baptisms will be recorded there and most deaths. Everyone was Baptised back then, and often they were recorded in the old church record books."

Celia remembered Hilton had worked for a newspaper company at one stage. Of course, he would know that sort of thing. She looked around at the family. "Most of the really old broadsheets are kept in the Mitchell Library in Sydney, really? Then I am guessing that we will take a trip down there when the school holidays start next week." Celia turned to Jenny. "Interested, poppet?"

Jenny's head nodded like a bobblehead toy. "Is that the library in Sydney? The big one that we walked past on our last visit?"

"Yes, poppet," Celia said with a grin.

Morning tea stretched until noon, and Iain arrived home for lunch. As Jenny heard the front door open, she was up on her feet and shot downstairs to meet him. The conversation upstairs had ceased in anticipation of Jenny's excitement. They were not disappointed.

Jenny's joy was evident. "Papa, Papa, do you know there are convicts in your family, and guess what?"

Iain hugged his daughter. "What, my poppet?"

Jenny was positively bouncing. "Mama and I will see if we can learn more about them. Isn't this exciting? Gramps said we could, and it wouldn't worry him." In the time that Iain had entered the house, removed his hat, and placed down his bag, she had filled him in with the morning's revelations. By the time he was ready to join his family, he had stripped off his coat. His tie was carefully placed on the tie rack so it was ready to wear when needed again.

Jenny was waiting outside their room and took his hand as she tugged him upstairs. "Papa, did you know about the convicts? Did you know that Gramps's family has that history?"

Iain could see the faces of his family waiting for him. "Hi Bev, Hilt, Dad, sorry I'm a bit late. A late customer came in just before closing time." He bent down to kiss Celia. "Hi, sweetie, sorry I'm late for lunch."

Celia gave a small gurgle of happiness. "Iain, we've been so busy we have not even thought about food. We're still sitting here from morning tea. Your Father has been letting some family secrets out."

Hilton almost had come alive now that his brother-in-law was home. "Iain, did you know about the exciting revelation?"

Iain met his father's gaze and shook his head. He knew his own first name, William, had a family connection but was unsure how. Iain had been his maternal grandfather's name.

Gramps gave a shrug. "It never occurred to me that anyone would be interested in such old history. Celia, you really want me to record the stories I can remember?"

There was a chorus of "Yes, please" from everyone.

~

The school holidays saw Celia and Jenny make their long-awaited trip to Sydney. This involved a car trip to the railway station in Gosford, a train trip to Central Station and then a bus to the Mitchell Library in Shakespeare Place, Sydney. The bus route took them past the Hyde Park Barracks, Government House, and some other old buildings that Jenny later discovered were the hospital and Parliament House.

Jenny's discovery was helped by an old lady sitting next to her mother. "Mum, these buildings are old, but what are they?"

The lady emitted a friendly-sounding chuckle at Jenny's comments. "Dear, I work at the library and can tell you some of their histories. Are you here for a visit?"

Jenny nodded vigorously and proceeded to explain the reason for the journey.

Again, the lady laughed. "It seems that we were destined to meet. I am one of the archivists in the library, and it's to me that you would have been sent. I am pretty sure that I have some of the information that will start you off. However, the Genealogical Society in Kent Street will have more information on microfiche. I love that place and haunt it too."

Both Celia and Jenny asked in unison, "What is microfiche?"

The lady's eyes twinkled as she explained. "They are miniaturised books that are kept on film. You place the sheets into a reader; they will make you seasick if you are not careful."

Jenny frowned. "How can you get seasick on land?" She had been seasick while fishing in their boat. It was an unpleasant feeling.

The lady explained. "It's the eyes, dear. The movement of the pictures upset the stomach. However, with my help, I think we'll start with birth records rather than newspapers. They are now on file."

They arrived at the library, and the lady punched her card in and unlocked her room. Celia and Jenny followed with passive excitement. They had no idea what discoveries were before them.

After telling her of their quest, she knew just where to start. She asked a few questions and then set about working backwards from Gramps.

Mrs Fox set them up on a microfiche reader in her office. "You know, dears, you should really be in the public rooms, but I can help you a lot more in here. I have more than what is available out there, both reels and sheets. The machine you are on can read both." She flicked through a carousel of things and found the birth of his father, Christopher Kellow, in 1880. Gramps was nearly ninety, and although his hands and hips had aged, his mind was clear.

Jenny had sat with him and written down the few dates that he thought would be useful. It was minimal. His birthdate, his parents' names and their dates, but he didn't know his grandparents' first names. He had drawn a little family tree on the front page of her book.

Christopher (Toff) Kellow b 1880 (Popa)
m 1908 Mary Lance
    *Logan Kellow (**Gramps**) b 1910*
    m 1930 Sylvia Wallace b 1918 d 1962
        *1. William **Iain** Kellow b 1931 (Papa)*
        m 1958 Celia b 1939 (Mum)
            *1 **Jenny Kellow** b 1959 (Me)*
        2. Beverly Phoebe Kellow (Bev)
        m Hilton Barlow (Hilt)

Jenny showed Mrs Fox the family tree. "Apparently there is one of my ancestors called Jennifer and it's really her we're looking for."

The lady smiled and nodded, flicking through the carousel. "Ahh! This is what we need. This one includes your great-grandfather's dates, so I'll show you how to find him first, as it will be the most accurate description. The newspaper will normally only have the father's Christian name and the gender of the child. It will be something like a birth on Sept 9th last, a son to Jack Kellow and his wife'. However, you know his birthdate, and it's an unusual surname. Once you have him, you work backwards and then fill in more details. You go back until you find out as much as you can. So I would suggest you do your grandfather's, Logan Kellow's, marriage searches first as births are only available one hundred years before today; then check about twenty years back to find the next generation as they married quite young back then." Mrs Fox spent another fifteen minutes overseeing the research. When she saw they were proceeding well, she went about her work. They had already found Christopher, Gramps' father, born in 1880 to Jacob and Isabella, but not Gramps, as 1910 had yet to be filmed. That was the easy bit, but then they had to find out the next generation backwards. Gramps' marriage record in 1930 listed his parents, Christopher and Mary. Within two hours, they had another generation but still no convicts. Where were the convicts? Was Gramps wrong? How far back did they need to search? She found a Logan whose father was Jacob but sometimes called Jack in the birth records. Was it him?

His grandfather was another Logan, but still no convict. After lunch, they set to work again and found another person, Christopher's wife, Catherine. That was a baptism record with Logan's parents, Christopher and Adelaide. So it was not the right one, but there was another one earlier, and that Christopher was born in the colony too, only much earlier. It was so confusing. Jenny now had her eye adjusted the microfiche machine and could flick through the pages quickly while Celia recorded the finds. Jenny was thinking and learning. "Mum, if the first Christopher was born in Parramatta in 1821, that's pretty early. When did the convicts come?" Celia didn't know and suggested they ask Mrs. Fox when she returned from her tea break.

The older lady returned refreshed from her break and came over to see how they were going. "Oh, now this is exciting. Look, he was born in Parramatta in 1821. I wonder…" She bustled off and grabbed a large volume that looked like a record journal. She pulled on cotton gloves and flicked open the cover of the tome. "The fiche is good, but the original records can't be beaten." She carefully flicked open the first few pages of the leather volume. She carefully ran her finger down the page. Then the next page… and the next… "Got him. Look!" The page she had opened had a blank page next to it.

Jenny and Celia stood on either side of her and gazed. Christopher Logan Kellow was born to Jennifer Kellow. After that entry, there looked to be letters, bc FF. "Oh, now this is interesting, as Jennifer was a single convict; therefore, she has given him her surname; however, there is another name added later, look." Williams was added later in a different ink. Mrs Fox met Celia's eye with her eyebrows raised.

Celia gasped. "But he's Kellow not Williams; he was illegitimate? What does the 'bc FF' mean?"

Mrs Fox smiled. "Looks like it, dear, but the dates also mean that he may have been born in the Female Factory in Parramatta. That 'bc' usually means born in the colony." She saw the frowns on the faces of her guests. "Do you not know about the Female Factory? It's the female prison that was opened on February 1st, 1821. That was the day this child was born. The girls had a tough time there. Maybe it is an area you could do some future research? It's worth a look through the place if you ever get a chance. I went once as a child when it was all but derelict, but I believe it's used for other purposes now. Um, it's a school, I think."

Celia and Jenny were astounded. Gramps's story about convicts sounded as though it may well be true. Mrs Fox said, "If this girl, your ancestor was a convict, as it looks, then I suggest you go to The Society of Genealogy in Kent Street, Sydney and see Jess Hill. She is doing a study on convict women and will be able to point you in the right direction. She may even have the records you are looking for."

Chapter 4 Jennifer's Experiment 1817

*J*ennifer's first commercial batch of hard cheeses was ready for market by the spring of 1817. At nearly seventeen, she was excited to watch the first of her half-wheels of cheese being packed in special straw-filled boxes and sent to London for sale at the markets. Along with one hundred regular large cheese wheels, Mr Williams was finally selling the first of her gourmet ones. The samples were brilliant. The two families had spent the week dipping the cheeses in various wax colours. This was always a messy job, but it stopped them from being contaminated on their journey. The different coloured waxes made identifying the flavours easy. A new brand label was placed into the hot wax.

Jennifer had also made some small cheeses for taste testing rather than cutting into the larger wheels. She knew that the blue triple flavour batch was good, if not superb. She had watched them maturing, gently rubbing them with lard for six months before they matured for the remainder of the year. These cheeses were very hard, and they needed time for the flavour to be fully developed. As she had been making them in commercial volumes for a year, she had hundreds more in varying stages of maturity. It had taken a full year before she could get the flavourings just right. Now they were also trying different ages from the normal three-month small wheels, which were a medium cheese, to six-week-old new cheeses that had a creaminess that held the subtle flavour well. Mr Williams was correct; the stinging-nettle one had a kick as an after-bite, and the addition of pepper enhanced this. It was delicious, but would the cheeses sell? Twenty-five of each of the four new flavours were being sent to London. The one that had been exceptional was now blue waxed. It was a pure Guernsey cream, triple-flavoured cheese. Her last experiment with the extra creamy milk had worked.

When the two families had gathered around to taste it, Billy had forgotten himself and given her a congratulatory peck on the cheek to show his pleasure; however, he had waited until they were alone before doing it. Her hand flew to her cheek, and their eyes met in a secret understanding.

Billy said, "I'm so proud of you, Jen. If this sells well, I might even be able to leave the mine and come and work with you."

Jen blushed. "You would want to do that?"

Billy chuckled. "Heck yes, Jen. I may even do that anyway." Knowing that they should not be alone in the cheese cave, he moved to go, then turned back and said, "Jen, have you no idea what you mean to me?" He bent down and kissed her forehead. "I'll wait for you, you know." He cupped her cheek and gave it a gentle caress with his thumb. He had kissed her cheek this time; a smile settled on her lips. He dropped his hand and left her alone with her cheeses. One day, he would claim her lips.

His action had made her day, but she had work to do. Jennifer oversaw the containers being packed for transport. She knew little of this side of things but was willing to learn all she could.

The carriage was finally loaded and sent off with a prayer. Phoebe, Isla, and Polly stood beside Mr and Mrs Williams as the wagon trundled down the dusty track. The sale of these two hundred cheeses could make both families wealthy. But it would be months before they would know if they were enjoyed. Mr Williams has said that a good hard cheese in London costs about fifteen pence per pound. Hopefully, her flavoured ones would bring more money, but they needed to figure out how much more. The wagon was being sent to the cheese agent, who was instructed to sell half to the highest bidder. The remainder he was to offer to some of the biggest houses in London. The large aged wheels were about twenty pounds in weight each. The flavoured half-sized wheels weighed less than ten pounds but hopefully would bring in more money. Mr Williams sold his standard cheese wheels for £3 each and hoped he would get the same for the smaller ones. The samples were also packed for the agent's use. Jennifer had also made minute bite-size samples cut from a long tube-shaped cheese she had made, as well as the half-pint ones. Each tiny cheese was individually waxed with flavour-specific colours. This stopped the cross-contamination of flavours.

Time would tell. Now, they had to wait.

The London merchant, Bertram Tremayne, a Cornish man who had grown up in Newlyn, was not surprised when the carrier arrived with an accompanying letter. However, he was astounded when he tasted a sample of the cheese. Each flavour was better than the last. He had received an order for special cheeses from a duke's mansion at St James' Park and had wondered what to supply them with; now he knew. The blue waxed cheese was superb. He hoped all the samples would not get consumed as he wished to keep some for himself. He had not tasted a flavour like this. Some other makers had tried adding dried herbs, but the speckled cheeses were not as popular. Some had even gone off, as the herbs and additives had not been treated properly. These, though, were vastly different.

Bryn had not told him the difference, only that they were special and each wax was a different flavour. These cheeses were top quality and, as such, could be served in the best houses and even palaces in London. It normally took him some weeks, if not months, to dispose of a wagonload of cheese wheels. More often than not, some ended up in his small cold store for months. He took a wheel of each to the big house along with a sample of each taster. He was sure of at least one sale there but had no idea what the French chef would purchase.

An hour after arrival at the fancy house, he left with a wad of money and an empty basket. They had purchased all five wheels. The large plain twenty-pound wheel brought in £5, each of the three single flavour ones brought £15 each, and the blue triple flavour one was £20. A haul of £70 for the one sale was astounding for just five cheeses. He decided to hang on to the rest of the shipment until after the duke's dinner party and see if it would produce further sales. He expected that it would. He knew the chef and asked him to pass on his details to the butler.

On return home, he carefully stowed the money in his safe. He was on a 10% commission, meaning he earned £7 from this one sale and had ninety-six more cheeses to sell. This money was more than he earned all of last year. With many more wheels yet to sell, he hoped the prices would be as good.

~

By the end of the month, all the cheeses had sold. None had gone to market as word had spread through the kitchens of the big houses after the duke's dinner party, and the remaining products had fetched an astounding price.

The eighty plain cheese wheels had brought in £10 each instead of the usual £3, and the flavoured *Kellow Special* ones had been sold at £20 each for the single flavour half wheels. Amazingly, he got £25 each for the *Southern Belle*, triple flavour ones. The haul for the sale was £600. He was reeling. He had been happy with a £7 commission but with another £60 to add to it. He still had a few more to sell. They were sold that week.

A week later, having sold all his stock, he decided to take the money personally to Cornwall. Knowing there were highway robbers, he decided to travel by ship. He felt flush in his pocket as he had made so much money in less than a month. However, he also wished to discover the secret to the new variety of cheese. Why was it so different? And more importantly, how much more could they produce? Bertram also wished to negotiate an exclusive deal as the only merchant handling the new products. This meant a trip to Cornwall was required. Even the quality of the ordinary cheese had improved.

His arrival in Cornwall at the end of summer surprised his old friend. Bryn Williams could not believe his eyes when Bertram walked toward him from the harbour. It was only two months since he had sent the wagon to London, and he doubted he would hear of any sales for six months. For Bertram himself to be here was a worry. He stood waiting as he walked up from the town; however, he noticed a big grin on Bertram's face.

Bertram gripped Bryn's hand with a vice-like grasp. "Hello, old friend, I have news; where can we be private?" He glanced at the girls' hard at work in the dairy.

Bryn nodded, wondering what the news was. Bertram's smile was at least encouraging.

No sooner was Bertram ushered inside the farmhouse kitchen and served a mug of tea than he checked that Bryn, Delen, and he were alone in the kitchen. "Bryn, I have sold them all and brought you the money personally." He pulled out a leather pouch tied with two straps and unrolled it. The fat wad of notes he pulled out brought gasps from the two others at the kitchen table.

Bryn was the first to recover from his astonishment. "How much is there, Bertram?"

Bertram chuckled before saying, "Patience, dear friend." He pulled out a document and flattened it before pointing to the various sales. Line by line, he pointed out the individual costs. "Bryn, the entire sale was £1160 for all two hundred cheeses, less my 10% commission; you get £1044 for all the wheels. I have come to see if you can supply me with more; many, many more, and I would like to have the exclusive rights over the flavoured ones."

While Bryn gasped, Delen giggled and then burst into tears. Bryn reached over and patted her hand.

Knowing the difference that this sale would make to the Kellows. Bryn smiled, then laughed. He would keep Jennifer's identity quiet for as long as possible. If London found out the latest craze was made by a teenage girl, they would rebel. Even before he sent his new products to London, he had decided not to tell Bertram about Jennifer's additives or how to make them.

The various kinds of cheese had been marked just single and triple flavours, and each colour wax was different. As expected, the *Southern Belle* blue had been snapped up by the top chefs in London and the surrounding big houses; the palace kitchen had even purchased one.

Bertram hoped he would be asked to stay for the evening as his folks' home was a few miles away. He would catch the mine wagon to their house in the morning.

With the afternoon milking yet to occur, knowing that the milk that day was to be made into plain cheese, Bertram was invited to watch the girls work and turn the curd into the beginnings of the wheels. The process took a few hours before the fresh wheels were put into the cheese presses.

The following morning, Bertram departed none the wiser of what flavoured the gourmet cheeses were. Bryn waited until the wagon carrying his friend left before walking into the dairy. The last of the cows had headed into the stalls, and Isla was settling herself to milk. Bryn called for Jennifer to follow him and waited at the door for her.

Jennifer had no idea who the departing visitor was and willingly followed her boss into the kitchen.

Delen was waiting for her and ushered her into the parlour, then turned and hugged Jennifer. "Jennifer, dear, Bryn has some news for you. But I think you had better sit down first, for this may come as a shock."

Billy was on the afternoon shift for work, so he stood hovering, waiting to see if he would have the chance to comfort and encourage her. He knew how the news would change both families. With this money, he hoped he could now court Jennifer, but he had to wait until she was old enough to marry. She was just too young. His father would protect her for as long as he could. Billy sighed in frustration.

Once Bryn and Delen were in bed the evening before, they discussed how much to give Jennifer. They had expected £300 from selling the plain cheeses; now, if they kept £644, an even £500 would be Jennifer's cut. This amount of money for such a poor family would be life-changing. Jacob was on a yearly salary of £12. With more cheeses to sell, this was just the start of what they would get. They had decided that instead of the 30%, Jennifer would get a 40% cut of whatever Bryn received after this payment. Knowing this would be life-changing for the family, he was determined to do all he could to assist them. Bertram's future cut would also be raised to 15%, making him happy, too. He had mentioned an exclusive contract, and as Bryn realised this would protect them both, he willingly shook hands on the deal.

Bertram spent a week with his family before returning to the farm, at which stage Bryn showed him the storehouse with the stock cheeses awaiting sale. He also asked Bertram about possibly adding some soft cheeses to the sale catalogue. He had tried some at various stages, and the three-month ones were soft and creamy with a deliciously subtle flavour. The six-month-old ones were slightly stronger in flavour but were not crumbly like the year-old mature ones. He wondered if they could sell all four varieties at various stages. However, he would reduce the volume sent for sale to keep the competition and demand for the product high. London now had a taste of what their dairy could produce, well, what Jennifer could make, and he had watched how she made the flavours. The new strained, caramelised onion salted slurry she added to the milk worked as an enzyme to curdle the liquid and make the cheese. Jennifer had taught Isla how to make the flavourings and then salt them, so they had plenty on hand. It was this flavoured brine that produced the top-quality cheese recently sold.

As the single flavour half-wheels brought in twice as much as a full plain cheese, they would now make more of the flavoured varieties, thus doubling the volume as they were only half-wheels. Thankfully, the three ingredients were easily accessible. However, it was the triple flavour one, made with the morning milking of full cream from the Channel Island cows, that was the cheese in demand.

Bryn knew that this money would bring immediate relief to his friends. After Bertram had gone to bed, Bryn walked the few hundred yards to Jacob's cottage and left him a note to come for a visit after work. He could now make sure that Jennifer, Isla, and later Polly would be guaranteed employment at the dairy. The two younger boys could choose the mines or dairy for employment when they were old enough. Bryn hoped his son, Billy, would now leave the dangerous mine. Billy had mentioned some time ago about coming on to help in the dairy. Both men were thrilled.

Billy had arrived home while Bertram and Bryn were stretching their legs on an evening walk. Delen took the opportunity to tell him he could finally leave the mine. He was their only child and would one day inherit the farm, so knowing the ins and outs of the daily requirements would be necessary. Knowing that he had a tender spot for Jennifer certainly didn't hurt. Delen had caught the odd glance between them and wondered if Billy had made his feelings known. Jennifer was getting close to the age where she could contemplate courting, but according to his father, she was still too young to marry. Billy sighed in frustration. With the cheeses now making more than he could at the mine, even if he reached the top rung as mine manager, quitting and learning the ropes at the dairy would be more financially sound. The profit that they had made from the first sale would well and truly make up for the loss of his mine salary for the rest of the year.

The downturn in the tin profitability and the danger of the depth of the mines were now worrying. Some shafts were over six hundred feet deep. The temperatures were extreme, and the conditions were poor. The water table had been hit, and the miners' lives now hung on the reliability of the pumps. If they failed, the miners had only minutes to get out. Often, they were working in a section where they could be trapped. They regularly worked waist-deep in filthy water. Billy had to inspect the mine shafts daily and was pleased he no longer had to work the pick and shovels. Coming up from hundreds of feet below ground was a difficult feat as it was.

Jacob and Bryn wanted their boys out of there. Jacob was now in charge of the pumps above ground at his boys' shaft. The responsibility of all those lives was eating at him. Some of his boys had already left the underground tin mines and headed to the open-cut copper mines owned by the same group of investors. As more positions became available, more of the lads would follow. The copper mines were more profitable at the moment, and as long as the mineral seams lasted, the open-cut copper was easily sourced.

Logan was able to access the malachite seams using his explosive skills. As soon as he had gone, he sourced some jobs for his brothers. The work was mostly outdoors but at the mercy of the elements, though the conditions were much safer. Logan was working, blasting the cliffs and veins apart, then the others had to retrieve the shattered rock and haul the rubble up the escarpments with baskets and ropes.

The money from this enormous cheese sale gave both families some breathing room. The two fathers would finally have a way out of the poverty that had hovered over them all their lives.

When Jacob arrived at Bryn's house, they sat and enjoyed a home brew apple cider. The delicious tipple had a kick, so after one mugful, Jacob quenched his thirst with water.

Bryn waited until Jacob was ready to chat, then told him of the windfall from the cheeses.

Jacob choked on his third glass of fluid. "How much did you say?"

Bryn smiled, expecting this reaction. "Five hundred pounds is your share, Jacob. Well, it's Jennifer's share, if the truth be told. But she's underage, so I'll give it to you. She is happy with that, so don't worry. I've guaranteed all the girls jobs, and Jennifer has already taught Isla the technique of how to make these delicacies, which included her secret ingredients."

The conversation fell silent for a while as Jacob digested the information. He would first do some much-needed repairs on their home; the roof leaked, and Phoebe also needed a new hob cooker. Jacob decided that she needed far more than that; their tiny cottage had been outgrown years before, and she had slaved over a single pot belly stove for years. It was now on its last legs and about to fall apart. How she coped feeding so many, well, he had not really thought about it. Phoebe never complained; she just got on with her work. He was listening to Bryn talk, but his mind was swirling, and he planned on building her a brand-new kitchen with a proper cooker. There was also enough money to get some help with the laundry or even send it out to be done, thus helping another family. He would also buy some new clothing for his family. The boys working in the shafts needed warm jackets when they emerged into the frigid temperatures above ground. Jacob shook his head to concentrate on Bryn's words.

The conversation between the two men delved into a full-time partnership, a larger storeroom and more hands working the cheeses. All the unwaxed cheeses needed rubbing with lard before setting to mature in what Bryn called his cheese cave. With the quantity that they now planned, they would need more workers. It would benefit both if they could keep the family employed instead of bringing in more workers. The village girls would still be employed to milk the cows, but the secret of the flavouring and handling needed to be kept quiet.

~

When Bertram returned at the end of the week, the two families had met and nutted out a way forward for the business. Deciding to trust him, he was shown the entire stock of special cheeses. Bryn asked if he would like to taste some of the soft cheeses.

Bertram wondered what other goodies were in the cheese cave. He had no idea what he was in store for when he followed Bryn from the kitchen. On his visit to the cave, he was astonished that none of the cheeses were waxed. All were sitting on the shelves in their cheesecloth skins. A girl was sniffing one when they entered; then she rubbed the wheel with some white goo. He asked, "Excuse me, miss, but do you have to do that to all the cheeses?" The two men had taste-tested a dozen or so of the new cheese flavours.

Jennifer had hardly noticed the men as they were at one end of the room. She had been absorbed with her work; her nose had picked up the scent of a bloom of the wrong mould on one of the old, nearly ripe wheels. She kept a bucket of heavy brine nearby for this eventuality. Beside the bucket was a box that contained a handful of clean cheesecloth squares. Dipping one in the heavy brine, she carefully wiped the cheese with the heavily salted cloth. The mould had not penetrated the rind, and she set the wheel aside in case it bloomed again. This one would need special attention over the next week. Once dry, she would add a thicker layer of lard. She looked up and simply replied, "Yes, sir."

Bertram watched her as they walked around the room. He realised she knew exactly what she was doing. The lovely young lady would spin each wheel and check it all over. She would then scoop a few fingers full of white lard and massage this into the cheese. Bertram watched spellbound while they talked. He was astounded that the cheeses sat up on their sides rather than flat. The wooden racks were piled as high as the ceiling would permit, and the spaces between the cheeses allowed air to circulate. The racks themselves were designed to permit the air to flow freely. Bertram's cool store was nothing like this. All the wheels he handled were already waxed, so they had little need for airing, however, they were kept cool. After this visit, he would ensure that the care he gave them befitted the time and effort that was lovingly put into them.

Bryn smiled, realising what had caught Bertram's eye. Since their few words, his friend's eyes had hardly left Jennifer. Bryn realised that he needed to introduce her to his friend. He needed to know the whole story so they could all keep the benefits. Introducing Jennifer properly was now paramount.

As they walked back down the aisle towards the teenage girl. Bryn filled him in on the history of new cheeses, then said, "Bertram, please keep her identity secret, not only for our business but for her sake, too. She is an innocent in an evil world, and I don't want her tainted. Our Billy is keen on her, but she's too young yet, so he has not declared himself. There's plenty of time for that."

Bertram was overwhelmed that a girl in a small Cornish village was creating something that had been served at the King's table. "Bryn, I keep being pumped for information about these delectable creations. If she's responsible for them, she may need to come and settle the rumours that I'm not importing them illegally."

Bryn gasped and shook his head. He made the introductions and Jennifer bobbed a curtsy to the newcomer. She was aware of how important the sale of their product was to their project. She knew this man was the London agent for their products. She had promised her boss that she would not share her secret with anyone unless he gave her leave to do so.

Bertram could hardly believe that he was meeting the young girl who was the brains behind the gourmet cheeses. As he spoke, Jennifer resumed her work. The old cheeses were lovingly caressed and covered in a thin layer of lard as Bertram plied her with questions. Her hands dug into a tub of white lard, and she scooped out a lump and smeared it over the cheese in a thin film. By the time their conversation had finished, she had repeated the process on the entire shelf of wheels. Bertram was intrigued. Behind him, Bryn would give a nod or a shake, determining how she would answer the quizzing. They did not reveal the ingredients, only saying they could be found in any cottage garden.

Bryn and Jennifer explained that the waxing was done before packing and was purely for transport. It was for the protection of cross-contamination and for identifying the flavours.

Bertram's trip back to London on the ship gave him time to think. He had tasted many of the new varieties and ages of Bryn's cheeses in his cheese cave, so he knew his business was about to pick up. He needed someone who knew about the quality of what would become available. If only he were married, he could ask Jennifer to come and assist in selling the product. Her beauty was enough to win over the toughest client. She had such unaffected grace that stopped you in your tracks, but she was needed here.

Even so young, but for her deplorable outfit, she could take London by storm. Her family were obviously poverty-stricken, but her elegance made her stand out. He had seen the tiny cottage she lived in and met her parents and some of her siblings, yet she had overcome her poverty and held her head high. She was no ordinary peasant. Jennifer Kellow had a joy of life that many would envy. She had pride in what she did, and she did it well. He would give it a year or two and see if the new batch of cheeses he had with him sold as well as he thought. It was a pity he was so much older than her. Maybe this year, he would hunt for a wife. He now had enough money to buy a small cottage or a house with a cellar and set himself up so he would not have to pay rent anymore. In the meantime, he would set about finding new customers, and they would no longer be from the markets. Having tasted the fresh products and knowing what would soon be on offer, he had much work ahead of him. He encouraged Bryn to permit Jennifer to increase the volume of the single-flavour ones but not the triple variety. That way, he could demand top price, if not higher. The sky was the limit on what they could make with this. Some of the chefs demanded perfection in their products. Well, the triple cheese was just that. He had never tasted anything equal to it.

~

Back on the farm at Newlyn in Cornwall, Bryn could see that there was the possibility that Jennifer may have to head to London to promote their cheeses. He and Delen had discussed this idea, but until Bertram had a wife, it would not be possible for her to stay with him or anywhere else alone in the big smoke. He sighed, leaning against the door frame and looking down the hill to the all-but-derelict cottage. He had always had dreams of Jennifer marrying Billy when she was older. He loved her like a daughter; she would be so good for the farm's future and new business. A smile settled on his lips as he thought of the future. Billy and Jennifer already liked each other; in another couple of years, she would be old enough to contemplate marriage. The thought of grandchildren again made him smile.

Delen came to his side and slid her arm around his waist. "If you're thinking of matchmaking, give her a few years, Bryn. Billy won't need any pushing, but she's not ready yet."

Bryn glanced at the lovely lady who was snuggled up to him. "You know me too well, my dear one, and yes, I know it will be a few years before she's ready to settle. She has seen too much birthing already, and the earlier she marries, the more children she will bear. As much as I want grandchildren, I don't wish her to be burdened as Phoebe has been. At seventeen, she is just too young." He kissed the top of Delen's head. She had carried but one child to term, and both had wished for more. However, Billy was healthy and a good and loving son. They had lost count of the times they had nearly had a second child, then lost it. They did not dwell on that sadness, only on the joy in the one child God had blessed them with.

Billy had come home that day and told them that he had already handed in his resignation. He was a son they were proud of and one they loved dearly.

Chapter 5   Old Sydney Town 1975

*E*xcitement grew as January 26th 1975, drew closer. The official opening of Old Sydney Town at Somersby was about to occur. Not that they would be permitted to go that day; however, the following day was open for young and old.

Celia had been busy making a brown paisley gown with a matching mobcap and reticule for fifteen-year-old Jenny to wear, and she explained that the convict women back in the early days only wore blue or brown, drill or serge gowns. Jenny had never heard of a mobcap before and had no idea what it was. However, everyone was supposed to be in costume, so she didn't mind the odd fashion.

On arrival on the big day, Jenny was disappointed that many visitors wore ordinary clothing. However, enough people were in period costumes that she didn't feel too awkward. Celia explained that many others had their outfits in the bags they carried. She had seen a few interesting things poking out of a couple of bags. It began to feel like the modern-day world was being left behind. The car park was full, and the immense crowd was transported into the past and hid the journalists with cameras slung around their necks.

Jenny noticed that many carried bags, and as the crowd surged towards the entrance, the mood changed from the noisy, raucous children's laughter to a more subdued and even respectful behaviour. As Jenny was, their parents dressed them in period costumes.

Soon, tickets were purchased. $2.50 for Celia and 75c for her. The turnstiles clunked as body after body passed through the gift shop and made their way to the wonderful square rig ship models. The displays of miniature square-rigged ships showed the primitive transport the confined and bound felons had to endure.

Jenny had spent many enjoyable hours on some boats in the

Whitsunday Islands in Queensland, but these strange ships looked nothing like the almost luxurious tourist boats up there. Jenny gazed in awe at all she saw.

Celia held her hand tightly and had to drag her away from the display they needed to pass by. Everybody was perspiring in the January heat, and Jenny could feel rivulets of sweat trickle down her back.

Once out of the main building and shop, they walked with the crowd past old carriages and assorted things to look at. The snake-like trail wound its way towards a double archway to what looked like a barn door. It did not look too inviting. To the left, it said ENTRY in bold red letters, with instructions of what would follow. However, above the arches was a big sign that read NEWGATE WHARF. Celia explained that this was where the convicts were taken from the prison and shipped to New South Wales or New Holland, as Australia was first known. They followed the people through the open archway and saw a shop where you could have your photo taken in fancy period costumes.

Celia didn't hang around that area, and Jenny couldn't take it all in at one glance. She tripped along in her mother's wake. As they walked deeper, they entered into a darkened tunnel-like void.

It took a few seconds for her eyes to adjust, and when they did, Jenny's eyes caught sight of two manikins dressed as convicts. There were various dioramas of the convict's scenes. She jumped. The setting was all too realistic. The prisoner manikins were in a cell and didn't look happy. The conditions in the room were squalid, to say the least; they showed being arrested to the cramped ships' cells, then from convicts to everyday life. She realised that the barn doors were a time tunnel. The darkness seemed to eat the words of the river of people as they moved as they had fallen silent. Most now had donned their costumes and were now garbed in colonial outfits of one sort or another. Each step carried them further from the modern-day era and back into the convict past of their ancestors. With each step, the crowd grew quieter; each diorama drew gasps of awe and horror until, when they turned the final corner, they oozed out of the darkness into another earlier world, one of heat and glaring light.

The dust was the first thing Jenny noticed. A carriage pulled by horses had stopped just past the exit. Another was coming up the dusty road towards them.

Celia was about to grab Jenny's hand and walk past the carriages when a red-coated soldier rudely asked them why they were late for their morning work.

Jenny jumped, forgetting she was dressed as a convict. She shrunk closer to her mother for protection. She had not done that since she was a child. At fifteen, she was at eye level with her mother.

The soldier saw her subtle movement and played on it. "You girl, who are you assigned to? The candle maker?"

Jenny didn't know what to say, so she nodded.

The soldier told her to stand to attention; after eyeing her up and down, he circled her and then grunted. He pointed to a shingle-roofed building and told her to head down to the candle maker and get to work.

Celia grabbed her hand and dragged her away from the now laughing soldier. The man wolf-whistled at her as they departed. He turned to the next unsuspecting visitor. Jenny turned to watch his antics and muttered to her mother about her fright, then asked, "Mum, what's this about a candle maker? Don't people just buy them from a shop?"

Celia dug out her programme and the map. They walked past a few old carriages that were obviously not used today. Their shafts sat on the ground, and no horses were in sight. Opposite this was a dais with a flag flopping at the top of a pole. A breath of wind moved it, and Jenny saw that it was not the flag she was used to. "Mum, what's that flag?"

Celia followed her gaze and saw the British Union Jack up the pole. "That's the British flag, Jen; it's what the country used until 1954 when the Flag Act came into law. Australia became our own country in 1901, well long before that in the aboriginal times, but the English relinquished control at Federation, and our flag was designed soon afterwards; however, it was not adopted until a few years before you were born. This place is set about one hundred years before that. Old Sydney Town recreates Sydney as it was in about 1808, just before the Rum Rebellion, when the only coup occurred. The Militia overthrew the government. At the time, the legal currency was rum. Papa's ancestor's mother would have been about nine then, but I don't think she was out here yet."

Jenny had tasted rum and didn't like it. Astounded, she asked, "Rum! Why rum?"

Celia explained, "The first rum still was imported from England soon after the First Fleet arrived. A sailor named Thomas Webb brought it out as part of his salary. He and his brother, Robert, started growing grain and brewing rum. They sold some of it legally to Government Stores, but they sold the rest of the grain and, later, home-brewed illegally. It was quite lucrative for them. Others were soon following their example. I was reading about their history when I researched the family tree. Robert's daughter, Mary, married my great-great-great-grandfather, Joseph Huff, and then Mary died in childbirth. He remarried our ancestor, Mary Amelia Harlow. I was intrigued, so I looked it up. Joseph and Amelia were convicts too."

Jenny had heard about the rum still before but didn't realise there was a family connection. More convicts? The brief breeze dropped again, and the heat of the light-coloured road reflected the glare back at them as they walked. Perspiration dripped from them both.

Wiping their brows, Celia said, "It was hot like this when the First Fleet landed." Opposite the flagpole was Elizabeth Rafferty's General Store. It was busy with a queue waiting to enter. "I think we'll come back there on the way out. Let's have a look at the candlemaker. I've often wanted to know how they make tallow candles."

The odour of the clarifying fat was the first thing they noticed on entry. There was a rack of skinny candles cooling over a vat of some substance on the stove. Celia saw the lady getting ready to dip a row of candles. Celia asked, "Can you explain the process, please? I've been wondering how they made candles without beeswax."

The colonial-dressed lady willingly explained the process. "It's not that they didn't have beeswax; they just didn't have much of it. Most lighting for convicts was tallow candles using rush wicks. They are, as the name suggests, made from peeled, dried rushes that were soaked in fat and then dipped in tallow. The wealthier people used beeswax ones with woven cotton wicks, but the rush ones were the traditional ones for the colony."

Jenny listened but didn't really understand why they needed candles anyway. "Why don't you just turn on a light?"

Celia and the lady both chuckled. "Darling, in 1808, there was no electricity. If you wanted light anywhere, then it was candles or an oil lamp."

Jenny's eyes were as large as saucers. "No electricity? Are you serious? So, no streetlights?"

Both older ladies shook their heads. The candlemaker said, "Or television, or even record players, let alone fancy new cassette machines. Even the vehicles of the poor were what some called shanks pony, which meant walking. At best, they could ride a horse. It's why horses were so important. If you go down the hill, they will harness the bullock team just after ten o'clock near the flagpole. The bullock teams were the trucks of yesteryear. They pull all the heavy loads. Horses were the quick means of transport. Now, a car can do in a few hours what took a horse to do in half a day or more."

Celia asked, "Is it worth watching?"

The lady nodded. "Yes, see if you can follow the programme. After the team is harnessed, there will be a muster at the churchyard. The muskets will fire, and then the cannons. You may see a convict flogged while there, and don't worry; it is red ink and not blood, but it looks real. Normally, they don't put the flag up until half past ten, but a special guest came today, so it was done first."

Jenny nodded. She was beginning to wonder what she had agreed to by coming to this place. She had wanted to know more about what her ancestors had endured, but it seemed quite civilised so far. She tentatively asked, "What comes after that?"

The nice lady ran through the rest of the programme. "Make sure you see the cooper making barrels, casks, and firkins. Then, you'll be drawn to the magistrate's court and see another flogging. Inside is a schoolroom. For a lass your age, stick your head inside, and you will be stunned at how a classroom was run back then. There was very strict discipline. Mind you, at fifteen, the girls were often married."

Celia added, "They didn't have pens and paper in the classrooms; they used slates and chalk. The boys learned by *rote* that is, by repeating what they were supposed to be learning over and over. The girls were normally only taught at home. The teacher used to walk around with a cane in his hand and would hit the children who misbehaved. Classes are vastly different now, but it will be good to see."

Jenny wasn't that keen on school. She was not a good student, although she loved this era in history. Having family who lived through it made it easy to understand. Seeing it was even better.

The lovely lady who had finally told them her name was Mary said, "After the muskets fire again, head down to the tavern and have lunch. After that, go to the lake. The ship will get stormed, and more convicts will be in action for a mutiny." She chuckled. "Then things get fun. It's followed by a convict wedding, another magistrates court, and then a flogging, but you will have seen that, so until three o'clock, wander around a bit. See the brick kiln and the bond store, and watch the spinners. Wilma Bond is doing a demonstration today; she's often in the pottery room but on spinning today. She's one of the special people in the village, and she's a good friend. The programme finishes at four o'clock, after a funeral and grand finale. Spend time watching as many of the crafts as you can. What you will see today will stay in your mind forever. It's why hands-on learning is so important."

Jenny was listening. She understood the hands-on learning. It's how she remembered things herself. Her mum had learned that early on. She was having trouble understanding division in primary school. Her mother had picked up six books and shown her the concept. Six books divided into two piles were three each. Multiplication was basically the reverse; two piles of three made six books. The simple use of a physical prompt made the understanding as clear as crystal. After that, she'd never had trouble with them again. History was the same. The textbooks didn't make sense, but reading a book with pictures showing what happened seemed to untangle the concept of what she was reading.

After seeing Mary dip and cool each batch of candles, they purchased a dozen from her and left to watch the bullock team being harnessed. Jenny had seen this occur once before when visiting an old farmer in Kincumber. The old man had a fallen log to move, and with no tractor, he asked if she would like to watch while he harnessed up the gentle beasts. Mr Frost had eight huge horned bullocks, and Jenny watched as they walked into their positions without even using a rod, let alone a whip. One by one, they were tied to the heavy collars they wore to pull the load. The beasts at Old Sydney Town were similar. Instead of leather collars, these poor beasts had iron bars and a wooden yoke that paired them together. The load on this trip was a covered wagon loaded with sightseers. Like the other team, the bullock master only had a long, thin rod, and he would tap the rear of a bullock to make it move. The pace was slow and cumbersome, but that was the pace of the times. With the wagon load of laughing people moving down the road, the crowd flowed down the hill to where the muster would occur.

Celia and Jenny clung to each other as the convict and colonial-clad throng moved as one to the parade ground. A shout was heard over the cacophony of so many people moving and the shuffling of feet, and then a gunshot resounded.

Soldiers appeared behind them and shouted, "Move on, you bunch of lazy, misbehaved convicts. Move it. On the double!"

It only took a moment, but the group surged down to the parade ground. Once there, they circled the activities in the middle of the grassy area. Off to the side, more soldiers were dragging a bedraggled man towards them. He was shouting of his innocence. With activity all around, Jenny didn't know where to look, but soon, the captured man was escorted toward a pyramid-frame contraption and tied to it with his arms elevated. This evil device was apparently the whipping frame. Soon, the man's back was covered in red goo. Thankfully, Mary had told them it was ink, not blood; however, the reality of what the convict of nearly two hundred years before had suffered sank in.

Celia had explained some of the punishments, but until this demonstration, flogging had made no sense. Seeing the recreation brought the atrocities home. One of the cells in the black time tunnel was of some convicts with a ball and chain, and they looked tortured. Now she knew why. Up until seeing this demonstration, Jenny had always glorified what the convict life was like.

Rather than wait until the end, Celia snuck around the back of the crowd and headed down to see some of the other sights. There were convicts in stocks awaiting judgment; others were escorted under arrest to the magistrate's cells. Passing the King's Head Tavern, they entered the woodturners cottage.

The cooper was at work making staves for a wooden barrel. Other finished items sat around the shelves and awaited sale.

Celia and Jenny knew the cooper and greeted him by name. Celia greeted her friend. "Hi, Charlie; they are on the way down, so I thought I'd pop in before you became overwhelmed with questions."

He didn't stop working and used a small spoke shave tool to shape the staves for a barrel. "Hello, ladies; I have to get the stave done before they arrive, so I'll keep working while I chat if that's all right." They saw a pile of finished slats sitting on the bench.

Celia said, "That's fine, Charlie. We just popped in to say hello. We want to see everything, so we won't stay for this segment. We'll catch you at home sometime."

Charlie finished the stave and checked its measurements. With a nod that it was correct, he set about assembling the barrel. A set of loops and a pre-form insert held the staves together. In only minutes, the shape of the barrel appeared. Charlie was concentrating as he chatted. Then, with a tap of his hammer, he let the big loop drop, and all the segments collapsed. "Done; now I have a few minutes." He sank onto a wooden stool. "Let me sit for a bit; once they get here, I'll be on my feet all day."

They plied him with questions before they heard the noisy group arriving. Charlie waved a farewell and then fell into the character of the colonial craftsman. Celia and Jenny slipped out as the first of the new arrivals entered. Acting the part, he now spoke with a thick Irish accent.

Next door was a printer. Through the window, Jenny saw some blank *Wanted* posters on the walls and hoped she could buy some for school. She could think of a few teachers' names she wished to put on these, then chuckled at the thought and wondered if she dared put one up on the library door with the headmistress's name on it. A bell tinkled as they entered; again, they were the only ones in the shop. They had time to watch the printer ink the roller and print some *Wanted* posters. "Sir, are these for sale?" Jenny asked hopefully.

The man grinned. His teeth were blackened, and his reply was almost menacing. "Yes, miss. Have some names you want to be added?"

Jenny realised this was all part of the show, but she shuddered. She nodded in reply and said, "Can I just have some blank ones? How much are they?"

The printer gave a toothy grin. "Fifty cents a pop, love; how many do you want?"

"Twelve, please, sir." Jenny paid her six dollars, and the man handed her a bag with the certificates.

The man said, "Oh, there's a baker's dozen in there, love. It's no mistake, darlin'!"

Jenny looked puzzled. "What's that?"

Celia answered, "That's thirteen; I'll tell you why as we walk around." She turned to the man and asked for some certificates. "I'll have half a dozen of each of the *Ticket of Leave*, *Certificate of Freedom* and *Absolute Pardon* forms, please."

"Nine dollars, thank you, ma'am."

With the paperwork now stowed in their lunch bag, they wandered across the road, checked out the barracks and gaol, and then walked up to Rosettas Tavern. There was a small schoolhouse with a sign outside saying Kenny's School.

Knowing that the programme said there was to be another court case, flogging and musket demonstration, they headed down to the waterfront to eat their picnic lunch.

As they ate, Celia explained the term b*aker's dozen*. Celia looked at the small buns she had filled for their lunch. "Jen, back in Medieval days, that's around the 1100s, bakers sold bread by weight, and although they were all supposed to be the same weight, some buns and loaves varied in size as well as weight. So they added another one to ensure the weight was correct, hence the baker's dozen. Egg sellers did the same if the eggs were small. The practice has carried through to even today. There are many terms from yesteryear that we still use today. Many of our laws are as old, and even our language has roots back long ago." Celia watched the ship as the sailors on board prepared for the afternoon's activities. "Even nautical terms still exist. You have heard Dad say he's *rocked to the scuppers* over something?"

Jenny nodded. "What's a scupper?"

Celia had seen the small model ships as they entered. She had pointed out the decking, sails and a few other points of interest. As they were looking at the ship, she pointed to the slots along the decking. "The scuppers are the holes around the sides of the deck that allowed the water to escape. When a ship is rocked to the scuppers, it is tipped nearly on its side. Another one is when it's so cold that it *freezes the balls of a brass monkey*. The brass monkey is a brass sheet with studs, and a pyramid of cannon balls sits on it. When the temperature drops to freezing, the brass contracts and the cannon balls fall off it. There are more like *it's a long shot*. That is about aiming a ship's cannon. The phrase *taken aback* is describing the luffing sails against the spars and masts, and, of course, there is *batten down the hatches*. That is almost self-explanatory."

Jenny was munching on her peanut butter and honey roll. "You mean we still use convict-era terms today? What else?"

Celia was wracking her brain. "I know another one; when you say *Go with the flow*, it's talking about the ebb and flow of the River Thames in London. The sailing ships had no motors and went up and down the river with the tide. And I know you have heard the term *cock up*. That's about nocking an arrow into the bow with the cock-feather facing the wrong way so it won't shoot straight."

Jenny nodded again.

"Another one I say to you often. I say *pipe down*, meaning that you have to be quiet." Celia smiled. "That's what the captain says to the duty shift when they are to head to their hammocks. They have to be quiet. But that was originally a nautical term, as it is another term I say when you get moody. I say you are *in the doldrums*. In sailing terms, it means the wind has dropped, but we use it today to mean depressed. Can you see the similarity?"

Jenny was surprised at the existence of these phrases. "But Mum, what about from the convict days?"

Celia could only think of two off-hand. "We call a small child learning to walk a *drunk toddler*, right?"

Jenny had a mouth full, so she replied, "Yes."

"Well, a *toddler* is a convict term for an old and infirm person."

Jenny didn't reply, but Celia saw her surprise. She continued, "The other term is *topped*. It is what they say if a person has been hung. Not pleasant, but other terms have fed down through the years."

As they sat eating their pre-packed lunches, a soldier walked up behind them and shot some words at them. "Eh, you there, have you two got permission to laze about when you should be working? Anyone would think you was a *swell* or something."

Celia chuckled. "That's another one, Jenny; a *swell* is a well-dressed or well-off person."

The soldier laughed. "Well, ain't you a *game pebble* missus. If you aren't careful, then you'll both get *pulled up* before the magistrate."

Celia again laughed at the soldier's words; she knew he had been listening to them. "And that's two more words, Jen. A *game pebble* is a person whose behaviour is incorrigible, and getting *pulled* means being arrested and sent before a judge."

As Jenny was listening, the soldier moved towards the waterfront. Knowing that the next item of the programme was to be directly in front of them in half an hour, they took the opportunity to look at the blacksmiths forge. They had heard it working while they ate, so they headed up the street and stood watching the smithy hammer a red-hot horseshoe. The outside summer heat was cool compared to the forge, and the scalding metal made the heat worse. They stood watching the filthy man work. Jenny couldn't take her eyes from his sweaty torso. His arm muscles rippled with each hammer blow. The soot from the fire had coloured his skin and was smeared all over his leather apron. He worked steadily, and when the horseshoe was finished, he quenched it in a barrel of water.

Not wanting to miss the storming of the ship, the *Perseverance*, the girls thanked the smithy and headed back to the foreshore. They again took their places next to their picnic basket and waited. Half an hour later, they were ready to investigate the rest of the area. They had passed a few buildings they wished to see inside, so they retraced their steps. Soon, they wandered into Mary Bryant's shop, then Elizabeth Rafferty's general store. The pottery shop, bond store, tinsmith, and leatherworker were all investigated, and then they went to the Market Fair just before it packed up. They were able to get some good bargains and then headed back to the candlemaker to watch the duel that was to occur. All the while, soldiers were on the march, wagons were passing, animals were being herded, and life in the colonial village went on as though it were real.

Jenny really did feel she was back in 1800.

Celia had taken a few photos, and opposite Elizabeth Rafferty's store, she now took out her camera to take a snap of the windmill that had just started milling some grain. The door said, "No entry." They could smell the delicious crushed wheat. She had the strap around her neck when a red-coat soldier stepped before her. This man had been nearby throughout the day, and although they had not spoken to him, he had been plied with questions from others. Somewhat surprised, Celia lowered the camera and said, "Pardon, is there a problem, sir? Am I not permitted to capture this?"

With his musket on his shoulder, he said, "Nope, you can't do that, ma'am."

Celia wondered what the problem was when Jenny got the giggles.

Celia asked, "Can I take it from somewhere else?"

The soldier shook his head.

"Why?" She really wanted a photo of the new stone windmill.

The toothy grin of the soldier then broke across his face. "Got the lens cap on, ma'am." With that, he roared laughing and marched off.

Celia blushed, removed the lens cap, took the photo, and was about to turn to the next feature when they saw the soldier had returned.

"Follow me, ma'am, and miss." He walked toward the mill and didn't even check to see if they were following. The heavenly smell of freshly ground grain wafted from the opening upstairs. The flour dust could be seen in the shaft of sunlight. He opened the door and entered. For the first time, he was out of character. He turned to her and greeted her. "Hi, Mrs Kellow. You won't remember me, but I was in one of your Scripture Classes at the primary school in Avoca Beach. It's because of you that I got a job here. I had been told by other teachers that as I could neither read nor write, I'd never get a job anywhere. You were different, you see; you cared, which made a world of difference for me. You told me to use my memory skills, and I have."

Memories of Tommy Stork came flooding back. He had a reading difficulty, but his memory was photographic. It just didn't translate into reading or writing. He only had to hear something once and could remember every detail. "I see you have realised who I am. You once told me that if I lived back in the convict days when most others could also not read or write, I'd be no different from them. Your words stuck with me. I dropped out of school because of my reading and landed a job here as soon as I could. I've been helping build it and now work with the stock. They know of my problem, and we work around it without issue. My boss read me the history of the settlement, and now it's up here." He tapped his head. "Well, I'm a bit like a walking encyclopaedia. I simply adore this place. They gave me a job as a roving soldier to keep my eye on the tourists, but every now and then, I get to arrest one as they race by. To say it is fun is an understatement. But I would have hated to live back then. I do like my comforts at home."

Celia and Jenny were in awe at how this boy's life had turned out. He had often been the topic of a few discussions at home. No one knew what had happened to him after he left school. Tommy had just vanished.

Chapter 6   Cheese Wheels 1818

*T*wo years passed since Bertram's visit to Cornwall.

Jennifer now worked with Billy and all of her brothers except Logan. They were employed in the new Williams-Kellow cheese cave. The underground cellar had been extended to under both houses as the business had taken off.

Jacob also had resigned from the mines and had thrown himself into learning the dairy industry. This was a huge change from the way of life of his ancestors. They had always been miners or fishermen. Now, he and Bryn were full partners in the cheese industry. His job was to source and make the additives for the cheeses. Jennifer and Isla had shown him how to caramelise the onions and garlic before making the salty brine additive. The solutions were now made in huge vats and bottled. Jacob's main responsibility was quality control. Phoebe was also now helping where she could. Her job was mostly cutting the cheesecloth squares in the various sizes required. After the arrival of Polly in 1810, Phoebe had thankfully not conceived another child, and her health was improving. Polly, at eight, was now milking in the dairy with many of the family and was part of the growing business.

Bryn oversaw the milking shed and the herd. This had intentionally not been increased as they were finding it hard enough to keep up with rubbing all the cheeses they already had ageing. There was still enough milk left over for the village use, but now, none went to waste except the whey.

Angelina DeMartini, the Italian friend who had taught the girls poise and etiquette, described some cheeses they had in Milan. She knew about making soft cheeses from whey and was assisting Jennifer in experimenting with two new varieties. There had been many discussions about expanding the hard cheese flavour options; however, it was decided to stick with just the five options: plain and the four flavoured varieties. They did now offer various stages of the cheeses, from a mild three-month cheese, a medium six to seven-month one and the normal, mature twelve-month ones. The prices changed depending on the age. With the regular return of the funds from Bertram's sales, he often added a treat. Sometimes, a bolt of fabric or a set of hunting knives for the boys; once, there was an illegally imported French Camembert cheese, and another was an Italian soft, almost creamy one called aged ricotta. Because of these two cheeses, Jennifer had asked her Italian friend if she could tell her how to make soft cheeses. Mrs DeMartini mentioned that the French soft cheeses needed to be made with a raw milk base, not scalded milk. And they were not a rubbed cheese but naturally cultured. The special rennet in this cheese assisted in producing the white bloom on the skin of the cheese. Mrs DeMartini was about the same age as Jennifer's parents but looked younger. She had been married when very young to a much older man who died only a year after their marriage. Returning to Italy was not an option, as her father would have made her remarry as soon as possible. So she stayed away. She had enough money to buy a nice cottage overlooking the bay in Newlyn.

Jennifer had carefully extracted some of the creamy French cheese from the inside of the miniature round. She cultured some in a pot of warm milk and experimented with tiny four-inch wheels of cheese. She added culture to both raw and scalded milk and set them aside with the appropriate labels. This cheese was poured into a mould, set aside to drip, turned into some specially prepared cheesecloth, and left to bloom in the cheese cave, well away from the other cheeses. She had no idea if the French cheeses would work. These were not coated with lard but left in the cool room to mature and bloom naturally. Hopefully, if she had done it correctly, she would see the growth of the famous white mould rind. The soft white rind was as delicious as the cheese itself. The first batch of ten was placed in the cave to ripen. She had made five of the raw milk ones and five with the scalded milk. Even if they didn't work in commercial sales, the family would enjoy them. Trying new things made the business successful, and Bryn was not against her experimenting with new ideas. The family became used to eating many of her different tests.

Jacob had been in the village sourcing more onions when he arrived home with not only the onions but a bucket of juicy lemons. Jennifer's Italian friend had offered them to him. She always had lots of excess produce, and as she first suggested the flavourings, she had planted many rows extra of these garlic bulbs. She had a large lemon tree growing against the chicken yard. These were yellow, ripe and juicy.

Jacob loved Phoebe's lemon-delicious pudding and hoped she would whip one up for dinner that evening. Delen also received half of them, but her share had barely reached the kitchen before Jennifer pounced on some.

Jennifer handled the fruit and said, "Papa, these are lovely. Are they from Mrs DeMartini?" She had spoken to her after church last week. They had been discussing the Camembert experiment.

Jacob nodded. "Yes, love, there are hundreds more, and she's just letting them drop. That tree is loaded. I'm guessing that from the expression on your face, you have another cheese in mind?"

Jennifer was almost dancing a jig on the kitchen floor. "Yes, Papa. Do you remember that fresh Italian cheese Mr Tremayne sent us? I want to try some. Mrs DeMartini was telling me how they made it at home in Milan. It is only salt and lemon juice, and it's made from whey, not milk."

Bryn had heard their conversation from the sitting room. He joined them in his kitchen. "More ideas, Jennifer?" Bryn saw Billy outside listening; then, he vanished soon after.

Jennifer smiled at both men and nodded. "Yes, Mr Williams, I was thinking of trying my hand at some aged ricotta cheese. Mrs DeMartini told me about the soft cheeses she made at home. She said one was an aged ricotta, and the outside was smoked. But also there is a charcoal one. I thought I would have a bit of a play with some whey and see what happens."

Bryn looked puzzled. "You can make cheese from the whey? How?"

Jennifer shrugged and said, "Mrs DeMartini said so, but I haven't tried it. We have lots of whey, so I thought I'd have a go at it."

Delen joined the conversation too. "What do you need, dear? Is it a tricky process?"

Jennifer looked at the lemons. "Not according to Mrs DeMartini. She said I needed whey, salt, lemons, and cheesecloth. We have all that, and I can use the sample moulds as a fresh cheese." She stood waiting for the adults to decide for her to try.

As they stood thinking, Billy arrived with a large bucket of whey. He had been listening from the back door. "Hello Jen, I think I have everything. You said you have lemons?" He saw the large bucket of them on the table.

She said, "Oh! I don't think we'll need that much, Billy."

The five people set about making this first small test batch. The first thing needed was to juice the lemons and then strain them so there were no lumps, pips, or foreign bodies. Within an hour, the first fresh ricotta was hanging to drain. Delen was used to her kitchen being used for all sorts of test cheeses and flavours. Jacob now used her big stove to make the large vats of flavouring brines. All were keen to taste the fresh cheese. This one would be eaten immediately, but there was enough whey to make a few more.

The finished cheeses were left hanging and would be put in the smoker after dripping. These were not small wheels but more like a netted blob.

Bryn said, "I had presumed the whey was just wastewater. I had no idea we could have been making this all along. I had a pinch just before I tied it up; tangy but nice, with a very subtle flavour. How long do we have to leave it?"

Jennifer had finished washing up the dishes, Jacob was wiping, and Delen put things away. Jennifer replied, "Anything from one hour to overnight, Mr Williams. Pull one out tonight and leave the other overnight. We can try it on toast tomorrow morning. If it tastes all right, we might make more while we have the lemons. But we could smoke some so they can be taken to London."

The first cheese had not been permitted to cool before they cut open the tied cloth, and all tasted it. Half was devoured in a matter of seconds. The remaining half was set aside to cool fully and taste tomorrow. The smoking would enhance the delicate flavour of the cheese. This product would be another winner. However, these would mostly be for experimenting and family consumption. The flue had been used to smoke the hams and bacon they all adored for years.

By the end of the week, they had fifty small cheese balls either draining or in the kitchen stove flue smoking. The whey would now be processed into smoked ricotta. With a regular monthly delivery to London by ship, the cheeses arrived in far better condition. It took only a few days, and Bertram would have a wagon waiting as the ship pulled in.

~

1818 faded into 1819. Jennifer had just turned twenty.

The new cheeses were wending their way to their new owners only the day after unloading. They arrived in perfect condition and were an instant success. Sometimes, French chefs had messengers waiting for the ships to dock. As soon as the unloading started, they sent a maid or kitchen hand down to assist so they could be the first to obtain the new products. When the new smoked ricotta cheeses hit the market, they were instantly successful. So much so that Bertram was accosted by one of the French chefs and demanded information about where the delectable produce came from. It was rumoured that they did indeed come from the continent. Bertram stayed mute; however, he knew the time would soon arrive when Jennifer needed to be identified.

Unfortunately, that time came sooner than expected. He received a summons from the Duke of Shesham's residence and he demanded knowledge about the source of the product. Many presumed it was imported illegally from France. But the embargo had ceased some years before. The Duke insisted on meeting the maker to ensure he was not serving food that was not produced in England. Jennifer was required in London.

As the ship sailed with the latest consignment from the cheese cave, Billy was watching Jennifer's face. He could see that she was anxious. They had not gone down to the wharf; they left that to their fathers' as they could see the ship as it left the harbour.

Billy decided it was time to approach Jennifer and officially ask to court her. He would turn thirty-one next birthday, and at twenty, she was now ready to settle down and marry. They could have married two years ago, but his father had made him wait before declaring himself. Rather than say what was in his heart, he stood beside her and slipped his hand into hers. "Jen, I was wondering if you would be interested in taking our friendship to the next step. I want to court you officially."

Jennifer's reply was to take a step closer to him and rest her head against his chest. "I'd love that, Billy."

Those few words made his heart sing. He felt he had been waiting all his life for her. Waiting and watching, and not too passively either, he had nearly kissed her a few times. Soon, he would. Soon, she would be his. He dropped her hand and slid his arm around her shoulders, drawing her close. "I'll wait until you're ready, Jen, but I want to kiss you silly right now." He kissed the top of her head. "Just so you know."

With no one within sight, she turned to him and wrapped her arms around him. "I am ready now, Billy, except maybe not here as it's very public." She lifted her face to say the words.

Billy found it very hard not to do what he wanted to, and that was to kiss her as he wished. He did, however, give her a peck on the lips. "One day soon, I will properly kiss your red lips, Jennifer; one day soon."

Jennifer was thrilled, but she turned to him and said, "You really want me?" She was not a small framed girl but felt almost tiny in his arms. She felt safe and cherished. She had adored him for years, but he rarely showed her favouritism.

Billy drew her closer. "I do, and I always have, Jen. Have you never wondered why Father asked you to work with us? You were only ten, I was already twenty-one, and I was waiting for you to grow up even then. Now you have, but I have found those ten years hard."

"Billy," she was about to suggest something her parents would not approve of.

"Yes, Jen," he said as he flicked a wisp of her hair from her face. He wished to devour her lips.

Jennifer swallowed and softly said, "Billy, I'm ready. I want you to kiss me. I have wanted to be with you for some time, too." Her face radiated her happiness, yet she had no idea how beautiful that made her.

Without a second prompt, he lowered his head and did just that. He realised they would be seen if anyone looked up from the foreshore, but he didn't care. She fitted into his arms as though she was meant to be there. Neither heard the arrival of the wagon that had returned from the wharf. They didn't hear the squeal of delight from both of their mothers and the gasps of astonishment from her siblings. They were caught up in the moment and enjoying every second of it. Eventually, Isla's shout of delight broke them apart. Rather than fall apart in embarrassment, Jennifer rested her head on his chest.

Billy smiled at her almost possessive action. "Don't make me wait too long, Jen. I want to marry you, and soon." Billy dropped another kiss on her upturned lips before turning towards their family.

"Really?" she replied in surprise. He had only asked to court her moments ago; now, he had all but proposed, too.

"Really, Jen! And yes, that's an official request. However, I shall drop to one knee if you wish." Billy was grinning so broadly that she could hear the laughter in his voice.

"Don't you dare!" She was horrified that he would even contemplate that. They had discussed the embarrassment of public displays of affection, and yet they had been caught by their whole family in exactly that situation.

Billy smiled at her reaction. "I don't mean right now, sweet Jen, but I will when you're ready. You mean the world to me. I love you, just in case you are wondering. It's not just money or cheese or anything else; it's you. I just want to be able to call you mine. To keep you safe and protect you."

"I love you too, Billy. I have done so for a long time as well. It was that first kiss on the cheek about five years ago that made me realise you were not one of my brothers." She lowered her voice, saying, "I was very thankful for that fact. I was hoping that was what you meant by your occasional action or comment. I hoped you cared a little."

Billy felt like jumping and punching the air in delight. "I do, and now you know it. Let's go and face the music. At least we know that everyone will be happy."

The welcome was everything both wished for. Although not yet engaged, it was only a matter of time. Jennifer knew that as soon as they were alone, he would propose. Hopefully, that would be in the next few days. That they could walk holding hands was enough for the moment. Jennifer was ecstatic.

She was correct; Billy didn't wait long. A week later, she headed in to rub the cheeses but noticed the doors were shut. It wasn't cold, so they normally stood open. She pulled the door open and saw Billy waiting on one knee. He held a ring and broke into a beaming grin. "Private enough, Jen?" He chuckled. "Jennifer Kellow, will you marry me? Please say yes. Please!"

Jennifer gave a little squeal of joy. "Yes, of course I will."

Billy rose and slipped the ring on her finger. Years ago, she had said that a simple ring was all anyone needed as it was just a symbol of the promise. He had purchased a stunning ring, although it was also simple. It was gold and engraved with words of love. It had a small blue stone embedded into it. It fitted perfectly. She would not even have to remove it to rub the cheese. With the ring now on her hand, he drew her into his arms. "Don't make us wait months, Jen."

It took some time for her to reply. When she did, the words were not what he wanted to hear. "I won't, but Mama said that your papa had heard from Mr Tremayne, and he wants me in London to meet someone."

Billy already knew, and he was not happy. If she went, it would be better if they were married, for as a single lady, she would be at the mercy of the unscrupulous men in London. No, he didn't want her to go. He had a bad feeling about the trip. He held her as though his heart would break.

She said, "As soon as I return, we will marry. So be ready. I don't want a fuss, but I'll buy a dress to look spectacular for you. Like a real lady."

A frown crossed his brow. "I don't want you to be different from what you are now. I don't want you frocked and adorned in lace and satins. I want the drill-clad girl I've loved most of my life."

Jennifer giggled. "Then I'll buy a new drill gown and get married in a cheese apron."

Billy smirked as he said, "Do you really think either of our mothers would permit that?"

Jennifer wrapped her arms around him. "Somehow, I don't think so, but Billy, I promise we'll get married as soon as I return."

~

A few weeks later, just after Easter in 1820, Mrs DeMartini offered to escort Jennifer on her first trip to the Old Smoke, as the filthy, smoggy city was called. The lady was an experienced traveller after spending much time touring the continent with her husband for their year of marriage. Since she was widowed, she had returned home every few years. She knew the etiquette of a lady travelling unaccompanied. Jennifer had never even been to Truro, the main town in Cornwall, let alone any further. In the past years, her clothing had improved a little, but her gowns were unsuitable for an interview with a duke in London. She needed to sell her cheeses, so she needed to be presentable. One of the gowns she would buy would be used as her wedding dress. To say she was excited was an understatement, but she was fearful too. Money was now available, and she had instructions to buy a selection of items for her family. Isla needed new boots again. Polly had grown so fast that she had outgrown all her gowns. She felt spending their hard-earned cash on frivolous dresses was a waste, but they needed to be decently clothed, as did the boys. Still, this trip was required. Hopefully, she would return in less than a month. Having never been away from her family, she left with great foreboding.

As the ropes were cast off from the small jetty, Jennifer held back her tears. She had refused to let Billy come to the wharf, as leaving was hard enough. She knew she would fall to pieces if he were there. He stood on the headland watching her go. They had said a fond farewell in private earlier that morning. He stood where he had asked to court her only weeks earlier. Her parents had both come to the ship to say farewell. There were many hugs, kisses and tears before the travellers went to see the small cabin. The two ladies saw that their bags had arrived and were relieved they had a reasonable cabin; they returned to wave farewell from the deck.

Watching from his spot on the headland was a dejected Billy. He was standing all alone, and his heart was heavy. Something didn't feel right about this journey. He did not want her to leave. If they were married, he could have gone with them; however, Jacob did not wish to rush the wedding. Billy wanted to race down the hill and pull her off the boat. He did not want her to go at all. So he stood waving until it was too unsafe to get closer to the cliff's edge. He blew kisses and shouted his love until they were too far out.

This boat carried a batch of cheeses. It had loaded the new stock from the bay where they lived. Jennifer had also packed some fresh ricotta. She wished to see how it travelled. As this cheese needed to be kept cool, she wished to see if they would arrive in good enough condition to sell. Bertram had arranged accommodation for them at a genteel inn in London. From there, he would escort them to the various fancy houses and venues they needed to visit.

The trip to London was one of the most unpleasant experiences that Jennifer had undertaken. Mrs DeMartini had warned her about seasickness, however, she had no idea that it felt like you were turning your body inside out each time she vomited. The trip took a week, and only in the last few days in the river did her stomach feel it was back in its correct place. The only benefit was that it took her mind off Billy.

Over the days on board, Mrs DeMartini had insisted that Jennifer eat and drink, and if Jennifer had been a less congenial person, she would have shouted at her. However, the food made her feel slightly better until she threw it up again. The black tea certainly helped, even if only to wash the taste of the bile from her mouth. They were now slowly floating up the Thames River with the tide, but it was calm.

Bertram met them at the wharf and took them to the accommodation he had arranged. However, London was a rude shock for Jennifer. The city's smog, stench, and filth were vastly different from the crisp Cornish countryside. She quickly realised how it got its name, Old Smoke. Even the tin mine sites were cleaner than the filth-strewn streets; excrement littered the gutters, and chamber pots had obviously been emptied from the houses into the streets. Jennifer's eyes grew larger and larger the deeper they went into the rat-infested city.

The four-story high Angel Inn at Islington was the most prominent building Jennifer had been in. She clung to Mrs DeMartini as they walked through the foyer of the inn. It was quite clean inside, and the large scented floral displays had dulled the smells from outside. The heavy scents masked the unpleasant odours. What lay ahead would be a test of her faith.

Chapter 7   Premonitions 1820

$\mathcal{B}$illy stayed on the headland for some time. He felt so wrong about the trip. So much so that he was tempted to head to London by road as another boat would not come that week. He was so unsettled that his father found him sitting on the cliff edge two hours after the ship had rounded the headland.

Bryn lowered himself onto the grass beside his son. "She'll be back, Billy; you know that. She loves you."

Billy's sad eyes lifted to meet his father's. "I know, but I feel so wrong about this trip. We should have been married long ago, and then I could have gone with her. Father, I am seriously agitated." He punched his chest. "It feels wrong here. For some reason, I'm worried. I've waited so long for her, and I feel something is just not right."

Bryn knew his son would not speak unless he felt something deeply. "If you feel so, follow her. Go with my blessing. We can manage here but bring her home even if you must marry her there. I'm sorry we held you back for so long. We did it for her sake; you know that."

Billy sniffed and nodded, unable to trust his voice. Eventually, he said, "I know, Father, but I will go, for I am really concerned. My spirit is disquieted, for I feel she is not safe."

Bryn patted his son's shoulder. "Then go, son, bring her home."

By noon that day, Billy was packed and set off to walk to Penzance. From there, he would catch the mail coach to Truro.

The twenty-seven-mile trip would take the remainder of the day. From there, he would make his way to London. Like Jennifer, he had not ever travelled further than the nearby towns. Even contemplating travelling to Truro instilled fear into Billy. That he had to travel alone to London was daunting.

~

Eight days after Jennifer left Cornwall, she was overwhelmed by the big city and engulfed by Mrs DeMartini's expectations of her. She was being fitted for new gowns and hated this endless standing and pinning. It was the most trying and uncomfortable experience she had endured, even worse than the seasickness.

She refused laced-up, bone-lined corsets and insisted that her loose-fitting undergarments were perfectly adequate. She did accept new drawers and a chemise or two, but not in silk, only in cotton. The latest fashion of the split drawers was something Jennifer did not relish; however, with the new gowns and volume of undergarments and petticoats, she could understand their use. The split made using the chamber pot easy. She reluctantly donned the new apparel and returned to the inn laden with new clothing and wearing her new underwear. Her old apparel was tied in a bundle. She wore a new blue gown; the three others would be sent later. Admittedly, she had delighted in trying on silk night attire, and Mrs DeMartini insisted that she purchase a new silk night rail, even if only for her wedding night. Although she had blushed scarlet, Jennifer relented and permitted the purchase of one slinky night rail. It was so sheer that it was almost indecent. She could imagine Billy's embarrassment as he saw her in it on their wedding night.

Mrs DeMartini assured her that he would love it.

The remainder of the new gowns would be ready the following day, and in the meantime, Bertram planned to show Jennifer his small cheese storeroom in London. She wished to know how her cheeses travelled, and he promised to show them.

The new ricotta seemed to have arrived in good condition. One of the French chefs had already placed an order for some for the duke's table for the following evening. Bertram had yet to introduce her to the inquisitive duke, who had demanded her presence. Rather than take Bertram's word, he insisted he meet the maker personally. Bertram had even tried to get him to go to Cornwall. He had refused.

After their shopping trip, Jennifer was wondering how to occupy her time. The inn had no library, so she stood watching the comings and goings of the traffic along the road outside the inn. She was still not used to wearing her engagement ring and was often fiddling with it. She missed Billy, and she missed her family. She wished she had not come. Even alone in her room, she did not feel safe. She was used to the familiar noises of her family in the cramped cottage. Mrs DeMartini was only next door, but she felt like she was suffocating in the smokey fetid-smelling air of the city; the room was almost worse. She would insist on returning home as soon as the required meeting was over.

They descended the inn staircase to the dining room, and Jennifer felt all eyes were watching her. Her new drawers were breezy, to say the least, but as she had washed her old underwear and they were drying in her room, she had little choice but to don them. She may well look the part of a London lady, but she did not feel it.

She was not used to sleeping in, as she was normally up at dawn each morning to milk the cows, so dawn saw Jennifer awake and standing at the window again, watching the movement in the courtyard. Hackney carriages came and went along the busy street. Lamplighters snuffed the lamps, and flower sellers set up their stalls on the corners of the road.

In London, other than servants, nothing started until eight or nine in the morning; she felt it was a waste of the best part of the day. By now, at home, the milk would already be set to rise. Isla would be preparing the moulds for the afternoon's cheese-making. Today, part of the morning milking would be set aside to make the triple cream cheese. This was the first time Jennifer was not involved. Finding her clothing still not dry, she dressed in her new attire again and set out to deliver the cheese order to the other chef Bertram had mentioned. Having often made home deliveries, she could surely do one easy job like this without any problems.

~

Billy was trying to find where the mail coach left in Bath. It would take a day more to reach his destination. The only seat on the previous coach took a circuitous route. He had stayed in Exeter, then Taunton, before arriving in Bath. He realised that he now should have caught the Salisbury coach rather than the Bath one. It had taken a week to get just here, but he was over halfway there. Hopefully, from Bath, the trip would be quicker. He had travelled over one hundred and ninety miles so far. That was one hundred and eighty-nine more miles than he felt comfortable with. There were still over a hundred and eighteen more miles to go, but the roads should be better as they drew closer to London.

They changed horses every ten miles, and he often slept in the coach as it travelled late into the twilight. He was anxious, as Jennifer would have already arrived in London. He yet had to find where Islington was and then the Angel Inn. Bertram had told the two families the details of the trip. Billy had Jacob's permission to escort Jennifer wherever she needed to go, even to marry her if required. He was kicking himself that he had not brought any proof that Banns had already been read. They could have been married immediately, and he could have kept her safe. Now, he would only be permitted to be her fiancé. At least, that was something, and she wore his ring as evidence.

The miles ahead of him were as uncomfortable as the last ones. The bouncing carriage jostled the passengers, and although they changed with each stage, they were all as unpleasant on the nose as he knew himself to be.

In Cornwall, he had a daily swim. It was the only way the Kellow boys, and he could get clean after working in the mine. Many miners didn't bother to wash. He did, as did his friends. Unlike many of the village girls, Jennifer and the other two girls were always scrupulously clean. He knew Angelina DeMartini had been watching over them for many years, and they could easily pass as gentry. Even the way they dressed and their hair was fancier than a milkmaid would normally wear.

When he finally reached London, he had been in the same clothes for nearly ten days. When Billy arrived at the inn, there seemed to be some kerfuffle in the courtyard. A footman was holding the reins of a hackney carriage. His own conveyance, another hackney carriage, had not even bothered to turn into the courtyard but offloaded him in the street.

Billy paid and took in the chaotic scene before him and wondered how he would get around them. He asked a bystander, who explained the three uniformed men were Bow Street Runners, and a rowdy group of patrons surrounded them. Billy was going to skirt around the group when he recognised the figure of Mrs DeMartini in the centre of the ruckus. If she were there, where was Jennifer? He dumped his bag where he stood and elbowed his way to the side of Mrs DeMartini. She had now been pushed away from the centre of the group.

"Where's Jen?" was all he managed to shout as he approached. He saw her point to the collapsed figure being escorted by the Runners. Where was Mr Tremayne? What had occurred?

Billy kept elbowing his way forward and eventually drew close enough to identify Jen being held up from under the feet of the seething crowd. He attempted to gain her attention. "Jennifer! Jen, I'm here. I've come for you."

She stirred but did not lift her head. She thought she heard Billy's voice, but that was impossible.

Billy tried again. "Jennifer, it's me, Billy; I've come to help you."

Jennifer did then lift her head, and their eyes locked across the surge of people still separating them. "Billy, help me!" She mouthed and tried, struggling to get to him.

The two Runners only held her tighter.

Billy pushed himself closer; he refused to give up. "Let her go. She's my fiancé."

Eventually, the third Runner motioned for the crowd to permit Billy to get to her. Miraculously, they parted, and Billy wrapped Jennifer into his arms protectively.

Her swollen, tear-filled eyes looked up at him lovingly, and she asked, "Why are you here?"

He whispered, "I felt something was wrong. I left soon after you did, but I had to come overland."

Clinging to him tightly, only then did she weep. The relief at him being here to support her overwhelmed her. She had done nothing wrong.

With her safe in his arms, they would deal with whatever was ahead of them. As her fiancé, he would demand that the Runners discuss the situation with him. They planned to face the future together, whatever that entailed. He still needed to sort out what had occurred. A well-dressed gentleman stood slightly off to the side. His arms were folded, and the look of wrath he gave the embracing couple did not bode well. Ire and anger were etched on his face.

Billy disregarded him and turned to the closest Runner. "Can we find somewhere quieter to sort this out?"

The man nodded and set about shooing away the crowd.

The three Bow Street Runners eventually managed to dismiss the rabble, and only then did Mrs DeMartini make her way towards them. Behind her was a footman from the inn carrying his bag. Bertram was still nowhere to be seen. Jennifer had not moved from the circle of Billy's arms. Her head was hidden on his shoulder; an occasional sob gave her emotions away. It was where he wished her to stay. With her now physically safe, he began to wonder what all the hullabaloo was about. There was still far too much noise to ask many questions.

Billy saw one of the Runners in discussion with the angry gentleman, and he nodded and called for one of the watching footmen. All the staff from the inn still stood at the doorway gazing at them.

They quickly vanished after just one look from the angry man. The footman went inside and promptly returned, nodding. He had arranged for the small group to use a parlour in the inn. Two footmen followed in their wake, carrying not only the basket from the hackney carriage but Billy's bag too.

Billy shooed away the waiting hand of the Runner, and he kept Jennifer close. She was half leaning on him, and Mrs DeMartini stood on her other side if required.

Of Bertram, there was still no sign.

One of the Runners led the way into the parlour and checked to ensure the room was empty. With a nod to the others, he held the door open and ushered them to take seats. When the door closed behind Mrs DeMartini, all started talking at once.

Billy's angry voice topped them all. "Quiet!" he boomed. "You are all frightening her. What is my fiancé supposed to have done?" His angry visage took in the four men. He pointed to the lead Runner and said, "You seem to be in charge; what is Miss Kellow supposed to have done?"

With a somewhat nervous glance toward the angry, well-dressed man leaning on the mantelpiece, he said, "Accusations have been made that she has been passing fraudulent money."

Billy was astounded. The exclamation of "What?" escaped him. Looking at his beloved Jen and knowing she was innocent of this crime, he laughed. "You have no idea how ridiculous this accusation is. She has no more idea of what paper money looks like than the cows she normally milks. She's a cheese maker, not a criminal. She has come to London at the request of the Duke of Shesham. He demanded that he meet the maker of the cheeses he has been purchasing. Our agent is Mr Bertram Tremayne, and he insisted that she come in person. As we are not yet married, I had to come overland while she came by sea, with Mrs DeMartini as her companion and chaperone. How is she supposed to have accessed this money?" He looked at Jen's worried brow. It was furrowed, and she was on the verge of tears again.

Again, the angry man and the Runner started speaking simultaneously. The name of the duke certainly had caught the Runner's attention.

Billy lifted his hand to silence them. "One at a time, please." He pointed to the Runner.

"Sir, first, please introduce yourself," the Runner said.

Billy nodded. "I am William Williams, from Newlyn in Cornwall; I am affianced to Miss Kellow. However, I have known her all of her life. She works for my father and has done so since childhood. We plan to marry as soon as she returns from the trip. Banns have already been called."

The Runner seemed to accept his words. "Fine, then, as you are not yet married, she is still responsible for her actions. If you were, then it would be your head on the block, sir." The Runner glanced at the well-dressed, angry man. "Now you, sir. Please introduce yourself."

Billy gulped. He knew the Runner's statement to be true.

The gentleman bowed in acknowledgement. "I am Baron Mortonford." He turned to Billy and said snidely, "The Right Honourable Lord Mortonford, for your information, sir." He said it mockingly as though he had his cheeks stuffed full of plums. Spittle nearly hit the Runner as he spoke.

The Runner also nodded acknowledgement to his introduction. He turned to Billy and said, "This gentleman has accused her of feloniously passing fraudulent money. He purchased some of her wares and paid with a five-pound note. She produced three forged one-pound notes as change."

The well-dressed man near the fireplace had an evil smirk on his lips. He also had a set of nail scratches on his cheek. "She thought she could get away with fraud, but I'm wise to the tricks of people of her way of life."

Billy was livid at his innuendo. "And exactly what way of life would that be, sir? Exactly what are you accusing my affianced wife of?"

The man was a little taken aback at the question. "She provocatively sauntered into my house, selling her wares, then said she was affronted when I took what she offered. No honest, self-respecting lady comes calling on a single man's residence alone. I presumed the role of a cheese seller was a ruse, and when I offered to purchase her wares, she did not object. I merely took what was offered. I paid upfront, and it was only when I checked the change that I found them forgeries."

Billy was horrified at what he heard. "You defiled her? How dare you touch such an innocent?" He struggled to push Jennifer from his arms to exact his revenge, but she clung to him, not allowing him to leave her side.

The man shrugged. "How was I to know she was an innocent until it was too late?"

The Runner was aghast at what he heard. The Baron willingly admitted he had taken advantage of the girl and then accused her of passing forged money. "Sir, you did not reveal the entire story."

The man shrugged with a smirk. "She got what was coming to her."

Jennifer looked at Billy as though she was fearful he would reject her. "I had no idea, Billy. No one told me I should have asked to see the chef at the staff door. We don't even have a back door at home. I sold him some cheeses as I did at other houses, and then he... then he..." she looked at the well-dressed smug man with daggers shooting from her eyes, "... He abused me in a vile way. He... he stole my innocence. Even we don't do that, Billy. He's so much bigger than I am, and I could not fight him off me, hence the scratch on his cheek." Her voice dropped, ashamed she was now ruined. Ashamed and distraught that Billy would no longer want her. She wondered if he would cast her off.

Billy hugged her tightly. "I love you anyway, Jen, but we will deal with the consequences of that later." He turned to the man, his voice almost dripping venom. "Are you so cock-sure of yourself that you feel you can force yourself on any poor girl? The scratches on your face show she was not willing. And that you now accuse her of such a false crime adds to my anger. I would call you out for a fight of fisticuffs, but in London, you would probably demand swords or pistols. Neither of which I have handled before. We don't need much paper money in Cornwall, so I wouldn't know what it looked like."

The evil man sniggered. "My charge of fraud still stands. She may have unknowingly given me forged notes, but that changes nothing. I am within my rights to accuse her. She alone must face the magistrate for his verdict as you are not married to her."

Billy understood the consequences all too well. He also knew that more than one in ten one-pound notes in London were forged; however, he also knew that Jennifer had never seen any paper money before. The cheese money had gone directly to her father. She had never had reason to handle money other than a few coins. In his anger, he turned to her chaperone. "Mrs DeMartini, where were you at this time? You were supposed to be chaperoning her! She was under your care."

The Italian lady flushed scarlet. "I am in error, sir. However, I was not aware that she had even left the inn. It was very early morning, and I was resting after a busy day of dress-fitting yesterday. She was supposed to be in her room doing likewise. I believe that yesterday, Mr Tremayne sent word that she had been requested to meet with some of the chefs and had sent her a list of the addresses. Had I known what she intended, sir, I would have gone with her. However, she did not see fit to tell me."

Billy nodded. It was typical of Jennifer not to wish to disturb her friend. He blew his cheeks out in utter frustration. "Fine, then what next?"

The Runner realised that he must arrest her and take her before a magistrate. "Sir, Miss Kellow must come with us. I will give her time to change and gather her things; however, she won't need much." He turned to Mrs DeMartini. "Take her to her room and stay with her while she changes." He motioned for one of the Runners to follow them. "Wait outside her room."

Billy told her to leave and kissed her reassuringly. "Jen, it was not your fault, and I will love you no matter what happens. Be assured of that. Go and change. I'll be here when you return. Do not fear, for I'll stay with you as long as possible."

Jennifer was sore from the violation that had occurred. She wished to wash and put on her own clothing. She was emotionally fragile and still on the verge of tears. She knew she needed to clean herself up as she was sure she was bleeding, but she wanted to return to Billy as quickly as possible. Reluctantly, she followed her friend from the room. She vowed never to wear split drawers again as they permitted the man easy access to her privates.

As the door closed, Billy turned on the unsuspecting smug man and planted him a facer that sent him reeling across the room. The man crumpled from the power of the punch. Billy's fist had shot out with lightning speed. "You dare ever besmirch a girl or force yourself on my Jen again, and you won't know what hit you."

Hardly believing what they were seeing, the two remaining Runners turned their backs on the repercussions of the quick manoeuvre by the insulted fiancé. They smiled at each other at the results of the skirmish. The disrespecting fancy man had got what he deserved. Neither of the Runners went to his aid nor took action against Billy. He had the right to be angry and take his revenge as he wished, and this was less messy than a duel.

They cast a glance at each other and smirked. The toff had received his comeuppance, and his claret flowed freely onto the floor. His handsome visage would be permanently disfigured as his nose was now distorted. He would never forget this girl or this day and his abusive actions. The girl's fingernail marks had cut deep. They would probably leave scars.

The six-foot-tall warrior who defended his beloved's honour was still livid. Billy paced the room and waited for his lady to return.

The victim was still prostrated on the floor. If he were wise, he would remain there. Unwilling to move, the baron groaned in agony but realised that he had met his match. He could feel that his nose had been severely rearranged.

~

Twenty minutes later, a tap on the door signalled the return of Jennifer and her two escorts. The Runner carried her small valise, and Billy could tell Jennifer had been crying. Her eyes were red and swollen. Disregarding propriety, he held his arms open to her. She sank into them and wept afresh. She had not even noticed the man lying on the floor. All she saw was that Billy still wanted to hold her. "I'm so sorry, Billy. I'm so very sorry," she murmured into his shoulder. "I had no idea men were so evil. I am tainted and now unfit to be your wife. I release you from your offer." She struggled to be released from his grasp and tugged off her beloved ring.

Billy was horrified. "No, Jen, I do not want to be released. I love you even though this has occurred. I refuse to let you go. I waited long enough for you, love. If I balk at the first obstacle, I'm not worthy of being your husband. No, I refuse to release you." He drew her close again and kissed the top of her head. "I will marry you for better or for worse, and if the worse comes early in our marriage, so be it."

He felt her nod against his chest, but she remained silent. No one spoke, all waiting for the unhappy couple to have a moment together. Her accuser had barely stirred, and until he could bring forth his charges before a magistrate, there was no hurry. She was not going anywhere.

Jen pulled back a little. She realised she was mid-cycle in her monthly flow. "Billy, what happens if there is a child?"

Billy had already thought of this. "If that happens, I shall bring it up as my own. It will never know; even though I may not be the father, you will be its mother, and therefore I will love it wholeheartedly." Billy glanced at the man on the floor. He was eventually moving and was now being assisted to sit up. He held a handkerchief to his bent and bleeding nose. Billy said, "Jen, if there is a child, he will never be permitted to have a say in the child's life, but I will make him pay for it. He owes you that much."

The man was now sitting up and heard the conversation. Finally acknowledging his inappropriate behaviour, he nodded and realised all the Runners, and Mrs DeMartini bore witness to his vow. "But she still must answer for the fraudulent notes. I will not let her get away with that."

Billy was furious. For three measly pounds, he had ruined her life; no, he had selfishly ruined both their lives.

Two Runners heaved the baron to his feet in a not-so-gentle manner. They did not respect him now since his admission of violating an innocent girl, yet he still accused the girl of fraud, and she had admitted to it. The charges must be answered. They roughly ushered him out the door before Billy could land another facer. The baron's shirt was already drenched with blood, but it was nothing to what he had done to the girl. Her life would never be the same. The Runners knew Billy was within his rights to cast her aside. They could see that Billy was nearly unable to control his wrath. He only let the baron leave, as to retaliate again would have meant he needed to release Jennifer. She needed him and his strength.

~

Shortly before Jennifer left the inn, the Duke of Shesham had summoned Bertram. He was being probed for information about the cheeses while the fiasco at the inn occurred. Unaware of the events that would change Jennifer's life irreparably, they arranged a meeting with Jennifer for the following morning.

For Bertram, the interview had not gone as expected as the duke pumped him for details for nearly three hours. From the minute details of his early life in Cornwall, meeting Bryn Williams, his marriage to a childhood friend, and their life in the small coastal area. How Jennifer's family fitted in, and what life in a small Cornish village was like. Bertram liked the austere man. His visage was hawk-like, and his dark brows were furrowed with concern.

The duke learnt about Bryn's wife, Delen, and the small dairy she inherited from her family. Bryn Williams had willingly moved from Wales to marry her, and it was through that union that Bertram had found a new role.

Bertram had been itching to leave Newlyn and his tin mining life and move to London. Being Bryn and Delen's agent gave him that opportunity. He had been equally surprised when a new variety of flavours appeared in minute batches some years ago. More for his tasting and appraisal than in commercial volumes; they were still not large quantities, so he offered them only to his best customers. A quarter-size wheel occasionally came, and Bertram would offer taste morsels to his favourite clientele. He would then give feedback to Bryn. Four were superb, and these were put into production in the dairy.

The duke's chef had been a regular for some time and had, therefore, been one to benefit. When the new small wheels had finally matured, their reputation had already been murmured through the better kitchens of London. The king's chef had even requested one of the next batch of cheeses. The price the king's chef had paid after his first taste made it worth Bryn's while to expand his production. The duke's table, however, often was given free samples for the duke's personal consumption. He had contacts in high places, and a word in the right ear would ensure the venture's success.

When Bertram tasted the full-cream *Southern Belle* cheese, he realised that the price of this alone could be astronomical. He tripled what he thought he would get and was paid that price without question. Jennifer's new soft cheeses would take London by storm, including the smoked ricotta and the new white rind soft cheeses. She eventually perfected the Normandy variety and invented her own creamy variation. It was unnamed by the family, but as Jennifer meant *Fair One* or *White Wave*, Bertram started referring to this white creamy cheese as a *Cornish White Wave* special. The batches of the new ricotta-styled cheese she had brought with her had already found their way onto some of the more famous tables in London. It was this smoked delicacy that had brought the summons from the duke. He had never tasted anything like it before. When it was followed by the latest batch of the *Southern Belle*, he sent a carriage for Bertram to be brought immediately; no refusal would be tolerated.

Bertram did not even have time to pen a quick note to the ladies. He was bundled into the carriage and expected to be able to join the women at the inn at noon as planned. It was eight o'clock when the carriage arrived at the duke's door. He had been for a morning ride in the park, and Bertram had sat twiddling his fingers, awaiting the duke's return.

After the grilling, an appointment for ten the following morning had been arranged. Bertram was excited that the duke had promised his patronage to the dairy on condition that he be offered the first taste of all new batches and varieties. He would willingly endorse the locally made product over imported similar items. Bertram released a cheer as the carriage door closed and pulled out from the steps. He could not wait to share the good news with Jennifer and the lovely Italian lady who accompanied her. He instructed the duke's carriage to drive directly to the Angel Inn in Islington. As he entered the inn, two burly men were escorting a bloodied gentleman from the parlour. He walked to the door of the room to peek in. He was surprised to hear a familiar man's voice call, "Enter."

Bertram did and then froze. The last person he expected to see was Billy Williams. Jennifer looked up from Billy's arms as he walked into the room. He could see her eyes were red from weeping.

She gasped and said, "Mr Tremayne, where have you been?"

Rather than answer, Bertram looked at the rough-looking gentleman beside Billy and Jennifer. "Who are you, sir?"

The man pulled him up to his height before replying, "A Runner, sir, and whom may you be?"

Bertram's eyebrows shot up, and he enquired with a smile, "A Runner? Is their reunion that monumental?"

The Runner quickly shook his head. "No, but the accusations of passing fraudulent pound notes are enough to demand my presence."

The shock on Bertram's face showed he knew nothing of this situation. "Fraud? Jennifer, where did you get the money?"

She was about to answer when the Runner raised his hand to stop her. "Miss, you will be asked to answer all those questions at a later time. For now, please refrain from discussing the case."

Jennifer turned to Bertram. "Why didn't you tell us where you were?" Her eyes flicked to Mrs DeMartini's startled gaze.

Bertram saw tears appear in Jennifer's eyes again. He was stunned into silence as he knew he had paid for the gowns they had ordered yesterday as she only had a few coins on her; she had said she had no other money. Then he remembered that she had asked for some of the new cheeses yesterday, and he had supplied her with the addresses of the kitchens that had requested samples. She probably sold some, but where? With the Runner in the room, he could not even ask as they had been forbidden to discuss the case. He said, "Cheeses?" in such a way that she nodded in reply.

The Runner reluctantly permitted Billy to accompany Jennifer as he escorted them from the room.

Bertram and Mrs DeMartini were to remain at the inn in case required. Both were left standing in the middle of a disaster area.

A pool of congealing blood was near the fireplace, close to an overturned chair. A bloodied handkerchief was the evidence that some form of skirmish had occurred, but why?

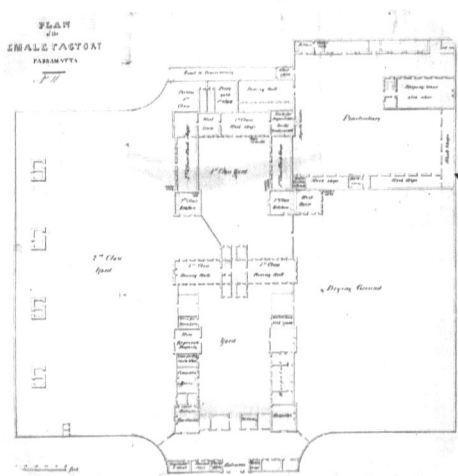

Chapter 8   Parramatta Bound 1983

*J*enny's interest in her family history didn't wane as She grew older. She worked with her mother on the family tree. They had taken the family tree back another two generations, finding out that her namesake, Jennifer, had given birth to a child. But they knew that already. They still had no idea how or why she had been sent out. Who was the child's father, and who was this Billy Williams, who was listed as her husband? He was not registered as the child's father.

Jenny had just received notification that she had been successful in getting a job at Rydalmere in the Department of Agriculture. She found a flat and moved in with the minimum of furniture. A fold-up bed, second-hand fridge, bean bag, and portable black and white television were all she had. Thankfully, her room had a built-in wardrobe, but she could survive until she could hunt around the second-hand stores for some furniture.

As she would be living in the area, Jenny was determined to do some more research. Hopefully, the library in Parramatta would be better than the Gosford one. There were new microfiche files that were stored in this more extensive library. Now a member of the Genealogical Society, Jenny had made many visits to the Society's records in Kent Street, Sydney, and she had learnt a lot, but how the convict history was linked was still an enigma. Her gramps said, "Start with yourself and work backwards." She had based her searches on her grandfather's tiny family tree but needed proof that he was correct. So, the starting point was herself; her father was William Iain Kellow, Gramps was Logan Kellow, and his father was Christopher, and she discovered that he was born in 1880. His father was Jacob William Kellow, born in 1860; he married

Isabella in 1880. Another Kellow was the next name they found, and it was his father, Christoper Kellow Williams, who had been born in 1821 in Parramatta. The Williams had obviously been added later as it was in a different writing. Baptism records listed his mother, Jennifer Williams née Kellow, born in 1799, who was now her goal in research. But the entry of her conviction had a line through it. All that she knew was that she was arrested in London. Five generations existed between the two Jennifers. Jenny was determined to learn as much as possible about the first Jennifer. She had been told that there were convict records and that she may need to go to the State Library in Sydney to access them.

On the first Saturday in town, Jenny planned to try the local library first and see what information they had. She found a floor plan of the Female Factory and wondered how much time Jennifer had spent there. She had the exercise book her grandfather had written his story in and the family tree they had filled in. Jenny's quest for her namesake was becoming an obsession. She checked in to the research section of the Parramatta Library and was escorted to the upstairs to the Family History Research section.

The nice lady about her age reminded her of Mrs Fox from the library many years ago. The lady showed Jenny where the information she sought would be found.

Jenny found a spare table and laid out her notebooks and pencils. She thought she would spend about half an hour looking to see what she could find. Microfiche sheet after sheet, Jenny searched. The fact that baby Christopher had been born under the name of Kellow but also had Williams added at his Baptism was a puzzle. Who was the Williams? Why did his children not use that surname? How was she to narrow down such a common name? Jenny felt she had been looking for nearly half an hour when she realised that not only had she missed lunch but that it was three o'clock.

The nice lady came over again, introduced herself as Michelle Fox, and asked how she was doing.

Jenny explained her search, and Michelle had found Jennifer's records in mere moments. Jenny kicked herself that she didn't seek help earlier.

Michelle flicked over the pages and turned to the 1820 listings. "Jennifer Kellow arrived in September 1820 on the *Morley*, and she must have given birth sometime after she arrived."

Jenny showed Michelle the listing. "I think this was contradictory to what the other records said as it said she came 'with child'."

The lady smiled. "Dear, the records were done and transcribed by semi-literate sailors and soldiers. Then, they were often transcribed again, and information was lost. The actual journal is in the Mitchell Library in Sydney. My mother, Janie Fox, used to work there. But 'with child' is the term they used before 'pregnant.' 'In the family way,' 'interesting' or 'expectant' were also used."

Jenny sat upright. With a beaming smile, she said, "I met Mrs Fox years ago. It was when I was only eight, but she was so helpful. After we left that day, she kept looking and found us some more information. Your mother found a record of the baby being born in the colony. But she sent us to the Society of Genealogy in Kent Street, Sydney, where we found more."

Michelle said, "Exactly, transcribing from the original to the official record often had errors like this. Mother loved picking them up. The poor women were convicts, so the soldiers didn't care much about them; some were just recorded as 'a woman'. The poor girls were treated like dirt, but most were only petty thieves. I'm sure many stole just to be transported, as their lives in England were even worse than they had here."

Jenny frowned. "How so, Michelle? Weren't they village girls and the like?"

Michelle released a long sigh. "Oh, if only they were. No, these poor girls often came from the poorest of the poor, from the slums like the Rookery in London and other big towns and cities. They had little hope of a decent life of any sort, you know, prostitution, starvation, and the like. They had no way out of the cycle of poverty, and even if they had some money available, their father would normally have taken it. Back then, women had no rights at all. Even in the upper levels of society, their marriages were normally arranged."

Jenny gasped.

Michelle nodded. "Moreover, they never married out of their class or would be shunned. The middle class may have had it a bit better, but rarely were they permitted to marry for love. The only life path a woman had was marriage. Anything else, and they were ostracised. If the nobility did marry outside their class, it was hidden as much as possible, and no one in the aristocracy or nobility ever had anything to do with trade. That was a dirty word. Occasionally, one married an American person who would bring in much-needed wealth. It was called *new money* and was frowned upon. Love was a word not often associated with marriages in the upper echelon. Men often had mistresses and kept opera singers and actresses for their dalliances. Their wives were kept at home and expected to breed heirs. All this, of course, is a huge generalisation, but it was often the case. We'll do some more digging on your namesake and see what we can find. We should be able to get her court record if it still exists, and it might give us more information about her background and details of her crime. Once we know more about her, we can delve a little deeper."

Jenny was so excited. She said, "Could we, really?"

As Michelle was speaking, she pulled up a chair. "Mum was good at this sort of ancient detective work. She, of course, inspired me. For you to have met her and also remember her is amazing."

For another half hour, the pair scrolled through the records. Michelle said, "Look, Jenny! Jennifer had not arrived with *a* child but arrived *with child*, as in she was expecting one, but she had not delivered it, so Mum was right." Something puzzled her. "I wonder why there is a line through the entry? I've not come across that before." She shrugged.

Jenny said, "I found that in another place, too. I don't know why either."

Michelle's face had a frown etched on her brow. The records seemed to infer that the child had been born in the colony. Michelle sat back in her chair, biting her lips. "I wonder!" was all she said before she walked over to another great leather-bound tome in the reference section. "Some of the surgeon's journals have been transcribed. I wonder if the 1820 voyage of the *Morley* is one of them?"

Michelle flicked them and shook her head. "Sorry, not yet; we may have to wait a few years before all the documentation is transcribed and printed. They have a swathe of work being done for the bicentenary in five years. We may have to wait that long or even a bit longer. Jenny, would you mind if I kept some of your convicts' details and your name and number and kept hunting? I feel that we have a connection through my mum. And as you met her, connecting with someone who knew her is a delight. I miss her so much. She started you off on your search. I want to help you along this path or even help you finish it."

Jenny gave Michelle her complete attention. "You would do that, Michelle? I feel so linked to this woman and know nothing about her. I want to learn as much as possible, but I'm floundering. I have no idea where to start or where to look."

"I have a few years of experience in this, Jenny. Leave it with me." Michelle was as excited as Jenny. She missed her mum so much, and to find a link, even though tenuous, was a delight. Also, the story intrigued her. Yes, she would follow this up. This story piqued her interest.

Jenny rewrote the tree she had so far. The details were slowly filling.

Chapter 9   Convicted 1820

$\mathcal{B}$illy had not even thought about accommodation. Jennifer was under arrest, and he refused to leave her side. The three Runners had a wagon with a barred cabin at the back. Billy insisted on accompanying her, even to being locked in the mobile cell. He vouchsafed to stay with her until he was no longer permitted to do so. If that meant he stayed with her in a prison cell, he would try to get permission.

The wagon was driven by one Runner and escorted by the other two mounted on either side of the wagon. Billy had been informed as they entered that their destination was the Bow Street Magistrate's Court rather than the Old Bailey. The Bow Street Magistrates would hear her case, and the sentence would be handed down immediately. If the baron was still intent on pressing charges, he only had today to pursue his case or it would be dismissed.

When Billy realised the baron had to appear in person, he hoped he would not turn up. He knew his punch had inflicted a busted nose and hoped that would not hinder their case. The man seemed to acknowledge that his carnal actions were inappropriate. Did he not realise Jennifer was utterly innocent of the accusation of fraud?

On arrival at their destination, the two mounted Runners handed off their horses to the attending groom and unlocked the grill door of the carriage.

Billy alighted and assisted Jennifer out. She was close to tears again, and he eased the tangled hair from her eyes and cupped her cheek. To comfort her, he said, "I promise I'll stay with you as long as I can."

No sooner had he finished speaking than two other Runners appeared from inside and attempted to wrest her from his grasp.

"Let her go! I'm her fiancé and intend to remain at her side." Billy allowed one man to take her arm but refused to relinquish his hold on the other. He would be permitted to stay with her for the preliminary hearing.

They were taken into the fancy three-story building and shown into a small private cell. For the first time since his arrival, he had a few private moments with Jennifer, with no one listening. Even in the barred carriage, the driver could hear their conversation.

After an initial hug, Billy kissed her tears away; he asked, "Jen, what happened? Where did the money come from?"

Jennifer was still reeling from the unfolding events. To have Billy with her during this trauma was wonderful. "I sold some cheeses, Billy. I had a basket of them and had been asked to take them to the baron's chef and two other places. I packed more than he had ordered, hoping he would purchase more. Just before I entered, a man who said he was from the next house asked if I had any spare. He bought three and paid a pound each for the small ones. These were the new smoked ricotta cheeses, and I needed to sell them while they were fresh." She gave a hiccough and continued. "You know, I have never seen paper money before. I thought I was clever in making a sale. I knocked at the front door and was shown inside, then… then… everything went wrong." She dissolved into tears again.

Unable to talk for some time, Billy just held her. Her hacking sobs tore through him.

In a trembling tone, she said, "He hurt me, Billy; it hurt so much when he forced himself on me. I fought as hard as I could, and all the while, I was screaming for you. Then, I couldn't believe it when you appeared at the inn."

Billy was gutted. It might have shaved off a day if he had taken the southern route. He would never know now, so it was a moot point and useless stressing over that decision. He told her of his feelings of disquiet and that his father had told him to follow.

They had barely finished recounting their tales when interrupted and informed that her case would be up next.

The baron had appeared and still intended to press charges.

This Runner who had come to collect them was the same one who had stayed with them at the inn. "Miss, you will be charged with 'Forgery and uttering circulation of counterfeit notes.' This crime is punishable by death, miss. If you plead guilty, then if you're lucky, you will be given a lesser term of fourteen years and transportation to New South Wales as it was under £5." The look of horror on both their faces made him sad. He realised that this girl had indeed been an unwilling victim of this crime, in more than just being handed forged money. She had been violated and ruined to boot. Goodness knows what would have occurred if her fiancé had not appeared when he did. Shaking his head with sadness as he departed, he thought he would keep them together as long as he could.

Jennifer clung to Billy's hand as they walked from the cell. At the door of the magistrate's room, they finally had to separate. Billy was shown to the gallery, where he was permitted to watch but not to talk. From this stage on, she was in God's hands. He could only pray for her safety.

The baron had cleaned himself up as best he could and glared at Billy, seated in the front row upstairs. The man seemed to have time to think about his actions and was not pleased with the outcome.

Billy realised that from his ire, he would accept no responsibility for his words and probably none for his actions. He felt the impending doom of the upcoming case. He knew now that Jennifer would be convicted and possibly transported. Following her was not a decision to be made lightly. He was his parent's only child and the heir to the dairy business. It was far more than just money that was involved. The entire Kellow and Williams families needed to discuss what to do next. If he followed Jennifer, he may never see his family again. His heart hurt either way.

The nice Runner had suggested that rather than give a yes or no answer; she should attempt to explain that she was an unknowing recipient and passed them off in all innocence.

It was to no avail.

The magistrate seemed intent on punishing her to the full extent of the law. He was livid at her pleas of innocence.

She tried to explain that she had never seen money before this week, and he laughed at her. "Sir, I am but a Cornish milkmaid who makes cheeses. Any money I get paid goes directly to my father. I have seen and used coins before, but never paper money."

The magistrate's face went a profuse shade of purple. He exclaimed, "Balderdash! What sort of poppycock story is that? Not seen money before; that's ridiculous! Do you think I'm that gullible?"

Jennifer's pleading face turned to Billy. "Tell him, Billy, please tell him."

The magistrate's ire exploded. "I gave no permission for you to talk. Did you or did you not give the baron forged notes?"

Jennifer nodded. "But I didn't know that's what they were, sir; I mean, Your Honour. Honest, I didn't."

The gavel struck the bench top with an echoing bang. "So you do admit it! Guilty as charged; transportation to New South Wales for fourteen years. Next case!"

With these words, Jennifer collapsed.

The two attending Runners had been given no chance to intervene, and Billy had not been permitted to assist or speak for her.

Billy flew down the gallery steps and went to her side.

One of the Runners had scooped her up to vacate the courtroom. And he willingly handed his unresponsive burden to the imposing young man who had come to her aide.

Billy took his beloved burden from the Runner like she was a featherweight.

Her arms wrapped around his neck as she came to, and she began to weep softly. "I'm being banished, Billy. Abused, violated, accused, and now I'm to be transported." She hid her head against his neck and sobbed. She wondered that her tears had not run out, such was the volume she had shed.

The wetness of her salty tears trickled down his neck. He was gutted and didn't know what to say. He had been in London for under six hours, and his world had fallen apart. He held her tighter. Hopefully, they would have more of a chance to talk. Hopefully…

~

Billy had been permitted to stay with her for another two hours before being escorted away. The look of fear on her face as they parted tore at his heart.

One of the Runners awaited his exit from her cell.

Billy heard from this man that she would be taken to Newgate Prison, and he would be permitted only one more visit later that afternoon. He was aghast. Even in Cornwall, he had heard about this hell-hole of a gaol. For his beloved Jen to dwell in the horrific place was appalling. His hands were tied. In her own words, she had been vilely abused, falsely accused, and now transported for fourteen years to the other side of the world, and there was not a damned thing he could do about it. Billy was winded with the revelation that he could lose her completely if he didn't make some very hard decisions. Yet those were decisions that he could not make unaided. As he had been assured he could see her again that afternoon before she would be moved, he did not wish to leave the gate. Not being wed, he would not be permitted to visit her in gaol. He decided on the spot that after the visit, he would return to Cornwall and discuss the situation with their families before making any further decisions. He would supply her with money to purchase food and necessities in prison. He had left his bag at the inn, and hopefully, Bertram and Mrs DeMartini would have it safe. There was little else he could do.

As he exited the Magistrates Court building, Bertram and Mrs DeMartini awaited him.

Somewhat dazed, they took him back to the inn and ushered him into Jennifer's room. His bag sat on the bed. Jennifer's scent met his nose as he entered her private portal. He walked to the window where she had stood only hours earlier, and as she had done, he gazed out the glass into the street below and prayed. He could do no more.

Bertram and Mrs DeMartini joined him minutes later. A tea tray followed, and they sat in the privacy of her quiet room to discuss the next move.

The upshot was that Billy would return to see her that afternoon, and then he and Mrs DeMartini would return to Cornwall by ship. Bertram would oversee Jennifer until she was transported.

With a strength he didn't know he had, Billy returned that afternoon to say farewell to Jennifer. He held back his tears and handed over a small bundle of clothing and some money. He insisted that she place the small coin purse down her bodice as it was less likely to be stolen.

Bertram assured him that he would bring more things if she needed them, but even he could not see her again. The bulk of her luggage, including her new gowns, would be returned to Cornwall with Billy.

Billy knew that he had waited for her two years longer than he wished so she would not be burdened with the strains of bearing too many children too early. Now, he could lose her completely. Added to that, she could already be carrying another man's child. He was angry, confused and upset, but he couldn't let that show as he met for their final visit.

In the intervening hours, he had already decided to follow her, but that meant leaving his parents alone. If they had been married, as her husband, it would be him facing deportation, not her. He would have borne the punishment willingly. However, the law did not permit a fiancé to take this sentence for her, only a husband. She now was to be banished to the other side of the world.

Putting on a brave face, Billy, Bertram and Mrs DeMartini fronted up to Newgate Prison at two o'clock. The overwhelming feeling of oppression hit all of them as the huge gate clanged behind them as they entered.

Each jumped as the sound of the huge bolts slid home.

The warder, who called himself a turnkey, led the way to the cells.

Billy followed on his heels, and Mrs DeMartini clung to Bertram's arm. Unbeknownst to Billy, Jennifer's Italian friend had turned to Bertram as they were taken away earlier that morning.

Bertram found that the petite Italian lady fitted nicely into his arms, and he quite liked the protective feelings she stirred in him. He had not met her in Cornwall when he had visited. Now, he hoped she would stay longer. He had already sewn the seed for her to remain in London.

The turnkey arrived at another huge barred door. He called for Jennifer to come over to them. He unlocked the cell door for her to exit.

She had already discovered that any possessions left unattended would vanish in moments; her shawl had already gone. The few possessions she still had, she carried on her person.

Billy took in the squalid condition in a single glance and gagged at the appalling conditions. The facilities were only a bucket that was not hidden from view; the convicts had no privacy. From the stench emanating from the bars, there were no washing facilities for any of them. The odour was overpowering, and his beautiful Jennifer was forced to endure this vile hardship.

In the few hours she had been in the overcrowded cell, her clothing already reeked with the stench of the other occupants. Regardless of her filthy condition, Billy enfolded her in his arms as soon as the grill opened. His admiration for her stoicism in the unfortunate circumstances she now found herself in reinforced his protective feelings for her. He turned to the warder and asked, "Can we have a little more privacy somewhere? Our friends will join us, so there will be nothing untoward occurring. You may stay yourself." A coin passed hands.

The warder gave a simple nod. "Follow me." He led them along the corridor and ushered the four of them into a small room with a barred grill window in the door.

No sooner had they entered, they found themselves locked inside.

Knowing time was short, Billy again took Jennifer in his arms. He would hold her for as long as he could. It could well be the last time for a long time. He sat on one of the chairs and cradled her in his lap.

Bertram knew that time was short, and they must set a plan in action. "Miss Jennifer, we have had a short meeting and feel that the best plan is for Billy and Mrs DeMartini to return to Cornwall and discuss with the two families the next stage. I will stay here and bring you whatever you require. I notice you are already without your shawl, but we have brought some clothes to tide you over until you set sail."

Jennifer drew back a little from Billy's arms and then stood up. "You'll leave?" Her tone was borderline panic.

Billy's heart was breaking. "I must, my love, as I will not be permitted back into Newgate after today. It will only be until I can work out the best action plan. Being my parents' only child, Jen, I cannot make this decision lightly. I must return home in person to tell both families what has occurred. I dare not do that by mail. Your family will be distressed enough with your news, but I have no siblings, sweetheart. I must let my parents know that I intend to follow you. The Runners have told me that I should be able to have you assigned to me once I get there, and you can serve your time out there with me. I can protect you but can't travel with you, Jen. I asked, but they won't let me. Even as a husband, I could not sail on the same ship."

A sob escaped, and her tears overflowed the already swollen eyes that he adored. Once more, her legs buckled. Billy caught her and continued, whispering, "Bertram will stay here and see to your needs. But be assured that I love you and will do everything I can to be reunited. Stay strong, my love."

Jennifer was now beyond sobs. Against his chest, she shook her head. "I can't, Billy; too much has happened. I've failed you and been besmirched. I can't believe that God has let this happen. He has failed me."

Billy jerked. "Jen, God didn't fail you. Sweetheart, sin is all through this world, and this situation is a consequence of that. Reverend Tyzzer explained it to us. My beloved, I know you really believe that too. It's mankind who has sinned and moved away from God. What has occurred is the result of that sin; God loves us, Jen; you know that, don't you?"

She nodded.

He continued in such a loving and caring way that it made sense. "We don't see what He sees. We have to trust Him that somehow He can use this for good. Jen, I'll come with you, and we will make our life over there. Maybe this is what God wants us to do, but, sweetheart, we will be together."

She gazed up at him so lovingly it broke his heart. He knew his following words were ones he had no wish to say but something they both had to do. "Jen, we both have to forgive the baron."

The look of horror on her face made him gasp. She shook her head against his chest again.

Billy rested his cheek on her hair. "Jen, we need to find peace in our own hearts, and the resentment burning within us will not give us that. We are told to love our enemies, but that doesn't mean we must like what they have done to us or our loved ones."

Jennifer lifted her head and met his pained look. After some moments, she said, "I'll try Billy, but it's so hard. He has stolen our lives." She once again rested her head against his wet shirt and clung to him. She found that the pain in her heart was already easing.

Mrs DeMartini had been rethinking her decision. "Billy, I think I'll stay in London awhile. As a widow, Mr Tremayne will be an adequate escort for me, and I will be able to see Jennifer in prison, where he will not."

All three pairs of eyes swung towards her.

Bertram was delighted and nodded his willingness to do so with such a big grin on his lips that the widow drew in a quick intake of breath.

Billy thanked her, and Jennifer smiled with adoration and murmured her thanks.

Angelina DeMartini raised her eyebrows at the smile on Bertram's face. He was attractive, and she had found he was only a year older than her. He had been the first man to stir an interest in her since the death of her husband, not that she liked *him* much. It seemed to be reciprocated, but that was something to consider later. She was responsible for chaperoning the girl, and she had failed dismally. She should have instructed her not to wander about alone. For Jennifer to have been abused and arrested devastated her. Staying was the least she could do for her. "Billy, I think you should head home as soon as possible. Tell her family and discuss what you will do with your parents." She moved to Jennifer's side. "Oh, my dear girl, I am so sorry for failing you so badly. I should have explained that wandering around London alone is just not done. I should have known better, and I have let you down."

While not fully releasing Billy, Jennifer reached out a hand to her friend. "I already knew, Mrs DeMartini, but I didn't think visiting the kitchens in one house would be a problem. I just had no idea how wrong I was."

Mrs DeMartini had indeed told Jennifer years before in the classes she gave to the Kellow girls. She was unsure if Jennifer had remembered the instructions; obviously, she had, but she had chosen to ignore them.

The conversation of the four turned to cheese. It was one subject they all had in common. It was also the reason they were all in this predicament.

Bertram filled Jennifer in about where he had been. The meeting with the duke the following morning could no longer occur, and Bertram sent a note to the duke explaining her situation. Rather than be put off, the duke mentioned that he would keep the appointment, but he would come to see her.

At the end of the hour allotted, the lock's jangle signalled the turnkey's arrival.

Billy's heart was almost breaking as he gave her a long last kiss. How she felt, he had no idea. But she was already withdrawing into herself. Rather than be taken back to the cell, she was locked into the room with the small bag they had brought. Billy's last sight of her was her arm reaching for him through the bars, calling his name, and saying, "Billy, don't leave me here." His heart broke. He returned to the grill and kissed her through the bars before he was roughly pulled away from her by two warders.

Billy slept in her bed that final night in London. Jen's scent was on the pillows, and he wept into it while holding the pillow and her silk night rail.

~

The small vessel that carried Billy back to Cornwall left at dawn the following morning. Even if he stayed, he would not be permitted to see Jennifer again. Bertram would escort Mrs DeMartini to and from the prison while Billy returned to break the news at home to their families. This was not information he willingly carried, but he realised it was best to hear personally rather than relaying the story in a letter. Knowing that she had also been ravished would distress her family. He would make sure only her parents discovered that information. It certainly upset him, but he didn't blame her or love her any the less. He would stand by her, loving and cherishing her as always.

The trip gave him space to think. He had almost too much time on his hands, but he decided to follow her. His distress was in leaving his parents. As an only child, he realised this was a bitter pill to swallow. Thankfully, the Kellow's would step up to fill the void in the dairy. Some of the younger village boys could leave the mines and work for the farm, but that would not be the same for his family. He would miss his parents and his life in Cornwall. Life for him was now to protect Jennifer from more harm. She needed to be his priority; otherwise, she would be entirely alone.

His arrival at the small harbour in Newlyn passed unnoticed. No one was at the wharf to meet him, and of this, he was somewhat pleased. To have remained silent in front of others would have been difficult. The morning milking was over, and he knew he could gather the four adults to explain the situation privately. The weight of his bags was nothing compared to his heart as he trod the well-used path up the hill towards his home. He did not see the beauty of his surroundings as he walked the dusty track. His head hung with sadness and of the forthcoming revelations he must make. Releasing a long sigh as he entered the gate to his home, he was met by the stunned gaze of his father.

Bryn looked down the bay and asked, "Where is Jennifer?"

Billy shook his head and motioned for him to go inside. He swallowed and replied, "Bring Jacob and Phoebe." Then, he brushed past his parent to his room.

Bryn noticed Jennifer's carpet bag slung over Billy's shoulder but remained quiet. He went towards the dairy to summon his two friends.

~

The explanation of Billy's arrival in London was a shock to everyone. The story unfolded as the five sat in the farm kitchen with mugs of tea.

Each was deep in their own thoughts as they sat silently staring into their now empty mugs. All hurt.

Bryn was the first to reply to the situation; however, he addressed his wife rather than his son. "Delen, although I love this area and the work, our young ones now need us. Jacob, I shall discuss this in detail with my family, but I propose that you and your family take over the dairy and this house, and we will move to New South Wales with our two children. We will become partners in the business, as we shall endeavour to start a similar concern in New South Wales and send our products home to sell."

The astonishment of the four at the table echoed in his own heart. He loved his home and farm but loved his son more. As head of the household, he was responsible for making decisions for their benefit. This was the only solution that would keep them together. Jacob knew the business, and it was because of his family that it was now a raging success.

Further conversations would be required, but he would not waver in keeping his family together. Billy needed to be with Jennifer, and he and Delen needed Billy. At fifty-two, he would need to start again in a new land, but Billy would be with him.

~

Time passed slowly, but much had been sorted.

Three weeks elapsed before Billy stated that he wished to return to Jennifer's side. In London, he could be on hand if she needed him. With the planning for their departure now underway, Billy wanted to be close to her in London. The families had packed up Jennifer's few personal belongings, and Billy added some warm handmade items to her bag. Bryn and Delen would follow when they could. He went to the wharf to ask about booking a passage to London on the next available boat and found that a vessel had just arrived carrying a long letter from Bertram. He ripped it open and realised he would not need the ticket. She was no longer in the prison but on a ship. His father arrived at his side as he read the screed; Billy passed the first page to him.

The Angel Inn
Islington, London
April 28th 1820

Williams Dairy
Newlyn, Cornwall
My Dear Bryn,

  I bear news of Jennifer. She has already been loaded onto the ship.
  First, I am so very sorry for the situation that has occurred. At the time of the incident, I was meeting with the Duke, who had demanded her presence in London. Believe it or not, he visited Jennifer in Newgate the morning Billy departed. He had her moved into a solitary cell if it's any consolation. She is now safe from the rabble. However, that only lasted for a week. More about why later!
  A lady named Mrs Elizabeth Fry has visited and met with every convict lady being transported. To each, she gave a care bundle, which included clothing and activities: cloth, sewing, yarn and the like. We happened to be at the prison and met her outside as we headed to see Jennifer. As she was in a solitary cell, we were both permitted to visit her. She is well and sends her love. She was informed that she would be transported soon but did not know when.
  We sat conversing for some time when we heard footsteps approaching. It was Mrs Fry coming to see her. However, she was followed by two prison guards. Without warning, Jennifer was told to bundle her possessions, and they took her to the convict ship waiting in the Thames River.
  She and thirty-nine others were taken in hackney carriages and loaded on board the Morley. Apparently, others will join them later, but Mrs Fry had already been given permission to see that she is well cared for. The one blessing about the Duke's patronage is that she has been assigned to care for the Captain's children for the duration of the voyage. She will, therefore, not be confined to the hellhole with the other convicts.
  Oh, Bryn, this is such a blessing. Mrs Fry was very informative about the horrific conditions on board these vessels. She met with us the following day and said she visited the ship and met with the doctor. He had 'rescued' a couple of better-class women to help with the sick bay. Both can read and write, so they were also put in charge of teaching some of the fifty or so children on the ship. The majority are convicts' children, but like Jennifer's charges, they will need things to occupy them.

  Bryn stopped reading. His gaze fell on Billy, knowing he had delayed his departure so they could travel together. Now, she was already on board the convict transport. He swallowed before continuing. He wondered why Billy did not hold the entire situation against him. He shook his head and read on.

  Billy, I wish you to know that I went to the dockland and waited until I could speak to the surgeon on board. His name is Thomas Reed, and he seems like a caring chap. With Mrs Fry and him overseeing Jennifer, he will do all he can for her. He also knows of the Duke's summons of her to London.

Mrs DeMartini will stay until the ship sails. She will accompany Mrs Fry on board for her visits and ensure Jennifer has anything required to make her trip tolerable. I ensured that Jennifer received the shawl Billy purchased for her before he left. Jennifer has enclosed a letter for Billy.

Be assured that we are doing all we can.

Again, know that we are very apologetic for this situation. We are doing everything to assist where permitted.

Bertram

Billy hardly noticed they had walked up to the house as he read. He devoured every word and read between the lines. She was well-cared for. But it did not make him happy. Now seated at the table in their kitchen, Billy saw a sealed note fall from between the sheets of the letter, and with it was her ring. He picked it up and saw that the letter was in Jennifer's writing. The paper it was written on was filthy, the ink had been thin, and it was hard to read.

My dearest Billy,

I cannot thank you enough for being here in my hour of need. As we are to be torn apart, I wish again to say I release you. The reason for this is now apparent. I missed my flow and am now absolutely ruined. Billy, I am probably carrying another man's child, and although I do not wish to live without you, I must for the sake of this new life within me. This child is innocent of the crime its father did to me. Mrs Fry has me under her care while I remain in London, and two other convict girls have been assigned above decks. We are the lucky ones. I know I am being watched over by our Lord above and will continue to trust in Him, as you encouraged me to do. I received your gift, and thank you for it. I will treasure it always.

I am now on the vessel that will carry me to the other side of the world. On board, we have a doctor. He is known as Surgeon Superintendent Reed. And he also knows of my suspected condition and has already eased my lot in life by assigning me to the Captain and his family. I understand a Reverend and his large family will also be on board, so I shall be kept occupied. I will not see you again, Billy, and knowing that is hard.

Be happy, my love. Marry Isla instead or some other girl; have lots of beautiful children. Know that you have my blessing.

I am returning your betrothal ring, but know it was much kissed.

Goodbye, dear Billy, live a good life and try not to think too harshly of me.

Jennifer

Billy stood so abruptly that the chair was sent flying across the kitchen floor. He let out a howl of grief and, without a word, left the room. The letter fluttered to the floor, but they saw him slip her ring on his little finger.

Delen watched her son walk down the garden path and out to the headland. She picked up the letter and read it for herself. "Oh, Bryn, she is with child from this abuse and has released Billy from their betrothal."

Bryn nodded. "Billy said she had already tried to do that, but he refused. Regardless of this letter, I know he will still go with her. He will now quite literally go to the end of the earth for her. I should not have made them wait, Del, but... No, it's too late for buts. We shall move to New South Wales and make cheeses there. I will not lose our son."

Knowing that Billy needed time and space, they left him alone. He would return and prepare for their move half a world away. Even though Jennifer had released Billy, he would not let her go. They would be leaving all they knew, including their farm, life and possessions, to their friends. Jacob would continue the business with the assistance of his family.

Bryn replied to Bertram and asked him to find the three of them a passage on a vessel to New South Wales as soon as possible. They would travel together and take their two special cows with them, and Jennifer could make her cheeses there. He had just finished his letter when carriage wheels were heard on his driveway. A knock on the door followed, and Bryn answered it to a hook-nosed, well-dressed gentleman.

Chapter 10   Transported 1820

*T*he *Morley* departed Deptford in London on March 17th 1820. However, only hours before this occurred, a small watercraft approached the anchored vessel. It contained three well-dressed men. The first was the Solicitor from the Bank of England; the second was the Governor of Newgate Prison; and last, but far from least, was the Duke of Shesham.

The solicitor from the bank was here to give £5 to each female who was convicted of forging money, fraud, or other crimes. They had no idea why but were willing to accept the funds. The convict women convicted of fraud were told to form lines on the main deck and were each given a five-pound note.

Appearing at the end of the line, puffing, Jennifer had never even seen a five-pound note before and took it somewhat hesitantly. The last time she had handled paper money, it had been her undoing. She took it and rolled the money, intending to tuck it away somewhere safe. She kept it in her fist and shoved her hand into her pocket for the moment.

An hour earlier, she had heard the anguished lowing of the distressed cows on the vessel. She had found them at the end of the convict cell deck, and as the door to them was unlocked, she attended to their distress. Her heart raced at their pain, but she could not leave them in discomfort. The three cows each turned to lick her as she settled down to strip their excess milk; consequentially, she had been late joining the line of women. She had arrived puffing, but she was in time to hear the reason for the muster.

The duke's eyes met hers as she skidded to a stop on the deck. He had a hint of a smile on his thin lips. As the three guests were welcomed on board, her eyes sought the hawk-nosed man who followed the Governor and solicitor. He glanced her way, and she saw him smile at her.

After receiving the £5, the Duke of Shesham beckoned her to follow him. They mounted the steps up two more decks to the top poop deck. They could not be overheard there but were within full view of the assembled multitude below. There was no impropriety in their meeting. The duke had spent time with her in gaol the morning after her arrest, and she had told him of the cheese-making process. They also spoke of her home and family and her love for Billy. Bertram had already made an appointment for them to meet; however, with her arrest, the duke came to see her. She had no idea he would deign to visit her in prison, let alone come onto the convict ship. His interest in her cheeses was obviously more than a passing fancy. For him to be here proved that to be so.

She sank into a deep curtsy with her money still held tightly in one hand. He took her other hand and lifted her from her prolonged bow. She dared not meet his piercing stare. It was as though he could see right through her. She still had her head dropped in subservience.

He lifted her chin and asked, "Jennifer, are you housed out of the hellhole below?"

With her head still lowered, Jennifer nodded. She was somewhat surprised he would be concerned about her accommodations. She murmured, "Yes, thank you, Your Grace." Jennifer watched the captain wander up from the quarterdeck and stand nearby. She wondered why she had been singled out by them both. Had she done something wrong?

The duke turned and spoke to the captain, who stood beside him and addressed him. "Captain, see that Miss Kellow is looked after, for this young lass has great skills that will be put to good use once she arrives in the colony. She is here because I summoned her to London. She would be safely ensconced with her fiancé in Cornwall, but for my summons and insistence to meet her. So take care of her, for she has been abused by one who should have treated her better. Her crimes are trumped up. Unfortunately, she admitted to handling the fraudulent notes but had no idea what they were, having never seen paper money before."

Her head flew up. Jennifer could not help it; she nodded in agreement. A tear rolled down her cheek. He believed her. Her lips turned up in a shadow of a smile.

The noble but austere-looking man with a hook nose was tempted to thumb the tiny drip away. It took all of his discipline not to touch the girl. She was nearly as beautiful as her volatile sister, Isla. He smiled at the thought of the Cornish firebrand he had met. She had verbally shredded him. Jennifer, however, had already been manhandled inappropriately by one of the nobility. He saw her sadness.

He turned back to her, saying, "I can't change the outcome, miss, but I can ease your journey." Knowing that her interesting condition would shortly be known if it wasn't already, he said loud enough for the captain to overhear,

"Miss, I'm sorry that my summons to London has caused this and that one of the nobility has let you down."

Jennifer gave a nod of thanks. Another tear slowly slid down her cheek.

The girl certainly did not realise how lovely she was. The few freckles on her nose added to her attraction. Again, she reminded him of her sister; he found that the younger girl haunted his dreams, yet she was only a milkmaid. This girl was so natural and innocent that he felt like giving her a hug. He was overwhelmed that this young woman triggered his protective instinct. He had only met her once before, but since he had met her family, he felt she was his responsibility. He had felt the same for her sister, especially when she raged at him for putting Jennifer in this situation. Isla had just discovered that her older sister had also been defiled, and she was livid. Her fists had flayed against his chest, and he stood and received her just chastisement. The girls were only milkmaids, but if both had been well-dressed and had been of noble blood, they could have taken London by storm. They had more elegant grace in their little fingers than many of the blue-bloods he had met all too frequently in the overcrowded ballrooms in society. He shook his head slightly to get his thoughts back on point. He saw that Jennifer was smiling at his distraction.

The duke said, "I have made sure that word spread of what occurred. The baron has been shunned and will retire to his Sussex properties for some years. No innocent girl should be treated disrespectfully and violated in such a way. Your innocence should have meant you were safe, not abused by a peer."

Jennifer could not believe this man had taken an interest in her welfare. She presumed all toffs were like the baron, yet this man really seemed to care. "Thank you, Your Grace." She bobbed another curtsy. She had noticed a softening of his features moments ago. She realised that his air of arrogance was but a veneer. She had seen through that tough crust in the gaol. Having never met a person of such rank before, she was somewhat intimidated. Unsure if she should say more, she fell silent.

The duke glanced towards the man next to him. He ensured the captain could hear and said, "I have something for you, which I'm sure the captain will store away until you arrive."

The captain looked up with interest.

The duke dug into his inside coat pocket. "Mrs Fry let me know of your unfortunate condition after the abuse, and Baron Mortonford has sent £1000 compensation as he promised your fiancé he would do, should the situation arise. It is enclosed here, along with a letter of introduction for you to my friend, Governor Lachlan Macquarie."

The captain gasped.

Jennifer saw the fat packet the duke held.

The look on the captain's face showed his astonishment, but he remained silent. The duke had forced a fallen woman on him to care for his family.

The duke continued, "The baron has been informed that he is to have nothing more to do with you or the child he fathered unless you or the child contact him. If you wish to do that, do it through me. I have ensured that he is willing to pay should you wish for more funds. His only stipulation was that if the child is a boy, he would like to see it well educated. What you do with your life is up to you; however, this money should set you on your feet. My letter will ensure that you are not imprisoned with the multitude. It also contains another for my friend Perry, who lives there."

Another tear or two escaped Jennifer's eyes and rolled down her face unheeded. As she took the fat letter, she realised it was addressed to her, not the Governor. Her eyes flew to meet his. "This is for me?"

Again, their gazes met, and he smiled, realising she had read the addressee. He gave a half-laugh. Of course, she could read; why was he surprised? The duke waved away the captain but motioned for her to remain. He watched as the captain returned to his duties and other guests below. When they stood alone, he said, "Yes, Jennifer, I have also included a letter to you. However, it seems you will not have to have it read to you. I was going to ask the captain's wife to do so, but it seems that is now unnecessary."

He saw her shake her head.

"I can read well, sir," she said quietly.

One dark, winged eyebrow raised in amazement. The duke smiled; this girl was full of surprises. "My letter to the Governor explains my interest in your skill. However, you may wish to read the other interesting letter in the envelope first. It is from your fiancé." He heard her quickly draw in a breath. "Mr Williams junior wrote to me hoping I could pull some strings to permit you to at least stay in London. I tried but could not change the conviction; however, the official letter to Governor Macquarie means that you will be assigned to your future family on their arrival in the colony."

She gasped. "Billy is still going to leave Cornwall? I released him from our engagement."

The duke's big grin gave her confidence. "He is, Jennifer. He refused your offer." He dug into his pocket and pulled out a small velvet pouch, which he opened. And tipped Billy's ring onto his palm. He held it out so she could slip it on her finger. He also handed her the bag and also pointed to a small parcel at his feet. Meeting her eyes, he said, "Jennifer, his parents will accompany him to New South Wales. Your family will continue your work in the dairy in Cornwall, and I will now be a sponsor for the business to increase productivity. The *Southern Belle* cheese is too good to let the business fold. An endorsement of more from me in London and this product will be one of the most sought-after cheeses in England. Those in the know understand that I only put my name to the best of everything. It's one of the benefits of being a duke. Open this parcel, dear. It's from Billy for you."

Jennifer untied the string and saw a lovely, warm shawl. She remained silent, but the smile on her lips told him of her delight. Even her eyes now glinted with happiness. She pulled the shawl around her shoulders. It was lovely and warm.

One winged eyebrow lifted again as he heard a chuckle. He was a duke, and she a convict, but he felt she could see through the impenetrable tough exterior he had built around himself. His appearance was enough to put fear into most people, but not this young lady. Her own cocked eyebrow showed she waited patiently for him to continue his story, so he did. "A new cheese cave is being constructed as we speak." He noticed the look of happiness that settled on her face. He noticed that she bit her lip to avoid interrupting him. He paused, knowing his following words would astound her; he glanced up, checking that no one was listening. "Jennifer, I went down and stayed with your future family for two weeks after your arrest. I met your parents, too, and, dear girl, you have a wonderful support base. Your sister, Isla, took me to task in such a way that I felt like a naughty child. I deserved her wrath. You could say I have become obsessed with them all, as well as your cheeses. Those, by the way, are so good that I am determined they will become one of the must-have items to finish the finest meals in the Kingdom. The King is considering a Royal Warrant for the *Southern Belle* cheese."

He was expecting tears or a squeal of delight; however, she stood silently. All she did was give a slight nod. She knew her produce was good, but he could tell she was hanging on his every word. She did none of the things he expected, but neither did Isla. She had given a fleeting benign smile when he told her of Isla's verbal attack. He was impressed by the fact that she also was not overawed by him or his rank, so he continued again. "While I was there in Cornwall, your father took me to inspect the mines. I had asked him how I could assist, meaning the dairy; however, he took me on a tour of the area. One of the tin mines is now currently closed due to flooding. Some of the lead mines are not much better; however, I will try to help them all."

Knowing how vital the mines were to the families employed there, he saw a frown settle on her brow. He thought, "Ahh, she is interested in their welfare, not the money." Her frown remained until he explained. He said, "You see, I bought the mine when I saw the appalling work conditions, then closed it until it's again safe to work. Therefore, there is a great need for income in your village. Consequently, I have employed them all at double their pay." He paused to see if she understood the implications.

Although astounded, her eyes nearly popped. Though she merely said, "All of them?"

He nodded with a lop-sided smile. "The dairy operation on your farms will be expanding tenfold or more. The young ones are starting with a paid holiday until the new cows arrive. I've sent them to learn to read and write at the new temporary school. The men have already been put to work on the next stage of my project. It will still be a hands-on dairy, but the work will also be safer for the miners. The mine owner will not lose out, as I purchased it at twice its value. Also, more cows will be arriving from the Channel Isles, particularly the Guernsey Islands, as I believe they are some of the best cream cows."

Her shy smile showed. She said, "We only have two from Alderney, sir. I used to make the *Southern Bell* from their full cream milk. However, we always wished for a Jersey cow or two. Oh, what I could do with their cream-rich milk!"

He nodded, then continued. "So I heard. Now, what I hope to hear after your arrival is that you, Miss Jennifer Kellow, will establish a new cheese industry in the colony. From what I read in the papers, what they are currently making is fit for the convicts on government rations but little else. My friend, Lachlan, said he won't eat it."

Her interest was certainly piqued, her head tipped as though encouraging him to expand on his explanation.

The austere facade had vanished. He almost looked embarrassed at what he'd done for her. "That is the only deal I could work out for you. I already know that Governor Macquarie has a dairy behind their residence in Parramatta. I met Lachlan in London before he left. He is a good man, even though he's Scottish." He gave a chuckle. "Jennifer, as I said, I will be buying some Guernsey cattle for the dairy, but I shall hunt for some Jersey cows for both venues. Mr Williams senior may be bringing some of his own breeding stock when they come later this year; if not, I will send them on later. I have already been investigating passage for them. The main dairy herd and equipment for the cheeses will arrive next year. So, you must survive the first months and your child's birth alone; then, they will join you. Having a child while unwed will have its drawbacks, but Mr Williams junior, Billy, said that he intends to acknowledge it as his as he knows the situation."

Jennifer only nodded in understanding, but would Billy really do that? She twisted her ring again, and a quick smile licked at the corners of her mouth before tears again filled her eyes.

The duke saw her suffering. "I must admit I am impressed by your young man. We had many discussions during my stay at his farm. He is a lucky man, my dear. Anyway, my letter to Governor Macquarie requests that they fast-track your permission to marry. I will book a passage for them as soon as I find another ship heading that way. As the silent partner, I am sponsoring the building of the new dairy there, too. They should only be months behind you."

Jennifer recalled her letter to Billy, releasing him from their betrothal. Her heart had sunk when she had penned her words, relinquishing him. Now, her heart soared, and now she knew Billy was coming to claim her even though it meant uprooting his life. He had even trusted the duke with his ring. She beamed at the duke as he spoke. Unable to stop herself, she grabbed his arm. "Thank you so very much. I'm just a simple milkmaid. Thank you from the bottom of my heart."

The duke covered her hand with his own. Then he took it and upturned it; he gazed at the elegant and delicate fingers. "There is nothing simple about you, Jennifer Kellow. The skill in these small fingers will create a new industry for the growing colony, so don't waste your talents, my dear. Trust the good Lord that you are where He wants you to be. Let Him use you." Realising he was beginning to show the turmoil in his own heart, he saw she was gazing at him as though seeing deep into his soul. He saw her give a micro nod.

Jennifer's situation was only part of his attraction to Cornwall. Her teenage sister, Isla, had pierced his tough exterior like no other woman had. His hawk-like visage did not deter her, nor did his gruff facade. She did not stand in awe of him as every other debutante did. Isla called a spade a spade and frequently laughed at his lack of knowledge of the smallest things in life. His first attempt at milking saw her almost writhing on the floor in laughter. It was not that she had no respect for him, but she thought it funny that although he was a duke, he had never had to do even the most basic chore. She could not believe that he even had a valet to dress him. Although his pride had been pricked, he didn't mind and found his heart was becoming seriously involved with this girl, which was concerning. Isla was only a dairymaid, but she was not the sort of person who would tolerate a casual relationship. He realised that he, too, would no longer seek his pleasure without the bonds of marriage. She had challenged his faith, and he found it again, buried deep in his being. But how could he consider a teenage milkmaid as a wife? Plus, at thirty-six, he was twice her age. He fled to London to meet with Jennifer when he realised how close he was to declaring himself to her, and he had only known her for two weeks. Even now, he could feel his pulse racing just by thinking about her.

Jennifer saw the emotions flicking on his face. His smile softened, and then it was followed by a frown. Shocked at his thoughts, he caught the interest in Jennifer's face. The duke realised that she, too, was also not afraid of him. This was so refreshing. A deep grin creased his cheeks, and this transformed his entire appearance. Returning to the topic, he continued, "Jennifer, I am also sponsoring the sending out of a large herd of more appropriate dairy cattle for cheese production for the governor and your family. The only payment I ask is that you teach others so that the knowledge does not die."

She frowned, and then it cleared. She nodded her willingness to do this. "I will, sir, but not the special cheese; I promised Mr Williams I would never share that secret."

Seeing her interest, he said, "Agreed, but do you know, I had no idea that cows produced different sorts of milk until our conversation in gaol."

She nodded again and blushed at his praise. "The Jersey cow has the richest milk, but they are near impossible to buy since the French wars."

Realising that he still held her hand as he spoke. He looked over her head and saw the assembled crowd gazing at them. He knew she needed to leave, so he quietly asked, "Do you have any messages for your family? I shall let your fiancé know I have spoken to you again and ensured your safe placement with the captain's family." He motioned with his chin towards the clergyman, standing to the side. "I believe the reverend and his wife have a tribe of young ones, too. Do you read well enough to teach them to read and write?"

She nodded. "I was first taught at Sunday School by Reverend Tyzzer, sir, but I loved it so much that he kept the lessons and reading going. He had a library we were permitted to use. I read history and geography and know Latin, and I can speak Italian fluently and a little French and German. I learned Italian from my friend. I think you met Mrs DeMartini? It was she who first told me about the idea of adding flavourings and making ricotta and other soft cheeses. Italian is very similar to Latin, so it came easily to me." She blushed as she admitted that. "Isla can too. She also speaks French very well."

Eventually, he released the fragile and talented hands of the well-educated but shy milkmaid. He was astounded at her knowledge. The dairymaid who reads Latin and spoke Italian differed from the uneducated girl he had first expected.

Jennifer's eyes again clouded with tears. "In answer to your question, sir, just let my family know I'm sorry and that I love them. I will pray for them all, and sir, I will endeavour not to let you down."

The now not-so-stern duke smiled at her. "I am proud of you already, Jennifer. I look forward to tasting your new cheeses from the colony. I should have mentioned that Bertram Tremayne and Mrs DeMartini are to be married. She has moved to London and is a resident at the Angel Inn until their nuptials. She will assist with the new cheese warehouse, and, for my convenience, I have purchased her house in Newlyn. Sorry, I nearly forgot to tell you." He looked over her head and saw the captain now beckon her. He gave a nod of acknowledgement. He knew that the tide controlled their time of departure.

She swallowed before once again thanking him. Her gaze followed his. Until now, she had her back turned to the rest of the ship. She suddenly realised that everyone else but herself and the duke were now on the main deck. "Oh sir, I must away." Rather than await dismissal, she squeezed his arm, murmured "Thank you," and fled. She left him on the poop deck, watching her race down the sidesteps.

Jennifer was the only one missing from the assembly; all eyes had turned to them, watching. The entire ship's complement had been waiting for their conversation to finish.

While their meeting had taken place, all the other women had been individually marched up on the quarterdeck. They had been given a half-crown from the Governor of Newgate Prison. The money was from a charity for this purpose and was supposedly used to better themselves. As they filed past, each received their coin; then, they were told to be seated on the main deck.

As Jennifer headed down the steps to join the other women, she dug into her pocket where she had shoved her £5 note, and she also now clung to the letter and money tightly. The future was now in her hands, but at least she had one. She clutched Billy's letter and knew it contained good news. He was coming to claim her. She twisted her ring again with her thumb and smiled. She couldn't wait until she was alone so she could read his letter. She shook her head as if to clear her thoughts, and, still smiling, she turned her face to Doctor Reed. She was relieved that Billy would not abandon her, but he had to be free to make that decision. She stood listening with a big smile that went right up to her eyes.

The doctor and captain motioned for her to stand where she was rather than join the other women and wait for further instructions. Clutching her treasure in her pocket, she waited silently. Her eyes roamed, and nearby were the reverend and his family. His seven children ranged in age from small to young teenagers. She eyed them with interest, wondering if she would be teaching them too. From what the duke inferred, she would be.

Doctor Reed stepped forward to speak. This was not his first convict voyage; he had assembled everyone, sailors, soldiers, convicts and free settlers, on the deck and read them all his rules. Knowing that few were literate, his sonorous voice carried across the multitude. "Although my rules are intended specifically for the convicts, they will also apply to the sailors and soldiers guarding the said prisoners. I will not countenance immoral behaviour coming from any quarter. Please listen carefully. However, I will repeat the rules for the first few days. They will be in writing and pinned to the walls in a few places. Please note that any breach of the regulations or any person attempting to deface or destroy this paper will be punished severely, and the person offending will be brought to the notice of the Governor of New South Wales on arrival. Now listen well. Break them at your own peril." He looked at the filthy group of women who stood before him. He would have difficulty ensuring they stayed alive, let alone not force themselves on any willing sailor rather than vice versa. However, he would guard them with his pistol if required, and he intended that they should know that. Shrugging at their contempt, he read aloud. "1. *The care and management of each mess shall be instructed to a Monitor, who will be held responsible for any irregularities committed by those under her direction; it is expected that everyone will behave respectfully and be obedient to the monitor of her particular mess.*

2. Cursing and swearing, obscene and indecent language, fighting and quarrelling, as such practices tend to dishonour God's holy name and corrupt good manners, will incur the displeasure of the Surgeon Superintendent and be visited with punishment and disgrace.

3. Cleanliness, being essential, is necessary to the health, comfort, and well-being of every person on board; it is desired that the most scrupulous attention in this respect shall be observed on every occasion.

4. The monitors are particularly enjoined that the utmost vigilance in taking care that nothing disorderly shall appear among the members of their respective messes.

5. Anyone convicted of disturbing others whilst engaged in reading the Holy Scriptures or other religious exercises will incur special animadversion, and such misconduct will be entered in the journal.

6. A proper reserve towards the sailors will be held indispensable, and all intercourse with them must be avoided as much as possible.

7. A daily account will be kept. A faithful report will be made to His Excellency the Governor of New South Wales of the conduct of each individual during the voyage for those who behave well. However, they may have come here with bad characters, will be represented favourably: the Surgeon Superintendent pledges to use his utmost effort to get everyone settled in a comfortable manner whose behaviour shall merit such friendly interference."

Point 5 made Jennifer's head jerk up. She glanced at the Reverend and saw him nodding.

The duke still stood watching and noticed her interest in that rule. He had learnt that the two families had a strong faith. What intrigued him more was that no one mentioned it, but they lived it. Oh, how they lived it. Their conversations had stirred up the beliefs of his youth. But more than that, Jacob and he had sat on the headland, and he had unravelled the intricacies or the complicated theology into a simple belief in God's love for him. The scales fell off his eyes to sin and the folly of his youth. He was selfish and knew it.

When the doctor finished reading the rules he could read anger on the faces of some and relief in the faces of others. These rules were for their own benefit and safety. Doctor Reed said, "I shall read them again tomorrow and the day after and daily for the next week. This is for those who are unable to read for themselves. Sailors and soldiers, this also pertains to you. To protect these women, I have a pistol, and I will use it. The reverend gentleman and I intend to oversee your physical and spiritual well-being. Mrs Fry has already read you her charge, and she and her friends…" He motioned towards the duke, "…have generously provided slates, chalk, Bibles, and women's activities for you to occupy yourselves while on board. You will be allowed to learn to read and write and supplied with sewing, knitting, weaving and plaiting straw to keep occupied. We have chosen one of you to teach the upper-deck children." He motioned to Jennifer. "Good behaviour will be rewarded with more privileges and rations. Use this time to better your situation if you can. The cruise ahead of you will take at least three months. Use that time wisely. There are other occupations for those with varying skills. Are there any on board who know much about milking cows?" He doubted many country girls would be amongst this unruly rabble but thought he would ask.

Jennifer's hand rose as she stood near him, and surprise showed on his face. "You know about milking too?"

She nodded; she had just stripped the milk of the three lowing cows. She had heard their distress and had gone to attend to them. Her eyes flicked at the duke standing watching on the upper deck.

He met her glance with a smile and gave her a nod of approval.

As her arm dropped, the doctor's gaze met hers.

Doctor Reed turned to the captain. "Can she milk before she comes on duty for you?"

The captain nodded, then shrugged. "As long as she gets the work done, she can be useful wherever possible." He, too, looked towards the duke. He responded with a nod of his own. "There are only three cows that will require milking. The others are due to give birth on the voyage, so they will only require watching."

The doctor smiled and replied, "I know you are literate, too, so I'll send some slates and things to your quarters."

This time, it was the captain's eyebrows that rose in surprise. He found he had some interesting convict women on board this journey. He gasped and said, "You read well enough to teach my children?" He had realised she could read her name, but many had that basic skill.

Once more, Jennifer nodded in reply. She could elaborate later if required. She stole another glance at the austere duke. He was leaning on the railing, observing the activities below. Her glance elicited another smile from him.

As the doctor still had to tell them of the daily routine that would be observed on the voyage, the convicts remained seated. He turned to the women and said, "You shall be awoken at seven each morning if you are not already awake. Your morning meal will be served at eight; your bunks and persons must be cleaned and tidied by then. At nine, I shall open the clinic for those needing treatment. I have the mercuric treatment for those of you who have the clap. If there are other conditions you need to be treated for, I shall do my best to keep you healthy. Your midday meal will be served as close to noon as possible, and the evening meal will be provided as close to six o'clock as is able. These times are dependent on the seas. In times of storm, dry rations will be provided, and water will also be available in barrels. Times of hardship will occur, and you are all expected to obey orders when given them. Your lives may well depend on this. Those behaving contrary to expectations will be confined to quarters and, on arrival in New South Wales, will follow you to the colony. Conditions in that settlement are primitive already. However, should you require further punishment, this will not be withheld. Crew, soldiers, this goes for you too; you will leave the women alone."

Although his words seemed harsh, many had already needed to use his medical skills. They realised that these were for their protection rather than a severe chastisement. In reality, the man's bark was worse than his bite. With the riot act now read and the rules laid out, the convicts were returned to the prison deck below. Jennifer was told to stay put until the doctor reappeared from the store room with the writing materials. She took the opportunity to turn again to watch the official group leave. Jennifer saw the guests escorted to the ship's side and assisted down the rope ladders. Before the duke disappeared from view, he raised a hand in farewell and dropped lithely into the small craft awaiting them.

The doctor quietly reappeared beside her with his arms full. He said so only she could hear, "The duke works with Mrs Fry, you know. He's one of a growing group of peers who assist the underprivileged. One of his friends, another peer, is severely burned. Lord Perry is the Earl of Collingsford, and although he is now overseas somewhere, he has quietly garnered support amongst the nobility. Due to his friendship with the earl, the Duke of Shesham was among the first to aid Mrs Fry's work. Many have risen to the cause and now do all they can to help those they deem worthy of assistance. They help in many ways, from sponsoring a locally produced product to paying for things like these slates and chalk."

Jennifer gave a small gulp of surprise. She watched as the small craft pulled away from the ship's side. She said softly, "I had no idea the nobility did things like that. I always saw them as too good for us poor villagers. I've only met two, and one wasn't nice."

The doctor looked down at the lovely face of this girl. Freckles sprinkled her nose, but they added to her beauty. She had reason to believe that men were crass and debased, yet she still seemed to be able to trust. She had put that trust in the nobility of London and had been vilely abused. She had to live with that stigma for the rest of her life. Carrying a child when unwed was enough to make many girls jump into a river and drown themselves; such was the shame they felt. Having heard the story from two different sources and knowing the Duke of Shesham endorsed her background and publicly singled her out kindly, he ensured she stayed as safe as possible. "Miss Kellow, I wish to say something, and I may be jumping the gun, but I have heard a few whistles from the sailors. I have already thrown three of the crew out from the deck below. They were wantonly cavorting with the women, and I will not permit this to occur under my watch. You must not be alone under any circumstance, do you understand me? When your condition becomes more advanced, they may leave you alone, but you do not wish for a repeat of the abuse. Once the captain's family has dismissed you at night, you must stay in your cabin unless called by them, the reverend's family, or myself. Will you promise me this?"

The concern etched on his face reminded Jennifer of Mr Williams's fatherly worry for her when she started to work for him ten years ago. He insisted that Billy walk her home if she was working late. Even as a child, it was Billy whom she turned to for safety. As a little girl, she had fallen asleep after work more than once, and Billy had carried her home. Because of her, the Williams family were uprooting themselves and travelling halfway around the world. She would probably never see her family again, but she would have Billy and his parents. Thankfully, she could write to her family. She was still clutching the letter and the money she had been given. £1005 was nearly as much as the first sale of cheeses had brought. She had not mentioned that the family now had access to money. She had never seen it though.

The duke knew, and he, too, had stayed quiet. With his help, her future and a cheese-making business should still happen. She stayed watching until the small craft reached the shore. Again, a small catch of breath escaped when the duke lifted a hand in a final farewell. Her return wave was automatic. Then he was gone. It had been a month since her arrest. A month where her life had undergone trial, torment, and a new path. She had experienced highs and lows in the last four weeks that she had no idea existed. Up until now, her life had been one easy plane of happiness.

~

With the ship underway, it was not long before the seas became progressively worse. The convict women now understood the warnings about hard-tack rations and access to water. In the middle of the Atlantic Ocean, the calmness of the Thames River and estuary was a long-forgotten memory. Jennifer's tiny room was a luggage store room with a bunk. Thankfully, this had a mattress, and she was given a new blanket. Even at home, her bed had been a straw-filled sheet she shared with Isla and later Polly. Her duties were not onerous, but she found them difficult due to reoccurring seasickness. She attended the cows each morning and afternoon, and one of the soldiers carried the milk to the galley. Then, she would return to the captain's quarters aft of the ship and entertain his children while his wife strolled to stretch her legs. In the rough weather, this was more often than not just up and down the corridor. On her return, Jennifer would settle down and start lessons. The children were young, and she started them learning a nursery rhyme that she had been taught. It was the alphabet, and once they mastered that, she taught them how to write their names. Progress was slow, but she relished the challenge. The children, however, were a delight. They reminded her of her siblings when young, and their antics at avoiding work were the same the world over.

Initially, the minister at the local church and his wife had run an after-church school for all the village children. When they had first arrived in the area, her parents had laughed about the children being taught to read and write. However, this had been a blessing in their young days. Mrs DeMartini had seen their progress and taken a special interest in the two older girls. As she was bored, she undertook to teach them grooming and deportment, then later Italian and French. When Jennifer started making cheeses, she could write recipes and keep notes of how the processes were done. This permitted exact repetition of the process. She recorded weights, volumes, quantities, and temperatures.

Eventually, each of the children was permitted access to a library of books to read and return. It was a children's library of sorts, only it was not of children's books. Jennifer devoured the stories, and when the minister mentioned the odd Latin word in his sermon, Mrs DeMartini spoke Italian and explained the similarity between the two languages. From then, Latin became easy. She found she could read aloud to her mother when combing the fleece for her to spin or even when spinning. Both of these activities occupied her hands but not her brain. Reading filled a void in her life. She read of travels in far-flung lands and stories of savages, lost kingdoms, and Bible times past. Her interests were such that Mrs Tyzzer, the minister's wife, had even permitted her to read some books from her husband's reference books. The minister had a set of Clarke's Bible commentaries, and Jennifer devoured these as she had children's books. Isla, too, discovered them and remembered even more of what she read. Reading had been a treat for them and had opened up a new world. Now, it was paying off. Word by word, the children started playing a game. She would write a word on the slate, and they would have to find the item without being told what it was. Soon, each wanted a turn. As they now knew their letters, they learnt their names, and they would attempt to spell them out. Often, the results were quite funny, but the game meant they were learning in leaps and bounds.

As the children were on the high seas, the captain brought them two books: *Robinson Crusoe* and *Swiss Family Robinson*. The first she read to settle them when they were getting somewhat irascible. The other she set aside for use during rough weather. This story she knew was only recently published, and she had not read it herself. Having skimmed it, she realised it was of a marooned family. Mayhap a storm would not be a good time to read it after all. It was about a family stranded on the way to Port Jackson who became shipwrecked. Considering they were doing the very same thing, only with a shipload of convicts, she wondered about the wisdom of bringing this book for them or even reading it to them. She would ask the captain if she had a chance. It could well scare them.

The voyage continued with scuds, storms, and squalls interrupting the otherwise calm weather. After the first two weeks at sea, she had felt the first presence of the child she carried. She woke one morning needing to throw up, but she had not been seasick for some weeks. But when everyone else had been prostrated, she was fine. Now, the sickness surprised her. It was six weeks since the abuse, and she hoped that she would have lost the child. However, her flow had not returned, although she was relieved about that, as coping with that on a ship would have been awkward due to the lack of washing facilities.

Throughout the afternoon, she again fled for the chamberpot. The seas were not even rough. Mrs Reddall, the minister's wife, and Mrs Brown, the captain's wife, took her aside while the children were occupied, and they explained what was ahead of her. The three women had grown close in the few weeks they had been at sea. Jennifer occupied the children, and already their parents had noticed a difference in their behaviour.

Captain Brown had explained to the minister what Jennifer had been arrested for and that the Duke of Shesham was sponsoring her. After the duke's visit on board, some of her history had been revealed. The fact that the duke had also given her a letter of introduction to the governor of the colony assured the Browns that Jennifer was a suitable person to teach their children. Her letter to Governor Macquarie and her money now resided in the captain's strong box. She may well only be a milkmaid, but Mrs Brown soon realised that Jennifer was as genuine as the Duke assured them she was. Mrs Reddall discovered that she also had a deep faith and willingly spoke about it to anyone.

After the Brown children were asleep, Mrs Brown sat Jennifer down and explained what was before her. The morning sickness should only last six to eight weeks, but the tiredness would soon mean that she would feel she could hardly pull herself around. Mrs Brown would take the children for half an hour after luncheon, where Jennifer would be permitted to have a nap. She was expected to eat her meals with the children, so her food allocation was far better than she would have received below deck.

By the time they had been at sea for eight weeks, the morning sickness had all but abated. The tiredness was overwhelming, as was her hunger. Each day, Jennifer put some of the hard-tack rations in her pockets and nibbled on these as the day progressed. She craved freshly steamed cabbage with butter, which was unavailable, but she discovered the doctor had brought barrels of pickled cabbage on board. Jennifer asked for a ration of this as often as she could. Knowing of her condition, the doctor gave her a serving of the sauerkraut as often as her cravings demanded. Others below the deck were not even able to stay clean.

As the voyage progressed, the doctor spoke to the captain and Mrs Brown, "Captain, is there nothing you can do to halt the activities of the sailors? I found an area where some of your crew have broken down the bars dividing the passageway and forced themselves upon three of the younger girls. I arrived in the nick of time while on my rounds and banished the offenders, but the girls are now locked in the hospital rooms for the moment. More for their safety rather than need."

Mrs Brown showed a look of horror. "No! How deplorable!" She left the men to discuss the invasion below. She returned to Jennifer and the children.

The captain, likewise, was not impressed at the behaviour of his crew. When his wife had gone, he said, "Believe it or not, there are few rules as to what they can and can't do. Mutiny is forbidden; unfortunately, nocturnal activities with the inmates are not. Mayhap some women may be willing to indulge them." The captain knew it was not a perfect solution, but it might suffice.

The look on the doctor's face showed his disgust at the suggestion. "Captain, I shall protect the convict's honour with my pistol if required."

The captain's brow creased into a deep frown. "You would put your life at risk for... for such as them? Many of them made their living on their backs." He almost spat the words.

The doctor's ire was raised. "Admittedly, many came on board with the clap; however, it is degrading for any woman, and I will not permit them to be further abused. Many listened to Mrs Fry's words in London and have reformed their ways. Many were forced to make a living that way, and they are the ones complaining to me about the nocturnal visits."

The captain looked long and deep into the doctor's eyes. He was wondering if the man was serious. "Are you really serious about defending them?"

The doctor nodded.

With a resigned sigh, the captain finally answered, "Fine; then I'll send the carpenter to repair the entry and exit points from the convict deck. I think we'll have our hands full keeping the crew out. However, we will try as hard as we can."

Within an hour, the carpenter was hard at work sealing up the holes in the dividing barricades. The women below would be safe for a few days.

Chapter 11   Document Finds 1988

$\mathcal{A}$t eight o'clock on Saturday morning, Jenny was looking forward to a long sleep-in, but the phone rang its incessant jangle of unharmonious clatter. There was no option but for Jenny to get up and answer it. "Yes, how can I help you?"

The excited voice at the other end of the line woke Jenny quicker than being splashed with a bucket of icy water. "Hi Jenny, it's Michelle Fox. I've found a journal from the *Morley* from 1820. I have left it under lock and key at the library. Can you make it in this morning?" Michelle needed an answer immediately.

"Yes! Heck yes!" Very little else would have made Jenny so wide awake at this time on a Saturday morning. It had been a great time at the movies last night, but she was so tired. Yet, this discovery of Michelle's was amazing. "I can be there in thirty minutes if you can open early."

Jenny washed her face, had a lightning-fast shower and walked out the door twenty minutes later while munching on a banana. The library was only ten minutes away. The walk in the cool morning air was refreshing, and by the time Jenny arrived with her genealogy bag, she was sparking on all cylinders. As she walked, she thought over what they had learned before. Over the intervening five years, the two girls had met at least once a month to delve deeper into the archives. Jennifer Kellow Williams' name kept popping up in various paperwork; however, it didn't fill in much information about her life. There was a mention of a conviction for fraud, but they could not find a better explanation of the meaning.

Last year, Michelle had made the startling discovery that Jennifer had been arrested and convicted in London in 1820 and charged with fraud of all things. However, she was not sentenced at the Old Bailey but at the

Magistrates Court belonging to the Bow Street Runners. That discovery had brought another early morning phone call.

In the following years, only small discoveries had been made. A name or two here or there, but both ladies became sidetracked with life.

Earlier in the year, the two girls had joined many of the other Sydney-siders who had dressed in period costumes; they joined the huge throng of Australians celebrating the bicentenary of the founding of the British colony. They knew that one of the bicentennial projects was being sponsored. The Government was having many of the old colonial documents transcribed and made publicly available. Knowing they would one day be available for public perusal would be wonderful. Jenny had been searching for twenty years already; a few more years would mean that many old journals would be photographed and hopefully transcribed.

The ladies greeted each other with a hug, and Michelle tugged Jenny in through the staff entrance. "Shh, you should not be in here, but I'm making you a volunteer for the day. Here's your badge, and stick close to me."

Jenny had the calico bag containing her research books still over her shoulder.

Michelle turned to her as they reached a locked door. "Jenny, unfortunately, you can't bring the bag in here, so just grab your book and a pencil." She waited for Jenny to get her things and place her bag on the table within view.

Michelle pulled out a chair for Jenny, and the two waited for the Microfiche machine to warm up. Michelle slipped the film she held under the reader's glass, and the pages of the surgeon's journal lit up the screen.

Jenny opened her notebook as they scanned through the pages.

Michelle read from the surgeon's journal. "*18th April, four women from Devon Gaol; 21st April, seven women from Horsemonger Lane; 22nd April, two prisoners from the county gaol of Kent; 23rd April, forty women from Newgate were brought to the ship on a lighter; three more women followed from Exeter and one from the Justitia Hulk at Woolwich. Later, two women from York and three from Winchester were brought up, and another three from Newcastle, one of whom was so old and infirm as to require assistance to get up the side of the ship. On the 27th, three more women arrived from Shrewsbury, two from Carlisle and four from Lancaster. They were all cold and wet and were given dry clothes and refreshments and allowed to retire. Eighteen more women arrived on the 28th and displayed riotous conduct and mischievous disposition. Most of these were from Lancaster. The women who arrived from Ilchester a few hours later were of a more decent and modest appearance than any yet seen. On the 29th, eight prisoners arrived from different country prisons.*"

As Jenny took notes, she said, "I wonder if my Jennifer was one of the ones from Newgate. You said she was tried in London, but have we been able to find out more about her?"

Disappointed, Michelle kept scrolling. "Nothing here, Jenny, lots about the weather and the many attempts of the sailors trying every way possible to break into the women locked up below."

Jenny shuddered. "I can't believe our poor convict women were so set - upon by the crew. As if they did not have enough to cope with. How did they survive such abuse?"

Michelle flicked further down the journal. "From what I've read about Doctor Reed, he seemed to be a special sort of man. Apparently, these rambunctious sailors did not give up. They made a secret passage from their area down to the store deck, through the storeroom and then through the vessel's hold. They made a hole in the fore-hatchway bulkhead from there and broke into the ship's hospital. Thankfully, he had locked some of the women inside that area and heard the disturbance while on his evening rounds. The crew were caught in the act of attempting to open the hospital door with a key. He met them with his pistol and sent them packing. Did this man never sleep? He seemed to have been on duty at all times."

The two chattered about the lack of discipline from the captain until Michelle found another entry in the journal. "Jenny, listen to the lengths the sailors went to. This is horrible. *The surgeon feared the sailors were no longer willing to conduct themselves within the bounds of propriety and felt completely at the mercy of these vile men who were now incited by their worst passions, and this success may further extend their daring to acts of mutiny, and gratify themselves by open violence. Captain Brown's hands were tied as he had no power either to restrain or punish the sailors and offered 'to share the fatigue' of being on watch and allow the surgeon to get some rest. But the surgeon could not accept this kind of offer as the Captain was needed to command and navigate the ship.*

Nevertheless, the surgeon, resolute on keeping watch in prison and armed with his brace of pistols, was ready to defend the women from any violence, 'even at the peril of my life.' The sailors' nocturnal annoyance continued, but this time with added malice: a cat attached to a cord was forced down through the fore-hatchway, and it piteously meowed, which upset the women. Their daring became more desperate when they broke down two of the bars over the prison fore-hatchway with a boat-hook staff but abruptly stopped, no doubt sensing the surgeon was 'determined to fire on anyone who should have the temerity to venture in'."

Jenny listened and noticed that her heart beat faster. "Michelle, imagine we are two of those girls locked below decks. Can you feel their terror knowing that lustful men were attempting to break in and ravish them?" Jenny shuddered. "This man must have put his own life in danger for him to need a pistol."

Day by day, they read through the journal, skimming many entries. Michelle read of wild weather and found a record of the crew passing notes through small cracks in the bulkheads and decking. She gave a long gasp. "Oh no! That's all he needed. He found one note, but this was not about meeting the women. Listen, *An unfortunate incident occurred on 21st August, which could have had serious consequences. The bars over the prison fore-hatchway were accidentally crushed by a small cask as it was being hoisted from the hold, and the surgeon became aware the sailors were 'ready to take advantage of incomplete repairs.' That night, at about 2 a.m., he heard the locks on the grating over the hatchway open and shut, 'no doubt by means of a duplicate key.' There was also a rustling sound as if the men were descending, but it suddenly ceased. Nothing further happened that night, and the women slept soundly."*

She paused reading aloud but kept perusing the words. "I wonder if the reverend was helping him? Here's another entry, *'The paper, written by a sailor who had tried to break into the prison, was addressed to one of the women. The handwriting was disguised, and its contents disturbing; as soon as it was ascertained that the surgeon was weary of watching, they would break down the bars to the prison:* There are plenty of us to do it, *it said. There were threats of violence towards the surgeon, and they 'have an eye towards my pistols,' and other expressions which 'are too indecent for publicity,' The designs of the sailors were hampered by the surgeon's constant watch, and they gave up on their annoyances at night. However, the surgeon feared their simmering disappointment might ignite further attempts 'should any opportunity offer'."*

Jenny looked puzzled. She asked, "Did they mean mutiny?

Michelle shrugged. "Look, they had another storm in August. So they must have been nearing Tasmania by then." Michelle was equally shocked. "I think it must. I wonder what else the doctor had to cope with. They must be nearly at Hobart by now. And where was the Reverend who was on board? It makes me wonder what he was doing all this time. I know his wife and children were there too, but surely he could have done some shifts with the doctor."

Jenny was still taking notes as Michelle made each comment.

Michelle kept moving the microfiche tray. "Yes! They have arrived in the Derwent River in Hobart. But listen to this. *'There were only a few days before landing, and the prisoners' thoughts now turned to being separated from those who were disembarking in Hobart Town and the others who were proceeding to Sydney. For many, the end of the voyage was the end of comfort and peace of mind that they had never experienced and may never again. 'A thoughtfulness marks every turn and action,' mingled with sadness, resignation and regret. The surgeon repeated his sermon on the benefits of observing the rules of moral and religious instruction and was full of praise for those who showed the benefit of his wisdom by their behaviour. In this state of reflection, Ann Farrell's old habits unfortunately resurfaced, and she lost her temper over a trifling issue, beating up one of her companions. The surgeon's appearance promptly put an end to their disagreement 'which was instantly succeeded by tears of sorrow'."* Michelle gave a bit of a giggle. "Some of those women were real tartars. This Ann Farrell sounds like a bit of a problem."

Michelle kept scrolling. "Here's another entry that shows the women did appreciate his efforts. Listen. *'The following day, 28th August, a heartfelt letter signed by one hundred and twenty-one female convicts was presented to the surgeon by the Reverend, who helped write the letter. It expressed their deep feelings of gratitude for the great deprivations he had endured on their account and through his good advice, moral and religious instruction 'shall benefit by your counsel…'.*" Michelle sat back and smiled. I thought the Reverend would have a hand in helping him. By the sound of it, they were caring for the girls equally, only as it was the doctor's medical journal, of course, it would be from his view."

Jenny wondered about the mutinous sailors. "Is there anything more about the mutiny? I noticed very few women are mentioned by name and normally only if they are bad."

Michelle flicked through the next page. "Yes, here we go; they are now anchored in the Derwent River at Hobart. It was still called Van Diemen's Land back then. This was August 29th. Just three months after leaving London, so they had a speedy trip. It being Hobart, it had been snowing, and I bet there were no warm clothes like we have now." Michelle took a deep breath before reading the entry aloud. "Listen, *'Most of that day, the surgeon watched over the prisoners until about 8.30 p.m. when he retired to his cabin to prepare notes for those who were to be landed. This took about an hour, and on returning to the prison, he found that four females had been lured away. A search soon discovered three of them in the hammocks of three of the sailors, and the fourth came out from her hiding place. The women were immediately restrained, and early the following morning, the surgeon laid the whole affair before the Lieutenant Governor. He ordered a police constable to arrest the four sailors, also a fifth who was principal in arranging the dalliances. As they were being led away, three other sailors forced the constable to arrest them too. The remaining crew united in the most violent and mutinous manner, stopped work and to a man went below'.*"

Jenny said, *'They do write differently, don't they?"

Michelle nodded and kept reading. "There's more, *'The Police Magistrate, followed by the Sergeant with a file of soldiers, arrived. Captain Brown urged the sailors to return to work, but they obstinately refused. The Magistrate tried to reason with them, pointing out the seriousness of the situation. They accused the surgeon of threatening to shoot them and took little heed of the Magistrate's remonstrances even though 'the soldiers were drawn up under arms beside them.' The surgeon challenged them to advance any charge they wished that he was acting perfectly within the law and warned them not to interfere with him performing his duties or they would 'repent of their folly.' There was loud and vulgar bragging by the crew, but they suddenly changed their tone and, one by one, returned to work'.*"

Jenny had taken notes again as Michelle read. "So it seems the doctor was justified in what he did. I knew he sounded nice. I'm sad that my Jennifer is not mentioned anywhere in the journal." Even though they had read through the entire book, they were a little crushed that they were none the wiser over Jennifer but now better understood her situation.

Michelle read of the death of a convict's three-year-old child the day before they left Hobart. It was buried onshore. "Do you realise how little there is said about the children? With fifty of them on board, surely someone was occupying them. The captain is supposed to have some, and the reverend and his wife had seven. Maybe they used some of the convict girls to help care for them. Hopefully, that was where Jennifer was."

Michelle had finished the journal and skipped down to another reference she had found. "Hey, Jen, this is from the newspaper a short while later in September 1822. Listen, '*Some of the most curious facts relative to the treatment of the prisoners may here be stated. Previous to their sailing, the Solicitor to the Bank presented £5 to every woman convicted of uttering forged notes or having them in her possession! This practice appears to be more philanthropic than judicious, for the money, according to Mr Reed, was either misapplied on its receipt or at the first subsequent opportunity. The Governor of Newgate also visited the ship and gave every woman from that prison half a crown out of some idea devoted to that charity. This donation also led to quarrels and blows. The prevention and punishment of such misconduct are to tie the pugnacious combatants back to back and leave them pinioned in this inoffensive attitude till their passions cool. For graver offences, confinement to the hospital and exclusion from the deck are the awards. The latter is a severe visitation under the circumstances of the voyage'.*"

Michelle glanced at Jenny. "That means your Jennifer will have had some money. Well, half a crown may not seem like much to us, but for them, it was a gold mine. A year's wage for many of them would be £1. So if £1 was the same as $2, then it was still only about twenty-five cents. However, we already know she was done for fraud so she may have also received the £5 for forgery."

The girls looked at each other in astonishment.

Jenny said, "Why would they bother? It hardly seems worth it, doesn't it? Half a crown is two shillings and sixpence, isn't it? I wonder what that would buy back then?"

Michelle reached out and pulled a sheet from the shelf behind her desk. Running her finger down the list, she said, "The actual value compared to today is about $50, but the buying power would mean it's ten times that. So we're talking big money. I certainly would not mind being given $500. Food was mostly home-produced, and needs were few. Cloth would be one of the biggest purchases, and boots, of course. Hats and warm clothing were normally all homemade, but they needed to buy their own fabric unless they had a fine-weave loom. There were no off-the-rack dresses as we have, so you either received hand-me-downs that were normally well worn, made your own, or paid a dressmaker. The latter would only be for special occasions."

Jenny wondered what shops there would have been in Sydney back then and even if the convicts were permitted to use them. She made a few more notes and then asked Michelle, "It's okay to have money, but as convicts, they could not get to the shops. Where would they have spent it?'

Michelle didn't need a book for this question. "Back then, there were various stores and shops at the dockland at what is now Circular Quay. You know the Campbell's stores building and where the Argyle building is now?"

Jenny nodded. She loved that area and haunted the shops as often as possible. There were many really old buildings, and some were even being restored. "I love the Argyle stores."

Michelle kept hunting while she chatted. "Well, sadly, they weren't built until about six years later, but there were other shops, and I think the original Campbell's stores were there at that time, but they are not the buildings we know. Those were built in the 1850s. Mum and I used to haunt the place. Anyway, there was a stack of imports coming in all the time. Rum, of course, was the main currency in the colony until Governor Macquarie bought about twenty thousand Spanish coins and punched the middle out of them. Have you heard of the holey dollar and dump?"

Jenny still had a souvenir from her school days when commemorative coins were issued to all school children in 1970. "Yes, I do."

Michelle kept moving the sheet reader as she chattered. "Well, Mr Campbell was a man who stood against the militia who caused the Rum Rebellion that overthrew Governor Bligh. He had to go to London to stand witness at the trial, and when he was away, his business suffered to the point he was bankrupted while he was gone; even his fleet of ships had been wrecked. Anyway, on his return in 1815, Governor Macquarie put him in a position of trust, and soon, he had his businesses rebuilt, and they were bigger and better than ever. Hence, Campbell's store is still there. Others were built nearby, and Mary Reiby's store opened when the Argyle Bond store did in about 1826. So, a lot of stock was certainly available, but probably not for the convicts. Their problem was accessing things. Many would probably have asked or bribed a soldier or gaoler to buy them things. The fabric would always have been popular, but the convict women probably spent it on grog. Remember, the majority would have been the poorest of the poor and willingly returned to the gutters from whence they had come in London and other places." She sighed. "I haven't found much about your Jennifer, but I'll keep looking."

Michelle had not even looked up as she spoke. It was a subject that she obviously knew well. She spieled off the names and dates with ease. The stories were as well known to her as her own family history.

As Jenny had taken notes, one name was suspiciously absent from the journal, and that was of Reverend Reddall. "Michelle, is there any information of the reverend?"

Her question was answered with a chuckle from her friend. "I presume you have never heard of him before?"

Jenny shook her head.

Michelle switched off the microfiche machine and pulled out the sheet she had been perusing. She set about putting away the things around her and then pulled out a big blue book. "This is volume two of the Australian Dictionary of Biography. It was published in Melbourne in 1967. He's in there."

Jenny put her pencil down and listened. "What did he do?"

Michelle flicked the tome open to the man's entry. "Let's see, will we? She abbreviated as she read, "Thomas was born and raised in England where he attended Oxford and was trained for Colonial Ministry. He, Isabella, and their seven children arrived in Sydney on 14th September 1820. We know that as they were on the *Morley*. Anyway, once here, although it doesn't say where he preached, it may well have been St. James, but he soon was involved in education. Only three months after his arrival, the Governor had leased *Meehan House* for him, and he had opened it as a private school. The Governor's son, Lachie, also went there, so he must have been a good teacher. By the following year, he was not only running the school at Macquarie Fields with Lachie Macquarie but the Lieutenant-Governor of Van Diemen's Land's son, too. But he also worked as the minister for Airds, Appin and Minto; then, he was made a magistrate in August 1821. It seemed things went well for him until he took his eyes off the ministry and focused on a bigger house and his farm. His wife Isabella and some of his daughters changed the private boys' school into a select girls' school. It seems that he overstretched himself somewhat; as it says, '*he ran into financial difficulties.*' It doesn't say much more than… '*A man of taste and refinement with a bright and active mind, an excellent conversationalist, cultured and capable, with a pleasing personality, he misused his talents.*' It says he died on 30th November 1838, aged 58." She closed and put away the book.

Sadly, it was now time for the library to close for the day. They had spent hours searching, and little more information was forthcoming about Jennifer. The fact that she was not mentioned was a good thing as it meant that she was unlikely a bad prisoner.

They would keep watching and waiting.

Chapter 12 Mutinous Crew 1820

*H*obart was cold and bleak. Snow lay on the ground, and the cutting breezes from the river were frigid. The wind cut through Jennifer's gown, and the thin shawl she had pulled tightly around her shoulders was all but useless. At four months gone with child, the crew left her alone, but this was not so with the other convict women. The fact that Jennifer was assigned to care for the children of both the captain and the reverend also gave her a measure of protection. Several small children often accompanied her on deck, which was enough to make the sailors leave her alone. That didn't mean that she was immune to the insulting wolf whistles of the crew. There were four men in particular that she had learnt to stay well away from. Even the captain wouldn't permit her or the children on deck when these four characters were on duty.

Reverend and Mrs Reddall were also wonderful. While they had taken to teaching the women to read and write, she educated their children. Their eldest son, John, needed little assistance from her, but she oversaw the work his father had set for him to achieve. Her education was extraordinary, and it had been more than adequate for her needs in Cornwall. The books supplied by Mrs Fry, the captain and the Reddalls stretched her to her limits as she had never taught small children who knew very little.

An incident occurred while they were anchored in the Derwent River, and it frightened Jennifer. She had visited the cows to strip off their milk when muffled sounds were heard from the hammocks just beyond the stock. Realising that the ship was currently being searched for some missing women, she slipped out as quickly as she had entered. Returning to the captain's cabin, she reported the noises and stayed put until the four convict women and the four sailors hiding them had been apprehended. It didn't take long before she could return to the cows. After so many months at sea, their milk was drying up. There was little enough for the ship's use, but the captain told her to have a mug full before it was taken to the galley. She loved this and craved the creamy drink; she willingly helped herself. The calf was now weaned, and she loved stroking the nose of the small heifer. It would nuzzle her as she sat and milked her mother. It would grow up to have big horns like its mama, but for now, the calf head-butted her lovingly as she set about her duty.

As the vessel was at anchor, she carried the milk to the galley herself. Rather than go through the shortest route down the corridor to the galley, she climbed the steps and then walked across the deck, heading back down the aft steps to the galley. The captain's quarters were just above this area, and she was already late in helping get the children out of bed. The routine was somewhat out of kilter, as today, fifty of the women were to be landed. It was four of them who had gone missing. Three had been found hiding in three sailors' hammocks, and another emerged from another hiding spot with another sailor in tow. By the time Jennifer returned to her tiny room to change from her milking apron, the ship was once again quiet. Apparently, all eight had been arrested and taken ashore.

Mrs Reddall mentioned the evening before that their family would take the opportunity to permit the children to stretch their legs onshore. Jennifer hoped the Brown family would do likewise, and she could have a long rest. The voyage had been almost enjoyable. Thankfully, she had not been required to teach the other eleven children belonging to the four female passengers. She had needed to care for them when one or other of the mothers had been ill, but it was beyond her ability to care for twenty-one children. Ten children of assorted ages were stretching her patience and her skill; however, her condition meant that tiredness was sapping any energy she had. She folded her apron and dragged herself to the captain's quarters.

On knocking, Mrs Brown called for her to enter. "Dear, as you can see, you will not be required today. We are going ashore with the Reddalls, and I want you to take the opportunity to rest. I have no idea what your situation will be in Sydney; I may even try to keep you on board with us for a while. But the captain said he and the doctor will introduce you to the Colonial Secretary. Plus, you will need to deliver your letter to Governor Macquarie anyway. Robert has it safely stored for you, but I'm not sure there is a bank in the colony yet. Mayhap the governor will keep the money safe in his office."

Jennifer had never needed a bank before. There was certainly none in either Newlyn or Penzance. "Do you really think he would look after it for me? I have no idea what to do with five pounds, let alone one thousand. Billy and Mr Williams will need it to build a dairy. I don't want it, Mrs Brown. I've never needed money before. Sometimes, I would have a penny to buy something for Mama, but I had never seen paper money before London. It was for that reason that I found myself in trouble." Jennifer paused, thinking back to that day. She had momentarily been elated from making her first cheese sale to only minutes later trying to fight off a lecherous lord wanting and eventually succeeding in violating her. Her hands fell to her stomach. His child was now growing within her rather than Billy's baby. She should have been married for four months by now and should have been carrying his child.

Mrs Brown saw the wave of sadness cross her face. "Dear, I know you believe in God. You have proven that more than once on this trip. Do you remember me stitching my big tapestry?"

Jennifer nodded. A tear dripped from her eyelash as she did, and she angrily wiped it away.

Mrs Brown saw and admired this girl even more for her attitude to her abhorrent situation. "When you first saw the tapestry on the frame, you could only see the back of the work. All you saw were the knots and the backs of the stitches. You could not see what I saw: the beautiful picture of the sailing ship and a stunning sky."

Jennifer shook her head. The lump in her throat stopped her from commenting.

Mrs Brown continued, "God is like that. We can't see the plan He has for us and our lives. All we see are the knots. They are the hard situations that we must face on our road to life. All the while, God is carefully placing us in situations that are not of our own making and setting us like stitches on a tapestry. What you are going through, my dear girl, is not what you and Billy had planned. You should be with him, looking forward to the birth of your first child together and not sailing the high seas away from him and being banished to the other side of the world. I freely admit that I was very hesitant when I heard that Robert had been requested to have you assigned to us for the voyage. It only took minutes in your company to see that the duke was correct." In the time the two women had been chatting, the children had sorted themselves out and were now waiting for their mother to lead the way ashore.

The cabin door was flung open. Captain Brown was flustered. "Oh, thank goodness. I thought you had all left. I need you to all stay inside and lock the door. Barricade it and let no one in but the doctor or me." He quickly kissed his wife. "The crew have mutinied. I'm pretty sure there will be no trouble, but I need you to all be safe. I have told the reverend the same, and his family are locked in too." He was about to leave when he pulled his wife back into his arms. "Stay safe, love!" He kissed her again and pulled the door closed behind him. "Barricade the door while I'm here. Put a chair under the handle and then the full cases on either side." He waited until the door was secure before he departed.

The cabin was aft of the ship and, therefore, had rear windows that they threw open to gaze out. As the tide was incoming, the ship swung so the stern faced the shore. A longboat had been lowered, and they watched as Captain Brown, the reverend and the doctor were rowed ashore by some of the soldiers supposedly guarding the convicts. All the crew were already ashore and standing in a group that did not bode well for the remainder of the voyage. Captain Brown had drawn his sword, but although he was holding it aloft, he was not actually threatening anyone. The crew was obviously livid over some issues. Those observing the activities had no idea what they were. As they watched, an official man who looked like a policeman arrived with a line of soldiers. The situation suddenly exploded. Scuffles erupted amongst the groups. The new soldiers arrested the four obnoxious sailors that were pointed out by the doctor. Although they had been taken off the ship with the convict women, they had been released once on shore. Now, they were being escorted away, and their shipmates did not like this situation. Only moments later, the soldiers had shouldered arms and readied their muskets.

The sailors decided they were not going back on board without their shipmates. The crew were about to charge when the soldiers took aim directly at the angry, mutinying crew.

There was a stalemate onshore, and the ladies and children watched with bated breath. Slowly, the crew advanced upon the waiting soldiers. The captain, reverend and doctor all stood unmoving and waited.

First, they heard Doctor Reed challenge them, and he called them out for their abhorrent behaviour. Then, the reverend called for them to repent of their folly. The crew replied by yelling vile abuse and shouting vulgar bragging at those behind the armed soldiers. The captain stepped forward and spoke; the women could not hear what he said; however, they saw a visible change in the stance of the crew. All the crew turned and looked at one of the more vocal men in their group. Little by little, they backed away from him. Soon, the man was all but standing alone. The uniformed officer who had first arrived arrested him and handed him off to the waiting armed soldiers to join the other four offenders.

With the five instigators now dragged away, the rest of the crew slowly returned to work. The entire incident had taken an hour, but the women watching remained nervously locked in the cabin.

The captain, doctor and minister returned to the ship, and soon, the long-awaited knock was heard at the cabin door. The children and ladies pulled back the heavy bags and opened the door to the much-relieved captain. Without apologising to Jennifer, he ignored her and pulled his wife and children into his arms. "Thank goodness you are all safe. I think that we will be able to leave now, but onshore excursions will be cancelled; sorry, love." He turned to Jennifer, "Help the children get settled again, Jennifer. We won't be going ashore after all. I want to reach Sydney safely, and I will weigh anchor as soon as I can arrange it." He pulled away from his family and said, "That means leaving tomorrow. I don't want to waste any more time here, and I don't want the crew to mutiny on the way. Jennifer, I need you to remain vigilant, and you are never to be alone. That includes when milking. Take the children with you if you must."

For the remainder of the day, the tones on deck were hushed. The children changed out of the shore clothes and settled back to another day on board.

Jennifer was so tired. She wanted to curl up and sleep.

As she sat at the table, Mrs Brown saw that Jennifer's eyes were closed. She sent her off for a nap while taking all the children onto the poop deck.

Jennifer slept... and slept... and slept. She didn't hear the small cabin door open and close numerous times throughout the afternoon when Mrs Brown or Mrs Reddall checked on her. Eventually, the distressed mooing of the cattle awoke her. She could hear the pain of the cows' lows. Realising that she had slept way past her half-hour nap, she struggled up and washed her face in the small basin outside her room. Grabbing her milking apron, she headed down to the cows to relieve them of their milk. She passed the minister on the way down to the stock and apologised profusely, and he only answered with a chuckle. She looked puzzled but continued on her journey. As she drew closer, the sound of children's voices grew louder. They were all with the stock. On entering the area, the children giggled while watching their mothers try to get some milk from the cantankerous bovine animals. Jennifer's gasp brought sighs of relief from both ladies.

Mrs Reddall asked, "Jennifer, how do you get them to let their milk down? I'm having no luck at all." She willingly relinquished her stool.

Jennifer first rubbed her hands to warm them up. She had tucked her hands under her arms as she had descended the steps to the beasts, so they were already quite warm. She answered, "They have their own likes and dislikes. Most prefer a certain way of milking them. In a dairy, they will often choose their own milkmaid. Each girl has their own way of stripping the milk, and the cows can be fussy about who does their milking. If you watch a dairy herd carefully, cows will rarely have to be herded, but they will file up to the dairy and move into their chosen cubicle in an orderly way and without fuss." By now, she had seated herself beside the first cow. "Here, they have no choice." This gentle beast turned to see who was at her side and lowed her thanks softly. Jennifer chuckled, moved the bucket under the teats, and took hold of two of them. She started with a gentle push upwards that mimicked a calf's sucking action. The steady flow of milk was soon heard going into the wooden pails. The children watched in awe, and after Jennifer had finished the calm one, she moved to the cantankerous cow. More of the herd had given birth shortly before reaching the Derwent River, and the first three had been offloaded in Hobart. They were back to only three cows again. Jennifer started milking this cow. Having had the first pint stripped, she was far more forgiving. "Children, how would you each like to have a try?"

All ten children tried their hand at getting some milk from the teats. The two smallest children stood between Jennifer's legs and squeezed until they managed to get a squirt of milk into the bucket; knowing that the third cow yet had to be started, she made the last five children wait until she had made the last cow comfortable.

Their lessons for that day were far from their normal learning, but they may need to milk their own cows or goats one day in the colony. As she stripped half of the milk from the last cow, she let the remaining five children have a try. However, she removed the full bucket and placed an empty one in situ. It was just as well she did as when the oldest boy sat down to milk; he squeezed too hard, and the cow gave a kick, sending the empty bucket flying.

For the remaining voyage time, Jennifer extended the children's lessons to include milking. Their mothers would join them. None had ever needed to milk their own cows before, and all realised that in their new lives, all knowledge would be useful. The trip down the Derwent the following morning occurred while Jennifer was milking. The ship was carried eastward by a fresh morning breeze. By the time Jennifer emerged, followed by a trail of laughing children, the ship was within sight of the sea. The breeze carried them past the northern headland, and they watched as the crew set the sails to catch the new sea breezes.

An elevation of speed was felt as the wind filled the snowy sails above them. However, the icy winds cut through Jennifer's thin clothing, but the children were warm as toast. They were wrapped up and sitting out of the wind. The captain was at the wheel behind the mizenmast on the deck below them, and they were watching him as the ship tacked to turn northward. It did not take long before Jennifer was shivering badly.

The minister's eldest son, John, first noticed her blue lips. "Miss Jennifer, you don't look very well. Are you all right? Your lips are blue."

Jennifer was feeling quite light-headed and ill. She was about to reply when she heard footsteps behind her. She spun around to see who it was; that movement was the last thing she remembered. The captain caught her as she collapsed. He had heard John's comment and turned to look at her. He could see her shoulders shaking from the cold. His concern was such that he handed the wheel to the first mate and took the steps two at a time. She fainted in his arms, unaware of the turmoil she now caused. The children clustered around her, and the captain felt how cold she was.

The ten children scurried down the steps from the upper deck and into their cabins. They opened doors for the captain as he walked with his burden in his arms. Rather than take her into her small storeroom cabin, he placed her on the floor beside the brazier in the family room.

Mrs Brown sent the children into the Reddalls' rooms as she set about warming Jennifer. Her thin shawl was almost threadbare, and the gown was unlined and had no warmth in it. No wonder the poor girl was cold. She should be resting in her condition, yet she worked hard while the ladies read or embroidered. Shame swept over Mrs Brown, and she stripped the blankets from their bed and wrapped Jennifer in them while cradling her to warm her. Jennifer's shivering slowly decreased, but she had still not come around. However, the girl's blue lips slowly returned to their customary pink.

After some time, Jennifer's eyes fluttered open. Finding herself enclosed in her mistress's arms on the floor of the captain's cabin was not where she expected to find herself. She struggled to right herself and started apologising profusely, ashamed that she had let her down by her physical weakness. Tears followed from Jennifer, but also from Mrs Brown.

Mrs Brown caressed her cheek lovingly. "Oh, my dear, I had no idea you had no petticoats or undergarments to keep you warm, and although the shawl is pretty, it gives you no protection."

Astounded at the empathy, Jennifer replied, "Billy sent it to me." She looked down and stroked the Angora shawl. "It's the warmest thing I have." The thought of Billy brought tears to her eyes. "I'm so sorry to be so weak and silly."

Mrs Brown helped her up as they heard a knock at the door. The captain entered carrying something, followed by a sailor bearing a tray. There was a bowl of hot soup and some delicious creamy porridge. The concern on his face was echoed in that of his wife. When the three were alone, she said, "Robert, she has no warm clothing at all. How did I not notice? All this time, she has been selflessly giving, and receiving nothing from us but more work. I cannot cope with three children in a cramped cabin, but she not only must milk the cows but care for ten young ones." Turning back to Jennifer, who was eating the lovely hot porridge, she again apologised.

Jennifer paused in the consumption of her tasty meal. "Ma'am, sir, I have worked all my life. I'm normally up at dawn at home, and there were twelve, and then later thirty cows to milk. I come from a large family, and our clothing was always hand-me-downs from another family. I'm used to being cold. However, this little one…" she touched her stomach, "seems to have affected my cold tolerance." At nearly five months along, the child could easily be felt moving. Her thin frame now showed her bump clearly.

The captain sat at his desk and gazed hard at the girl and his wife. He, too, had never thought about what life was like for those who needed to work hard for a living. His life had always been about the sea. He had met and married his wife on a rare trip home; she now travelled with him when she could. The children were soon of an age where their sons could do the job of cabin boy, but that would only be if they wished to stay at sea. He would not force them. He had never thought much about their education but realised how necessary it would be for them to read and write. As a captain, he needed to keep a ship's log. Shaking his head to banish those thoughts, he turned to the girl in their quarters. "I brought you an oilskin coat, Jennifer. If you venture out again and it's cold, I want you to wear it. However, I also want you to keep it as your early mornings will be cold when you start the dairy. The dairy may not be close to your dwelling, and you will need the warmth. This one is too small for our sailors, so you are welcome to have it." He held the coat out to her.

She saw that it was made so the seal fur was on the inside and the leather was oiled on the outside, therefore making it waterproof. As she finished her food and felt better, she stood and slipped on the luxurious coat. The warmth enveloped her, and she felt like she was being hugged. "Oh sir, truly this is for me? I've never seen anything so, well, splendid."

Mrs Brown went to her closet and rifled through the drawer at the bottom. From right at the back, she pulled out a fur cap. "Add this to your ensemble, and that will keep you warm. It's not fashionable, but it's cosy. I have never worn it, but purchased it on a previous trip. The earflaps tie under your chin like so." She tied the brown ribbons in a bow.

The remainder of the day was spent in the large cabin with the children. Now, the captain was aware of how cold the biting wind was; the children were told to stay indoors until the weather warmed.

All the young ones and their mothers accompanied Jennifer below decks to the cows at milking time. The other four female passengers had also asked to learn this skill, and Jennifer's milking school brought much laughter and merriment to them all. Twenty-one children and seven women soon had the work done. John and Thomas, the minister's eldest sons, would then carry the full buckets of milk to the galley and then return for Latin lessons before supper. Jennifer adored teaching the two boys as it refreshed the lessons her minister had given her.

Now warm, Jennifer and the four eldest children would head on deck to watch the sunset. They were never permitted off the top two decks, and they only stayed until the sun sank, then would head inside for story-time. She had long since finished reading the two books and now sat retelling stories of her childhood in Cornwall. Their reading had improved so much that one of the older children often read a story that she had written for them. For the remainder of the short time aboard, the discussion turned to the colony and life ahead. The Browns thought it was time to discuss Jennifer's astonishing bequest from the child's father and what she would do with it. The money was safely locked in the captain's strong box, and he would give it to her when the governor boarded in Sydney. The captain said, "Depending on his reaction to what the duke has written in his letter, your future is unsure. You must serve your term of fourteen years regardless of any outcome. However, he may assign you immediately rather than spend time in prison."

The duke had made her aware that only the governor could change how this was done. It could well be served in the female prison in Parramatta, or she could be assigned elsewhere until Billy arrived. Even though she had the duke's letter, it did not assure her of anything, but it gave her a fighting chance. Jennifer had not spoken to the Browns about her conversation with the duke before they left. The details were stored in her heart, but now she replied, "Sir, ma'am, the duke has not just sent a letter, but he has given instructions to the Governor, whom he met in London, that I am to start working at the Government Dairy. He has requested that I start a commercial cheese industry in New South Wales and train others with the required skills. He is personally sponsoring the project. When Billy comes, he and his parents will bring out the beginning of a dairy, and a full herd of special cows will follow with more equipment. The duke is also now sponsoring our old dairy in Cornwall. I have not told you before, as I'm still unsure how his plans will pan out. I will put half of the money from the child's father into this project. Mayhap, the governor will not wish me to work there as I have yet to have this child. I may not even live through the birth. If I do, then the duke asked that Billy be permitted to marry me, and together with his parents, we will build a cheese dairy and establish the new industry in town."

The astounded look on both their faces showed they had not realised how much responsibility this girl had in front of her. "You know that much about cheese?" How had she kept this hidden from them?

A subtle nod was her reply.

The captain was intrigued. "How do you know the duke?" This was something that had puzzled him since the eagle-nosed peer had boarded his vessel.

Jennifer smiled. "Well, I would not say I know him, but he knew of one of my new cheeses. It was he who summoned me to London, and therefore, he felt responsible for all this." She placed her hand on her stomach. "One of the new cheeses I made was called *Southern Belle,* and our agent supplied the duke's chef with samples. The duke demanded that the maker come and answer questions to prove that it was an English-made product and not illegally imported from Europe. Impressed with the cheese, he wished to sponsor more of it to be made." She paused but saw the captain wave his hand for her to tell the rest of the story.

"I came to London to meet him, and another chef had ordered one of these special cheeses. I was to deliver it but went to the front door instead of the back. I was innocently selling my wares, as I used to do at home, but the baron mistook the purpose for my arrival at his home. He did buy some small fresh cheeses, and I gave him the change of three pounds with the money I had received from another sale. I intended to give the chef a smoked ricotta cheese and had some products with me. It was two of these I had sold. I had never seen paper money before and had no idea they were forged. The baron realised they were forgeries after I had departed, but by then, he had had his way with me." Tears welled in her eyes as she told the whole story. She had not fully revealed that morning's activities before, except in court. Even to Billy, they had so little time together that she had left bits out. She then told them of the affray in the inn courtyard, of Billy's arrival and then of Billy punching the baron and breaking his nose. It was because of the promise extracted before witnesses that morning that the baron had sent the money. She had revealed all this to the duke when he had come to the cell with Bertram the following morning at the prison. It had been the duke who obtained the money and made sure the baron would be shunned for his actions. Now, his money would be used to build a new dairy industry. He had told her that cattle and their attendants would arrive in about a year, and she hoped the Browns would now vouch for her to the governor. She handed the duke's personal letter to her over to the captain and sat quietly while he perused the screed; Billy's letter she had reread numerous times and almost knew by heart.

After the captain handed the letter to his wife, he stared at Jennifer wide-eyed. "Why didn't you tell us? I knew he had singled you out, but now I understand why he wanted you with us, not down with the rabble below."

Jennifer said softly. "I'm but a simple milkmaid with the knowledge of cheese making. I experimented with some additives, and they worked. If the King had not demanded the history of where the duke sourced my cheese, it might never have been more than a nice cheese. However, my parents will now oversee the Williams Kellow dairy in Newlyn, and we shall start a branch out here."

Mrs Brown finished reading the letter too. "The King wanted your cheeses?"

In her understated way, Jennifer just nodded. "The duke said something about a Royal Warrant, but I'm not sure what that is."

Alderney Cattle.

Chapter 13 Long Farewells 1820

 $\mathcal{B}$ illy, Bryn, and Delen packed their belongings, and with Duke Felix's sponsorship, the four of them set about purchasing new items to start a dairy from scratch.

Only weeks after Jennifer's arrest, the duke had come for a visit and, having no inn in the village, he had stayed with the Williams family for two weeks. He had Bryn and Isla teaching him to milk a cow and saw how time-consuming cheese production was. He had no idea of the requirements needed to produce this staple food, but this stay opened his eyes to the need to support small local businesses.

The Duke of Shesham's friend, Perry, had challenged him to look deeper into what makes England tick. He had only recently discovered from his father that Perry was in New South Wales and living in Parramatta under his untitled name of Perry White. Hopefully, they would return soon, but he had written immediately to tell him about Jennifer. Their tale was long and twisted; with his wife presuming infidelity on Perry's behalf, she fled, but she had been mistaken, and after intentionally stealing something, Katy was arrested and convicted of theft. Perry caught the next ship and arrived soon after she had. Like Jennifer would need to do, Katy had to serve her term as a convict before returning to England. She still had a couple of years left to serve, but their work with Lachlan Macquarie had interested Felix, Duke of Shesham, and he had kept in regular contact with his old school friend.

Perry had written to his friend and told him of the appalling condition of the convicts and how they still preferred this new land to what they had left behind. One of Perry's last letters challenged him to try to improve the lot of some poorer people in England, so when the *Southern Belle* cheese landed on his table one evening after their meal, it opened a door for him.

It had taken nearly two years for Duke Felix to trace the source of the gourmet product to Jennifer in Cornwall. However, as Bertram held back as much information as he could, bluffing and forestalling further enquiry made him even more intrigued. It also made him doubt the validity of the source of the product. To confirm Jennifer's story, he realised that he needed to see for himself that what she said was true. He knew that he finally must take a journey.

The visit to Cornwall had seen Jacob take him for an in-depth tour of the lead, tin and copper mines, as well as showing him the cheese process. It was eye-opening.

Bryn and Billy then showed him the hands-on requirements of manufacturing cheeses. He had spent time talking to the people in the village and getting to know the Williams and Kellow families. The initial tour of the dairy took nearly three hours, but even then, he wanted to stay and watch everything. He was promised that he would get a chance to do that each day he was there. The few days he initially planned to stay turned into a two-week-long visit. He was enthralled.

Although poor, the families were scrupulously clean and surprisingly happy. From the youngest child, Polly, to the eldest two sons, Logan and Billy, each pulled their weight without their parents being continually on their backs. Jennifer's sister Isla had taken over making the special additives with her father. This left the young boys now having to cure the set cultured milk before adding the brine flavouring. With only one cheese press, it was a time-consuming process. When only three wheels of cheese were made, one press was adequate. With the increase in productivity, this step was the main area that held up production. He sent a note to his secretary in London to immediately source ten more twenty-pound cheese presses and twenty-five smaller ten-pound presses for the *Southern Belle* half-wheels. Regardless of the outcome of his propositions, these items would be a gift of his thanks in the way of an apology.

Bryn and Billy walked him through the process as they made the cheese that afternoon. With a notepad in hand, the Duke wrote a list for himself of what they needed to speed up production.

With the planned outing on the first morning of Duke Felix's visit, Jacob left the kitchen to Isla and accompanied the duke on a tour of the area.

As they viewed the various mines, the hazards miners and their families faced tore through him. In his discussions with Bryn, Billy and Jacob on the evening of his arrival, he informed them what he would like to do.

A new partnership had been formed before they had retired for the evening. His offer to sponsor the significant growth of the business as a silent partner took their breath away.

Felix went for a walk outside while they discussed his offer. The peace of the evening quieted his soul. He had been in turmoil for some time, knowing he needed to marry soon. He had cast his eye over the new batch of simpering debutantes and immediately rejected them all. Knowing that some would try to even compromise themselves with him so he would be forced to marry them, he shuddered with the thought of being trapped into a marriage that way. No! He had an unreasonable desire to find someone who loved him for himself, not his wealth and title. It would certainly not be because of his looks as he realised his hawk-like visage was enough to scare off most girls. He sat on the grassy headland, watching the sun sink. He blew out his cheeks in frustration. A face forced its way into his mind. Her laugh and joy of life made him smile. Isla Kellow was so pure in comparison to her London counterparts. She had a joy of life that had nearly knocked him off his feet. Her joyous laugh made him smile. Something he had not done for goodness knows how long. He frowned, trying to remember when he had last enjoyed himself as much and could not pinpoint any such time. The thought shocked him. Again, the thought of Isla made him smile. She was also so beautiful that her father had noted his small gasp and cocked an eyebrow at him.

Felix shook his head, sending the inappropriate thoughts flying. No, to distract him, he would completely bankroll a new dairy in New South Wales as well as an expansion and upgrade of the facilities of the existing dairy here in Cornwall, not to mention the mines and, therefore, the entire village.

Billy was sent out to get the duke back in to hear the verdict, which was, of course, supportive of his idea. Rather than bring him inside, Billy was caught in a discussion with him about Jennifer. Felix discovered he was only four years older than Billy, who mentioned that he intended to follow Jennifer as soon as possible. Billy told him about his feelings for the young lady in question.

Having briefly met her, Felix could understand Billy's attraction. She was indeed a beauty. Isla, though, was the rose of the two young ladies. He knew she was yet to discover the full situation of her sister. He expected and deserved any chastisement that would follow.

Once Bryn and Jacob had accepted the duke's offer, Bryn mentioned that they also intended to head to Sydney to be with Jennifer. Although this had not been mentioned until Billy's conversations with him, he knew that Billy at least would follow her. The Duke was pleased that Bryn and Delen would be with him. This actually suited his purpose.

The New South Wales plan was shelved for later discussion.

After the tour of the mines, the duke realised that the immediate need was for a larger cheese cave. This needed men to dig it out; currently, none were available. With this at the back of his mind, when the duke saw some half-naked miners emerging from the tin mine, he asked Jacob for an explanation of what it was like.

Jacob's friend, Dylan, was the mine manager, and he suggested that the duke go down the pit and see for himself. Jacob made the duke strip down to his undergarments, then handed him some dungaree coveralls and a small candle lantern.

Small dust-covered humans pushed a blackened carriage of the tin-laden ore out of the mine.

The duke was horrified when he realised the filthy naked bodies were children. "Jacob, do all mines have children working in them?"

Jacob nodded. He was unsure of what to call the duke. He had initially Y*our Graced* him a few times, but *Sir* didn't seem appropriate. Now, he just tried not to call him anything. He pinched himself a few times to think he was in the presence of a real duke. He had stolen the odd glance at the young peer but was caught by the hook-nosed man's penetrating, enquiring eyes.

The duke smiled. "I don't bite, you know, Jacob. We are partners, and I think you can call me Duke, Shesham or, if you can bring yourself to do it, then Felix. It is my Christian name, and my friends use it. It is Latin for happy or fortunate. Admittedly, I do consider myself to be so." The austere-looking man felt that this older man could become a friend to him. One who did no asking but freely gave of the little he had. Felix wished Perry White lived closer as he had been one of the few friends from school who liked him for himself. Another had been Sam Garney. He, too, had vanished from his life. He shrugged off the thought and turned to the older man showing him around.

Jacob had seen the wave of sadness pass across the brow of the young duke. He nodded with a knowing smile. The man's appearance was an acquired taste, but a smile could transform his face; however, a frown from him sent shivers down the spine of the toughest man. Jacob dropped his head and smiled to himself. Having the name of Felix, the fearsome duke was somehow more human. After biting his lips to stop a laugh, he grinned. "I think I'll stick with Duke for the moment, sir, and see how I go with that." Jacob continued watching the full carts come out of the mine. "Are you ready, Duke? Once the carts are emptied, we will join them to return to the mine face."

The two men climbed into one of the carts that were then let down on a rope.

The children that had helped push them up the hill were also inside the wagon attached behind them, and a giant pulley and a thick rope let them down.

The ten-minute descent into the dark bowels of the earth took all Felix's willpower not to shout out in fear as they descended into the abyss. He had never been so terrified.

The horrendous conditions were not only dangerous but downright scary.

The blackness was both overwhelming and oppressive.

Upon their arrival at the mine face, he was met with the sounds of picks sparking as they hit the quartz and the sound of running water. The mine shaft was half full of water, and the workers were waist-deep in some places. There was no way that he, as a duke, could in all good conscience permit men and children to work in such conditions. Before reaching the surface, he had decided to buy and close the mine until conditions could be improved. Water pumps, fresh air, and new dual chains on the wagons were the first safety things to be implemented. He also realised that new roof supports would be needed, as the timbers in the mine were obviously ancient; some had broken and had not been replaced.

The tour below ground was over, and the duke could not walk up the tracks fast enough, so much so that Jacob had a tough time keeping up with him.

On arrival at the surface, the duke almost doubled up, drawing deep breaths and fighting for fresh air. The air below was so oxygen-deprived that Felix felt dizzy. "Jacob, how could you permit your children to work in such vile conditions? I could hardly stand it for thirty minutes."

Jacob shrugged. "We have no choice, sir. We all need to eat and need money to live. I won't permit my lads to work in the lead mines, for they are even worse. We have three main industries here: fishing, mining and milking. The latter is where we choose to work, but most of us do not have the luxury of choice. I lost my father at sea, as the waters here are dangerous." How did one admit to the duke that he drowned while smuggling? "Let me just say that I prefer to keep my feet firmly on solid ground. Therefore, this is preferable. Call it the lesser of two evils."

Felix straightened up and started peeling off the coveralls.

Jacob saw that the young man's torso was not flabby but muscular, well-toned and fit. For some reason, he did not expect this.

The duke stood in his fine linen draws and reached for his clothes. "I'm going to buy this mine, Jacob, and I will close it until I can get some urgent repairs done. That will include new pumps for both air and water removal and chains for the carts with new tracks and a ratchet system so that they will not require the children to do more than push around the empty wagons on the mine floor. Not to mention new lighting." He shivered with the memories of what he had just experienced.

The tour of the various mines continued until two o'clock when they needed to be back for the cheese-making that afternoon.

Jacob had taken him to the open-cut copper mine where Logan worked with the explosives. A blast occurred as they were driving along the road towards the site, and they saw a cloud of dust rise from a desolate valley. The shockwave startled the London horses, nearly causing them to bolt. Thankfully this mine was entirely above ground but also involved makeshift pulley systems and unsafe mine practices.

Although interested, Felix did not stay long as he wished to see the cheeses made. That was the purpose of this trip.

Seeing the state the duke was in on his return, Billy took him to the beach for a swim in the ocean. Felix donned some of Billy's shorts to swim in. The pair went down to a secluded cove and dived into the sea. The chilly water refreshed him, and he rubbed himself with sand to remove the grime. There were no baths in the village, and Billy had already mentioned his daily swim in the bay. Now clean, although chilled from his dip, Felix returned to the dairy. He observed the process of adding the flavoured brine, then dicing the curd, scooping out the congealed milk squares and placing them in the cheese moulds. It certainly did not look like cheese at this stage, but after the curd had been left to drain for a short while, the filled cheese moulds were placed in the press. Twenty minutes later, the now pressed curd at least looked recognisable as a cheese shape. These new cheeses needed to cure. He was amazed to learn that this stage could last up to one year.

The second evening, after dinner, more discussions were held, and the partnership was expanded to be a dual-country one. Bryn and Jacob were stunned to hear that the duke was prepared to finance the foundation of a new venture in a new country. But that was not to be the priority.

The following morning, he realised that Isla had discovered the full extent of her sister's disgrace and that the Duke of Shesham had essentially been responsible. He arrived at the dairy as she finished milking, and she turned on him.

Her fists pummelled his chest in her anger, and her beautiful face distorted in rage. "It's all your fault. We were happy until your blasted demand that she leave her home to attend to your whim. You throw your title around as though it is worth something. But, oh no, you sit on your ivory chairs, not caring about the little people who work hard to put food on your plate. You could have come and seen for yourself, but that would have been too much effort."

He could have dodged the kick to his shin, but she was right about everything. Felix's heart sank. Every word she threw at him was accurate. His ego made Jennifer travel to him rather than come to see if the story was true. He felt like enfolding the angry but beautiful girl in his arms, but she had gone.

By the time he left at the end of two weeks, he had purchased the mine and closed it, then set the miners to work on what they did best: digging. His first thought was for a new colossal cheese cave. The miners could make a start on that immediately. He had already chosen and purchased the land next to the dairy. At the end of the first week, many had said they were willing to change roles and never return to mine again. Other older miners were employed to sink new, safer shafts near the old mine. This had been something they had wished to do long ago but had not been permitted to do as the minerals were deep, as there would be no profit until the mineral layer was reached. Logan and his explosive team were employed to blast the first sections of the area away. Only then would they really start digging. Two new water pumps were purchased, and another one was bought to pump fresh air below for the workers in the lower levels. New lighting was also purchased, and the tunnels would now be lit from the entrance to the mine wall.

Seeing the improvements, other mine owners were challenged to improve their shafts.

On return to London, Felix had arranged to see Jennifer on the ship shortly before she sailed. He was able to buy a new herd of cows from various sources. Two-thirds were already available, and he sent these to Cornwall for the newly expanded dairy, and the remainder he would send to Green Park in London until the ship to New South Wales was ready to sail with the Williams family. He didn't want the milk, so he employed some girls from one of his orphanages to strip the milk from the herd and give it away to the poor nearby. He needed the thirty cows to be in calf and preferably to a Guernsey bull. First, he had to find one. Bryn was correct; no one wished to sell these beasts. He discovered money talked, and he hired one to impregnate his cows. He also wanted the herds' milk to dry up for most of the journey, so he had to time the mating of the herd. Hopefully, the calves would be born shortly before arrival in Sydney. He expected the cows' milk would dry up shortly after sailing, as the trip out to the colony was now three to four months long. He had found three orphan girls nearing the age they would need to leave the orphanage, and they were willing to travel with the cattle and to be employed as milkmaids in the new dairy once there. He provided a ten-pound dowry for each of them, knowing that this would set them up for life.

He had outlined his plan to Bryn; all the family needed to do was pack their personal belongings and go to London to catch their ship. The *Juliana* sailed from London on September 3rd and would head directly to the colony.

Bryn had given the duke a final list of items required. It was so detailed that it even included the colours of the blocks of wax and the various shades needed. They would use different colours for the English cheeses to be easily identifiable. Bryn also included a plan for a cheese cave and what his ideal dairy would look like. How deep it should be and what temperature it needed to remain at. The duke realised he also needed a thermometer. On receiving the instructions, Felix set to work. He had returned to Cornwall a few times to check the progress of things.

Four months after Jennifer set out on the *Morley*, Bryn, Delen, and Billy returned to London with Felix, as the *Juliana* was due to leave in September 1820. It would head first to Hobart in Van Diemen's Land. Once there, it needed to offload its convict passengers before heading to Sydney.

Before embarkation, the Williams family stayed with Felix in London and, while there, attended the wedding of Bertram Tremayne and Angelina DeMartini. The Italian lady had eventually returned to Cornwall to pack up her house and move to the Angel Inn in London until their wedding.

Unbeknownst to either family, Felix had purchased her home for his own use and arranged a wedding luncheon for them at his London mansion, and while there, his staff moved her luggage into Bertram's new house above the new storeroom. The house was an old mansion in a nice part of town.

This particular place was close and chosen as it had the most amazing cellar that was the perfect temperature for the cheeses that would be stored there. The mews at the back of the house had access directly to a second underground storeroom. A secure door had replaced the existing one; a barred steel gate was installed in front of that one, thus securing the precious products.

~

Finally, Bryn, Delen and Billy were *en route* on the *Juliana*. They, too, carried a letter for the Governor from the Duke of Shesham requesting a land grant of some suitable dairyland. They also carried mail for Felix's school friend, Perry White.

Captain Ogilvie had one hundred and fifty-nine male convicts on board with a contingent of soldiers from the 34th regiment. They had met the doctor, the surgeon superintendent, Doctor Graham, and another family on board. They saw first-hand how they were treated. After the family's departure, Felix made some more visits to Cornwall, again, ostensibly to check on the progress of the construction. However, Isla's tuition and disregard for his title were a delight. He consulted Jacob and Phoebe about the business extensions and found that one more thing was required to make the business successful: sorting out transport. Felix purchased a small ship with a special room and purpose-built shelving for transporting the precious cheeses. He had already chosen a name; it would be named the *Jennifer Belle*. All approved of the choice.

For the equipment to travel after the Williams family had left, the Duke was as good as his word, and he had hired a warehouse at Deptford, and soon dairy supplies were piling up, waiting to be shipped out.

A vessel, the *Royal George*, was due to sail on May 18th, 1821, and it was initially considered until it was found to be carrying the new governor, Thomas Brisbane, who would replace Governor Lachlan Macquarie and was planning to be diverted *en route* via Rio De Janeiro. He decided to find another vessel.

Chapter 14 Jennifer's Landing 1820

*A*s the *Morley* was drawing near to their destination. The captain suggested that the families and free passengers stand on the poop deck behind him and watch the almost magical opening of the harbour appear. He had sailed these seas before, and yet the sight of the magnificent heads always made him draw a deep breath. He referred to it as the best harbour in the world. He had learnt to avoid approaching the bay from too near the shore. The land had been in sight since leaving Hobart, but as they neared the harbour, he had headed a little further out to sea. Once he tacked and turned westward, it looked like he was heading directly to the cliffs. But they weren't; they towered on either side of the opening. As they drew closer, the children were worried that the ship would crash into the rock walls.

The *Morley* tacked again, and then the order came to drop half of the sails. The activity above them drew their eyes. Jennifer had seen this activity in the rigging before, but ahead of them was the land that would soon be her new home. With a gentle easterly breeze moving them forward, the ship slowed. The headlands looked like they parted, but she saw that the escarpment was broken into three as they entered the majestic harbour. There were two large bays, and Captain Brown turned the ship to the southern one. Anchored vessels dotted the coves as they sailed past. Jennifer knew she should be locked down with the other convicts, but the Browns and Reddalls wanted her nearby.

Even the baby seemed excited as she felt it kick. Her hands rested on her growing stomach. She had her new coat on as it was cold in the breeze. She felt an arm slip around her waist.

It was Mrs Brown. She asked, "Are you nervous, Jennifer?"

Jennifer nodded. "Yes, but excited too. In the past months, I've realised that too much has occurred for God not to be in control. I must trust Him that I will somehow get through the months until Billy arrives. I hope it's soon, but I don't think they can pack up the business that quickly. They will have to make sure Papa knows exactly how to do everything. I doubt they will come on a convict ship, but they may. I just wish Billy was here already. I miss him so much." She brushed a wayward tear away. She was getting used to the melancholy that came with her growing condition. The gown she wore covered her growing bump, but soon, her gowns would need to be exchanged for voluminous empire-line frocks that she had made for herself while on board. The new high-waisted gowns were full at the front, and Mrs Brown showed her how to gather the fabric and add volume to the stomach area. In the colony, she wouldn't have any option to purchase more material.

Captain Brown carefully dropped more sails until just one small sail caught the wind. It was still billowing in the evening breeze, carrying the ship towards their anchorage. Tonight, they would sleep in the calm waters of Sydney Cove, and tomorrow, the Colonial Secretary and a detachment of officers would come on board accompanied by the senior surgeon. He would view the condition of the women and read the doctor's report. No sickness was on board, and as no one had died, there would be no need for quarantine.

As the children wished to stand on deck and watch the goings-on that was occurring around them, the group stood at the railings, and she had them spell out things they saw. The word *wharf* threw the little ones, as did *quay*.

The sun sank, and twilight passed quickly. The ship sat peacefully with new noises permeating the hull. Jennifer retired to her small cabin and set about tidying it. She didn't have much but knew that she would have to pack her possessions into something. As she stood beside the bed looking at the pile of belongings, there was a tap on her door. Mrs Brown had an old carpet bag for her to use. However, she was teary. "Jennifer, we've just had word that you are not permitted to stay with us. You must front up for assignment with the rest of the girls."

Jennifer was resigned that from now on, her life would be uncertain at best. She had been hoping to avoid the situation of being confined with the rabble below. Thankfully, the worst women were offloaded in Hobart. Tears didn't come until the door closed behind Mrs Brown. She sank onto the narrow bunk and wept. Her respite was over. She praised God that she had been spared a horrific trip at least. Hopefully, the duke's letter may yet bring a reprieve.

~

The morning sunlight was warm as Jennifer made her way up from the cattle below. She had no idea if this would be the last time she stripped her charges. The three cows were each given a hug before she left them.

The bucket of milk was taken to the galley by a passing sailor. For some reason, not one of them had made a pass at her. She went up on deck to greet the morning, see what activity was occurring onshore, and noticed a long boat drawing closer.

"Morning, Miss Jennifer," came a call from behind her.

Jennifer turned and saw Captain Brown approaching. He leaned on the railing and said, "When they arrive, you must make yourself invisible, dear. This should be the Colonial Secretary and the chief surgeon coming to give us the all-clear from disease. The doctor left his report with me as the doctor and the reverend left at dawn to visit the governor in Parramatta. They had to file a report about the mutiny."

She stayed until the longboat drew alongside. The captain was waiting for their visitors at the top of the rope ladder. He turned and waved for Jennifer to go below. She slipped through the door and went to help Mrs Brown with the children.

For the next forty-eight hours, Jennifer remained below deck. She kept her eye on the ten children as they each took turns milking the cows for what could be the last days. Word had come that the cows would soon be unloaded. All were keen to see how they were off-loaded. There was much discussion about how this would occur. They had been loaded by ramp from the wharf in London, but there was no such facility in Sydney. The ship was anchored well offshore, making manoeuvring to the small jetty unlikely.

Jennifer agreed with John Reddall that it was likely that the cows would be lowered by a net into the water one at a time, tied to a boat, and they would need to swim to the shoreline. The calves would be placed into the long boat in canvas sleeves, thus ensuring the mothers followed.

The event of the cow transfer brought all twenty-one of the upper deck children up onto the poop deck. Seven of the reverend's children, three of the Brown's and the remainder travelling with the four mothers in the other cabins, the seven women oversaw their behaviour. Jennifer was thrilled she was permitted to watch. By rights, she should be forbidden on deck.

The manhandling of the cattle was fraught with difficulty, and eventually, Jennifer was called to settle them before being tied into slings and lowered into the water. She had milked them again shortly before the delicately choreographed manoeuvre occurred. Once a cow was in the sling, Jennifer had to stand well back.

Each beast kicked as its feet left the deck.

By noon, the beasts were on the foreshore grazing on the native grasses. They seemed no worse for wear.

With the cows gone, Jennifer was able to sleep in the following day. It was something she had never been able to do before, and she felt guilty about not being up before dawn. The Brown children were all that were left onboard. The Reddalls and the four other women with their children had all disembarked the previous afternoon. Jennifer stretched and enjoyed the peaceful morning. The child's movements were much stronger, and she could feel it moving as she lay on her back. If only it were Billy's child, she would be thrilled. Knowing he was on his way, or soon would be, was wonderful.

As the duke had said, it was not the child's fault, and she must love it as much as any other children she and Billy had later. Surely, God had a plan for it. At least the baron had supplied for it and even assured her that more money would follow if it were a boy. She left that in the hands of the duke. If it were a son, he would be well educated; she would ensure that. All her children would be taught to read and write. She started thinking about names for the child. She didn't wish to use family names for this one, so those were out. She loved the name Christopher. Mrs Reddall said it meant *Christ-bearer*. If it were a boy, she would teach him that he had to stand firm in his faith. If the child were a girl, then she loved the names of Clara or Christine. She heard the family moving around, languidly stretched, and rose to get on with the morning.

Breakfast that morning was sadly missing the fresh milk they had so enjoyed. The porridge didn't taste quite the same, as it was made with just water. A plate of the hard-tack biscuits sat untouched, and Jennifer had been peckish the day before, so she filled her pockets with a few. She had learnt not to try and bite them, but if she could not smash them into smaller bits, then she would leave them in her mouth, and her saliva would soften them. It was not ladylike, but then she was no lady.

Mid-morning brought the sounds of another boat arriving. She was busy cleaning the Reddall's cabin, ready for the next occupant whenever that may be, and she didn't know who had arrived. She had nearly finished when she heard the captain calling for her. Leaving what she was doing, she went to his cabin to find not only the Browns but a tall man and the doctor.

The captain greeted her with, "Ahh, Jennifer, I have something from the duke you need to deliver personally." The grin on his face was repeated on both Mrs Brown's and Doctor Reed's faces. The captain held out the duke's fat envelope to her.

The tall man turned around, and Jennifer realised it was Governor Lachlan Macquarie. She fell into a deep curtsy. "Sir, I am honoured," she murmured softly.

His Scottish lilt was a delight to listen to. "Miss, I believe you have a letter from a friend of mine. Duke Felix seems to have befriended you from what I hear."

Hearing the Duke of Shesham's Christian name almost made her chuckle. It suited him so much. He was undoubtedly blessed with prosperity. She opened the fat envelope, pulled out the sealed letter for Governor Macquarie, and handed it to him. She held the letter to Perry White in her hand, along with her money.

He took it, then walked to the windows at the back of the cabin and flicked the seal to break it, unfolding the sheets of fine parchment. The occupants in the cabin stood silently until he had finished reading.

Jennifer held the envelope containing the wad of notes that sat untouched. She had placed the duke's other letter to her back into her pocket along with the money as she did not wish to lose it. Billy's letter she kept close and reread it often.

The governor was half leaning on the window in a very casual manner. An occasional hum or har would be heard. And he even glanced up at her a few times. He finally finished reading. "Well, that was unexpected. I had no idea that cheese came in various sorts. In India and Egypt, it was mostly fresh cheese, but hard cheeses in England are often very similar to each other. He says you are to start a dairy." He walked closer and took her hands. "Duke Felix says that these hands are very clever ones and that I am to employ you in my dairy until such time that your betrothed arrives and sets up a new industry for my colony." The Scotsman looked at Jennifer directly. "My dear, he also mentioned the child. He explained in detail his part and the repercussions of the said visit to London. I will pull the strings he asks, but you must stay nights at the female prison for your safety. I will have a trustworthy escort assigned to you and the other girls you are to train. One man, in particular, I have come to trust implicitly. Major Grace is a soldier in a million. He has already placed a few of the quieter girls in safe houses. I'm not supposed to know of his actions, but little passes my eyes and desk unnoticed. He only arrived this year, and for those in situations similar to yourself, he vets their placements and assures the young girls' safety. I believe the first such rescue was on his first day on duty. That lady is now working as his cleaner whilst assisting his friend. I'm sure you will meet Sal Lockley and her husband, Charles. Both are assigned to Perry White." He saw her startled jump at the mention of that name. "That is all beside the point. As Duke Felix is now a partner in this venture, he said your beau will soon arrive with his parents. They will have funds to build a dairy, and we all have twelve months or so to prepare for this new venture. Miss, he also mentioned that you have funds to leave with me for safekeeping." He gave a chuckle as he looked around the room.

Jennifer nodded, drew out the wad of bank notes, and passed them to him. "I have a letter for Mr White, too, sir."

After tucking the envelope full of money in his inside coat pocket. The man drew himself to full height and turned to the captain, "He also said something about sending me a gift."

The captain nodded and drew a large parcel from under his desk. "He brought this on board the day before we sailed. I have had it in the lowest part of the ship as it's the coolest. I do hope it travelled well, as it was a test run for transporting said product."

The governor took the wrapped box and, untying the string, opened the box. He tipped out a blue half-wheel of cheese.

Jennifer gasped. The duke had sent the governor a *Southern Belle* cheese. Not only that, but if she could have some of it, she could make a culture for the new dairy. Without being asked to comment, she said, "Sir, this is the *Southern Belle* variety. If I may be so bold, please don't eat it all, as I can make a culture from it and make more here." She swallowed nervously. She realised she had spoken to the governor without being permitted. Her hand flew to her mouth.

The governor was not used to convicts speaking so freely, but this was no normal convict. He remained silent, but his cocked eyebrow showed his surprise at her comment. In the ten-plus years he had been in the colony, he had learnt that many had sad pasts, and more often than not, they had a root of poverty in their story. Not so this girl; she may have been poor, but she had been an innocent victim twice over. She had done no crime, and with the duke's letter, they would try to ensure she had a future. He looked at the blue waxed wheel. "Would you recommend that we had a taste?"

Jennifer wished to know if the cheese had travelled well. She nodded.

"How about you show us how to cut it?" He handed Jennifer a sharp knife pulled from a sheath on his calf. The captain was stunned the governor trusted her with a lethal weapon.

She carefully felt the wheel and flipped it over. With the tip of the knife, she gently cut into the wax rind and peeled it back. She had cut a 'V' shape into the wax coating and carefully pulled it aside. Before proceeding, she sniffed the cheese to check its condition. A smile lit her face. With a deft twist, she then dug in the cheese and cut a large cone-shaped section out of the block with a swift, practised movement.

The cone was placed on an empty plate that Mrs Brown supplied. She cut the cheese into even-sized bits and stood back and waited.

Mrs Brown offered the plate to the gentlemen and then took a segment herself.

Jennifer was itching to have some but had not been offered any. She stood waiting for the verdict. She nervously was biting her lips and felt much as she had when Mr Williams had first tried it.

The silence was deafening. She could hear the roar of the blood pumping in her ears, and her heart was racing with anticipation.

The governor reached for a second sample.

This boded well for Jennifer.

The vice-regal gentleman turned to Jennifer. "My word, my dear, this is extraordinary. I can definitely call it *feabhasaich,* which means superlative, excellent in Gaelic, it is simply outstanding. If this is the sort of product you can make, then I think we have a deal."

There was one small sample left, and she asked, "May I have the last bit to see if the quality is as it should be?"

The doctor reluctantly held the plate for her to take the last sample.

All watched her face as she first elegantly sniffed it and popped it in her mouth. Four pairs of eyebrows rose as they now waited for her verdict.

She didn't notice them, as her eyes were closed, savouring the flavour of home. The rapturous look on her face made them all smile. She opened her eyes to see that she was the centre of their attention. She said, "It has travelled perfectly, Captain Brown. This means we can now send home the ones we make here."

Mrs Brown came to her side. "My dear, when you said you made cheeses, I had no idea that this was the sort of product you produced. If the governor permits you to work at the dairy until Billy and his parents arrive, then you may also be able to teach some interested persons the secret of your product."

Jennifer smiled. "There are some secrets I have sworn never to discuss, as they are not mine to share. This particular cheese is one. However, there are many things I know about cheese making that I'm willing to teach anyone as I promised the duke I would do." She turned to the Governor. "Sir, if I may be so bold, I'm serious about requiring some of this block of cheese so I can culture it. I don't need much, but I would be able to make some plain cheeses from this, too. Every cheese needs to have a culture added to make the initial curdle. I also need fresh rennet, and this involves using part of the stomach lining of a calf. It's this that then turns the milk curd into what we know as cheese. I will tell you that until Billy arrives with the Guernsey cattle, there is no way we can replicate this product. It must be made with full cream-rich Channel Island milk cows. We had two of these cows, and I use only their milk to produce this special product."

The governor was eyeing his blue waxed parcel. Having tasted it, he did not want to part with any of it. "How much will you need?"

She saw his glance at the box. With a small gurgling laugh, she said, "Only a spoonful of the inside of the cheese, if not a bit more. However, I need to be in the dairy and a clean environment to ensure I can keep the sample uncontaminated. In our dairy, once the milking is done, it passes through the dairy room door, and everything must be washed and scalded. If things are not clean and kept covered, then the cheese will go off. It will get blooms of fluffy mould on it that will sour the cheese." She saw that she had won her point and met his smiling eyes.

The governor sighed with relief. "I thought you would need much more than that." His face showed his delight that he could keep most of this himself.

She shook her head. "May I ask you to keep it cool? If it's not, as it has now been cut, it will bloom. I will need to get the sample within a day or so, your excellency. But can we keep a chunk until Billy arrives?"

The Governor grinned wickedly. "You may miss; however, Mrs Macquarie and my laddie will wish to have a sample. If you don't come soon, I don't guarantee much will be left." He turned to the doctor. "Reed, make sure she is in the first to be unloaded. Take her to the prison yourself and ensure she is allocated a special bunk, if not placed in the special room downstairs. I know they are overcrowded, but the new prison will open soon. I know there is a single secure cell or two downstairs. See if one is vacant. If matron gives you any trouble…" He glanced at Jennifer, "If matron complains, tell her that you are to escort Miss Jennifer to Government House yourself, and she can stay there." His smile instilled confidence in Jennifer. "Yes, bring her tomorrow, and we'll go to the dairy there. For yourself, book a room at the Rear Admiral Duncan Inn. I hand-picked the owners, and it's a clean and safe place to stay."

Doctor Reed gave a half bow. "My pleasure, sir."

~

By noon the following day, Jennifer, Doctor Reed and four of the younger convict girls were travelling to Parramatta. All the girls had been made to bathe and were given new gowns.

Jennifer sat next to the window and gazed out at the dusty road. The doctor sat on the other side with one of the young girls separating them.

The doctor had made this trip before and was expecting a gasp or two from the girls. He had seen a kangaroo and knew that it would soon catch the eye of the girls.

Jennifer was unseeing at what passed by. She may be facing the scenery, but she noticed little. Her mind and heart were back with Billy. Where was he? Had he left yet? Would he make it in time for the baby to arrive?

One of the girls opposite Jennifer exclaimed, "Cor, well, I'll be blown, doc. What the bloomin' heck is that bouncing thing?"

Doctor Reed chuckled. "That, my dear, is your first sight of one of the native animals in this strange country. I believe there are many strange-looking beasties here, but that sort is the most common. I have only seen ones this size, but apparently, there are some twice as big. Many creatures in this land either jump or hop, even the birds."

The gasps of awe from the five girls made him chuckle again. "Girls, I was not going to tell you sooner, but be careful not to leave any clothing on the ground in this country. There are creepy black spiders that crawl into your clothes. These beasties bite, and according to the natives of this place, I hear they can kill."

The journey continued with much discussion about the changes in the animals, climate, and various other topics. The reverse of the seasons was one he still found difficult to get his head around.

The carriage passed various cleared areas that were now being farmed.

Jennifer thought it strange that the trees were often not cut down, but the ground beneath them was obviously being cultivated. The absence of stock was noticed by not only her but the other girls, too.

~

On arrival in Parramatta, the carriage drew up to a double-storey timber building in deplorable condition. The doctor alighted and told the girls to remain until his return. He vanished inside as they waited. It may be September, which, according to the doctor, was spring, but it was so hot. The perspiration trickled down Jennifer's back, and she needed to use the facilities. The baby began pushing on her bladder, and it had been some hours since their comfort stop.

After another five minutes, she could not hold on and opened the door to see if she could find somewhere to relieve herself. No sooner had she done so than an armed red-coated soldier met her.

He challenged her. "Hey, miss. What are you doing? Ain't you a convict?"

Jennifer nodded. "I am, sir, but I'm with child and need to find somewhere to relieve myself." She could hear the sounds of water flowing and presumed it would be a river. The walls of the prison obscured her view.

Finding a tree was not an option as they were in the middle of town.

He grunted in reply. He stayed within view of the carriage but showed her the outdoor privy. She was about to head inside when he called, "Watch out for the small red-back spiders under the seat. They bite something fierce, miss."

Jennifer carefully checked the seat before finding relief. As she exited, she gazed around at what would be her new home. The building desperately needed repairs, and she wondered how many would be housed there. She meandered her way back to the carriage and noticed the doctor awaiting her.

"Sorry, Jennifer, I forgot you must use the facilities. I had to do some swift talking. As the women's room upstairs will be overcrowded, Matron has permitted the five of you girls to use one of the isolation rooms downstairs. You will be squashed wherever you are; this way, at least, you will all be together. Upstairs has room for thirty, and some are already *in situ*. With seventy-one more arriving, cramped is an understatement. If I were you, I would accept her offer. The room at least has some stone walls and will offer you some protection from the elements."

The five girls followed him inside, and they were, in turn, followed by the guard Jennifer had met earlier.

With Jennifer's bag now stowed in the tiny room, she returned to the carriage with the doctor. With just the two of them in the carriage, the doctor gave her a running commentary of what they passed. They turned in through the gates to Government House. Off to the left was a collection of timber buildings, and much of the area had been trampled down by the constant use of many feet and horses.

The doctor explained, "Over there was the original military redoubt. The town has a new barracks, and this facility is rarely used. The new barracks had not long been started when I was last here, but now it's complete, and on the whole, the soldiers have moved down there. I think a few guards sleep here, but most have moved into the new building. We didn't pass it on the way in, but it's walking distance from here." He chattered until the coach pulled up to the front of the Georgian house set on the town's highest hill.

The governor was waiting under the small porticoed awning, and guards stood at his sides. "Good afternoon, Miss Kellow; did you have a comfortable journey?"

Jennifer sank into a deep curtsy. Her condition would soon not permit this to occur, so she was making the most of the ability to do this. "Yes, thank you, Your Excellency. I saw a wallakey...no, a wallaby," she said with excitement.

The governor laughed, "You will get sick of them. They eat nearly everything we plant. However, they are cute little beasties, and their bairns are more than just adorable. The joeys, as they are called, live in their mother's front pockets." He patted his stomach.

Jennifer had no idea what he meant. Her tummy bump was already showing; she rubbed her own stomach as the baby made its presence felt with a kick.

Realising she had missed the joke, he asked, "Are you ready for a tour of our dairy?"

She nodded enthusiastically. "Yes, please, sir." She was so excited to see her future workplace that she forgot that the man in front of her was the head of the colony and the king's representative. Recalling her surroundings, she fell silent.

Chapter 15 The Dairy 1821

The governor's coach carried the three along past Government House and towards the farm at the back of the expansive estate. A small building was visible in the distance, but the coach travelled past it. The governor said, "I thought you might like to see Elspeth's gardens. She's very proud of them and likes them being admired. Please do comment on them when you meet her. We will do a circuit of the domain gardens and approach the dairy from the other side." The austere man reminded Jennifer of the duke until he opened his mouth. The Scottish lilt and the Gaelic pronunciation of his wife's name made her smile slightly.

Jennifer gave a nod in acknowledgment of his request. They travelled on, and she admired the farmland and gardens as they drove. Here, at least, there was some stock. She noticed the cows were long-horned cattle, and although good milkers, they didn't have as much cream in their milk for cheese.

She remained mute, absorbing everything she saw. She wanted to see the building and equipment. The doctor said it became really hot in this country, so the dairy needed to be kept cool. She wondered how they would achieve that, maybe by digging it into a hillside; eager to see everything she could, she swivelled around and gazed at the farmland they traversed. She knew little about farming. But cows… with them, she was in her element.

As she absorbed the life on the farm, the governor gave a subtle running commentary of what they saw. His wonderful Scottish lilt was such that she could listen to him talk for an hour about the colour and price of coal, and she would still listen. He pointed out the extensive gardens and various flowering plants that they had cultivated in the gardens. He told her about the acquisition of the dairy from Mr Salter in 1813. "Miss Jennifer, when I purchased the thirty-acre farm, Salter was using it for crops. I have not continued with crops but have installed thirty beef cows that are occasionally milked, but it is still a working farm, as we also grow vegetables. The Salter house has since been converted into a dairy, and I added a verandah to protect the western side of the building. This cooled the inside of the room considerably." Noticing her gaze had now settled on the cows, he said, "There is only a small herd of mostly beef cows here, but we need milking cows more than beef. We personally don't use much of the milk; it gets sent to the gaols or sold or distributed through Government Stores. More than half of the herd is not currently being milked as they are due to drop calves soon. Most of what we do produce is put to government use. I really must arrange more milkmaids, but I need someone to oversee them; if you can inspect our building and suggest some improvements, I would appreciate that."

Jennifer jerked her head up in stunned surprise at his request. Was she to have control of this dairy? A smile briefly flicked across her lips. As yet, she had no questions.

The carriage eventually pulled up at the back of the small shingle-roofed building.

Jennifer alighted with the doctor's assistance. The roadway was rough, and she stumbled. She still didn't have her land legs and was also off-centre because of the child.

The doctor hooked her hand through his arm. "No use tripping now, Jennifer. Hang on, and we'll do the tour."

Jennifer nodded, then smiled her thanks to the kind doctor.

The governor led the way onto the building's verandah and pushed the door open. It was pristinely clean inside, having recently been whitewashed, and she was surprised at how cool it was, considering the temperature outside was swelteringly hot. The room was indeed set on a hill, but the insides were now dug into the earth. On entering, what met her eyes was a surprise. From outside, it looked like a single-story dwelling, but she saw steps leading down to a lower level.

The governor explained the obvious. "Down there is the milk room; the milking shed is up on ground level, but it is next door. The milk is brought down here to separate. More than that, I have no idea. My housekeeper, Elizabeth Eccles, oversees this facility. The sunken room used to be a cellar, but we had it excavated and turned into what you see now. I believe it has to do with temperature control."

The three walked down wide stone steps and into the milk room. In the middle of the floor was a sunken area that had obviously been used for milk separation. It was even cooler down here, which was excellent for cream raising, but she noticed two fireplaces. One on either side of the room. Each had an arched top, and she wondered about the possibility of using them to make smoked ricotta. Releasing the doctor's arm, Jennifer paced out the size of the room and discovered it was twenty feet by fifteen feet. Looking up from the floor to the overhead window, she realised they were now about five feet underground on the western side. There was a circular milk-settling area which made her screw up her nose. This was not sterile enough for cheeses. The lime-lined earthen pit was fine for cream settling but little else. Her lips twisted with concern.

"It needs work, doesn't it?" The governor's voice made her jump.

She nodded. In a building like this, she felt at home. She met his worried look. Without thinking, she started talking to the two learned gentlemen. She walked around the room, caressing the walls, including the big coopered vat. After checking to see if there was a bar across the chimney flue, she smiled as her hand felt a smoking rod, but it was rusty.

She absentmindedly began audibly reviewing the cheese process. "This is fine for milk, butter and cream, sir, but for cheese, it will need a vat we can both heat and sterilise. Metal is best for that, but it will need to have coopered barrel-like inserts, as you shouldn't put cheese milk directly into copper. But you can't put the wooden coopered vats over a flame. The fireplace over there will need to be used to heat the room; however, if we can get it to the required temperature, it may suffice; otherwise, I will need a brazier."

The governor nodded. "I'll get on to that!"

She saw that the doctor was listening and continued. "First, you add the starter culture, like the one from my blue cheese, to the warmed milk, and then the milk needs to be kept at a specific temperature of about blood heat and then left for coagulation. After some hours, the set milk then needs dicing: fine cubes for hard cheese and large cubes for soft ones. You can either use a dicing fork or two wire dicing frames, depending on the size and volume of the milk. That is when you add the flavouring and brine to the curds and whey. This stops the fermenting. The curd needs to saturate for a short while; then the diced curds get scooped into the moulds."

She checked the coopered butter churn that sat on the fire shelf. She saw that it had not been cleaned properly and was mouldy inside. She screwed up her face in disgust. Shuddering, she put the lid back on and continued her perusal of the room. "Over here, you will need to build a drip rack with either a bucket under each mould or a tilted shelf that drains to a bucket at the end." She motioned where a shelf needed to be added.

The governor asked, "Would timber suffice?"

Jennifer nodded. "If smoothed and oiled, then yes, sir. The shelf would need to run from the top of the fireplace to the other side of the wall." She looked around and saw very few items that were required equipment for cheesemaking. She continued her almost automatic verbal review of her requirements. "You need to obtain cheese moulds, not to mention a bolt of cheesecloth, curd scoops, the coopered vat, dicing wires, and some urns for transporting the milk and cream from the dairy, and that is just for starters. Oh, sir, there is much needed to turn this dairy into a cheese dairy. Not to mention, you will need a cheese cave to mature the wheels."

The governor's face had lit up when he heard her list. "Oh, we already have cheesecloth. My Elspeth uses it for insect screens on the windows." He was pleased that he could at least supply the fabric.

She smiled in acknowledgement and gave a nod. She said, "Good idea, sir! I will do that, too, as flies can contaminate the cheeses. Each cheese mould needs to be lined with the cheesecloth. It is then filled with diced curd before being left to drain. As I said, the curd must be finely cubed if making hard cheeses. Oh, you'll need a draining spoon. Did I say that already? The cheese mould must be filled and placed in a cheese press." Realising that she had not added that to her list, she said, "You'll only need one of those for the moment."

The governor smiled and replied, "You will need to write it all down for me."

Jennifer nodded again but remained quiet for a while. Going through the process in her mind, she explained the need for the rack and shelf inside. "The filled cheese mould needs to be set on a drain rack, so each will need a whey bucket under it until they have drained and they get put into the press. They remain in the press for about twenty minutes at least, and you need to continually tighten the screw, as if done too quickly, the new cheese can be damaged by screwing it down too fast. The longer the mould is pressed, the firmer it will be. Afterwards, you can turn out the cheese and fold the remainder of the cheesecloth over it until it's properly set. Then it is placed in the cave and massaged with the clarified lard." She released a long sigh. "That's when the magic happens." The tone of her voice changed. She spoke as though she were addressing her beloved rather than a lump of curdled milk.

The doctor chuckled. "If it tastes like that blue one, then it certainly is magic."

Forgetting where she was and to whom she was talking, her melodious voice contained the passion for her craft. "Oh, sirs, I am sorry." She explained further. "Once the cheeses are placed in the cheese cave, they need regular rubbing. You can use a heavy brine solution or lard. The blue wax cheese you tasted had a rind of lard before it was waxed. This also helps preserve the flavour, as the clarified fat permeates the cheese. It takes over a year of daily care and rubbing to produce top-quality cheese, sometimes longer, if you want it more mature or crumbly. Regulating the temperature of a cheese cave is also vital." Realising she had been speaking without having been asked for a description, she spun around to the men. "I do apologise profusely, sirs. Once I start on my favourite topic, I forget everything else. I really do apologise!"

The governor laughed heartily. "You remind me of my mama. She was much the same when she made haggis."

Jennifer's face flushed crimson with embarrassment, but smiled at the simile.

The vice-regal gentleman was now sitting on one of the stone steps, watching the enchantment and passion for her craft that was etched on her expressive face. He continued, "So, it's doable? Can you write a list of what we will need, as there is no way I would remember all the items you listed? If you can find some girls whom we can teach to milk, then all the better. I'll start hunting for the various bits of paraphernalia required. We may have to substitute a few things, but I will order them from England. Mind you, the duke said he would be sending some equipment. Come back to the house and write a list. And I'm guessing we also need a proper cheese cave."

She nodded. She noticed he had said nothing about using the house cellar, so maybe it didn't have one. Jennifer realised that, yes, she could make cheeses, but they needed a large storeroom nearby to age them. A natural underground cavern would be perfect, but apparently, there was none nearby.

The doctor had been leaning on the fireplace and had listened with a grin plastered on his face. He knew which girls she would ask. After tasting the delectable cheese she had made, his admiration for her had increased. She had said nothing about the excellence of her product or her skill. He had nearly choked when he heard about the possibility of a Royal Warrant for her product. Now, things fell into place. He finally understood why the duke had singled her out and followed her. With her knowledge, she only needed the right cows and milk and a few specific items, and she could make a fortune. Or, in this case, as a bonded servant, she could make a fortune for the government. He had tasted the disgusting cheese currently made here, which was only fit for convict rationing. When he saw her inspect the churn and vats only to find them covered in mould, he now realised the reason for the revolting cheese.

They spent half an hour more before returning to the carriage and continuing to look around the area.

The coach completed the circuit of the government land, and on returning to Government House, Jennifer once again needed to use the facilities. The privy at this house was clean and airy; however, she checked the seat before sitting. She was thankful she did, as a small fat spider with a red slash on its back was in a spindly web at the side of the seat. She removed her shoe and squished it. This country was full of strange beasties. Thankfully, she had been warned to check each time, no matter which facility she used. She had not expected to find one in the official residence.

On return through the kitchen, she was offered a glass of cool milk. The cook had a pail of milk sitting under a damp cloth. The milk was delicious but had a strange flavour. This was something else she needed to discuss. She wondered if the native grasses flavoured the milk. On returning to the office, she knocked and was surprised that a lady had joined the gentlemen. Realising that this was the governor's wife, she sank into a deep curtsy even before being introduced.

The elegant lady with a riot of curly hair drew her to her feet. "Dear, in your condition, the last thing you need to do is to be off-centre. I know that from experience." Her calming voice and similar Scottish accent settled Jennifer.

The governor beckoned her to enter and then introduced her to his wife. "Sit yourself down, Miss Jennifer, and tell me what we will need."

Sitting opposite the governor at his desk is not how she expected to spend her first day as a convict in a new land. She was aware of the first lady and the doctor sitting off to the side. They were chatting privately as the governor addressed her.

She paused, thinking and trying to collect her thoughts. She then spieled off the list of what was required. The inventory was memorised. "Sir, as I mentioned earlier, I need a cheese press, a scoop spoon or two, brine buckets and pans, a large drum of clean salt, clarified lard, cheese moulds, coopered milk vats or, better still, a large cast iron one that I can hang over the fire, and wire cutting frames or a cutting fork."

The governor could not keep up with her. He chuckled. "Hold your horses, lassie; I can't write fast enough."

Jennifer was itching to write down what she had thought of. "May I show you what I mean, sir?" She requested a sheet of paper and drew a cheese curd cutter and, beside it, a drawing of a fork-like instrument that had two-foot-long tines. This was a rectangular frame made of lines of fine wire pulled tight. This would be dragged through the coagulated milk to dice the curd. The spacing of the wires determined the size of the curd cubes. Under the picture, she wrote more requirements in her elegant handwriting.

She was about to hand it back when he said, "Keep going, lassie."

With a nod, she added that the existing bar across the flue was rusty and needed replacement. Hopefully, they could add more. These needed to be strong, as they would be filled with hooks to smoke the ricotta cheeses. These would be the first cheeses she would attempt, as she really only needed the cheesecloth, vinegar, or something similar, and string to make this. She could test the quality of the milk and if the grasses tainted the flavour. At the very least, she could make a variety of soft cheeses for the governor's consumption, and they wouldn't have to wait to taste them.

Forgetting that she was now a convict, she jotted away in her calligraphy-like script and then handed the list to the astounded governor. Once more, she flushed with acute embarrassment when she realised she had confounded the vice-regal couple. She had not even noticed that Mrs Macquarie now stood next to her husband's chair.

Jennifer had been oblivious to her surroundings as she wrote.

Mrs Macquarie chuckled. "Dear, did you know that you are an *affineur*? It's the name of a cheese maker's craft."

Jennifer shook her head. "In Italian, it's *casaro*, but in Latin, a craftsman is *artufex,* but as I am female, I suppose it is, therefore, *artuficis.* But I really should be a *caseum factorem,* which means cheesemaker, ma'am. I presume the etymology is from the same root word."

The three other people in the room stood looking at her with their jaws dropped open. Realising she had revealed a little more of her astounding education, her hand flew to her lips, and she dropped her head and then fell silent. They did not see her cheeks flush with embarrassment.

The doctor was the first one to recover. "Jennifer, you speak Italian?"

Her head nodded, somewhat embarrassed.

The governor chipped in, asking, "And the Latin?"

She shrugged and nodded again. She replied, "The minister who taught us to read realised my interest in languages and kept teaching me. However, it was an Italian lady who taught me about the additives for cheeses. She explained the similarity between the two languages and the root words. They, too, became an interest. The passion for both grew."

The governor realised that the girl sitting in his office was certainly not the normal sort of milkmaid, let alone a typical criminal. It was at that moment that he decided she would be assisted as much as possible. His friend Felix had explained about her abuse and his role in her being in London. Having tasted her skill, he would now create the area she needed. The cheese cavern would be the most problematic as the area had no caves. He had heard rumours of some up the mountains, and he decided he would investigate these further.

By the time Jennifer returned to the gaol, most other women had arrived on a train of flatbed wagons. One vehicle was unloading as she and the doctor alighted from their well-sprung carriage. She had been permitted to ask the four girls to assist in the dairy, but they were already sharing her room.

The remaining cattle were due to calf any day, and she discovered the three cows she had befriended were being brought to the government farm. With the arrival of new calves, the milking would need to start in earnest. At the moment, only one of the existing beef cows was being milked, supplying only the Government House. By the week's end, she needed new pails and a bevy of trained assistants. She had her work cut out for her. She had seen the farm cows from a distance but had not tested their milk for cream content. It did have an unusual taste, and she would need to work around that. She wondered how much they would get each day. She expected that it would be about thirty gallons from the two milking sessions. They could send any excess milk to the prison and barracks, but she would make a selection of soft cheeses to share.

Jennifer was escorted into her new room by the doctor. The four other girls awaited her.

He was approached by the flustered matron, who was about to chastise him for keeping her out so long.

A single glance from him silenced her. Her mouth opened and shut just as quickly.

He saw Jennifer safely to her room, where her friends greeted her; then, he motioned for the matron to follow him outside. He did not give her a chance to object but walked off. Standing in the courtyard and within earshot of Jennifer's room, he turned to the matron and outlined the governor's instructions for the newest dairy hand and the orders he had been given to relay.

Jennifer could barely hear his words over the girls' chatter. She shushed the girls as they talked excitedly about their new roles. "Shh, listen!"

The girls fell quiet and came to her side. As she spoke, they heard the edge of anger in the matron's voice.

The small, barred window was visible to the doctor, and he saw Jennifer watching them.

Matron had her back towards them, but they could hear the ire in her voice as she answered his probing questions.

The doctor silenced her again. "Matron, regardless of your desires, dislikes, and setting a precedent, Governor Macquarie has requested that Jennifer Kellow choose four more girls, and they will prepare the dairy behind his house. They are to set it up for making cheeses for the entire colony. These girls are, technically, to be assigned to him, but they will stay here in the bottom room until you move. We apparently have little time to prepare, for the governor already has thirty beasts on his farm, many of which will also calve soon. The new girls must be taught to milk before this occurs. You will still benefit as the excess milk will be brought here, and if you are lucky, you may even be given some fresh cheeses."

Matron's arms fluttered in annoyance. She started to say, "But… um, so this female is…" Words were stripped from her.

Without permitting her to complete her comment, the doctor's hand raised, and he silenced her with the motion. "Per the governor's instructions, a wagon will arrive at dawn to collect them for work. Call it their assigned work. However, they will remain in the isolation room and not be put in with the remainder of the female convicts. Do you understand?"

Jennifer saw the matron's head nod, but she could tell she was not happy.

Chapter 16 New Cheeses 1821

$\mathcal{B}$y the end of the first week, the five girls had the dairy scrubbed from top to bottom. Elizabeth Eccles, the housekeeper from the official residence, came to assist with the cleaning. She showed an interest in learning the trade. She had done her best but had no actual training. She had not realised how vital it was to have everything sterile. She threw herself into learning all she could.

Elizabeth was a widow who had arrived as a convict. She had married another convict, and they had lived on Norfolk Island for years. Her husband died some years after moving back to Sydney from the island. Elizabeth, better known to everyone as Betty, was the housekeeper for the governor. She had been milking the cows by herself but wished to increase her knowledge of the industry. The beasts provided enough milk for the official house and officers of the regiment.

Jennifer was thrilled to have a mother figure to advise her on other things. She already missed Mrs Brown and the children. However, the dairy industry was in Jennifer's blood, and this dairy was calling her to bring it to life.

By the time the dairy was clean, the first of the governor's calves had been delivered. The cow had been lowing most of the day before, and on arrival the following morning, a new calf was suckling at her mother's side.

This happy event was followed by the arrival of a flatbed wagon. The driver greeted Jennifer cheerfully and handed her a letter.

The scrawling script on the front made her frown. The wax seal on the back made her realise who it was from. The governor had sourced some equipment for her work. The wagon contained a dozen large milk urns, but they were ceramic and not tin. They would have to do. There was a huge new one-hundred-yard bolt of cheesecloth in a calico covering. There would be enough to cover all the windows to keep out flies. She could even make a weighted cloth drop for the doorways. The wagon also had many wooden crates containing numerous basins, scoops, and other items from her list. The girls were about to start unloading when the driver said help was on the way. He gave a lift of his head and pointed down the hill.

Jennifer turned to see a small group of red-coated soldiers marching up the grassy rise, and in the middle of them were six convict men. She recognised the fair-haired major who had escorted her to work for the first few days.

Major Ned Grace greeted her with a smile and soon gave directions for the convict men to await her instruction.

She asked how long the men were available, and he said they were at her disposal until noon. The wagon was soon unloaded, and the men were set to scrub the new coopered milk buckets. The girls were asked to scour and scald the new equipment. Betty was set to cut up cheesecloth in various sizes.

Jennifer was keen to bug-proof the room, and that meant they had to cover the windows so they could be opened but keep out the insects and some of the dust. With access to the large bolt of cheesecloth, this would have multiple uses. There would be ample fabric for cheese, so Betty cut the window and door lengths first.

The first products Jennifer would make would be the soft ricottas and cottage cheeses, as they had no moulds. Stoneware basins lined with the cheesecloth were all that was required.

Until they could source proper coopered or woven cheese moulds, she would use some baskets she found stored in a box. There was plenty of cream for her experimental purposes and enough to make the butter as well. The cottage cheeses could be eaten that day, and she decided to make a few flavoured ones to test the additives available here. She only needed vinegar, pepper, and an onion or two for savoury ones, but she also wanted to make some sweet ones. Betty would bring some of these back from the house after luncheon.

While the work was proceeding around her, she set to work on a small basin of cottage cheese for the governor. This would be as a "thank you" until she could produce some quality products.

Major Ned sat with his arms folded, watching the girls' activities with interest. While she worked, he plied Jennifer with a vast range of questions about her craft and then asked that she tell him of anything else she needed. He had brought a small keg of vinegar to scrub the pails, but he knew she needed other things.

Jennifer had used some of the vinegar to make the first small cheeses. It was okay, but hopefully, someone would have some lemons, and she would use them to make a soft dessert cheese for the governor. She could also flavour it with honey, but she needed a delicately flavoured one. In reply to his question, she mentioned both ingredients. "Major Ned, do you know anyone that may have a lemon tree? Also, I would like some light honey, like clover or similar. I could make a dessert cheese for the governor's table."

Ned grinned, knowing his friend Perry had a lemon tree in his backyard and Molly Miller had a tub of clover honey. "I do; I shall bring you both when I return to collect you this afternoon. Is there anything else you need?"

Jennifer nodded her thanks and added, "Yes, sir, I'd love to have a rack outside on the sunny side of the building where we can place the clean pails upside down after they have been scrubbed." She saw a micro frown cross his brow and explained what it was for. "The shelf can be a simple two-post railing beside the building. After milking each time, the vats and pails need washing and preparing for the next session. I still scald them before each use, but I prefer they dry out properly between each milking as it stops them from going slimy."

Major Ned dug in his pocket and handed her a notebook. He asked her to draw the sort of frame she needed.

She did.

He attached his own note for the storekeeper and added requests for some bowls. He also asked that the spare milk vats be brought from the Government Stores in George Street to the dairy as soon as possible. He listed the timber required and which convict workers were to be sent to construct the frame. The guard outside was dispatched with the order. Ned would remain until he returned.

By noon, the dairy was all but fully equipped for the initial experimental products.

The governor had also written to Government Stores in Sydney, and more equipment would come from there. He had come up on his morning ride to let Jennifer know about the expected arrival of the equipment.

Ned had overseen the construction of the rack and ensured it was sturdy. As he left for luncheon, Jennifer handed him a small hanging cheese. This was the very first cheese produced from the revamped dairy. She had nothing more to give than her skill. She simply said, "Thank you, Major Ned."

He accepted the gift with delight. He loved cottage cheese but had yet to find any good enough to eat since he arrived the year before. He planned to share this with his friends, Perry, Buck, and Charles, over bible study that evening. He dropped his precious gift to the White household before continuing to the next venue. Before he left, he went into the garden to see his friend, Charles. He had boasted that the lemons on their tree were extra juicy as they had their roots in the cesspit runoff. They certainly looked good. He wanted to see if he had any spare. Even one or two would be a good start for Jennifer. He was astounded when he saw the tree was dripping with golden yellow orbs. "Charles, when you said you had some lemons, I had no idea you literally meant a hundred of them. Is there any chance I could have some for the governor's new project? If you like cheese, then we are in for a treat. Jennifer Kellow has sent one for us to try tonight, and these will go towards another variety."

Charles looked at his friend and smiled. He was still astounded that a major in the army had befriended him. He was a convict who had arrived at His Majesty's pleasure. For the major to befriend him and then find a placement with an acquaintance was wonderful. It was even better that the major had also rescued the woman who was now Charles' beloved wife, Sal. She had stood out from the filthy women at the gaol. Her clean blonde hair had been like a beacon in the summer heat. His delight was that Sal was now his wife and mother to their son. He could not do enough for the soldier. "Major, I have a calico bag that we can fill today, and the fruit will be fine on the tree for some months."

Charles vanished for a few minutes and returned with a flour bag. The men filled it with about twenty juicy lemons.

Ned was grinning. "I'm sure Jennifer will love these. I may swipe one or two for myself."

Charles chuckled. "Don't bother. I'll pick some more for you for tonight."

Ned nodded, grinned and waved a hand of farewell. "Thanks, Charles, I'd better be off. I need to visit Bill and Molly Miller at the Rear Admiral Duncan Inn and see if they have some honey for Jennifer." He knew they bought it by the barrel full from Hetty Walker out on the Hawkesbury River. He borrowed a ceramic cork-topped jar from the White's cook and headed to the Miller's inn. Jennifer said she only needed a cupful, and he was sure they would be paid with a soft cheese in return. Knowing what a good cook Molly was, he was sure she would agree to the swap.

On his return to the dairy an hour later, Ned had a small jar of honey and a large calico bag of a dozen of the juiciest lemons he had tasted in a long time. Molly had asked if she could have a couple, and he was happy to give her a few as a swap for the honey.

Jennifer immediately made a few small, sweet cottage cheeses for him to take to the donors to say thank you.

Shortly before they closed the dairy for the afternoon, she gave Ned a taste of what she had packed up for the gifts. She had made one for Matron, and Betty took a large bowl of sweet cottage cheese for the governor's table that night. Another tied bundle she handed to Ned. "Major, this is for you to share with your friends tonight. If Mr White doesn't mind me using his lemons, he can have one of these each day. Sir, would this be Mr Perry White?"

Ned nodded. "Um, Yes!" He frowned at how she would know his friend's name.

Jennifer nodded. "I have a letter for him. I shall give it to you when you return me to the gaol." She passed the spoonful of cottage cheese to him.

His eyes rolled with delight as he licked off every bit of it. Grinning at the delicious morsel, two large dimples popped in his cheeks. "Oh, Miss Jennifer, that is truly delicious." He was keen to share his bountiful gifts with his friends. He finally had something to contribute to the meal at his friend's place by supplying the two cheeses. He ate there as often as he possibly could. To be able to talk of home and familiar things with Perry was a delight. With Charles, things were not as straightforward. The two looked like they could have been brothers, but he knew of no familial connection. They even had the same last name, as Grace was a pseudonym, but only Perry knew that.

Jennifer was happy. With the first cheeses made, they were now set to become a proper commercial dairy. They still didn't have proper ceramic cheese wheel moulds, which didn't matter as these cows didn't produce enough cream for a good hard cheese yet. Plus, they didn't yet have a cheese cave to age the cheeses.

The governor had mentioned the caves in the mountains, but she explained how hands-on they needed to be to rub cheeses. Therefore, they were not suitable. A nearby cellar was what she needed. She wondered if the governor's house had an underground cellar. A smile crossed her lips; she bet he did, but would he permit her access to their official residence to caress the cheeses each day? If not, then Betty may have to learn to do them.

~

Christmas came and went. She had a group of Godly friends whom she had met at church. Agnes Rosedale, Charlotte Ellis and Molly Miller were wonderful moral support for her.

Jennifer was heavy with child and growing bigger by the day. Unlike other expectant women at the gaol, she was given leave to take things much easier. Her back ached, and she was often lightheaded. She was fully aware of what she had to face as the pain and danger of childbirth were yet ahead of her. The dairy work was exhausting her, but she would not rest. She knew she had to teach the girls everything she knew about the industry lest she die during the delivery.

As the weeks progressed, she was so ungainly that she sometimes had to forego the early morning milking. The girls could handle that, and Betty oversaw them. She knew they could set the milk to separate and then skim the cream for the afternoon butter and cheese making.

Mid-morning, Major Ned would collect Jennifer and take her to the dairy in a sprung cart rather than the unsprung wagon.

After escorting her inside, he would deliver the full stoneware milk vats to the gaol and then do his other duties. He left a guard on duty for their protection, but most days, he would return and personally transport the girls back to prison.

Jennifer usually stayed until the afternoon milking session was over, having managed to oversee the making of the fresh cottage or ricotta cheeses. With the cows all with calves at foot, they now had plenty of milk. With the availability of a culture from the blue cheese wheel, she made two or three half-wheel cheeses as a test to see if the local grasses would taint the flavour. The excess milk was distributed daily to various places, including the barracks and gaol.

Betty returned with reports about enjoying the various test samples of soft cheeses. Jennifer always gave one to Betty for the governor's table whenever she tried a new flavour.

While not giving away Jennifer's trade secrets, Betty was told about using pepper, garlic, and onion for savoury ones. For sweet cheeses, Jennifer discovered a local tree with delicious-smelling leaves that tasted of lemon. Lemon myrtle and lilli pilli, another local fruit that tasted like apples, the cheese had become a favourite for a dessert. Mrs Macquarie had strawberries growing, and she suggested that Betty suggest to Mrs Ovens, the Macquarie's cook, that she flavour the sweet cheeses with a fruit puree sweetened with some light clover honey. This could be eaten with the soft cheese tipped on a plate and served covered with a raspberry or strawberry puree. She had one fluted cheese mould, and she kept this for use on the governor's table. She even showed Betty how to make individual servings for special dinner parties at Government House. The cook made some shortbread wedges to place on the top as a garnish.

Still, they only had half-wheel baskets for moulds until Major Ned had ordered some woven ones from a farm on the Hawkesbury River. These wicker baskets seemed to be working. Jennifer oversaw the manufacture of the ricotta from the leftover whey. This product quickly became popular on the government tables, and soon, all the excess whey was converted into this delicacy. Some of these cheeses she set aside and placed in the fire flue for smoking and then hung in a fly-proof, cheesecloth-covered area to age. While not the quality of those made in Cornwall, the cheeses were still good. The entire dairy was now draped with cheesecloth to keep flies out of the room. The windows had been fitted with frames that worked like screens, and a double-thickness weighted curtain covered the door. An occasional fly made it in, and it was quickly swatted.

On tasting the first smoked ricotta that she considered ripe, Jennifer was happy with the product, but it was only a tiny bit that had oozed through the top. She and Ned nibbled the morsel. It had taken only days from her arrival to produce the first of the soft cheeses that she considered good enough for Governor Macquarie to taste. Now, the first of the gourmet smoked ricottas were ready for eating.

Major Ned was given the job of delivering it to Mrs Macquarie. Having tasted the smoked ricotta he was itching to try more. It was better than what was served at his father's table at home.

On the day she sent the sample to the kitchens, Jennifer knew the time was approaching for her to deliver her baby. She wanted the governor to taste one of her products, just in case she didn't make it through the birth. She had shed many tears of fear when alone, worried how Billy would feel about a wasted journey if that occurred. Jennifer had been busy skimming the cream when she heard a vehicle crunch over the gravel road. She handed the job to one of the girls and went upstairs to see who had arrived.

A small unmarked black carriage was pulled up at the front of the dairy, followed by Major Ned in the cart. As she peeked out the window, she saw that the first vehicle carried four well-dressed people who were alighting. Two of the visitors she had already met, and they were the governor and his wife; the other couple were obviously friends. However, she glanced at the man and knew he was the person she had heard about from the duke in London. She knew without introduction that this man was the Earl of Collingsford, although here he was simply Mr White. Ned had obviously delivered the letter she had brought from the duke. She also knew that his wife, Katy, was here as a convict. As they entered, she was about to sink into a curtsy when Mrs Macquarie reprimanded her. "Jennifer, if you go down in a curtsy, you will deliver your child before time," she chuckled.

Jennifer smiled and did a nod of her head instead.

The new lady greeted Jennifer. "Hello, I'm Katy White, and we decided that as you can't come to us, we've come to you." She turned to the soldier. "Ned, come and join us. If this young lady's reputation is as Perry's friend Felix says, we are in for a delightful treat." Katy turned back to Jennifer and thanked her for delivering the letter.

The young major came at her call. He already knew what they were about to taste. The governor waved for his driver to bring in a tray. It contained some freshly cooked crusty breadsticks sitting next to the cheese. He handed the knife to Jennifer and asked her to do the honours.

Jennifer snipped the string, opened the cloth, and cut into the smoked cheese. The bowl-shaped morsel was soon cut into many small wedges. When done, Betty offered these around for everyone to taste.

The governor noticed Jennifer's anxiety while the tray was being passed around. She took a small slice and nibbled at the cheese. She grimaced. The flavour was robust, almost to the point of being unpleasant; considering she had made it identical to those made at home, the flavour was vastly different.

Ned saw her frown.

Jennifer realised the smoky taste had more than a bite, but it added a depth missing with the Cornish cheeses. Those were smooth and mellow; although the peaty smoke preserved them, the flavour did not penetrate the cheese. This cheese seemed to absorb the almost acrid smoke, which permeated almost to the centre of the small knob. It was just too strong. It would have gone well with a cigarillo or a pipe, but that's not what she wanted.

It was good but certainly different from those she had produced before. She realised that the gum tree timber she had used was the difference. She could taste it in the flavour. She was slightly upset, and her face showed it.

Ned saw her disappointment. "Jennifer, it's brilliant."

Jennifer shook her head but said nothing. She didn't like it.

Betty had also taken a small slice. She was keen to learn the skill of cheesemaking and watched everything Jennifer did. This was her first taste of smoked cheese, and it was certainly different; her eyebrows shot up in surprise at the richness of the flavour.

The governor, however, adored it. "This is good, really good. I'd be quite happy to serve this at any official function. Perry, what do you think?"

The severely scarred earl agreed. "I love it, Lachlan! Strong and smoky with a hint of... is that onion? It's no wonder Felix recommended you, Miss Jennifer. In his letter, he asked me to watch over you, miss. I will endeavour to do so with the governor's permission, of course. Our household would also be interested in obtaining some of your cheeses, should you have any spare."

Jennifer shook her head again. "It's not bad; it's just not what I wanted it to taste like. The smoke is too strong. Ricotta should be subtle." She walked over to the fireplace and reached up inside the chimney. On the new bars, many cheeses were being smoked. As she had little space, she only made six each day. But there were seven bars, and each row represented a different day. She unhooked a cheese that was currently three days into the smoking process. "Sir, this one has been smoking for half as long. The strong gum scent has overwhelmed the delicate flavour of the cheese." She sniffed the cheese she had just removed from the hanger. "I feel this may be ready to eat. If so, we can hasten production, as smoking will only require half as long."

The earl's wife, who had asked to be called Katy, said, "Can we try it too?"

Jennifer nodded and set about preparing the new cheese.

Again, Betty passed around the tray.

Jennifer was correct; this one was much nicer. The smokiness had flavoured it without overpowering the cheese.

A smile hovered at the edge of Jennifer's mouth. "Yes, this is better. Sir, I will only require a three-day period to have these ready for use or even sale. They are firm enough to transport and yet perfect to eat. Any less and they won't transport well. Fresh unsmoked ricotta should be kept cool and eaten quickly, but here, I believe there are no cold larders, so the smoked versions will remain viable longer." She took another nibble. "They will still need to be transported carefully, sold as a fresh product, and preferably kept in a cool room. They should be eaten in a day or so from purchase."

The expressions of delight on the faces of everyone showed that they all agreed with her.

Elizabeth Macquarie took a bite of this cheese. The overpowering smokiness of the last one had kept her silent. "Oh, Jennifer, this is delicious!" Her nibble turned into a big bite of the gourmet cheese. Seeing her encouraging reaction, the others all tried their sample. She was delighted that, finally, she could serve a half-decent dessert at the official table. "The cottage cheeses you make are fabulous with the berry *coulis* and shortbread. Mrs Ovens also loved the fluted mould it came in. I can finally hold my head up regarding a spectacular dessert." She took another nibble of the new cheese. Her eyes rolled in the enjoyment of the gastronomic delight. Moans and groans of pleasure echoed around the room.

Jennifer could tell they needed no false bravado with this one. This cheese was perfect.

The governor finished his serving and brushed his hands together, removing the crumbs of the crusty bread from his hand and jacket. He licked his lips and said, "Well, Miss Jennifer Kellow, if that is the quality of the fresh cheeses, then what awaits us with the gourmet hard wheels? As my lady Elspeth says, the sweet cottage cheeses you have made for us are delicious. We tried one with an orange glaze last night, and it was superb. I had never thought those two flavours would work together, but they do. I will write to Felix tonight and thank him for bringing you to our attention."

Jennifer smiled. "I have another flavour for you to try soon, sir." The appley lilli pilli cheese she had made gave her an idea for an apple and cinnamon one. Betty had brought a small curl of cinnamon bark for her to taste. She wondered if it would work in a cheese. Another spice they had maturing was grated nutmeg. The flavours she could make in fresh cheeses were endless. Anything from savoury to sweet was possible. Sending those to the market was not an option. However, they would enjoy experimenting on Ned, the Whites, and the governor. They could be sold fresh on market day in town, but they would need to be consumed that day.

By the week's end, Jennifer felt she was ready to explode. She felt huge, and her stomach was so ungainly. Her belly button was sticking out through her gown, and her feet were swollen.

Matron had come to assist her in dressing and said, "The babe still has not dropped, dear, so you will have a day or so to go yet."

The summer heat was overwhelming and sapped her remaining energy. Knowing that the days at the gaol for the majority of women were limited, as they had been notified about their imminent removal to the new women's prison. The Female Factory was completed, and the new weaving looms and wool carding areas were ready for use. The five girls were the first residents but were to stay in one of the lower rooms. The seventy-five other women were to move on February the first.

By the end of January, the matron was caught gazing at Jennifer's stomach. "The baby has dropped Jennifer. It should be soon." Matron had insisted that they settle into the facility first as her hands would be full overseeing the majority of the inmates transferring later that week.

Jennifer had packed her belongings into her carpet bag, and the day before the official move, Matron moved the five girls into their new abode. They settled in a small room near the matron's quarters in the new prison. Jennifer wouldn't admit it, but she had been having back pain most of the day before they moved.

In the dark of the night after their move, Jennifer was awoken by an excruciating searing pain that cleaved across her lower stomach and lower back. She knew her time had come to have the baby. Knowing the first contractions were hours apart, she tried to sleep. When another pain hit, she could see the first glow of the dawn light, and although she tried as hard as she could, Jennifer could not hold in the groans any longer. She knew the baby was coming but was unprepared for the agony that ripped through her. Her mother had never told her it hurt this much. Mrs Brown had advised her to breathe deeply through the pain when the contraction first hit. She was still trying to rest between the contractions; her mother had done the same. The pains were still about half an hour apart. Progressively, they got closer and stronger.

When Polly was born, Jennifer was eleven; she had been through the birth process with her mother and thought she knew what to expect. She was wrong. So very wrong. This pain was agony. Mrs Williams and Jennifer had been the only attendants for the birth. This pain passed, and Jennifer returned to her bunk for another rest. Again, she dozed before the next contraction hit with a vengeance. This time, the wave of pain hit to such a degree that she could not stay quiet. She had groaned into a rag through the first ones, but this time, the excruciating stabbing pain that hit caught her unaware. This contraction hit so hard that she could not hold her cry in. Her wail stirred not only her roommates but the matron, too. Bleary-eyed, caring friends soon surrounded her small bed.

The matron had apparently been expecting this to occur and bustled into their room, fully dressed and carrying a lamp. Following her was another lady who carried a bucket of hot water and a towel. She took one look at the situation and then carried them out again. With one look at Jennifer, the matron saw the fear etched on her face. "Now, now, dearie, try not to disturb the others; they have a big day later today. We will take you into the infirmary." She released a long sigh of frustration.

Rather than abusing her as expected, Jennifer was comforted by her soothing voice. The matron seemed to have backtracked on her initial reservations about her.

Matron waited until that pain had passed, and then they escorted her from the room.

Chapter 17   New Arrivals 1821

*C*hristopher Logan Kellow arrived just before dawn. He was a healthy eight-pound baby and had a mop of fair hair. As the matron held the squirming infant aloft, the little boy released a bellow at being subjected to the indignity of ejection from his warm and comfortable home. His lusty scream brought Jennifer's roommates into the room. They were so excited that the child had arrived safely and wished to ensure Jennifer had survived. Although she had yet to deliver the afterbirth, she was cradling the naked child in her arms. He was still attached to her by a pulsating cord. She adored the innocent child she now cradled. He may not be Billy's baby, but he was one of God's creations.

Matron waited until the cord emptied before tying, cutting it and wrapping the babe in a swaddling cloth. The new arrivals were soon involved in post-birth excitements.

Matron was watching Jennifer's face. "Melinda, quickly, take the babe."

Melinda was hovering expectantly, and Jennifer knew why. She remembered the bloodcurdling screams emanating from her mother when the afterbirth came away. Jennifer was pleased they were alone in the new gaol as the spine-chilling shriek that emerged from her would have woken everyone in the building. No sooner had she delivered the afterbirth than her roommates had to leave. They each kissed her in congratulations and then fled. Their escort had arrived with the cart.

Knowing the worst was over, Matron cleaned her up and handed her the baby. Matron had things to check for the transfer of the new women arriving today. She was tired even before the day started.

Jennifer had seen her mother put her child straight onto her breast, and she did the same. She discovered that the other woman who attended her was a midwife, and she oversaw Jennifer after Matron left. She bustled around the room and set about cleaning up the birthing area.

As Matron washed the blood from her hands, she sighed. The inconvenience of the birth today of all days made her late. At least Jennifer had made it through the night until dawn, so she had managed to get some sleep. Thankfully, she had slept fully dressed. The child was healthy, and that was a blessing, she supposed. Knowing the girl's story, she wondered if she would reject it when it arrived, but the little boy was a beautiful babe. He was not wrinkled as some babies were. She was sure the governor would call him a bonny babe.

Matron had quickly come to realise that stories about this girl were true. Jennifer truly was a lovely girl who had been badly put upon by a member of the nobility. She quickly came to understand why the governor had personally taken an interest in her. Also, Major Ned from the 48th regiment had been given oversight of her activities at the dairy. He was one of the few soldiers she trusted. However, it was when Jennifer brought her one of the early sweet cottage cheeses that her attitude changed, and she realised why there was such a fuss being made over her skills. Rather than condescending, Matron became very supportive and somewhat protective.

The four girls were collected in the pre-dawn light and driven to the dairy. News of the birth spread quickly, and Betty Eccles sent word to Sydney with the morning despatch. After a few months of instruction, the girls would now work exclusively under Betty's supervision for the next few weeks. Jennifer had been told that it would be some weeks before she could return to the dairy.

From the old gaol, the girls were occasionally permitted to walk back to the prison, as it was just across the river. There were men around, both emancipated and still serving time, that would probably attack them, so their escort was to protect them rather than stop them from escaping. However, with the move to the new Female Factory, the distance had tripled; therefore, so had the danger. From today onwards, the cart would collect the girls to and from the Government Dairy.

While Jennifer was off work, the dairy would only produce milk, butter and cream, although Betty had told Jennifer that she might try to make some cottage cheese while she was away, but nothing more adventurous. There were now thirty cows to milk as all the herd had calved, so for the following weeks, most of the milk would be sent to the prisons or government stores to dole out. More stoneware milk urns had arrived, which were delivered to many of the houses in town. As the herd grew, so would the requirements of the town.

Even the gaols had to pay for it, but it was sold to them at half market cost.

~

The *Juliana* arrived in Port Jackson on the evening of January 27th. The ship had first docked a month before in Hobart and offloaded the consignment of male convicts but had been held up leaving. The captain kept apologising, but the ship stayed anchored for two weeks. Finally, in mid-January, the vessel weighed anchor, set sail back up the Derwent River, and headed to its final southern destination. Sydney beckoned.

Billy paced up and down the deck, wishing the wind would carry them northward quickly. He knew the time for Jennifer to give birth had been and gone. They left Hobart a little before the nine months after her attack. His mother had explained that that was the length of time to have a child. To say he was frustrated was a vast understatement. The breezes held until they crossed Bass Strait, then as the ship turned at Green Cape, the winds dropped again.

For two days, they were almost becalmed. After the lull, the winds sprung up again; however, this time, they were from the northeast. Although the winds were gusting strongly, the direction meant tacking and wearing all the way to Sydney.

When Billy first heard these terms, he questioned the captain's use of the word. "I presumed it was actually tacking both ways. What is wearing?"

In the months at sea, the captain had become fond of this tall young man. He wanted to learn everything he could. The kindly captain simply said, "Tacking is one way, and wearing is the other. Sometimes, it is referred to as weaving, but that is wrong."

When off the country's west coast, Billy had assisted with the stock they carried, as did his father. One of the cows on board was having difficulty calving. The two men heard her distress and, without a qualm, assisted the birth. The bull calf was a big boy. Knowing they would need an unrelated bull for their herd, they offered to buy it. The calf's mother was from Jersey in the Channel Islands, and its father was a Guernsey bull. The cow was much smaller than their stock, and having met the gentle cow, the men attended to her health for the remainder of the journey. Within minutes of the birth, the bull calf nuzzled his mother for milk.

Over the weeks, Bryn watched the growth of the calf. Seeing how fast it was growing, he wished to see what the milk was like and quickly stripped a half bucket to test for creaminess. He was astounded at the rich consistency of the milk. This milk had nearly twice the cream of the other cows. No wonder the calf had a phenomenal growth rate. He also had inherited his mother's buckskin colouring. The head of this animal was not as finely boned as his mother, but he should sire calves with better cream content. Bryn decided to ask if he could also buy the mother as well. If nothing else, her milk would increase the cream volume. Jennifer would probably make some unique cheeses with this liquid.

With the *Juliana* now nearing its destination, Billy's anxiety grew.

Once they arrived, they found that they first needed to be cleared through quarantine, and then they had to deliver Duke Felix's letter to Governor Macquarie. On some days, he felt he could swim faster than the ship was moving. The evenings, however, were magical. Dolphins often joined them and performed in the bow waves. As they played in the sea foam in the darkness, they set off fireworks in the water. Each flip of their tails made an explosion of lights occur.

At the end of January, they finally arrived at the towering cliffs of Sydney Heads. All the passengers were crowded along the upper railings and watching the ship head directly for the solid wall of the cliff. The captain had previously permitted Billy to steer the ship for no reason other than to occupy him, but negotiating the entry of a sailing ship through the massive headlands could be tricky, so he took over the wheel.

Billy wondered if Jennifer had been able to see the parting of the cliffs as their ship made harbour. He hoped he would find out soon.

Shortly before the sun sank, the ship could finally drop anchor. Relief! They had made it. There had been no real misadventures. Their dairy cargo was yet to arrive later that year. They had decided to write to the duke and ask him to see if he could find some Jersey cows for both dairies.

It took three days before they were permitted to disembark.

Billy nearly crawled out of his skin when he climbed down the rope ladder to the waiting longboat. He was so worried about Jennifer, but he knew he had to find her first. His father had a letter of introduction to the governor from Duke Felix, which had yet to be presented, but they had heard the gentleman lived some hours west. Another delay! He groaned.

They found accommodation at a fancy-looking hotel on Pitt Street. The King's Arms Hotel was an establishment obviously trying to mimic the Angel Inn in Islington in London. Although it paled in comparison, it was comfortable and also central. They had thought of taking a hackney cab up the hill to Government House. The cabbie said he would arrange a wagon to bring their personal luggage from the ship to the hotel. The bulk of their items in the hold would stay in *situ* for some time as the ship was to stay in the harbour for a month or so. This gave them time to find Jennifer, arrange accommodation and storage and enquire about land suitable for the new dairy.

As they booked into the hotel, they discovered from the manager that the governor was not in Parramatta. He had gone to visit Botany Bay with Commissioner Bigge.

This delay meant that Billy was able to relax a little and have a look around town. There were new attached cottages being built and inns along the foreshore at Dawes and Millers Points, not far from Government House. He dressed in his new town clothing, a gift from the duke shortly before sailing, and stretched his legs for a long walk. His parents had headed along the foreshore eastward, but he headed in the opposite direction. He stopped on the headland of the Dawes Point Battery and sat watching the activities in the bay. A ship had some sails up and was heading out to sea. Others swung on their anchors with the tide. The shops on the harbour side were a hive of activity. As he sat on the rock wall near the cannons, watching the people buzz thither and yon as they went about their daily duties. On the other side of the point, there were various unusual-looking buildings that caught his eye, and he wondered what they were. He was about to wander down the path when a red-coated soldier arrived beside him with a musket slung over his shoulder. "Afternoon, sir; new to town, are you?"

The accent of the man puzzled him. "Yes, sir, my family has just arrived on the *Juliana*." Billy was itching to find some information about the area. "Would you mind if I asked you a few questions?"

"Be pleased to I would, young sir. What can I do you for?" The soldier's terminology needed some explanation.

Billy frowned, then smiled. "First, where do you come from?"

The filthy teeth of the soldier made Billy grimace. His breath made Billy sit down so he wasn't as close to him.

The man with the bad breath said, "I'm from a wee place named Butterburn, just south of the Scottish border. It's not far from the famous place, Gretna Green."

That was as far away from Newlyn in Cornwall as one could get in Britain. With that question answered, he pumped the man for information about the two odd-looking half-buildings on the foreshore.

The soldier released a throaty chuckle. "Oouch man, that is the Whaler's Arms and the Hero of Waterloo. The Whaler's Arms be my favourite drinking hole that be. When you go down that way, stop in and ask for a local rum. I must away, laddie; I'm on duty, so can't chat too long." The man walked off and continued his circuit of patrol.

Billy kept walking out to the point. Windmills twirled above his head, and the waft of freshly ground grain met his nose. He realised that he had been gone for some hours and he was hungry. The sun was nearly overhead, and it was hot. He returned to the hotel, hoping his parents would not be waiting for him.

They were. Billy's return was met with his father pacing the foyer. "Where have you been, boy? The governor is waiting for us, and we're due up there in twenty minutes. I thought we'd need to go without you."

Billy and Bryn quickly walked upstairs to prepare for the meeting.

~

The governor had been waiting some months for this interview due to the regular reports on Jennifer from his housekeeper and his occasional visits. Ned also kept him up to date and often brought samples for him to try. When he received the news about the birth of her child that morning, he was sad that her man had not arrived; but he had, Lachlan just didn't know that yet. He had missed the news of the *Juliana's* arrival as he had been away.

Later that morning, when Lachlan received word of the Williams' arrival Lachlan sent a note for them to come. He had an hour gap in his schedule and adjusted his arrangements for the day.

The three visitors stood in the foyer and gazed around them. They had expected grandeur like the duke's house in London, However, the modest dwelling was still one of the best and biggest in the area but was not much bigger than Bryn's two-story home in Cornwall. Mr Stewart at the hotel had told them that the governor's principal residence was in Parramatta, and the governor had only come to Sydney as he was showing a man around the settlement.

A door off to the side opened, and a tall, grey-haired soldier entered. His Scottish lilt gave his identity away even before he introduced himself. "Welcome, welcome. I have been awaiting your arrival for some time. Please come in and take a seat." He ushered them into the office and set about making them comfortable.

Delen took a seat, but the two men waited until the governor sat before seating themselves. The discussion that ensued was eye-opening.

Lachlan sat and waved for the two gentlemen to relax. "Now, I presume Duke Felix has sent you with another informative letter for me."

Bryn dug into his coat pocket and produced the bulky envelope. He passed it over, and the governor sat back and read it. Page after page flicked over. Eventually, he placed it on his desk. "As I thought, Felix has a swathe of instructions for me. The first of which I fully intended to do in any case. I am returning to Parramatta this afternoon, and you will accompany me."

This was not an invitation but an instruction.

"My carriage will collect you at... Where are you staying?" His brow furrowed.

Bryn replied, "We are at The King's Arms, sir." He swallowed nervously. "Sir, we are simple farm folk from Cornwall. We can make our own way to wherever you say."

Lachlan smiled and folded his arms. "Yes, you could, but as Jennifer had the baby last night, or should I say early this morning, I dare say Mr Billy wants to see her. She will stay in the new Female Factory until you find a home; then, I will reassign her to you after you are wed. I already have given permission for your marriage." He passed Billy a document. "All you have to do is see the minister and have Banns called; the ones in England won't apply here. Sorry! At the duke's instruction, I have had the Colonial Secretary hunt out some suitable land, and it's not far from the back of our domain in Parramatta. Jennifer may well be reassigned to you, but I still want her to work and teach at my dairy. She has already been making that delectable smoked ricotta and a pink, apple-flavoured cottage cheese that is to die for. When she arrived, Felix sent me a gift. The captain of her vessel carefully transported a cheese clad in blue wax. On tasting it, she said it was perfect. Unfortunately, she has forbidden me to eat much more until you arrive. Apparently, your first chore is to make a new culture from this blue wheel. She would have done it herself but decided to hold off until your arrival as she was unsure how long it would last. She did extract a small amount to make a culture for some plain cheeses."

Bryn's face lit up. "You have a *Southern Belle* cheese wheel? It never occurred to me to bring one. Oh, this is truly wonderful, sir."

Billy had caught on to a different topic. "Jen has had the child? Is she well?" He had almost pushed himself off his seat. He wished to be with her.

Lachlan's smile reassured him. "I hear she is, lad. I will not tell you about the child, but it too is well. Good lungs, so I hear from Matron. The other girls she works with were with her soon afterwards. My housekeeper sent me the news this morning, which I have only just received. I will tell you no more as Jennifer can tell you herself tonight."

The chuckle he gave made Delen reach and squeeze her son's arm. "Billy, you would not have been permitted to be with her during the delivery anyway. It's not like home." She motioned for him to relax, and he did so.

~

The trip to Parramatta was accomplished with interest from the new arrivals. Delen sat next to the governor and watched the scenery pass by. The three gasped in unison when a mob of wallabies in flight was seen bounding away from the road.

Billy was not one to normally swear, but his exclamation of "What the blooming…?" He was silenced by a filthy look from his mother.

The governor spent the next hour explaining the uniqueness of this ancient country. Then he said, "As I know you realise the importance of education, I do too. I have endeavoured to build schools for everyone who wishes to learn. The native children are encouraged to do the same, so I have built them schools, as well as the Irish orphans. Sadly, none of the groups will intermingle, but I do what I can. There is now a large orphan school at Parramatta, and the female waifs and strays from the colony are fed, clothed and educated there. The boys' orphanage is in Sydney. They are there until about age ten to thirteen; then, they are apprenticed throughout the colony and farms. They at least have a better life than on the streets of London. They all leave the school here being able to read and write and with a skill that suits them."

The vehicle's arrival in Parramatta was achieved a few hours before dark. The carriage stopped before a nice-looking place called the Rear Admiral Duncan Inn.

Lachlan alighted, speaking as he did so. "You will be able to stay here. I have arranged two rooms for you. Bill and Molly Miller will cater to all your needs. They also have a room of sorts below, where your excess luggage can be stored until required. Theirs is an interesting story, but they will tell you if they wish. Make sure you ask them about the books in the sitting room. They have a fascinating history. You see, Bill is extraordinarily interesting. His education runs rings around Jennifer's. While you are here, you may find it worthwhile to get to know them." By the time he had said his piece, they had arrived at the front door.

The governor did the introductions. "Bill, Molly, this is Bryn, Delen, and Billy Williams. They are dairy farmers from Cornwall and friends of Jennifer."

Hardly acknowledging the governor, Molly drew her breath and said, "You're Jennifer's new family, the cheese makers, aren't you?" She ushered them inside and showed them their rooms.

Lachlan pulled back Billy. "Throw your bag in your room, laddie, and I'll take you to see Jennifer now."

Billy didn't need a second invitation. As soon as he discovered where he was sleeping, he did what he was told and whispered to his father where he was going. The two men slipped out quietly while Molly and Delen were getting to know each other. Bryn just wished to put his feet up. He hated travelling backwards in a carriage.

Back in the carriage, Billy was now able to question the governor about Jennifer and if she really was well.

Lachlan proceeded to reassure him. "She is lad; I tell no lies there. However, she will be sore as she has just had a large bairn. It, too, is well, and I have ensured she was kept safe from the day she arrived. I believe we have a mutual friend in the Duke of Shesham. Jennifer has rescued four more young girls and is teaching them dairy skills as per his instructions. This includes my housekeeper. Betty is also learning to run a dairy properly. I have a team of convicts digging out a small cheese cave down on the flat, and until it's complete, she is only making soft cheeses. However, she has some unflavoured half wheels in our larder. Betty seems almost to caress them each day."

Billy nodded. There was far more to making hard cheeses than having a cheese cave. They need the right cultures. The *Southern Belle* one was a great start. "Sir, do you by any chance have a cellar? It may do in the meantime. Even if only to make up the blue wax culture that you have."

Lachlan smiled. "Of sorts, I do, laddie, and Jennifer has already put it to good use. It's more of a larder. I think we will need to work something out if more room is required. I propose you first build a cheese cave on your new land." The vehicle was only travelling at a walking pace.

Billy noticed the dirt roads, which were not so bad to warrant the slow pace. He was agitated, and the governor could tell.

Chapter 18 The Female Factory 1821

*T*heir slow arrival at the prison tested Billy's patience. The governor's driver seemed to be ambling along. When they eventually pulled up, the governor made no effort to alight. He saw Billy's impatience and said, "I'm not dawdling, you know. It is the first day in the new prison, and the women should be at meals. Therefore, the matron will need to unlock the door to the room Jennifer is in. In the new gaol, the soldiers of my regiment act as warders. This is the first day the women have been here in this particular facility, although Jennifer and her four friends moved in earlier. Matron wanted her here for the birth. The small infirmary here is clean and new." He opened the door and finally got out. He relaxed against the outside of the carriage for a few minutes. "This gave us time to chat, lad."

Billy nodded his understanding and looked around the area. For a prison, it looked neat and tidy. The blonde sandstone shone in the late afternoon sun. The walls around the gaol were only eight feet high, and some had toe holds on the top of each block. He wondered just how secure they would be. He could easily give someone a leg over them and clear out, let alone stop men climbing in. However, it was not his place to question its non-secure construction. Footsteps crunching on the gravel made Billy turn.

A uniformed woman approached, and she greeted the governor with a curtsy, then waited to be introduced to Billy. Once done, her abruptness shocked him. "So, you came for her then? I wondered if her words were just stories, but I was hoping you were as real as she said, but you sounded too good to be true." She beckoned him to follow.

Billy frowned and swiped at a fly. He was unsure exactly what she meant, so he remained silent. Leaving the governor to kick his heels outside, Billy followed her. She walked to the building beside them. It was two stories at one end and a single story at the other. She withdrew her jangling charlatan from her pocket and unlocked the door. She said, "This is more for her protection. She's vulnerable in here alone, so when I'm away, I lock her in for her own safety. She's in that room, lad."

As they walked inside, he noticed the whitewashed walls were pristinely clean. But Billy stood frozen on the spot. "She's in there, Mr Billy." Matron touched him on the shoulder, then gently pushed him towards the door.

He nodded. He had heard her the first time, but he was now filled with nerves. Billy didn't hear anything, so he walked slowly towards the open door. Looking inside, he saw a bed, and his beloved Jennifer was asleep. She had not changed, but he had not seen her asleep since she was a child. She had only been ten, and he had carried her home one night after she started working for them. Now, he crept across the floor and sat in the chair beside her bed. Her hand was lying on the sheet, and he gently took her fingers in his and caressed her palm as he had done many times before.

The loving action made her fingers subconsciously curl around his. In her sleep, she murmured, "Oh, Billy, I miss you so." Her eyes were still closed, but she felt that he was close.

He realised that she was dreaming but replied, "I'm here, love." His words sounded trite, but he had sailed halfway across the world to sit beside her as she slept, and he would be there when she needed him. To gaze on her while in slumber was comfort enough. His old life was not worth living if she was not in it. "I will always be here, my lovely Jen."

At those words, Jennifer's eyes fluttered open. "Billy, you came? Only you call me Jen."

He grinned. "I did and will always be here for you, sweetheart." His fingers eased from her hand to brush her hair from her forehead. He leaned over to kiss her brow. She struggled to pull herself up. A tear of joy escaped and trickled down her cheek. He leaned over, kissed it away, and said, "I love you."

She replied by reaching out to him. "I love you so very much. I need you close to me."

Billy was beside her on the bed in an instant and pulled her into his arms. He fully expected he would be weeping with relief, but he was far too emotional for tears. They sat on the bed and clung together. The months apart had not lessened their feelings for each other.

Now awake fully, she rested against his chest. It took some minutes before she said, "I missed you so much, so very, very much." She pulled back a little in his arms, and only then did she lift her head invitingly for a proper, deep kiss. He noted that she wore his ring, and with joy filling his heart, he accepted her offering with delight. Her lips were soft beneath his. They had kissed many times before, but this time, the promise of a future together meant so much more than it had previously. He would have liked to deepen his kiss, but she pulled from his arms a little. He forgot that she would be sore and almost crushed her to him.

Jennifer had been asleep for some hours, and her breasts were now tender as her milk had come in while she slept. She had already fed Kit twice, then slept the afternoon away. She had never experienced such pain as the birth, yet it was fleeting and now had passed, but it had left her so drained that she had slept for hours. Her breasts hadn't been sore when she went to sleep.

A small noise broke them apart. Billy eased from her arms and stood up. "Jen, the governor only told me you had delivered the baby and that you were both well, but he would not say more. What did we have? And what did you call it? I told you I would bring it up as our child. I mean that, sweetheart."

Jennifer gently eased herself up in bed. Her bottom still hurt, but it wasn't too bad. She said, "A boy, Billy. I have named him Christopher Logan, but I will call him Kit, after my brother Kitto. Kit Kellow, I like it; what do you think?"

Billy walked over to the tiny child in the cane basket. The infant was just stirring and was about to release a bellow when Billy stroked his cheek. "It's grand, love. Kitto was also my grandfather's name, so it's on both sides. I like it, too, but we'll add Williams when we're married. He can wait until then to be Baptised." The baby was obviously trying to focus on him. A frown settled on his brow, and he took a deep breath to release a hungry bellow.

Jennifer watched her fiancé anxiously. "Bring him to me, Billy, and I'll change him." The look of horror on Billy's face made her laugh. He shook his head. Jennifer said, "You won't break him, you know, Billy. Just pick him up and pass him over. Make sure you support his head."

The last thing Billy wanted to do was to hold the moving bundle. However, glancing at her pale face made him do as she asked. He pulled back the blanket and saw the child was fully swaddled. He gingerly picked up the small human, who would soon be his stepson. The baby opened his eyes and gazed blearily at Billy again. Now elevated, the tiny mouth opened in a yawn, then before it closed, his face screwed up, and he saw he was about to cry. Billy quickly shoved the baby at his mother.

Jennifer accepted her son with another chuckle.

Matron came in at the first squark of the child. "Sir, she will have to feed him, and this will take time. May I suggest that you say farewell and that you return tomorrow? If you were married, I could permit you to stay. However…" She looked a little embarrassed and left her comment unfinished. "You can spend most of the day with her on your return tomorrow. It's enough for you to be reunited again." As she spoke, she picked up a clean flannel napkin and placed it at the end of the bed. She then took the baby from Jennifer and laid him next to the clean napkin. She unwrapped the child with deft hands and cleaned his bottom while dodging his golden shower. Lifting both feet, she changed the napkin and soon had the clean one pinned in place. She swaddled the child again, only this time quite loosely, so his tiny hands were left free.

Billy watched in awe. He kissed Jennifer a fond farewell and promised he would return the following morning as soon as he was permitted. He stood at the door watching his soon-to-be family, then realised that as they were not yet married and she was about to expose her breast, he reluctantly left her to her motherly duty. He was still within earshot when he heard her say, "I love you, Billy, and thank you for coming."

Billy's emotions spilled over. "I love you too, Jen; I'll see you tomorrow." He had completely forgotten the governor was still waiting for him. Knowing that, he hurriedly returned to the carriage. Now that he had seen Jen, he was content. The only benefit of leaving was that tomorrow, he would get to spend the entire day with her.

Before Billy turned in that evening, he stood on the wide verandah outside his room, listening to the river in the dim light and praying. As the stars appeared above him, he thanked God they would soon be together for the rest of their lives. He eventually settled into the big double bed. Having never slept in such a huge, soft bed before, he tossed and turned for some time before getting comfortable. As his room overlooked the river, the double doors were flung wide open, and he lay in bed listening to the unfamiliar sounds of the new town. His new town! He now had to turn his mind to making a living in this hot and dirty, fly-ridden place. He was now thankful his parents had accompanied him. He had been in this brown country for only a few days, and instead of February being cold like it was at home, the perspiration dripped from his forehead even when he was sitting still. Kicking off all his bed coverings but the linen sheet, he turned his head and slept.

Dawn saw Billy, Bryn, and Delen start awake to a cacophony of morning bird calls. There was one that sounded like a volley of almost musical musket shots. Others gave cries that sounded like many screaming, strangled babies. Some were melodious and were a delight to lay back and listen to. The chorus of calls continued for some time before falling silent again as the sun rose. Now awake, Billy dressed and headed into the kitchen for food. Molly was already there, and he asked her what the birds were.

The young innkeeper laughed as she cooked their eggs and bacon. "The birds certainly take some getting used to. We call it the dawn chorus. We were the same when we first arrived from London."

A kookaburra was sitting on the verandah, waiting for a treat.

She smiled as she tossed out a bit of bacon gristle. "This one is the laughing bird, but it sounds like a gun being fired very quickly or like a deep-throated laugh," she said as she threw some more uncooked bacon fat towards the bird. It hopped off the railing and collected its treats.

"The screeching ones are cockatoos." A flock of white birds took off from a tall tree. "Look, that's a flight of them calling as they fly." They watched as she pointed to the six white birds flying along the river.

Bryn and Delen joined Billy at the kitchen table.

Molly served their hot breakfast, toast, and marmalade. She continued, "There are also bellbirds, crows and all sorts of others that I don't know. But the parrots are really pretty and come in all sorts of colours. From pink to red and green."

Billy ate quickly and soon was on his way to see Jennifer. The morning was cool, and the gaol was only about half a mile away. On entering the gates, Jennifer was waiting to greet him. Matron trusted her, and she was free to leave if she wished. However, she wanted to see him in private. Billy's form filled the doorway of the infirmary, and they stood looking at each other. He opened his arms to her, and moments later, she was enfolded in them. "Marry me, Jen; marry me soon. I find you are far more than just necessary to my well-being."

She was in complete agreement. "Willingly, my darling man." She reached up and pulled his head down to hers. There was no more discussion for some time. Neither heard Matron come or leave again. The world had become unimportant to either of them.

~

Jennifer remained in the temporary prison infirmary for another week before returning to her room with the girls. She stayed there until their wedding, four weeks after Billy's arrival. Banns had needed to be called again, but everything else was already prepared. On Thursday, March 1st, they celebrated their union. Molly even loaned Jennifer her own wedding gown. The fabric was stunning and so beautiful that Jennifer felt like a princess.

Molly and Sal added flowers to her hair, and she carried a prayer book that Reverend Marsden loaned her.

Billy wept when he saw her walking down the aisle on his father's arm.

The rotund Reverend Samuel Marsden did the honours, and the small group of friends, which included the governor and his wife, Perry and Katy White, the Millers, Lockleys and, of course, the four girls and Matron with Major Ned, entered the church and waited for the bride.

Bryn gave her away, which he thought was somewhat funny as she would be living with them as family. He realised she was sad her parents and siblings couldn't be with them, but the Williams family had known her all her life, and now she would be part of their family.

After the ceremony, the governor handed Billy an envelope. Jennifer's indenture was transferred to her husband. She was delighted that she was now officially assigned to him. She had asked the governor to keep hold of the money from the baron until Kit needed it.

On return to the inn, Molly and Bill Miller welcomed their new guest. As newlyweds themselves, Molly had decorated their bedroom with as many flowers as possible. Her one sadness about her marriage was that she had not conceived after two years. She desperately tried to put on weight but was still stick thin. She was somewhat jealous that Jennifer had conceived so easily after just one encounter that it was a bitter pill to swallow. Molly shed a few tears in the privacy of her room before appearing once again with her bright and happy face.

Jennifer had told Molly the entire saga and had kept nothing back. Molly realised how easily this could have been her situation if she had not hit her attacker with a skillet. It was, however, the reason she had been transported. Her husband, Bill, had hit her abuser a little earlier, and he, too, had been convicted for striking a member of the nobility. With only a few years between the two girls, they had become good friends.

Delen had taken Billy shopping in Sydney, and he had chosen a wardrobe of new work clothes for Jennifer. They had brought the gowns she had ordered in London, but none were suitable for work. Kit had a new woven rush basket, which sat in their room on the chest of drawers. Bryn and Billy met with Duke Felix's friend, Perry White, and the architect, Francis Greenway. They needed to draw up plans for their dairy. The governor had gone about his business and left them with Perry. As soon as the land had been chosen and the paperwork completed, a convict team was set to work excavating a cavern under where the dairy would eventually sit. The stone removed would be used to construct the building above. The house also was to have a cellar that could be used as an overflow for the cheeses should it be required. The Jersey cow and its growing calf were finally moved onto the farm. He was three months old and would be ready to mate with the new cows when they arrived. Hopefully, one of them would have had a bull calf to mate with this calf's mother.

After the family had departed London, it had taken the duke six months to source all that was required to start a dairy from scratch. Although Bryn, Jacob and Billy had left him an exhaustive list, he wanted more from what he had found and kept hunting. He had also found some Jersey cows and split the small herd between the two dairies. The farmer had told him not to purchase a Jersey bull as they were cantankerous beasts with a foul temper. The cows were just the opposite. In the weeks since his purchase, he had put his hired Guernsey bull over the smaller Jersey cows, and all were now in calf. He wanted the cattle on a direct voyage that would travel as quickly as possible. The *Brixton* was due to sail about twelve months after Jennifer's arrest. Hopefully, the ship would meet little rough weather. Finding the right sort of milking cows had been easy compared to getting the cheese moulds and bolts of cheesecloth and other paraphernalia, and then finding a way to transport the dried cultures and even purchasing the right sort of covered pans to make the flavoured brines. The duke had also found two huge coopered milk vats, wrapped them in oiled linen cloths, and added them to the stock awaiting their transport. Both had external copper sleeves so they could be heated over a flame.

The three orphan milkmaids were given instructions about caring for the newborn calves. The girls were so excited to leave London that they hopped from one foot to another. The duke could only smile at their antics. They were aware that the captain had an envelope for Billy. It contained the three ten-pound notes for the three girls' dowries. He read the letter from Billy about their safe arrival and the safe delivery of the baby boy. He knew he had to let the baron know. He would make him set aside funds for the child and book him into the best schools in England.

After reading the story about the scare Jennifer had given the captain about being cold, the Duke outfitted the three young girls with warm climate clothing and more gowns, underclothes and boots plus winter overcoats for the voyage. He had not realised the girls had no other clothing than what they stood in. Having discovered that he ensured that the occupants at his three orphanages were also supplied with vast quantities of more food and clothing. The duke also added a crate full of cheese moulds in various decorative shapes to the consignment to Sydney. Jennifer had told him she had one ceramic fluted one and asked him to find a couple more. He was sending more than a dozen in different styles.

Captain Lusk was honoured to carry the beginnings of a new industry. He personally oversaw the placement of the freight for the duke. As he carried no convicts, the herd of dairy cattle filled the deck and kept the vessel in milk for the entire voyage. This was a great luxury for the passengers. As there were also crates of chickens on board, the cook made a variety of custards and rice puddings. The ship had its own supply of beasts to consume on the voyage, which became somewhat like Noah's Ark. Felix found that estimating the volume of food the huge herd required was a nightmare. All the cows were in calf, and once lactating, they would need more feed. Then, he had to allow for water-damaged produce, so he doubled the provisions.

After leaving Portsmouth mid-summer, the *Brixton* traversed the seas in safety. It docked in Hobart only a little over twelve weeks after leaving England. Some of her cargo was unloaded before quickly setting off for Sydney with the duke's consignment of the new herd and the remainder of the dairy equipment; this included two large coopered vats that Bryn had only dreamt about. The thirty-five cows sent by the duke had all given birth *en route*, as he had hoped, and the calves were permitted to drink as much of the milk as they could. There were twenty-three heifers and twelve bull calves.

The duke had eventually been able to source ten Jersey cows. Five were included with this consignment, and the others were sent to Jacob in Cornwall. The three dairymaids from London were beginning to earn their keep. Until the calves arrived, they had had a leisurely cruise as their milk dried up. The Captain insisted that the girls always stay together. To keep busy in the first months, the girls occupied the children of the cabin passengers. They were not much older but used to many little ones. As the girls had grown up in an orphanage, part of their jobs was to care for the younger children. With the calves' arrival, they were milking almost constantly. The cook in the galley used some of the milk to make the morning porridge, and he scalded it and served it for the passengers to consume.

The ship docked in Sydney at the end of September 1821. It was just a year after Jennifer's arrival on the *Morley*. The harbour master sent word to Bryn the morning after the vessel anchored.

Knowing that livestock would be moved more often, a portable loading ramp had been constructed and could be pushed to the side of any ship. Passengers and stock could now walk ashore. All seventy beasts were walked down the ramp in fifteen minutes.

~

In Parramatta, Billy and his new wife found that living in this new country vastly differed from their life in Cornwall. Their new farm, which they named *Park Meadow*, was only a short distance from the Government Dairy, and Billy had been busy in the nine months since their arrival. As soon as their land was chosen, Major Ned had arranged for a convict team to make split rail fencing, and it had been completed only a fortnight after their marriage. Their one cow and calf now had the run of the large paddock. They let the calf drink as much as he wished, saving them from worrying about milking her until their dairy shed was built. The governor instructed Ned and two more convict teams to make the dream dairy a reality, including excavating a cheese cave.

Meanwhile, while living at the inn, Jennifer kept working at the small dairy on the hill behind Government House. With the new dairy under construction, Billy's thoughts turned to their future home. He discovered the benefits of a verandah from the existing dairy and sketched an idea of what he wanted.

Billy adored Kit, and he quickly became confident in handling his stepson. Usually, Billy rose to change him in the night until he began sleeping through. As Jennifer had to rise before dawn, Billy would care for the crying child. He learnt that Kit loved being cuddled back to sleep in a rocking chair. Delen had laughed and told him he was making a rod for his back. Although he was Jennifer's child, he loved the little boy unconditionally, as promised. One day, they would have their own. Billy would travel with Jennifer to the Government Dairy and assist her in the work. He would only leave her side when it was time to feed the baby. Then Kit was placed in his wicker basket on the floor of the bug-free dairy and was kept out of the way of the workers. He was the most adorable child. His big blue eyes and gurgling chuckle won the hearts of all who met him. Delen and Billy would often take him for a long walk while Bryn, Jenny and the girls made the cheeses.

Life in the colony was settling into an easy routine. Jennifer was overwhelmed that they were building a new house and that she would even have a room for their children, should more arrive. Life was good. Billy had planned that the new home would have six bedrooms.

Chapter 19 Discoveries 2008

Saturday morning, Jenny looked forward to a sleep-in. Now married with three children, such a morning was a rare treat. This weekend, the children were having a weekend with Mark's parents. He was away at a conference, and she looked forward to a lazy day.

A noisy kookaburra landed on the fence outside her bedroom window and gave his morning chorus. The earsplitting song stirred Jenny awake. With a groan, she rolled onto her back and knew the long-awaited slumber in bed would not occur. She rubbed her eyes and reached for the glasses she needed to read the time. Eight o'clock, oh well, that wasn't too bad. She had managed an extra hour but had no need to get up yet. Refusing to rise, she lay back and realised it was forty years since she had begun searching for her ancestors. The thought of "I'll just lay here for a bit longer" slipped through her mind. She rolled over, but the trill of her mobile phone brought another groan to her lips. While the children were away, she slept with the phone beside her bed, both for her safety and in case she was needed.

She reached out for the vibrating monster and sleepily held it to her ear. "Morning, Jenny here!" she said a little moodily and released a long sigh.

A bright and crisp voice met her ear. "Jenny, it's Michelle. You won't believe it, but I've found more about her at long last. I have found more about Jennifer Kellow Williams, and you're not going to believe her story. What do you know about the history of cheese in the colony?"

Jenny was now wide awake; she swung her legs out of bed. "What do you mean you found her? I thought we had before. We know she came to the colony and had an illegitimate child. Have you found more?" Jenny could hear the excitement in her friend's voice.

Michelle could hardly contain herself. "Yes! As you know, since we are both now married with a family, I only work on Saturday mornings as a volunteer. As the children are on a school camp, and David is with Mark at the conference, I had a hunch last night and came in early. I've been here since six, and I have found her. Can you come in?"

Of all the things that could have motivated Jenny on this particular morning, it was this. Today, her forty-year search may finally reach a conclusion.

"I'll be there in ten, Michelle. If it had been any other Saturday, we would have had sport and all sorts of crazy things, but I cleared my schedule of everything. See you soon." She pushed the button on the flip phone and climbed out of bed. She wished she had not read that extra chapter last night. Oh, well, too late now. A cold face scrub, a thermos of coffee, and a banana she would eat on the way.

By eight-fifteen, she was locking the door behind her. It had taken her five minutes to find her old genealogy notebook. She tucked it under her arm and then headed out the door. All thoughts of tiredness had fled.

Fourteen years ago, the girls had married brothers in a double ceremony. Michelle's husband, David, was eight years older than Mark. Nineteen years before, the four had met at Kent Street at the headquarters of the Australian Genealogical Society while hunting convict relatives. Having a like interest in this kept the four in contact. A passion for early Australian history and culture had seen them join the Bush Music Club. Once a month, on a Friday evening, they would meet up at Glebe High School for the regular bush dance. With busy lives, the four kept in contact and assisted with each other's research.

David and Michelle announced that they were dating at one of these dances, and it was not long before Mark officially asked Jenny out. The two couples became engaged only weeks apart, and the boys' mother had sown the idea of a double wedding. As they all lived in the Parramatta area, the choice of church was a given. St John's had seen the marriages of family members for over two hundred years.

The ceremony had been a delight. Although the brides walked up the aisle together, David and Michelle had married first, as they were the older couple. Mark and Jenny witnessed their signatures. They reciprocated for the second couple. Michelle signed her new married name for the first time as a witness. Having a best friend as a sister-in-law was a delight for the two girls. That their husbands were brothers with the same passion for family history was even better.

By eight-thirty, Jenny was at the staff entrance of the library. Michelle held the door open and handed her a visitor's pass. Security had tightened in all government buildings since the 9/11 plane crashes.

Jenny was used to the procedure. She had passed the security checks numerous times and had a permanent visitor's pass waiting.

Michelle no longer had an office, but these days, with computers, she didn't need one. Everything was now accessible online. The screen had flicked on to screen saver, and Michelle wiggled the mouse to wake it up.

Michelle grabbed Jenny's shoulders. "Take a deep breath, love, for we are just about to step back in time. What I discovered is going to rock your socks off, Jen. Pull up a chair, and we'll get at it." Michelle's excitement for their early colonial history had never waned.

Part of the problem of having a family with a common name is working out which they are amongst the hundreds with the same moniker. Williams was one such problem.

Many times over the years, they wondered if they had found the correct one, only to find that it was another dead end. Jennifer, Christopher and William were just too commonplace.

Michelle typed in her password, and the computer sprung back to life.

On her screen was an entry for a woman named Eccles.

Eccles, Elizabeth (Betty) (1742–1835)

"Elizabeth/Winifred Bird and John Love were accused of stealing a wether lamb; Mary Love was accused of receiving the stolen beast.

Elizabeth and John were sentenced to death on 15 March 1785 at Maidstone; Mary Love was sentenced to 14 years of transportation. Bird's death was later commuted to seven years of transportation. She and Mary Love were sent to Southwark gaol. Her age on embarkation was given as 45, and her occupation was 'in service,' She arrived in Sydney in January 1788 aboard the Lady Penrhyn *as part of the First Fleet.*

In March 1790, Bird was sent by the Sirius *to Norfolk Island, where she began living with fellow convict Thomas Eccles. They were one of nearly one hundred couples who were married on the Island in November 1791.*

In March 1801, the couple returned to Port Jackson on the Porpoise. *In the 1814 Muster, she was listed as 'Mrs Eccles,'*

In 1821, she was employed as a housekeeper. She died at Parramatta on 25 July 1835; her age was given as 105 but was probably nearer 93. She was buried the next day at St John's cemetery in Sydney."

Michelle read this entry aloud to Jenny and then quickly flicked to another one. "Listen to this; this one gave me the connection."

She read the entry. *"Elizabeth died at the Governor's Dairy, Parramatta, on the 25th inst, Elizabeth Eccles, aged 105 years. She arrived in the First Fleet at the age of 57 and has resided ever since in Parramatta, excepting the time of her going to England to see the Prince Regent, who settled upon her a small pension for life."*

Jenny wondered what that was for and thought they would look into that later.

"Elizabeth was born on the 18th of September 1730 at Stratford-on-Avon; her maiden name was Bird; her conduct was honest and upright, and she obtained the favour of all the Governors. She possessed her mental faculties till the last and died respected by her

numerous acquaintances. She was buried last Monday week at the expense of Governor Bourke, and her funeral was attended by His Excellency's servants and many of the old inhabitants of Parramatta."

Jenny was puzzled. "How is she anything to do with Jennifer, though?"

"Ahh," said Michelle. "Well, remember we found a reference to Jennifer being assigned to the dairy in Parramatta?"

Jenny nodded.

Michelle lay back with her arms folded and revealed the rest of the story. "Well, I didn't think much more about that for a while, but then I got to thinking. I wonder where Jennifer actually came from. We had looked before, but this time, when I checked, I found her records online from the Bow Street's Magistrates court. Jennifer came from Cornwall. It seems her family, and her husband were all in the business together there. There was a letter in her record that was produced after her conviction. Had it been available beforehand, I bet she would not have been convicted at all. This document tells the entire saga. And it was written by a duke. Would you believe that?"

Jenny was spellbound. "Well, go on, what was in it?"

Michelle grinned. "In a nutshell, the two families, Kellows and Williams, were cheesemakers in Cornwall; Jennifer made one in particular that a duke somehow got his hands on. This Duke Felix accused the agent of smuggling it from France and demanded that he meet the maker himself to prove the provenance of the produce. If she came to meet him in London, and her words proved true, he offered to endorse the product and tell his friends to buy some. She was reluctant, but eventually, she came. It was only the week before she and her fiancé were to marry. As an innocent girl in the big smoke for the first time, she decided to try to sell some cheeses herself. She had to deliver an ordered one to a chef at a baron's residence. I gather he was a bit of a horrible man as she knocked at his door to sell her wares, and he took advantage of her. Jenny, the scumbag raped her." Michelle was teary.

Jenny gasped. That would explain the illegitimate child. "Go on, so my ancestor may have been a baron, eh? What else did he say."

Michelle blew her nose while nodding.

Jenny could see how this affected her.

"Jennifer eventually escaped, but by then, it was too late. Having been raped, she was ruined. To make matters worse, she had sold another cheese on the way to the house and had been given forged notes in payment. She handed this change to the baron when he purchased the cheese that his chef had ordered. According to the duke, she had never seen paper money before and had no idea they were fakes. The baron who had just raped her then accused her of forgery and had the Bow Street Runners arrest her. Again, according to the duke's letter, Billy then arrived. Duke Felix writes that he only knew this part of the story as he met with her in prison the following morning. By then, she had already been tried and sentenced to fourteen years of transportation to New Holland, or New South Wales as it was known then. "While she had been selling her cheeses, her cheese agent met with the duke to make arrangements for their upcoming meeting. He visited her in Newstead Prison instead because she could not come to him. He eventually took her and the two families under his wing. He acknowledged that it was from his demand that she was in London and therefore, that she had been put in this situation, and he must have felt some responsibility."

Jenny was aghast. "Oh, poor girl, how horrible?"

Michelle nodded. "Well, there was little more in the letter, but I looked into the cheese that he mentioned, and it became a well-known and very popular brand in London, including on the king's table. This must have been due to the duke's patronage, or so I thought. I googled it and found a mention of this incredible product, which was known as the *Kellow Blue,* or its official name, the *Southern Belle* cheese, and there was a Royal Warrant for it. "

Jenny was stunned. "Jennifer was a cheese maker? Really? Gramps always said something about dairy being in the blood, but I never asked him what he meant. I wonder if Dad knows anything?"

Michelle nodded. "The article I found mentioned that the King himself had demanded the history of the product after a conversation with a member of the aristocracy; I'm guessing that man was the duke as he's written so much about her. I discovered the roots of this gourmet cheese go back to a young girl in a small family dairy in Cornwall. Jenny, this must have been your Jennifer."

Jenny agreed that this was possible. "Is there any way to see if there is a link?"

The wicked grin on her friend's face told her that she already had. Michelle was nodding vigorously. "Remember, Mum was an archivist at the State Library. Well, while there, she kept a journal of interesting finds she had to catalogue. There were heaps of irrelevant notes, which I admit I became bored reading, but she must have remembered your visit but had lost your number. In the margin of her last book, I found Kellow underlined a few times. One page was full of notes and journals, all under the Kellow name. Duke Felix wrote to Governor Macquarie and sent a letter of introduction outlining her story, conviction and relationship to… wait for it, one Billy Williams." Michelle punched the air. They had found the record of Jennifer's marriage to William Williams some years before at St John's Parramatta. Both girls had been surprised to see that both were not only literate but both had beautiful handwriting. "Mum also found this." She held a drawing by Henry Lawson of a dairymaid.

Jenny smiled, remembering the lovely lady. "Your mum contacted us a few times but never found much."

Michelle shook her head. "She didn't. She had taken notes about her conversations with your mum. Then, when Mum got sick and died so quickly, we didn't have much time for anyone else but us. Her diagnosis must have been just after this discovery. She has, however, written the references of where the letters are." Michelle's eyebrows raised in query. "Interested in looking for some? They are now online."

Jenny gave her sister-in-law a friendly arm punch. "What the heck do you think?"

For the following hour, they discovered a wonderful collection of material about the Government Dairy at the back of Government House in Parramatta. It tied Jennifer Kellow to Elizabeth, or Betty Eccles, as she preferred to be called. They found information that although Betty had been the housekeeper when Jennifer arrived, she quickly moved into the dairy and stayed there until her death. However, she had been taught how to make cheeses from an unnamed Cornish dairymaid assigned there before marrying and moving to their own dairy. A building with a cool room had been constructed nearby, and this stored and aged the cheeses.

There was little information about the Kellow Williams cheeses except for a reference here and there to the quality of the local product vastly improving after 1821.

The marriage registration between them was in both the St John's register and the Births, Deaths, and Marriages files. Four children were born to the couple in Parramatta. Jenny knew all that and had all that information. They did, however, also find mention of Mr and Mrs Rankin. They were a Scottish couple who had first lived in Van Diemen's Land and moved to New South Wales about the time that Jennifer and Billy's first child was born in 1822.

Michelle caught her breath. "Hey Jenny, look at this. A footnote in the history of the cheese file mentions the Rankins and the fabulous cheeses they made. We know that Jennifer was in Parramatta and assigned to the dairy there. I think that any link must be through hunting that way."

Both returned to the research, Michelle scrolling through the internet and Jenny reading the books.

The hunch paid off. "Da dar! Found her. Listen…" Jenny had been looking through some of the resources Mrs Fox had left Michelle. Jenny was obviously excited. She said, "Your mum found another few letters from Duke Felix to the Macquaries. They were unread as they had arrived after they had sailed in early 1822. She found them nearly two hundred years after Macquarie died; she opened the letter and saw it was again about Jennifer. She had marked it in red in her book. Listen, Michelle, the duke says the usual greeting and preamble, but then, and I will quote, "*…the first of the six months' cheeses have arrived in perfect condition, and while they do not compare with the Southern Belle, their quality is exceptional, and they were well appreciated by those at the King's table last evening. As requested, I hear that Jennifer has trained various new ladies in her skills. I heard from her, and she mentioned that Mr and Mrs Rankin from Scotland will now go* *into production in Bathurst. She also mentioned that Captain and Mrs Piper and Mr Innes had also been coming for lessons in the cheesemaking art, and the cheeses were already being sold in the colony to the appreciation of many. Her last letter informed me that your housekeeper, Betty Eccles, is now so obsessed with this new skill Jennifer has taught her that she has left you as a housekeeper for work in the dairy full time. According to Jennifer, Betty intends to spend her days separating cream and caressing cheeses. This made me laugh greatly. I'm guessing that Jennifer provides ample supplies for your table."*

Jennifer chuckled and said to Michelle, "You said there was a link to Betty and the Rankins. Now we've found them."

Michelle had exhausted her searches. "Is there more?"

Jenny scanned the letter and gasped. "Is there what! Listen!" She kept reading.

"My so-called silent partnership in the Kellow Williams Dairy in Cornwall now involves me more than I ever anticipated.

I will let you be the first to know that Jennifer's sister, Isla, has accepted my hand in marriage. I have written to Jennifer to let her know, too. Having seen the capers and behaviour of those in society, I am of the mind to retire from it and live in the simplicity of the wilds of the Cornish Coast with my beloved. I adore the straightforwardness of the village and that life is so uncomplicated. Lachlan, I now understand your desire to return to the wild islands of Scotland. By the time you receive this, we shall be married."

Jenny met Michelle's astounded gaze to each other at this news, making them both laugh.

Jenny said, "The duke married Jennifer's little sister? Ooh, I bet that did not go down well in London. A peasant and a duke, that's hilarious!"

There was another reference in the journal, and it was linked to another letter written that same week in the same handwriting.

Jenny clicked it, and it contained another previously unopened letter from the duke; however, it was addressed to Perry White. An old note mentioned that Perry had left the colony with no forwarding address.

Both ladies leaned over the screen and read the following letter. The crest on the paper showed the link. This, too, was from the duke.

Michelle noticed that her mother had penned a note on the back of the envelope before it had been scanned.

"Possibly Earl of Collingsford, who was later Duke of Cheatham, as the names match? Perry is Peregrin, and Katy is Catherine. The children's names are also correct, and some were certainly born in Parramatta under the name of White. Katy arrived as a convict."

Michelle squealed with glee as she read the note. "All these earls and dukes! Perry was an earl and later a duke. Pity, none are in your bloodline, Jenny."

Jenny chuckled. "Blow them, give me a cheese maker any day! Read on, Michelle."

"My very dear Perry,

I hope this makes it to you before you leave to return home. If not, then I shall fill you in on your arrival. I hope you are joining Lachlan on his return voyage. I have just written a letter to him, and although I am not sure when you leave, I look forward to renewing our friendship.

Perry, Jennifer's little sister, Isla has accepted my hand in marriage, and as you can imagine, this has set the cat amongst the pigeons in London. I expected Mother to be particularly distressed as Isla will be the first from non-blue-blooded stock in the family tree for two hundred years. However, I invited Mother to see the cheese factory, and she realised that the dairy was not what continually drew me. This young lady has more deportment and refinement in her little finger than most of the other London ladies put together. Mother was even won over to the point that she encouraged me to offer for her. After what occurred to Jennifer, I refused to let Isla come to London to meet her. I arranged for Mother to stay at my cottage in Newlyn, and I was stunned to find that rather than reject her, Mother embraced her. I suppose as I am approaching forty, she was just pleased to see me marry.

Isla is twenty this year, and I am eighteen years her senior. Yet, in many things, she is far more worldly-wise than I.

My darling Isla has a way of looking at life that makes me rethink all my priorities, and I realise that all that I have achieved is pointless. She is not impressed with wealth or fancy jewellery, but if I tell her I have purchased a new box of books for the children at the village school, she throws her arms around my neck and thanks me as though I have given her diamonds. Which I, of course, have, but she told me it was too big, and she made me swap the ring for one she could wear while working. I didn't return it but purchased another one for her.

Perry, this is so new for me. Consequently, last week, I supplied the entire school with new slates and installed a large chalkboard for the classroom in the new school I have just built for them. Her joy was great. The elderly minister has chosen two new teachers and will personally continue the education of the senior students.

Isla laughs at my attempts to do the simplest things. The first time I tried milking was a dismal failure until her hands closed over mine, and the massaging action of bringing the milk down and squirting it into the pail was the most sensual feeling I had ever experienced. However, it was because of this dear girl that I have reviewed my life. I may well be a Duke, and she a mere milkmaid, but in my eyes, she is a queen amongst women.

Dear friend, when I read of our friend Sam's possible plan to turn his mansion in West Sussex into an orphanage for the by-blows of the aristocracy, I was astonished and yet delighted. I will offer what assistance I can do and garner support for his work. Our time together at Christ's Hospital School was full of happy memories for me. Sam had a bad time at home, but I never knew the reason. Contact me as soon as you return, dear friend.

Perry, I wondered why there was no mention of Jennifer's special cheeses in your news sheets until Jacob said they were all being sent home. I thought that she may have kept some for sale there even though she assured me that she would not do so. I thought that she would sell some over there. She apparently does, but they are only plain cheeses with no branding.

The Jennifer Belle *carried a consignment of the new twenty-pound wheels, and*

Bertram and Angelina Tremayne will sell them in London as more of the gourmet cheeses. They no longer have to do the markets as they have opened up a store on the lower floor of their home. The Blue waxed Southern Belle *cheese that I sent Lachlan now brings in £100 for a ten-pound half-size wheel. A queue awaits each shipment, and it is a sight to behold the chefs fighting over the small quantity of the delectable treat. Chefs who battle over a recipe for a simple sauce stand side by side in the rush to collect the next gourmet offering that arrives from Cornwall. I never let on that the inventor is a slip of a girl who is now serving time in the colony. I merely said that the product was so good that, as a silent partner, we intend to keep the supply of the gourmet cheese consistent. My endorsement alone has brought new wealth to the surrounding villages. Not all are happy with the new attention, as I think some are still participating in smuggling, but all have benefited. Even the mines are now better supervised and far safer than before. The one I purchased on my first visit is now back open and is being worked safely. Air is now pumped into the mines, and working conditions are as safe as I can possibly make them. I am ploughing the profits back into the area. Hence the new school building.*

Perry, these people have become my people. How can I have never seen this side of life? My eyes were closed to many things before. They are now open to the lot of the poor in this land. What amazes me most is that the poor around me seem to be happier than the wealthy with whom I previously socialised. Here in Cornwall, I live in shirt sleeves and breeches and wash in the sea. I do not bring my valet but do have a cook and housekeeper. I am invigorated, my friend!

The last letter from Jennifer informs me that even though she is again heavy with child, their own dairy is producing the most wonderful creamy milk, and she is busy experimenting with new flavours for the next batch of cheeses. Someone gave her some dried truffles; she is currently experimenting with them.

Our mutual friend, your Major Ned Grace, as he chooses to call himself, sourced ten more girls from the women's gaol for them. More are promised as the need arises. I saw Ned's parents at the opening of Parliament, then later, after many conversations with him, Charles, Duke of Gracemere, spoke on the continuing use of children in the mines. Ned's brother, David, quickly married Ned's ex-fiancé. No wonder he broke off their relationship! If this woman's reputation is anything to go by, I wonder if any children they have will be his. This woman is one of the new breed of women that society is permitting to infiltrate their ranks. She has no morals! She introduced me to her cousin, and she is of the same ilk. No wonder I chose to marry a milkmaid."

His words made Michelle gasp.

Jenny was weeping softly as she read the lines of the letter. The salty drops had dribbled down her cheeks unnoticed.

This one letter had answered so much for them. They had found no record of the Kellow Williams cheeses in the newspapers because none were sold here under that name. The Governor's table must have been the only one to have tasted the products. They had discovered that, back then, a top cheese brought two shillings per pound. Jennifer's cheeses now brought in hundreds of pounds for the top-grade ten-pound half-wheels. Jenny could read no more.

The tears blurred the screen.

Michelle hugged her friend. They had met over this puzzle years ago, and her own mother had provided the answer, and they had never realised. "Are you all right, sweetie?"

Jenny nodded. "Yes, but I can't read the words anymore. Can you?" She sniffed.

Before Michelle took over finishing the duke's letter to Perry, she said, "You know I've heard of this Major Ned Grace before. His name crops up as the assigning soldier for many of the youngest convict women. From what I gather, he had safe houses all over the New South Wales colony. His name first appeared on the day after he arrived. He had signed out three convicts. There were two men and a woman, two of whom went to a man named Perry White. I presume it's the same person. It appears that Ned was here under a false name if I read between the lines in Duke Felix's letter and Mother's notes on the back. Major Ned left in 1842 after transportation finished. He married shortly before leaving, and I found he, too, was titled. He had just become the Duke of Gracemere and signed the marriage register as such."

Jenny blew her nose and nodded. Nothing would surprise her today.

Michelle mused, "I counted one day, and there were about sixty girls assigned to what was marked as safe houses. I have come across a few myself. There was Mrs Walker out along the Hawkesbury River and the Lacey's farm out near Mulgoa, which also had hired some dairy maids. There are a few rectories recorded that took the younger girls, and even an inn at Emu Plains that took short-term placements, and of course, there were two inns in town that gave refuge to the abused women."

Jenny gasped. "You're kidding!"

Michelle noted Jenny's astonishment. "I only found out about that from an article in the newspaper. This man, Charles Lockley from the Jolly Sailor Inn, was one of the first two men Ned assigned to Perry White. Charles later became an innkeeper and a man of note in the town, which included running Government Stores for the governor. I found later references to him being an earl, so there may even have been a connection between Ned and Charles. Charles had married the lady convict Ned assigned to Perry the same day. The article said that Sal and Charles had a safe room under their inn nearly two centuries before it became popular to help those experiencing domestic violence. Belting up your wife didn't even have a name back then. The newspaper article said that Charles and Sal were accused of running a brothel and taken to court more because they thought he was serving drinks on a Sunday. They had two very interesting character referees. One was Reverend Samuel Marsden and the other was Reverend Cowper. These two reverend gentlemen endorsed the Lockleys' work. Like your family, I gather these two convicts were people of faith. They certainly put it into action. Jenny, this man, Ned, really sounds like he would be interesting to know more about. It sounds like he was the second son of another duke when he arrived."

Jenny dried her eyes and agreed whilst chuckling. "Now that we've discovered more about Jennifer, Charles, Perry, and Ned, what might be our next projects? Now finish the letter, please. There are still some things I want to know." She was still holding the Henry Lawson drawing of the milkmaid. She glanced at it and smiled. She wondered if it looked like Jennifer.

Michelle found her place and kept reading. As her eyes skimmed the next paragraph, she said, "Cor, Jenny, wait until you hear this! He mentions Kit's father."

That comment made Jenny wipe her eyes, sit up and take note. "Who is he?"

Michelle giggled. "Patience, my dear, patience!"

One of the other staff brought in mugs of coffee for them. With a nod of thanks, Jenny picked up her coffee. The girls each took a sip of the steaming brew and returned to the unfinished letter.

Michelle scrolled down and kept reading.

"Perry, if Jennifer had remained here, then Kit's father, that appalling man, Baron George Mortonford, would have claimed his son, educated him, then dropped him like a hot brick when he reached his majority. The lad may well have ended up in a place like Sam's proposed school. Mortonford is still banished from society; if I have any say, he shall not return. I did inform him that he has a son. Thankfully, I still have some pull in society. Even His Majesty was disgusted at the behaviour of one of the peers of his realm. He took me aside when he realised I knew why the baron had vanished.

As Jennifer will soon be my sister-in-law, I find that forgiveness for his disrespectful actions toward her almost unforgivable. This black spot of anger sits uncomfortably in my heart. I have seen him a few times on visits to Malvern Hall down near your cousin Sam's place. Duke James Malvern tells me I must forgive him, and although I know this to be true, I find releasing that anger extremely difficult."

Jenny was reeling. "Kit's father is really a baron?" She released a long sigh. "It sounded like the duke insisted that he financially support Kit."

Michelle agreed.

Jenny saw there was more to the letter. "Does it say anything more about Jennifer?"

Michelle shook her head. "No, but I'll read it anyway."

"Perry, I saw your father at the House of Lords last week. He's well and misses you all. He's looking forward to you all coming home. He and your Mama are well, and he told me about a family of girls you sent him. He said to tell you that the Livingstone family have been rescued and have taken over his dairy. He's asked if I had any hints about cheese-making for them, and I suggested that he come to Cornwall and see for himself. He mentioned they would visit their cousin in West Sussex soon and may come down to us while there. He, of course, will not be told any of the special secrets, but even plain cheese has tricks in making it nice. I have become a dab hand at it myself.

On a slightly different tack, my work with our friend Elizabeth Fry had exploded.

Many of our peers have joined the cause. Her work is incredible, and I find that the more I assist the abused women she helps, the better I feel. Perry, when you come home, we will need you to assist in the next arm of my project. Through these abused women, we have discovered that many have turned to the streets as they have absolutely no other option to make ends meet. Often, their husbands are injured soldiers and sailors unable to work again. We must find a way to retrain them so they can find work. We shall discuss this in detail on your return. Perry, I know you hid your burnt face for years, and I know from Lachlan that you are accepted in the colony because of them, but these soldiers here will also identify with your wounds. Think about this, my friend. God can use you here, too.

Your brother in Christ
Felix Shesham"

Nearly the entire story of Jennifer Kellow's mystery seemed now unravelled from these two undelivered letters. Only a few questions were left, and one was about their farm. Another was why they vanished from local records, as the girls knew convicts could not return home. They had found no records of any deaths. They had just gone. But also, were there still Kellows here if the Williams' had gone? And why did Jennifer's convict conviction have a line through it? She still had no idea what their farm was called or where it was.

They now knew from the information they had found that Jennifer had first spent time in the old gaol and had moved into the Female Factory for a month before marrying Billy. However, it was unlikely she ever returned as an inmate as she was found on the staff list. She had thirteen years to serve after the dairy herd arrived. Then, records of the family just ceased. That was a puzzle for another day.

Jenny took the copy of the drawing of Henry Lawson's milkmaid and planned to frame it.

Chapter 20 A Legacy of Culture 1834

*L*ife for the Williams family in Parramatta was a delight. Kit was only six months old when Jennifer realised she was expecting again. Billy's joy was evident. The fair-haired cherub was a delightful infant that everyone cherished. Delen and Bryn adored Kit, but this new baby would be their first blood grandchild.

Their dairy had become a training farm for many girls at the gaol. Major Ned Grace was still there, frequently bringing them the youngest new arrivals to keep safe. Through an endorsement from Duke Felix, Ned had become a good friend. Jennifer was now listed as a staff member of the dairy and the Female Factory, so she could come and go at will.

On the whole, Parramatta was a wonderful place to live and work. However, on October 28th 1827, Jennifer and the girls were hard at work for the morning milking when the sound of shouts, musket fire, and running feet made her leave the cream vat to see what had occurred. She noticed a large group of convict women heading towards them. She knew many of them, as she took a class at the Female Factory once a week. She taught them how to care for cows. Many girls interested in dairy work were added to a roster of learning how to milk a cow and the general dairy requirements.

Once trained, these girls would be sent to Doctor Harris's new growing dairy on his farm in Ultimo or to other private residences that now had their own house cows. Every outlying homestead also needed someone to milk a cow and make butter. One was Lacey's farm out along the Nepean River, where they were also beginning to make plain cheeses. Numerous rectories were springing up in new areas, and Ned placed his young proteges in these safe houses. The girls' dairy skills could also be translated to goats and even sheep, should that be required. Milking techniques varied little between the various animals; the milk, however, had different uses. Goat's milk made better soft cheese, but cow's milk was easier to separate, and the cream made better hard cheeses.

Today, the convict girls had come to seek refuge at the only place they knew they would be safe. Jennifer stood waiting to hear what had occurred. On arrival, they told Jennifer and Betty about a riot that was underway at the Female Factory, and rather than stay and be accused of destruction of the property there, these girls had come to seek shelter where they would be protected.

Jennifer and Billy permitted nearly fifty of the unaccompanied women to take refuge in the dairy for some hours before Billy went to find Ned. She set them to weeding the herb garden, but she told them they must return voluntarily or they would never be permitted to return to the dairy.

All agreed willingly, but only when it was safe.

Delen and Jennifer fed them bread and cheese as hunger seemed to be part of the cause of their escape; then, after the gardening was done, they set them to work milking the herd.

A few years after their dairy opened, one of the cows became an escape artist. This gentle horned beast they had named Daisy, but to her, the grass was always greener anywhere than where she was supposed to be. Unable to keep her fenced in, Jennifer offered her to the Female Factory. There was a walled courtyard that was an airing yard for the convict women's work. The high stone fence that surrounded it had two small doors and would be escape-proof for the horned bovine absconder. She had sat in there to feed Kit. The high walls blocked out the noises.

While Delen minded the younger children, Billy and Jennifer had to walk the cow down the dusty road to the gaol. Kit insisted on accompanying them, and as Daisy was a passive cow, he rode on her back for the journey. While there, Jennifer decided to show them two small carved crosses she had found.

Daisy took up residence in the yard and was attended to by a roster of girls learning their trade. Having the sole care of a cow was a good learning experience for them. The milk from her was consumed at the prison. They learned to settle the milk and skim the cream to make butter.

Most of the cream and soft cheeses were still supplied from the Government Dairy, along with any extra milk required. Over the years, new stoneware flasks had been sourced, and these each held about five gallons. Depending on the number of occupants, up to twenty gallons of milk were consumed daily at the Female Factory alone.

A very flustered-looking Ned called into their dairy mid-afternoon, and he and Billy escorted the escaped girls back down to the gaol. Some of the more trusted girls in the group were encouraged to tell Ned the reasons behind the riot.

Jennifer heard only a little of the story, but for some reason, Matron had swapped salt for sugar, and this had been the proverbial straw on the camel's back. The riot ensued.

That night, the matron quit, and by the following day, a new one had taken her place. Jennifer had no idea if this was planned or an emergency placement, but realised that Daisy would not have been milked that day,

Jennifer entered through the small door leading into the walled drying courtyard. As she had done so many times, her eyes fell on the two small etchings carved into the sandstone blocks. As the crosses were at eye level, they were hard to miss. From the first time she had entered this yard the week Kit was born, her fingers were drawn to the convict maker's mark. The carver's marks were both of the sign of a cross, and she found her fingers tracing the shapes each time she entered. The first time she did it had been before she married Billy. She had found this safe yard where she could feed Kit in privacy.

The first time she had fingered these, the newly hewn sandstone was rough under her fingers, having only been carved the previous year. She had seen some people in church crossing themselves and wondered if the carver was one of the Irish Catholics who had been sent out here. Over the years, she repeated this simple caress of the stone whenever she entered this area.

The etchings had become smooth in the years since her arrival, so she presumed she was not the only one to be enthralled by this small tribute to God. She smiled as she thought of this and wondered how long they would last. One day, Kit would be tall enough to touch them by himself. As she entered the yard today, her fingers traced the dips in the stone; she looked at the pair of crosses and wondered how many there did the same thing. Alone in the large yard, Daisy came to her, and she sat down on the small stool she carried and milked the gentle cow into the pail that was ready and waiting.

Jennifer spoke to the warm beast as she milked, and Daisy lowed as a *thank you* when Jennifer had finished. Realising she must be lonely, Jennifer wondered if she should take her home soon. Hopefully, she would stop breaking out of the fenced paddocks. If nothing else, she would need to put her in calf soon.

Betty Eccles had now taken over the Government Dairy, and she continued the instruction of the artesian craft of making fresh cheeses. Their cheese cave had not fared well in a recent flood, and although the stock of wheels had been rescued, they now resided in the Government larder under the house.

The governor had decided not to continue with the aged cheeses in a cheese cave. They moved the stock from his cellar into the Williams' dairy.

Other students had come and gone, and one couple, the Rankins from Scotland, had arrived with some knowledge of the industry.

Jennifer was able to give them many hints she had learnt about making cheeses in the hotter climate of New South Wales and also about smoking the cheese for less time due to the strength of the flavour of the local wood. She only ever taught about plain cheeses and the fresh, ready-to-eat ricottas, cottage cheese and the like. The Scottish couple had recently moved to the new town of Bathurst and planned to set up a cheese dairy industry there.

Jennifer still had many years to serve, and their future seemed to be settled in the area.

Six months after the arrival of Bryn's herd, new cheese wheels appeared for sale at the markets. The varieties and qualities of these products were vastly superior to what had previously been available. The quality of this product was mentioned in the newspaper, and the price doubled. The first of their unflavoured hard cheeses were now ready for sale, and although not a named variety, they were given rave reviews in the newspapers. The normal price of cheese was 1s 6d per pound. However, the cheapest of the Williams Kellow plain cheeses available was bringing in 2s 6d per pound for a cut twenty-pound weight wheel. Few could afford an entire wheel, and the wedges were cut into blocks and sold in wrapped beeswaxed cheesecloth and all pre-weighed and priced. Their first foray into the local cheese was deemed a success.

The new light blue, triple-flavoured cheese was not sold locally, however, Governor Macquarie carried two of the first ripe wheels to take home to England. Perry and Lachlan and their families departed on a vessel in February 1822, and they had stowed the precious cheese carefully. Jenifer had waxed the first of their mature cheeses for consumption on the journey. They carried another for Duke Felix and the other to be eaten on the voyage.

Molly and Jennifer had promised to write and tell the Macquaries and the Whites about the news once their children were born. Molly and Bill had finally conceived, and Molly and Jennifer were due about the same time. Katy White hugged each lady twice and shed tears of sadness at their parting. Sal promised she would care for both of them. They were due about the same time, which was around Easter.

~

Bryn Jacob, known as Jack, was born on 25th March 1822. It was the same day Molly and Bill Miller at the Rear Admiral Duncan Inn had their long-awaited first child, Timmy.

Jack was born a little over a year after they married. Jennifer was stunned to find she had fallen again with her second child while still feeding Kit. Their boys were just under fourteen months apart.

Billy could hardly wipe the smile from his face. He had a son. Delen had made him sit in on the birth, and although nervous, it was something he would never let Jennifer do again without him beside her.

Molly had her friend Sal and her mother assist her, while Jennifer had the midwife from the gaol, and Delen helped deliver Jack.

Delen's calm and soothing voice was wonderful, and she knew just where to rub her aching back.

Jennifer was back in the dairy only three weeks after the birth. With so many helpers, the pressure on her eased.

Bryn oversaw the cheese-making in her absence, and Billy ran the rest of the farm and vegetable garden. Delen cared for Kit, and the work went on.

When Lachlan and Elizabeth Macquarie and the White family had left the colony together, their departure had left a hole in Ned's life, and he turned to Charles and Sal Lockley and the Williams family for friendship and fellowship.

Jennifer had admitted to Ned that she knew Perry's secret and wondered when Ned mentioned that he had been at the same school.

A look of almost horror whipped across Ned's face before he smiled. "Duke Felix gave me a hint that you may catch on. Please keep it quiet. I'm a second son, so I joined the army."

Jennifer's smile reassured him. "Trust me. I shall tell no one."

~

The years slid by almost unnoticed.

More children were born, and friendships were forged. Through Duke Felix's letters, Ned became a friend.

Ten years after Jennifer's arrival saw the birth of their fourth child. William Pascoe Williams, known as Will, arrived safely. Billy had been with her through the delivery, and she now lay cradled in his strong arms while cooing over their son. Tears of happiness rolled unnoticed down her cheeks. From the mess she had found herself in London, her happiness here had been unexpected.

Kit was nearly ten, Jack was now eight, Jennifer Delen, known as Del, was six, and Phoebe Isla, called Sis by everyone, was three.

Baby Will was the image of his older brother, Jack. He was dark with Billy's small, centrally dimpled chin.

Kit was fair and looked nothing like his siblings. He was already asking why he looked different, and shortly before Will's birth, Billy had taken Kit for a long walk and explained his story.

Expecting repercussions of rebellion, Jennifer awaited their return anxiously. His response was to throw his arms around her neck and assure her of his love.

Whatever Billy had told him drew him closer to them all rather than driving in a wedge. However, he no longer called Billy *Father*. His new term of *Papa* was much more affectionate and perfectly described their close relationship. They were father and son in all but blood.

In Cornwall, the town saw the refurbishment of the old DeMartini cottage into a lovely home. However, as Duke Felix and Isla now had four of their own children, they were in the process of building a larger house in Newlyn. Even though Felix had enlarged the DeMartini house, they had well and truly outgrown it. They had plenty of rooms for the family, but when his mother came for one of her frequent visits, her staff had nowhere to stay. Duchess Evelyn had never had to do anything *earthy,* as she called milking. The experiences of real life in Cornwall were grounding for her, and surprisingly, the Dowager Duchess relished her new, simpler way of life in the warmer climate of Cornwall. Summers there became a delight for her.

Isla adored her mother-in-law. The older lady was learning to look at life through new eyes. Isla taught her how to milk a cow. The regal lady was spattered with the unmentionable by-product of the cow's nether end before managing the first squirt of milk. From that tiny achievement, the Dowager Duchess was hooked.

Isla, of course, had the opposite experience; she had to learn to live in the other world. From a Cornish dairy, she had to brave the judgemental London Society.

Few, if any, knew her background, and when asked, she bluffed. "Yes, I come from Cornwall. And yes, it is full of miners, dairymaids, and fishermen. Do you think I grew up in a dairy or something?" She would completely flummox the enquirer, leaving their question unanswered. Sometimes, she would throw her hands in the air and mutter, *"Quanto sei stupido?"* Which was Italian for *How silly are you?* Then she would walk off.

Felix would smile as he watched on. He was absolutely besotted with his Cornish dairy maid, and everyone could easily see that.

After every such incident, every time she returned home, she collapsed into Felix's arms, laughing.

Isla was the Duchess of Shesham and had quickly learnt how to use her position in society. Felix was her champion in everything, and no one questioned her further.

Society knew that the duke was part owner in a Cornish dairy, but details beyond that were zero. They were known as Beauty and the Beast.

Visitors to their area were not encouraged, not that Felix had many friends. As there was no accommodation anywhere, no one could stay even if they did visit.

The staff had been sworn to secrecy about her birth status, but they adored their new mistress and her down-to-earth manners. She was not above doing some cleaning for herself rather than complaining if she saw something had been overlooked. She never called them out or growled at them, but it was more than that. She cared. Isla would send a maid to bed for the day if her monthly flow was causing pain, and she would make sure all her grooms, footmen, and drivers were well rugged up when their jobs required them to be outdoors. Even on a carriage trip, their staff were well cared for. Especially when travelling in cold weather. Hot bricks were ordered for them, and each coachman was gifted with new all-weather oiled sheepskin coats that would keep them warm in a blizzard.

By the time Isla had only been in London for a week, she already knew the names of all the staff, who their families were, and where they all came from.

Things in the household changed as more staff were employed, and each was encouraged to have a week off every three months to visit their homes and families. This period was chosen as it was as long as Isla could stand being without her family. This holiday time was also on full pay.

Felix had enough money to permit this luxury, and he was surprised to find the benefit this had in his household. The staff were happier. Even when he added some of the waifs and strays he and Isla had come across, they were embraced and shown the ropes of working in the big houses and estates the duke owned.

The poor houses were visited, but charity was not offered; love, care, and compassion were given. Isla did not use her title of duchess when she visited orphanages or workhouses. She became the dairymaid again and was known to them as Isla Shesham. She would spend a half-day at each venue, meeting the children and seeing the needy. Her visits were always followed by a large shipment of whatever was required by the occupants.

Once the London season was finished in August, they did a round of the duke's other estates before retiring to Cornwall for some months.

While Felix did the required business on each estate, she did the rounds of each village. She noticed things like the destitute widows and their rotting roofs; she saw the poorly clad children. Each she set to rights. Each estate manager had to justify their lack of oversight of the poor and needy. She quickly learned that the village minister or, if they didn't have one of those, the midwife was the two venues to find her required information about the village's needs.

Felix had never seen the state of the poorest villages and was ashamed when she ventured into the squalor of the most destitute areas. They were places he had previously avoided rather than did anything to fix the problem.

The first time she had encountered one of these tiny hamlets, she had come home in tears and flung herself into Felix's arms. Her eyes were red and swollen, and she was distraught. "Felix, I went to Swithern Balsam today and found this wretched village on our land. They are starving, and their houses are falling down around them; their well is dry, and oh Felix, we need to do something immediately."

Felix cradled his weeping wife. He murmured against her clean, lemony hair, "I ordered that place to be abandoned years ago. I built new houses and a school, but my darling, I never followed it up, but we will not leave until it is put in order."

After a short discussion, Isla ordered that the food being prepared for their meal that day be loaded onto a cart and taken directly to Swithern Balsam's village well, such as it was. The well had been dry for years, and the area was overgrown. Everyone at the big house would eat bread and cheese tonight while the villagers ate like kings.

From the supply they had on hand, warm clothing was also sent to the thirty destitute folks living there.

From that day onwards, things changed all over the Ducal estates. Each manager was put on notice and now had to supply a monthly detailed report.

Felix called in his estate manager and spoke about this village, and the man was hauled over the coals as to why this situation had not been brought to Felix's notice. Rather than dismiss him, Felix knew he lived alone in a large grace and favour house on the estate but had no family. He was moved into staff quarters, and his home was forfeited. The villagers of Swithern Balsam were soon housed in new abodes, with the sickest brought into the big house until they were well enough to care for themselves in new homes.

In the decade since the Sheshams married, many of their tenants had learnt Isla's secret, and none were prepared to betray her. Isla was a commoner and considered one of them, but she also stayed true to herself. She lived the faith that she had learnt at the feet of their minister. Like Jennifer, her education had astounded Felix. He had only ever had the head knowledge of faith. However, the Kellow family lived it, and Isla's Biblical history astounded him. She was fluent in Italian and French and also read a little Greek and Latin. It was her fluent Italian that had confused society. For surely no Cornish milkmaid would be so well educated and be able to fit into society so easily. Her passion for the ancient world meant that discussion with his peers was always unexpected. Dancing had been the one area she had no experience in, and Felix had delighted in educating her in that.

Isla's faith and simple views of life drew Felix on the very first visit to Cornwall. She didn't just believe in Christ and His teachings; she lived them. It had not taken long to realise that he had to make the decision to risk the social suicide of marrying not only a commoner but a peasant. Not that she was a typical peasant. Isla was far from typical on any level of society. It had taken him less than a year to overcome society's prejudice, but once he decided, he never regretted his decision.

Felix thought back to his proposal. His mother eventually took him aside and informed him that if he did not propose to the only lady who had stirred his heart, she would choose one of the silliest debutantes she could find in London next season. Felix had sought out Jacob for permission that very afternoon. He had not even kissed Isla until he proposed. He had walked her to the headland overlooking the bay and proposed on one knee, just missing a cow pat as he did so. For the first time in his life, he felt vulnerable.

The hawk-nosed, winged eyebrow face was cupped in two small hands, and his lips were kissed. Isla grinned as she kissed his lips. Then she stood. Rather than simply replying to him, she shouted her answer to the watching family. "Of course, I said a resounding 'yes'!"

There were shouts of joy, and they could hear the family applauding the reply.

Felix stood and drew her into his arms for a kiss. She felt tiny in his arms, but the protectiveness he felt for her was overwhelming. Felix adored this imp of a girl who had crept into his heart almost unnoticed. She was now vital to his well-being.

They had married quietly only four weeks later in the village church. The ageing Reverend Tyzzer did the service. He sent a notice to the newspaper two weeks after their marriage. They were pleased they weren't in London when word spread.

By 1834, Jennifer's time of servitude was nearly finished.

Billy had not discussed anything with her about their future. She did know that he and Bryn had been summoned to Governor Bourke's office the week before, and although they had come back smiling, he had not said anything to her.

On the fourteenth anniversary of her conviction, Jennifer returned from the dairy tired and looking forward to a nice mug of hot tea. She felt like falling into bed. The younger children would have exhausted Delen, and she knew she had yet to attend to their needs. Kit and Jack were normally helping Billy on the farm or tilling the house garden. Ten-year-old Del and Sis kept their eyes on little Will as they did their chores, combed the fleece, and spun yarn, but they tended to squabble. Everyone had their own chores, and Delen's job was running the household.

As Jennifer drew close to the house, she first noticed the silence. Their farmhouse was never quiet. The noise was constant, with five children and four adults in one building until the children were all in bed. She mounted the wide verandah and sat to pull off her boots. Still, there was silence from inside. She pulled open the new screen door and walked to the sitting room. Hopefully, everyone would be in there. Resigned to waiting for the family to return from wherever they were, she thought she would put her feet up first. As she twisted the handle, she heard Will chuckle. At nearly five, their son could not sit still or stay silent. Church services were somewhat of a chore as she often missed the sermon as she had to take him outside. As the door opened, Jennifer stopped mid-step. Not only the family waited inside, but all the milkmaids from the Government dairy, including Betty Eccles, Bill and

Molly Miller and their four children, Ned Grace, Charles and Sal Lockley, with their six imps and the midwife from the Female Factory. All called *surprise* as she entered the room. Jennifer had never experienced this before and was shocked. Tears threatened to overwhelm her as she sank into the nearest chair.

Billy came to her side and explained they had a big surprise for her. He handed her an envelope, and she recognised Governor Bourke's elegant but sprawling writing. He had often sent her notes of thanks for some new cheese sample she had sent him to taste. Other governors had come and gone in the time they resided in the colony. Each had become friends. Especially since they discovered her brother-in-law was a duke. She turned over the document and noted that it had an official seal. She eased it off and unfolded it.

The silence was almost deafening. Even her youngest remained quiet.

Two words met her gaze: *Absolute Pardon*. She wasn't just free; she could go home. She had expected a *Certificate of Freedom*. But this was astounding.

Billy was on his knees before her. "My sweet Jennifer, I will not presume, but we can go home if you wish." Unable to voice her joy, Jennifer nodded. Billy drew her into his arms and whispered, "We're going home, sweetheart. Home to your family!"

Jennifer was stunned. She would see her parents once again.

At forty-six, Billy's temples were beginning to grey. His physique was still lithe, and he and the two older boys worked hard on their farm. Even Will, at five, was in charge of his beloved chickens, which he called *chookies*. Each had a name and came at his call. Delen and Bryn had aged well. Now in their late sixties, they were beginning to slow down. Cornwall, home, now beckoned them all.

Recalling that they were in the midst of their friends, Jennifer gave Billy another kiss and then elegantly rose to face the multitude of happy faces. She was about to greet their friends when a thought occurred to her. She spun around to face her husband. "Billy, what about the farm? We can't just abandon it."

Billy was expecting this. "We aren't, love; it's why the governor called us in." He called a tall gentleman from the rear of the gathered group. "Darling, Doctor Harris has offered to run the dairy for us as he, too, is making cheeses. The only difference will be that he will not be exporting them. He owns Experiment Farm now and also has stock on the land surrounding Hambledon Cottage, across the creek from Elizabeth Macarthur. He is close enough to oversee the property and farm for us. His dairy there is small compared to the set-up here, so he will use our cheese cave. We will take our special cows home."

Jennifer knew this man well. He had been a friend of Perry and Katy White. The two men had arrived on the *General Hewitt* in 1814, and Perry had introduced him many years ago.

With the farm's future now settled, Jennifer circulated through the room with the ease and grace befitting someone from the upper class. The grooming and deportment lessons that Angelina DeMartini had given both her and Isla had held her in good stead all her life. Isla had blended into High Society with barely a ripple. Her letters were filled with hilarious antics of playing both sides of the unwitting upper echelons of English Society. However, when Felix and Isla returned to Cornwall, they were the happiest.

The last letter from Isla said that they had moved into their new house and wondered what to do with the lovely old home they had enjoyed so much. Isla had left the question unanswered.

Jennifer now wondered if Billy and Felix had already planned this. Her loving look across the room to him made her pause and draw in her breath. He stood leaning against the mantlepiece, gazing at her in adoration. It was written all over his face. Since she was little, he had never wavered in his love.

After some minutes, Jen managed to draw close to Billy once again.

His arm slid around her still-trim waist; he bent close and said, "Jen, I would sell the farm, but I feel Kit may wish to return. His life in England will be difficult at best; here, he fits in. He is a sensitive boy, and after much discussion, Felix and I have enrolled him at Eton. He will be there under the name of Williams and as Duke Felix's nephew. If John Harris can keep the farm going for five to ten years, Kit can return if he wishes. Oh, and we will be moving into Felix's old house, Angelina's place."

Words deserted her. She rested her head on his chest. Finally, she managed to whisper, "Thank you."

Jennifer's eyes rested lovingly on her eldest child. The lad was so different to his siblings in looks; however, he had not an ounce of resentment in him. They had told him four years earlier why his name and looks were so different, and he bore the stigma of his birth with grace. Ned had taken him under his wing, and the two often joined the Lockley family on some outings. Here in the colony, many were in similar situations. By thirteen, he was already at eye level with Billy. Jack and Will were probably going to be as tall as their father. Billy stood head and shoulders over most of his friends except Ned and Charles Lockley, who were eye to eye with Billy. She didn't remember much about her encounter with the baron, except that due to his superior size, she had no chance of escape when he attacked her. In that, Kit was like him. He also had his father's light colouring. His fair hair and deep blue eyes vastly differed from his brother's dark complexion. Although her own eyes were pale blue, Billy's were brown, and three of their children favoured him; only Sis had light brown hair like hers.

~

September 30th, 1834, saw the family on the *Harmony* waiting to weigh anchor and sail home. Captain Elley had loaded his cargo of colonial produce, which included all the Williams' cheeses possible from the maturing cave. The remainder of the unripe cheeses had been promised to the governor for his table. Doctor Harris had already overseen the placement of his own cheese stock in the better-built cheese cave.

Jennifer had packed a large tub of lard and a barrel of salt to make brine. The three-month voyage would see the final stage of maturing. Major Ned sent a team of convict men to construct spaced shelves on the lower deck so the cheeses could continue their maturation. He was sad to see them leave, but he still had his work to do there.

Some ingenuity was needed to stop the cheese wheels' movement in heavy seas, and the wheels were stored flat and packed so that they would remain stable unless the ship turned over completely. Even the wheels recently made eight weeks ago were loaded. Caressing and rubbing the wheels would keep the family occupied for the journey.

The colonial dairy was now empty of their valuable produce and waxes. For milk on the voyage, Jennifer and Billy took two of their favourite Jersey cows to milk *en route*. These two cows had become special, and their gentle nature had endeared themselves to Jennifer. Trixie and Bonniebelle also produced an incredible volume of cream.

Their farmhouse was now occupied by two of the orphan English milkmaids who had arrived with the bulk of the herd thirteen years earlier. They had married and had families of their own. The girls were sisters who had married emancipated brothers, and the two couples had lived in a one-room wattle and daub cottage on the estate. The third had married a soldier and moved to Sydney. These two couples would now be caretakers for everything in Kit's absence. They were to be paid well above award wage and did not need to pay rent.

The family found that parting with their friends was hard. Bill and Molly Miller and their four children were the hardest to leave. In the years they had been in the colony, they had grown close. Ned, Sal, and Charles Lockley had also been wonderful friends. The three couples often met after church on the riverbank for a picnic. Their children were all good friends. Bryn and Delen were surrogate parents to them all. Ellen, Molly's mother, and her second husband, Andrew, a doctor, visited often but now lived in England with their two children, and Jennifer promised they would be welcome in Cornwall. She had letters and messages to deliver from Molly.

Charles and Sal Lockley never mentioned any family back home, and as Jennifer didn't wish to pry, she remained quiet. She had learnt long ago never to ask about a person's crime or background. Some offered the information willingly, but most never mentioned their past lives. It was as though they didn't exist. Life here was a new start for many, and they were content to leave the past behind them.

The one friend who had become close was the young soldier who had first escorted Jennifer to and from the Government Dairy. Ned Grace had become a man of trust, and he and Billy had become firm friends. Since Perry and Katy had left in 1822, Charles Lockley hosted the men's Bible study around Perry's vast dining table that now resided at their new inn. Bryn and Billy attended most weeks, along with Bill Miller, and the bond between the small group strengthened through their faith. Others had joined the study or visited when in town. It was this support group that had eased the arrival of the Williams men. Bryn was by far the oldest; Billy was ten years Bill Miller's senior, and Ned and then Charles were each a year or so younger.

Ned oversaw everything. He arranged wagons for their cheeses, sorted transport for the belongings and even booked accommodation at the King's Arms Hotel in Sydney. Their farewells to him were the hardest as he stood alone on the dock as the vessel was towed away from the wharf. His red uniform stood bright in the spring afternoon sunshine, and he stood saluting them as the vessel rounded the headland.

Ned had a particular way of wearing his tricorne hat that almost made it look fashionable. Jennifer wondered about his background but figured that now she would never know; she realised there was a mystery, though, as Ned and Charles may well be related. They even had dimples in the same places. That the two tall blonde men were best friends made some eyebrows raise with interest.

One unexpected final visitor to their farmhouse had been Major-General Sir Richard Bourke. The governor requested that they take some official dispatches with them and handed them a large locked box. He stood, obviously wishing to say more.

"Sir, is there anything more we can do for you?" Billy asked.

Governor Bourke shook his head. "No, thank you, Billy; however, in a way, it's just the opposite." He reached into his inside jacket pocket and drew out an official-looking envelope. Turning to Jennifer, he said, "My dear, when you arrived on a convict ship, you carried with you a letter of introduction to one of my predecessors, which, by the way, he left on file. I want to reciprocate; only my letter is to the King. Your assistance in training many of those now heavily involved in the burgeoning dairy industry has been invaluable to our infant colony. Without the skills that you have taught, we would still be decades away from the quality products now produced here. With your instruction, the South Coast farms are producing excellent cheeses. And while still not as good as the wheels that have graced my table over my term here, they are delicious."

Jennifer bobbed a curtsy as he handed her the envelope. "Thank you, sir, but you do not need to do this. I am just an emancipated convict."

The governor shook his head. "You are far more than that, Jennifer Williams. Never underestimate yourself, dear. When I lost my beloved Betsy, you permitted me to find solace in a small corner of your dairy and watch you work. I knew I was amongst non-judgemental friends. Many would not have permitted that. But that time of peace let my hurting heart heal somewhat.

Over the past two years, my daughter also found friendship with you, and for that, you will always have my gratitude."

They had always intended to leave a gift for the governor. As he said, he had been a regular visitor at the dairy after his wife died. The distracting activity of watching the cheeses being made eased his grief. As Governor Bourke spoke to Jennifer, Bryn and Billy carried the last two mature waxed cheese wheels from the pantry and placed them on the small table next to the vice-regal gentleman. One had a two-tone wax coating.

Now, it was Jennifer's turn to say her thanks. The sad man had learned to cope with the searing loss of his wife. Mrs Bourke lay buried not far from their farm, and it was an easy walk from the cemetery to the dairy. The lowing of the cows had drawn him there soon after the funeral, and he had returned often. Jennifer had come to admire the lonely figure. Her parting gift to him was all she had to give. "I made these two especially for you, sir. These are not our normal cheeses, but these two are the local version of the cheese that His Majesty has issued his Royal Warrant for from our Cornish dairy. Over there, we call them the *Southern Belle*. This is the local version of that cheese. We have been transporting these to Cornwall and selling them as *Southern Belle Blue*. It is similar, but these have a blue vein running through them. There are also twelve more wheels of plain cheese maturing in the cave. Those will not be ready until next year as they have only been made this month, but Doctor Harris will care for them for you."

The governor's eyes twinkled with delight. "This is one of your blue vein cheeses? I remember a sample you brought me of that soon after I arrived. I believe it was from a wheel your family had kept. It was superb."

Jennifer nodded. "Yes, sir. I have shown Betty how to take a culture from it, and she knows how to make the veins in the cheese. Allow her, and only her, to have access to this cheese, please. Her cheeses won't have the same flavour as ours as I have not told her all of my tricks. I have not permitted her access to my secret ingredients, but they will still be better than merely good. We have also put some of our new wheels in your larder. So she will need to access to clarified lard to coat them until they are ripe."

The governor collected his gifts and departed, but not before giving Jennifer an unexpected hug and a peck on her cheek. "Thank you, dear girl."

~

The *Harmony* arrived in London a little over three months after leaving Sydney. Two days before Christmas in 1834, light snow covered the streets. It rarely snowed in London very heavily, so the white blanket was melting before they could disembark.

They wondered how they would get to Cornwall when an elegant carriage pulled up at the quayside. Jennifer then heard the familiar sound of "Jenny," being called as it had in her childhood. Only her sister could embarrass her like that. Her squeal of joy that was heard across the deck made

Jennifer turn towards the source.

Isla and Felix had arrived to welcome them home. With transportation now solved, the family disembarked. Isla embraced her sister; both were in tears.

Jennifer had left on a two-week trip from Cornwall and had been absent for nearly fifteen years. If she had been concerned with how the duke would welcome her, that was quickly abandoned when he initially gave her a bow of acknowledgement, then a big hug of welcome. He and Billy shook hands, and then Felix greeted Delen with a kiss on her cheek, which astounded her. The voyage home had been hard on her; a good hot meal and a bed that didn't move would be marvellous. As they were speaking, more vehicles arrived. One contained Bertram and Angelina.

More greetings ensued, and within an hour, the enlarged family group had left the unloading to the duke's staff and Bertram and Angelina, who were to oversee the unloading of the cheeses and moving them into their storeroom.

Felix piled the family in the first two carriages and accompanied them back to the ducal mansion near St James Park.

The edifice was somewhat overwhelming to Jennifer and the children. The foyer alone was bigger than their house in Parramatta. The divided marble staircase that met her eye brought forth a loud gasp. The red carpet that graced the stairs softened the sound of the multitude now ascending it.

However, Jennifer was happy, as after ascertaining that their parents were well, the sisters clung tightly to each other. They often talked over each other in excitement to relay their news.

At the top of the final bend of the staircase, four children were lined up and waiting to meet their cousins. Rupert, Karensa, known as Kerry, and twins Tristram and Rosen, called Rose, had been forbidden to come to the quay as the day before they had raided the kitchen. The cook's newly baked cherry pie had been partially devoured before their whereabouts were discovered. The four were, therefore, banished to the uppermost floors of the residence. After an initial eying off each other, a maid escorted the cousins to the nursery. Kit and Jack did not think that this sounded inviting. However, Billy had viewed this astounding room before and encouraged them to follow.

Jack did, but Kit chose to remain with Billy and the family.

The nursery was housed in the uppermost loft of the enormous house. The single room stretched from one end of the house to the other, containing everything a young person could dream about. From an indoor, elevated sand pit with complete sets of lead toy soldiers, there were rocking horses, two doll houses with accompanying dolls, an assortment of bears and other stuffed toys, to mechanical marvels that moved when wound up. The nine cousins only took a short time to become firm friends. Rupert and Jack were of an age and soon had the sandpit of soldiers engaged in a battle.

Downstairs, Felix settled his family into the parlour.

The staff had brought in the tea trays, and then, at the wave of his hand, they were finally alone.

The duke had a heavy parchment letter in his hand. "Before we do any more catching-up, I thought you may like to read this." He passed the letter to Jennifer and Billy, who were seated together on a settee.

They dropped their head to read the elegant handwriting of His Majesty King William the Fourth.

They read it through, and then Billy read the most important paragraph to his parents.

"With all due consideration, I have reconsidered your infringement of the law and your crime to have been unworthy of your punishment. Therefore, although many years late, your conviction has been expunged in all records, and I enclose a Royal Pardon. This should have been issued years prior to today; that notwithstanding, your crime, such as it was, has now been erased..."

WR

The letter thanked Jennifer for her work in the colony to start a new export line and the foundations of the now-growing dairy industry.

Knowing what this would mean to her, Billy gently slipped his arm around her and held her close. "You're free, sweetheart." He whispered against her forehead. "Free in more than just serving your time, but in every way. The shadow of your conviction has gone."

Her tear-filled eyes met his, and she merely nodded. While enfolded in his arms, she said so only he could hear, "Some things cannot be erased by this, though, Billy."

She pulled from his arms and looked at her son. Both knew she meant Kit. He would have to live with the prejudice of his start in life forever. Life would not be easy for him as an illegitimate child. This shadow of her past could not be pardoned. She adored her son, but he would forever remind her of everything that had occurred.

Her fifteen-year-old son, who had not joined his siblings, looked up from the other side of the room and met her teary gaze. He understood and gave a subtle nod and a half smile.

Chapter 21 The Way Forward 1834-39

The morning after the family arrived, Felix had his head in the estate books of one of his properties when a knock disturbed him. He had not long finished writing his speech to Parliament about the Poor Laws and was determined to do what he could to assist the underprivileged in London. Isla had opened his eyes to society's greed and how some of his Peers exploited the workhouses for their own purposes. Presuming it would be his footman with tea, he called, "Enter!"

His nephew stood on the doorstep, twisting his hands anxiously. His fair hair had been brushed into the latest style.

Felix beckoned him in. Realising something was eating at the lad; he sat his quill back into the stand. "Kit, come in and close the door."

Kit made his way forward and took the offered seat. He opened his mouth to speak, then closed it again. His nerves were showing.

Felix waited.

After shuffling his feet, he finally said, "Uncle Felix, I wish to meet my father. I dare not ask Mama or Papa, but… well, you know the situation." His embarrassment and confusion were obvious.

Felix realised the lad had been bottling up his raw emotions for some time. As a mid-teen, his voice had already broken, and there was a gentle fuzz of growth on his sideburns, but not what one would call whiskers yet. He looked long and deep at his nephew. Thinking about if he should go behind the lad's parents' backs, he asked, "Why?" He folded his arms and waited for an explosion. It didn't come.

Kit met his gaze with the innocence of youth. "When you only know half of your heritage, you don't really know who you are. I have known of my misbegotten start most of my life, as Papa told me when I was nearly ten. To answer questions about myself, I need to meet my father. Therefore, while I am here in London, I was hoping you could introduce me. I presume he lives here. My parents know little about him." Kit didn't shy away from his uncle's penetrating gaze but met and held it.

With an eyebrow raised, Felix asked, "And if you do meet him, what do you hope to achieve? He only met your mother once. I doubt he could even pick her from a crowd."

Kit's reply was almost instantaneous. "He may not pick her, but I'm sure he would know who I was the minute he saw me. I look nothing like the rest of my family, so I'm guessing I look like him?"

Felix nodded. "You do. I knew him when young, and you are a young version of him at your age."

Kit's face lit up. "Then you'll take me? I wouldn't like to go alone, but Mama wouldn't mind if I went with you."

Felix knew that he would do as his nephew wished. "Will you tell her?"

Kit smiled with relief. "Yes, I will, but not until after the visit. Is that okay?"

Felix nodded. He realised that now was as good a time as any. He knew the baron was in town over Christmas as his wife had banished him, and he had seen him at his club. An unannounced visit would be best in this situation.

The man's wife, a lady whom the baron had compromised years ago and had been forced to marry, had thrown him out. She remained in Sussex with their two children. She had banished him due to his continued philandering, but Felix ensured Lady Mortonford was well cared for.

As Kit stood at eye level with him, his gaze was fixed on his uncle.

Meeting his penetrating stare, Felix asked, "Have you an overcoat?"

Kit's embarrassed shake of his head made Felix aware that the first thing he had to do was arrange suitable attire for the entire family.

He huffed in frustration. "Follow me!"

As they were donning their coats, Felix had issued orders for suitable attire for the family.

Fifteen minutes later, the two fur-coat-clad gentlemen exited the mansion to a waiting carriage.

His butler merely gave a slow nod of assent as though dressing nine persons of varying ages from scratch was a regular occurrence. Isla had often turned to this capable man for many a strange request. This was one of the easier ones.

Felix expected that the house would be overrun with tailors and dressmakers by the time they returned.

The journey to the baron's residence was short and silent.

At home in Parramatta, Kit ran further to make sure a gate was shut. His gaze took in the sight and sounds of the winter morning in London. He intended to have a good look around the town. This morning, his mind was fixated on his father. The swapped change of seasons would take some getting used to, but he would deal with that later.

The small carriage pulled up at a large house. The pocket-sized garden looked uncared for. Not all of the autumn leaves had been removed, and this morning, they were covered in a light dusting of snow.

Kit followed his uncle up the three white marble steps.

The bell was a wooden handle on a wire. Felix tugged it somewhat violently. He waved for Kit to stand behind him.

The clang within was followed by a livery-clad footman opening the door.

Felix stood tall and said, "I am Shesham. Is the baron in?"

The elderly butler knew who the great man was. "Yes, Your Grace, please enter. I shall let His Lordship know you are here." The butler's eyes fell on Kit, and an astonished gasp escaped his lips. He bowed to them both and quickly sought out his master. He would make sure he would listen at the door for this meeting. The butler knocked on the study door a little further along the foyer.

Felix was hard on his heels, and Kit followed close behind.

The butler announced them. "His Grace, Duke of Shesham, to see you, my Lord and, um, a young gentleman accompanies him, sir." A smirk was on his lips. The butler didn't wait for an answer but bowed the two visitors into the room.

Although it was only ten o'clock, the baron was inebriated, and he found focusing difficult. He was swaying as he stood, trying to focus on the visitors. He turned slowly to face the man who had brought about his disastrous marriage. He had interfered with a debutante once too often at a ball and been caught out by her angry mother. Rather than slink off into the country, he found he was married by Special Licence that afternoon. His nuptials had been arranged by Felix.

The baron glared at Felix and wished he could focus enough to see just one of him. He hated him, as this hawk-beaked man had been instrumental in his downfall. The baron grunted and grabbed onto the mantlepiece to steady himself. He had been mulling over returning to his wife and getting some relief for his raging needs. He didn't like the cheap floozies as they laughed at his bent nose. His wife, Gwynne, had been delighted when he married her as she was not from a titled family, and her family was even more pleased. She bore him a son and heir; when she was expecting their second child, she had caught him *delicto flagrante* with a maid in this very room. She left that day, and he had never met his daughter. He had not seen his wife since. Now, as he was stuck in London after the season ended, he drank himself into oblivion every day.

After finally focusing on the hook nose of the duke, the baron angrily said, "What do you want this time, Shesham? I have paid for my crime to your milkmaid and promised to educate the boy at whatever price school you chose." His speech was slurred. He dared not let go of whatever he was holding on to.

Kit stepped out from behind his uncle. "Kit, sir, my name is Kit. Christopher, really, but like the rest of my life, nothing about me is as it seems, is it?"

The baron's mouth dropped open. He saw a young version of himself walking towards him. He blinked, then shook his head to make the approach of the young spectre vanish. He released his hold on the shelf and moved forward to greet his son.

Kit approached his drunken father menacingly. "So you do remember I exist? I wondered. From your comments to the duke, I gather you do acknowledge my existence and even know that am to be educated at your expense?"

The Baron's eyes tried hard to focus. He knew about the boy as he had paid the school fees. He nodded. His bent nose made his flushed appearance worse. Eventually, he realised that the vision approaching him was real. "You are my son? Christopher Mortonford, eh? You have my look about you. I don't remember what your mother looked like, though. Was she fair, too?"

Fire flashed into Kit's eyes. The meek-mannered boy suddenly vanished. His father acknowledged that he didn't even remember Kit's beloved mother. Kit was livid that this drunken sot was his father. "No, Father, I am Kit Kellow Williams, and I am proud of who I have become. I will never use your name, even if I was entitled to do so. I wished to meet you for one reason." He walked close to his father and looked him in the eye. His balled fist crashed into his father's stomach. "This is for what you did to my mother."

The baron doubled over in agony.

Kit did not step back. His fist balled again and smashed into his father's already bent nose. The tone of his voice rasped, "If you ever hurt another girl as you hurt my mother, I will track you down and... and...." His fist balled again for a third punch.

Felix saw the baron's claret flowing freely from the previously bent and, once again, broken nose. He grabbed his nephew's fist before he had the chance to throw another strike. "Enough, Kit!" His nephew had done what he had wished to do to the swine nearly fifteen years before. "I doubt his pretty visage will attract more innocent girls." The man's nose was squashed almost at right angles to normal.

Kit's aim had been perfect.

The baron had said nothing. He sat whimpering on the ground, holding a kerchief to his wobbling, bleeding appendage.

Felix was surprised he had not cast up his accounts.

Kit wasn't finished yet. He may not throw another punch, but he gave his father a tongue-lashing. "I am disgusted to know I have your blood running in my veins, but I will live my life assisting the girls that you and ones like you have ruined." He spat on him, and the glob of spittle landed on his father's cheek. Kit's anger was growing again, and he balled his fist again, ready to knock him out.

Felix realised he was about to throw either another punch or possibly even a kick. A hand clenched on his shoulder. "Kit, never hit a man when he's down, or you will become just like him. This man only picks on those who are weak and vulnerable."

Horror washed over Kit's face. He spun on his heel and headed for the door.

The butler and three footmen did not move quickly enough. They were all caught listening, as were the maids behind them.

Rather than be angry, Kit said loud enough for all those in the foyer to hear. "I hope you heard that. He violated my mother and then had her banished to the Antipodes. King William has expunged her crime, so spread that news around town. He may acknowledge me as his son, but I will not give him that pleasure. I am Kit Kellow, and I am my own man." He snatched his coat from the astonished butler, who still held it. He then stood to his full six-foot-two-inch height, gathering his dignity, pulled open the front door and stormed out. As he did so, an ancient Chinese Ming vase fell off a side table and shattered, and the glass panels beside the door cracked. Kit didn't care. He shrugged on his overcoat, and by the time he reached the bottom step, he had tugged it closed. He needed to walk off his anger.

Felix followed in his wake. He stopped long enough to grab their hats and his coat and to tell the staff they needed to call for a doctor. From their smirks, he wondered if they would.

Kit was angry at himself. He had lost his temper, and he had not planned that. He wasn't sure what he wanted, but it wasn't assaulting his father. As he stormed down the street, he realised he had dreams of having a relationship with him one day. Those dreams evaporated when he saw the swaying, debauched and drunken state the man was in so early in the morning.

Kit had seen red. Suddenly, he realised this depraved man was blood-related, and he could do nothing to change that. He felt ill. He turned and vomited into a nearby bush. This act made him even more enraged. He made it into the park down the street and released a howl of anger.

Unbeknownst to him, his uncle was close at hand. His strong hand on the shoulder was more comforting than any words could have been. Felix offered no recriminations or chastisement, only love and acceptance.

Kit shrugged off his hand and paced the length of the pocket-sized park.

Felix brushed off the snow, sat on a park bench, and watched the young man battle his emotions.

Finally, Kit sank onto the seat next to him.

Again, rather than words of retribution, Felix asked, "Feeling better now?"

Kit nodded. A sly grin settled on his lips. "Oh, Uncle Felix, that felt so good. I had no idea I was so angry at him." He took three long, deep breaths. His breath clouded as he exhaled the warm air. "I'm sorry, sir. I really don't know what came over me."

Felix grinned wickedly. "I do, and I nearly did the same thing myself fifteen years ago. I might add, though, that your Papa did just as you have. Like you, according to the Bow Street Runners, Billy let the swine have two of the hardest punches they had ever seen out of the ring. It's why the baron's nose was already bent."

Kit was astonished, and it showed on his face. "Papa did that? I shouldn't really be surprised, sir. He has adored Mama all her life. You know the story, of course. But Pop, Papa's father, would not permit him to court her earlier."

Felix knew the entire story much better than Kit did. "I know, Kit, your grandmother, Phoebe, has eleven children, and carrying them nearly wore her out."

Kit had yet to meet the other nine aunts and uncles awaiting him in Cornwall, let alone his grandparents.

His Aunt Polly, her husband, and their brood lived in the original Kellow cottage. The boys had all married, and most lived in a new row of attached cottages they had built with their share of the cheese money. Phoebe and Jacob lived in the old Williams home with their second son.

The two men sat in the park and talked over his history. Felix watched Kit fight his rampaging emotions. Eventually, the cold permeated their thick coats, and Kit realised they should return and confess to his parents.

One decision was now made. No longer would he claim a relationship with that man. Also, he would keep the name of Williams only until his return to Australia, as the country was now called. Only there did he feel he fitted in. No one ever asked about one's background in the penal colony. He promised himself that one day, he would return to their dairy.

The carriage was waiting for them at the gate of the park. Their return to the mansion in St James' Park was traversed in silence.

Felix watched the tortured feelings weave across the young man's face. As the carriage stopped at the steps, he grabbed his nephew's hand before he alighted. "Kit, they won't be upset, you know. You have done what they both wished to do. Your papa may, however, be jealous that you beat him to it."

For the first time in years, Kit felt his eyes water. He refused to let them fall and brushed them away angrily.

His uncle passed him a clean handkerchief and said, "Blow, lad, then chin up. I'll be with you." He pushed Kit back onto the seat as he climbed out.

Those few seconds of grace were all Kit needed. With his tears now under control, he exited the carriage with a small smile to the footman and followed his uncle inside.

Billy and Jennifer awaited their return. Both had guessed their destination and wondered how the meeting would go. They saw that the smile on Felix's face was not mirrored on Kit's.

Kit wondered what to say to them. He had never lost his temper before, and he felt guilty.

Billy slung an arm lovingly around his shoulders.

As he did so, Kit blurted out, "I punched his damned lights out, Papa."

Rather than be angry, Billy roared with laughter. "Lad, this proves that he may well have fathered you, but you are my son. I did the same thing and wished to do it again a few times. But Kit, I would not hit a man when he was down, and he fell like a stone and stayed down intentionally."

Jennifer just hugged her son and asked the same question his uncle had. "Feeling better now?"

Kit nodded, then grinned. "When I go home to Australia, which I will, Papa, I will be Kit Kellow, though. I will be my own man, accountable to no one but myself."

Billy smiled. "You already are a man, son, and one I'm so darned proud of that you can't believe how much."

Kit relaxed, and Billy drew him into a big bear hug.

~

Their return to Cornwall on the *Jennifer Belle 2* was another surprise. The first vessel had run aground on a voyage to Newlyn and had been replaced with a sleek new yacht that Felix used for relaxation as well as work. She was available for any of the family to use when they wished, as long as they did not interfere with transporting the cheese cargo. She had a permanent crew on board, and she also had her own jetty at Penzance. For most of the time, though, she sat at anchor in the Thames River near Deptford, as the family rarely used her. If the next consignment were nearly ready, then she would wait for it at her jetty in Penzance. The sleek luxury yacht carried the long-lost family home.

Billy moved his family, including his parents, into Angelina's renovated home. The ten-bedroom house was huge compared to their home in Parramatta, yet the luxury of the house needed some mental adjustment. The indoor privy in Cornwall meant they no longer had to traipse outside in all weather or check for snakes or spiders when nature called. There was much to be said about both countries, but the children pined for the hot weather.

Jacob and Phoebe stayed in the old Williams home with Oscar, his wife, Bronwyn, and their three children. They delighted in having their eldest daughter home. Phoebe was getting a little vague. She would forget years and sometimes treat the grandchildren as though they were her own.

Life settled quickly, and the new cultures that Jennifer had brought were made into cheeses and set to ripen in the new cave.

Kit never looked back. Now, he had met and flattened his nemesis; he held his head high and marched through life. At Eton, where he excelled, he was Christopher Williams, nephew to the Duke of Shesham. He was surprised that no one delved any deeper. He was careful never to mention Parramatta except to acknowledge it was where he was born.

Each Governor, except Macquarie, who had died, had been on first-name terms with his parents, and occasionally, they visited the school or met him at some official function, and they called him by his nickname. His standing at the school had shot up. Cheese was never mentioned. But soon, all his peers discovered that he had an open invitation at Government House in Parramatta.

~

In 1839, nearly five years after their arrival in Cornwall, word came from Parramatta that Doctor John Harris had died and that their farm needed someone to care for it. Their farm, *Park Meadow,* now only had the girls and their husbands looking after it.

His time at Eton was done and dusted. Kit, at nearly twenty, was already wishing he was back home in Australia's warm, sunny climate.

No sooner had word arrived of the need at home than he was saying a fond farewell to his family to begin his new life alone on his Australian dairy. Billy had signed over the title to him, and he would put it back into the production of the Kellow-Williams cheeses. He went armed with knowledge of cheesemaking, cheeses to culture and a desire to start his life anew.

~

Eight months later

"Billy, Billy, where are you?" Jennifer's excited voice told him she had news of some sort.

Billy emerged from his nap under the newspaper and saw the delight on his wife's face. "Yes, my darling love. I can hear by your voice that you have news?" He roused himself to sit upright.

Jennifer approached, waiving a letter. "It's from Kit. You will never guess what has happened."

Billy knew he shouldn't tease her, but he could not resist. "Let me see, he met his father on the ship and tossed him overboard?"

Jennifer chuckled, "No, but I bet he wished he had. No, Billy dearest, this is wonderful news. He met a young lady on board, and as they were travelling with a clergyman as a passenger, they married on the ship. Her name is Catherine Walker, but she is called Kitty. And Bill, she is already in an interesting condition and due early next year. We are to be grandparents, love."

Billy sat up quickly and was now fully attending to her. "He's married already? Really? Lucky chap! I had to wait years for you." His grin showed her that he was pleased with the information. "I'm so pleased that I gave him that letter of permission, as he is underage. It was meant to exchange ownership of the farm; however, I worded it in such a way that it could be used for this purpose if required." He lay back in his comfortable chair and folded his arms. At fifty-one, Billy Williams still turned heads. His wife had been beautiful as a young girl and then a young lady, but she now had a stately elegance that had been missing in her youth. He never tired of gazing at her. When she lay in bed with her halo of greying locks spread over their pillow, he rarely could resist kissing her. Other than visiting Will at school for his various awards, they now rarely left Cornwall, and of this, they were pleased.

Felix and Isla's children had the best of both worlds, and the ducal couple had promised to launch the Williams daughters into society if they wished. They had already been invited to Queen Victoria's coronation the year before Kit had left. She had reissued the Royal Warrant for their cheese, and on meeting Jennifer, she thanked her for the delectable gift she had sent. The young queen was honoured by the name of the newest cheese flavour. The *Purple Crown* was the latest variety to take London by storm. It was the blue vein version of the Australian cheese. Few knew of the connection except that it came from the Shesham estates.

The young queen had wormed the information out of Isla.

They discussed the cheese, and Isla said, "We made it from the milk of my favourite cow, Your Majesty." Her hand then flew to her mouth to cover it. She realised how much information that gave away.

For the first time in years, Isla's veil of secrecy had been penetrated. The Duchess of Shesham held her breath, waiting for them all to be banished. The young queen smiled and walked away.

Later, in a private conversation, she said, "We are amused that it has taken so long for your secret to be unveiled. We admire what you have done for the poor in your villages and how you have used your knowledge as well as your faith and then put it all to good use. Duchess, rest easy; your secret is safe, as is that of your family. Had you not been true to our King…" she pointed heavenward, then added, "…then things may have been different."

Queen Victoria was only two years older than Kit.

Jennifer stood watching their new monarch circle the room.

Billy came to her side and took her elbow. "Goodness knows how she found out, love, but Felix was worried for a while."

Felix said, "Her Majesty overheard Isla and me talking, and then my beloved mentioned that she had made her gift herself."

The four watched her from across the room, then saw her turn and meet their gaze.

Felix and Isla gave a slight nod and bowed from across the room.

Felix quietly spoke. "Methinks that finally, society will have to clean itself up. The immorality of the past will soon be frowned upon. And once again, we have a monarch that has her eyes on a higher realm."

Billy was surprised. "She has true faith?"

Felix nodded. "She was brought up as a pious Lutheran. The crown of England now means she is the head of the Church of England. They have very similar worship styles; she has embraced the role with gusto. Her stand will soon challenge many." He stood looking aloof with his hands clasped behind his back.

Jennifer would have thought he was angry if she didn't know him so well. She understood why he had previously been ostracised by society.

Isla had seen through his austere veneer. It was merely a front against the shallowness of peers in which they lived.

He had seen mothers try to manipulate him into compromising their daughters so he would be forced to wed them. Many peers, including the baron, had fallen victim to that ploy.

In the years since their return, Jennifer had seen the gentle, loving man that Isla had discovered. He had locked his heart away, and her sister had found the key.

Jennifer had already seen glimpses of his softer side when they had first met.

Billy watched her interest in her brother-in-law. "Jen, anything wrong?"

The adoring smile she gave Billy made his heart almost somersault. "No, Billy, I'm thinking back to the first few times I met him. He was so alone, and even though it was me who had been abused and convicted, I felt like reaching out to comfort him. Especially when he visited me on the ship. I wished to give him a hug. For Isla to break through and reach his heart... well, I was thrilled."

Billy smiled. "I know, darling. His tough exterior still frightens many."

Felix turned to them with a smile. "I can hear you, you know!"

His in-laws grinned wickedly. In unison, they replied. "We know!"

Chapter 22   Phoebe 2022
The Female Factory Parramatta

October 28th, 2022, saw the grand reopening of the restored heritage-listed Female Factory in Parramatta. This event was to celebrate the anniversary of the female convict riot that occurred on October 28th 1827. This was the escape of nearly two hundred undernourished convict women from the female prison. Some of the escapees were never caught; although many were rounded up quickly, a few were recaptured some weeks later.

Jenny and Michelle, with their husbands, were four of the first people to book the tour. Having found that Jennifer Kellow Williams had been incarcerated here for a month and was later on staff, it was a link to her past.

The day broke bright and sunny in what had been a very wet year. The two women were loaded up with hats, water, cameras, phones, and husbands. Jenny had a list of questions to ask the staff in the research centre. Her exercise book was now somewhat tattered and only had a few blank pages left in it before another book would be required. She wondered what they would discover today, if anything. Jenny was slightly dejected. Since they found the letters from Duke Felix fourteen years before, they had few finds of interest. However, this day out was really just for fun. Today was a step back in time to feel what being in the Female Factory was like.

On arrival, they did the tour of the site, and they sat through a lecture about convict women, which was incredibly interesting, but answered none of her remaining questions.

When it was over, Jenny sat outside the research room with her head in her hands. She had dropped her head and prayed that somehow, some way, they may be able to find out more about Jennifer's son, and especially about exactly where the dairy was, as there seemed to be no record of its location under the name of Christopher Williams.

Michelle brought out a coffee while the men were inside talking to the persons on the various displays. They were chatting to a man who had made a scale model of the site. Michelle had already purchased some of the books and was flicking through them. "Jenny, have you asked at the Government Dairy or at Government House about your family dairy? They might know something about it up there."

Before Jenny had time to answer, an old lady asked if she could sit and join them. They cleared the chair and made room for her at the table.

Once settled, the lady said, "Dears, I do hope you don't mind, but I heard you mention the Government Dairy."

The girls nodded.

After a sip of her coffee, she said, "I am a descendant of one of the families in the area. He came out free on a ship, and he married on board. He owned a dairy in the area, next door to the Government Dairy. Hence my interest in your comment. He had a lovely name, Kit Kellow."

At the mention of Kit's surname, both girls gave the old lady their full attention. "Kellow is the name I'm researching," Jenny said. "However, the name of the child I'm looking for is Christopher."

The old lady chuckled again. "Oh, dearie, Kit is a nickname for Christopher. His mother, Jennifer, came as a convict, but after she had returned to England, King William the Fourth gave her a Royal Pardon. Her conviction was expunged, and even the records here had her record crossed out."

Jenny teared up; she could not help but gasp. "Jennifer went home, and she was given a Royal Pardon?"

The old lady nodded.

That comment explained why the line was through her record. Jenny could not help but ask, "My name is Jennifer, too. I was named after her. I want to know about her, but it's like trying to do a jigsaw with half the bits missing. But how do you know all this?"

The old lady smiled knowingly. "When my grandfather came to live with us, he was bored stiff. He had grown up at the family dairy, and when he turned eighty, he sold it and moved in with us. That was in 1940 and during the war. My mother loved the stories he told us, and to keep them accurate, she purchased some exercise books and had him record them. We could not keep the lights on after dark as it was wartime, so telling the stories in the dark was great fun. I remember them all as I heard them often."

Michelle and Jenny caught each other's glances; it was exactly what her mother had done for her grandfather.

The old lady kept talking. "Popa filled ten books, most of which were stories about the dairy. I had no idea so much happened on a farm back then. I read them frequently until my eyes got bad. It was often used as a halfway house to keep young convict girls safe before their final placements. One of the soldiers had a chain of safe farms, and their farm was the closest to the Factory. When Popa was a lad, Gramps Kit lived with them for about ten years, so Popa knew him well. By the way, if you are related, then we are cousins. My name is Phoebe Kellow. I, too, am named after the family, as Phoebe was Jennifer's mother; therefore, she was Kit's maternal grandmother. I was the seventh child, as Jennifer was, and I was born in 1935, so I'm close to ninety."

Michelle and Jennifer grinned at each other.

Mark and David finally emerged from inside but stood chatting at the door.

The old lady, having finished her coffee, pushed her chair back. "I have something I need to show you. Will you take my arm, dear? I'm not so steady on my feet these days. It's the knees, you know. I should use a stick, but I refuse."

As Jenny took the old lady's arm, Michelle called their husbands. The small group walked past Matron's cottage, and Phoebe hobbled between the ladies. She showed them the courtyard on the other side of the matron's building. "This area was an assembly yard where the women were probably assigned, but where I'm taking you was possibly where they all assembled. I dare say we will never know exactly what each area was used for." Rather than stop, she hobbled past the gardens that filled the open space.

A small door was set in the wall just past the next building. She twisted the ring handle and opened it.

Inside was a vast, grassy courtyard surrounded by the remains of a twenty-foot-high wall. A roofed seating area was marked as a later construction.

Phoebe was puffing but said, "Jenny, see those walls? They were increased from eight feet to twenty feet high after the riot in 1827. Also, the big blocks had the tops chamfered off so the girls could no longer climb out. Later extensions were made totally smooth. But that's not what I want to show you. Our Jennifer had given the gaol a cow named Daisy. It lived in here; this was the drying area, and it was fully fenced back then. Jennifer had to come here and milk it. But it was also where she taught the girls about caring for a cow, so she also used Daisy to educate some of the girls in the factory." She paused and puffed from the slight exercise as she gazed around the empty yard.

Michelle and Jennifer grinned with delight.

Their husbands squeezed in behind them to have a look at the emptiness of the area. Not knowing the history, the empty courtyard was uninteresting. However, Phoebe telling them what this area was used for brought the yard to life. They could imagine a cow named Daisy, with big horns, grazing alone in the yard surrounded by clotheslines covered with the washed fabrics and things the inmates had used.

Phoebe had her breath back again. She released a long sigh as though she was reliving the stories of her past. Rather than walk further, she turned to face the wall.

She reached out and pointed to the sandstone blocks in front of her. "I have known about these carvings all my life. My papa showed me when I was a little girl. I can't remember what this place was used for during the war, but he was permitted here. It may well have even been derelict. I just remember these." She lifted her hand and traced a small cross carved into the stonework. A smaller stone beside it had another one the same.

Phoebe's gnarled fingers caressed the two carvings lovingly. She said, "Jenny, I want you to rub your fingers here."

Jenny did as requested. Her tears were already gathering; she guessed what was to follow.

The stone was warm to the touch and had obviously been rubbed smooth from two hundred years of being lovingly caressed.

Phoebe covered Jenny's hand with her own and said, "Jenny, our five-time great-grandmother, stroked these when they were new. When our Jennifer first found them, they were rough, but she traced the crosses on each visit. Popa told me that his Gramps Kit used to follow her example. When he returned from England in 1839, Gramps would come here and teach the incarcerated girls to milk and the basics of dairy work. He, too, used to trace these crosses on every visit. Gramps brought Popa and showed him, and he told him that his mama, our Jennifer, was the very first convict to touch them the week he was born. She and her husband, Billy, could sit in here alone."

Phoebe sniffed and wiped her eyes. She shook her head as if to stop her tears. "As we heard today, the gaol officially closed in 1847, and the Catholic nuns took over soon after transportation officially finished to New South Wales in 1840. More convicts did arrive until 1856, but not in the vast quantities they had before. Only fifteen hundred convicts arrived in the last ten years, but as most were male, they were not brought here. When the gaol finally closed, some of the remaining women went to Gramps Kit's farm nearby." She fell silent for a while, recalling conversations with her grandfather about the old days. "My Popa used to say that Jennifer wondered if an Irish Catholic convict carved these. Sadly, we shall never know."

Phoebe shook her head again to make her melancholy leave. She took a deep breath, stood up straight, and said, "To meet you here today is a Godsend, dear. You see, I never married or had children, and I would like to give you the books that I have. They are my Popa's notebooks, dear. None of my extended family is interested in the history, and I can see that you are. If you have more questions, I live nearby and would love to tell you what I know."

Jenny could not see the lady's face as tears clouded her view, but she was nodding vigorously. This lady had the rest of the answers and many more of Jenny's questions. "Phoebe, may I call you that?"

The old lady nodded and smiled. "I would love you too, dearie. After all, we are cousins."

Jenny asked for the last bit of her puzzle. "Phoebe, do you know where the farm was? I know it was nearby, but not exactly where."

Her search was now all but over. There would be no more shadows of the convict past to uncover. Even that had been obliterated. Tears rolled silently down her cheeks as Jenny stood looking at the cross in the stone. She was touching something her own many times-over grandmother and namesake had touched many times. Somehow, it brought the long-dead Jennifer Kellow Williams to life again. They were linked across the generations. Two hundred years had passed since she arrived in this place.

When a sob escaped her, Mark gently rested his hand on her shoulder, and one finger caressed her neck. He had walked this path with her for years. Somehow, he knew she would not let the story rest there. He wondered if she would now write it down. They quickly learned about her maternal grandfather, James Hunter, who was a Cobb and Co coach driver bushrangers had held up four times. That story and some of the others had been well recorded in the newspapers, as were his family stories. But Jennifer's story was more personal. However, the discovery of the crossed-out entry had intrigued them all. To find out it was because Jennifer's conviction had been expunged made sense of it all. It was just a convict shadow. Something he had not come across before.

Jenny stepped back into his arms and rested her head against his chest. His arm slipped across her shoulder, and he pulled her close.

Phoebe chatted away about more of their background, then said, "Jenny dear, as we are both named after the early Kellow ladies, as Phoebe was Jennifer's mother." She chuckled. "She was Phoebe Popplestone before her marriage. Anyway, I have decided that you will receive the box I have at home. You will treasure it as few would. I live at *Park Meadows*, which is built on the land that used to be our family dairy. That was the name of our family farm, you know. I was going to call a taxi home, but if I fit in your vehicle, I could give it to you now." Phoebe did not notice the gasp of astonishment from Jenny.

Was *Park Meadows* the Williams Kellow farm? Jenny brushed away another tear and blew her nose. She heard Mark and David both chuckle. Michelle met her eyes and smiled.

It took only a glance and a few nods between the four to start making their way towards David's big car.

Phoebe again clung to the arms of the two ladies as they left the walled courtyard, and David gently pulled the door closed behind them.

This history would be revisited. Only this time, Jenny and Mark would bring their children, Christopher Logan, Catherine Jennifer, and William Mark, and they would sit in the airing yard and hear the history of those early convict days. Each child would be encouraged to trace their fingers over crosses as their ancestors did long ago, and the past and stories would be retold.

For the short drive to her unit, Phoebe continued her historical chatter about the family. She had a vast knowledge about the family and their life in Cornwall. The information she knew was stored in her memory.

Jenny was determined to befriend her; however, she knew that two others would soon beat her to more questions. Her parents, Celia and Iain, were in the same village. She wished Gramps could have been told.

Phoebe was obviously lonely, but now she would have her family at hand. She had yet to tell the dear old lady of the other connection about where she lived.

David's large car pulled into the visitors' parking area. This was only two doors away from Jenny's parents' new unit at the retirement village.

Jenny said, "Phoebe, before we go to your unit, can I get my parents? They have recently moved in here. After a conversation with my Gramps in 1968, my mother, Celia, and I started on the search for Jennifer. Mum and my father, Iain, live here too." Jenny swallowed. "You see, back then, my grandfather moved in with us, and my mother set him to write his stories in exercise books too."

Phoebe's beautiful smile met hers. "I wondered if there was a connection when I saw their names on last week's new resident list. I fully intended to introduce myself this Sunday, but God put you in my path first."

Jenny smiled at the reference to the Maker. She smiled and said to Phoebe, "It seems that the Kellows also passed down their strong faith."

Mark quickly moved away from them to collect his in-laws.

Phoebe nodded but remained silent. She had been praying about meeting someone with a passion for their family history. As she unlocked her door, she was smiling to herself.

Soon, Phoebe's small unit was hosting six visitors.

For many years, Michelle and Jenny had updated Celia with every discovery. For the final revelations to occur on the very site where the dairy sat was fitting. They sat chatting and working out the relationship as about third cousins.

While Celia made coffee in the kitchenette of the unit, Phoebe struggled to her feet and called Jenny to assist her. They walked into the bedroom, and Phoebe pointed to a small chest that sat on the floor of her wardrobe. The beautiful brass inlaid wooden box was a big armful, but Jenny carried it back into the sitting room and set it on the coffee table.

Phoebe unlocked the chest with a key from a gold chain around her neck. Jenny noticed it also had a cross on it. Phoebe opened the lid and took out a parchment-wrapped bundle. The ribbon was ancient, and she gently brushed imaginary dust off the parcel and handed it to Jenny.

Jenny accepted it reverently and carefully untied the ribbon.

The parchment fell open, revealing a large wad of very old letters tied with another ancient string.

Jenny's eyes flew to Phoebe's. "Are these…?" She was unable to finish as tears of joy and amazement filled her eyes. A lump in her throat made further words impossible.

Phoebe nodded. "These are written by our Jennifer to Kit until she died in 1885. You are named after her, so they are now yours. Her Bible is in there, too. It was sent to Kit by Billy when she died. Kit had given it to her when they returned to England. It is filled with all the family details, dates and more of their story, but you can read those later. In the box are the exercise books with the farm stories and… well, everything else that I know. I have written my own story, including Popa's ones he did not write down."

Jenny sniffed and said, "Oh, Phoebe, this is amazing!"

Phoebe held out her hand to Jenny and placed the chain necklace in it that held the key. "This is yours now, dear. Keep the stories alive. And write the saga of your own search. One day, someone will wish to read about your passion."

Phoebe received the first big hug she had been given for many, many years. Many more would follow over the time they had together.

The gift was overwhelming. Jenny wept as she hugged the documents to her. Her tear-filled eyes lifted and met Phoebe's. "Thank you! Thank you so very much!"

Honest **Reviews** *of a book help bring them to the attention of other readers who are more likely to read something from a new-to-them author if it has more reviews (even if they are not five-star). Please leave a rating or a short review on Amazon or Goodreads.*

FREE Newsletter signup
https://preview.mailerlite.io/preview/41388/sites/
77987646202184961/wCAAcK

Author's Historical Notes

Jennifer's story is, of course, just that, a story. But it was inspired by our visit to the Female Factory in Parramatta in October 2022 for the anniversary of the riot. The crosses mentioned at the end of the book are really there and situated in the airing yard that is accessible from the parking area. Make sure you have a look if you ever go there. They have been worn smooth by many fingers caressing them over the two hundred years, and these two small crosses inspired this story.

My own three-times great-grandmother, Mary Ann Tyzzer née Harris, was a Cornish milkmaid in Newlyn Cornwall who came to Australia after her husband had died. She came free with her children to Victoria in the 1860s. Her husband and sons had been lead miners in Newlyn Cornwall, and it was a dangerous venture. Her son William arrived first, hunting for the gold rush in the 1850s; when widowed, she followed with the rest of her children. They settled in the area and later named their settlement Newlyn. Many others from their area must have come and settled nearby. There are still Tyzzers in that area in Victoria, as there are in Newlyn, Cornwall.

The dairy history for the colony is reasonably accurate, although the Williams-Kellow farm, *Park Meadow*, is fictitious. However, it was at this time that Dr Harris, Elizabeth (Betty) Eccles, Captain Piper and his wife, plus the Scottish couple, the Rankins, started their dairies... but someone taught them, and that person is unknown. The last two families went to Bathurst. Dr Harris's farm was in Ultimo and was the largest dairy in the colony for some years. Apparently, at one stage, he lived in a house next door to Elizabeth Farm in Rose Hill, Experiment Farm, and stayed there for a few years until his death. He died in 1838.

There are interesting articles in the newspapers (*available on TROVE*) that mention a substantial improvement in the colony cheeses in the early 1820s. The prices quoted are as accurate as I can find. The newspaper and diary quotes in italics are factual (not the letters from my characters, though), and quotations are from documents I found. (*see bibliography*).

The Macquaries were known as emancipists' friends, as were the Darlings. I wish to relay them as real and caring people rather than paper figures on a history page. I have used Macquarie's diaries (see *bibliography*) as my primary source of information. Elizabeth Macarthur was known to have dairy cows, as Elizabeth House has a small dairy. This venue can be visited today. The breeds back then were not as we have now, as they were large, long-horned cows. Due to the French wars, the Channel Island cattle were banned from being exported until the 1820s, hence their scarcity.

My husband and I visited these Australian Heritage sites as we discovered that our own five-times great-grandmothers, who arrived together in 1814 on the *Wanstead*, both spent time in both the old gaol and the Female Factory, in third class at Parramatta and, possibly, worked in this same courtyard. We felt that they, too, would have traced their fingers on these carvings, so the story was born.

Sara

Characters

Cornwall characters:
Jacob Kellow (son of Logan Pascoe Kellow & Jennifer Pollard)
 m 1787 **Phoebe** Popplestone
Children 10
> 1 Logan   b 1788
> 2 Oscar   b 1790
> 3 Samuel b 1792
> 4 Leo   b 1794
> 5 Oliver   b 1795
> 6 Alfie   b 1797
> 7 **Jennifer** b 1799 (convict. *Morley* 17/3/1820. arr 14 Sept 1820)
> convict in **Female Factory 1821** (returned to Eng 1834) Conv quashed
> d 1885 in Cornwall
>> 1 Christopher Logan (**Kit**) Kellow
>> b 1 /2/1821, *his father was Baron George Mortonford*. Returned to Australia in 1839
>> d 1914 in Parramatta
>> m 1839 Catherine (**Kitty**) Walker (1 child)
>>> 1 **William Logan Kellow** b 1840   d 1932
>>> m 1858 Mary (2 children)
>>>> 1 Christopher (**Chris**) Bryn Kellow b 1859
>>>> m 1880 Jane
>>>>> 1 William (**Billy**) Jacob Kellow   b 1881
>>>>> m 1915 Alice
>>>>> Children 7
>>>>> *6 older siblings*
>>>>> 7 **Phoebe** Kellow *met Jenny at Parr'a Female Factory*
>>>>> b 1935 never married - *Archive keeper*
>>>> 2 Jacob William Kellow b 1860   d 1950
>>>> m 1880 Isabella
>>>>> 1. Christopher (**Toff**) Kellow b 1880
>>>>> m 1902 Mary
>>>>>> 1. Logan Wm Kellow (**Gramps**) b 1903d 1974
>>>>>> m Sylvia Wallace b 1918 d 1962
>>>>>>> 1. William **Iain** Kellow b 1931
>>>>>>> m 1958 **Celia** b 1939
>>>>>>>> 1 Jennifer (**Jenny**) Kellow, b '59 researcher
>>>>>>>> m 1989 Mark Donovan (in a double wedding)
>>>>>>>> 3 children
>>>>>>> 2. Beverly Kellow (**Bev**)
>>>>>>> m Hilton (**Hilt**) Barlow
>> m 1st March 1821 **Billy Williams** in Parramatta
>> Children 4,
>> 1 Bryn Jacob (**Jack**), 25/3/1822
>> 2 Jennifer Delen (**Del**); b 1824
>> 3 Phoebe Isla, (**Sis**) b 1826
>> 4 William Pascoe (**Will**) b 1829
> 8 **Isla** b 1802 - M 1822 **Felix**, Duke of Shesham
> Children 4 Rupert, b23; Karensa (Kerry) b25; Tristan b29; and Rosen (Rose) b29
> 9 Kitto   b 1805
> 10 Pascoe b Easter 1807
> 11 Polly   b 1810

Mr **Bryn** Williams - Dairy owner
m 1787 **Delen** (means *tiny petal* in Cornish)
> **Billy** Williams -b 1788
> m March 1821 **Jennifer** Kellow in Parramatta - See Kellow tree

Bertram Tremayne - Cheese Merchant in London
Mrs Angelina DeMartini, an Italian lady, married 1821 Bertram Tremayne Sept 1820
Felix, Duke of Shesham, In London, demands to meet Jennifer
Baron George Mortonford: The Right Honourable Lord Mortonford abused her

Modern Australian Characters

        Christopher (Toff) Kellow b 1880

    m 1908 Mary Lance

        Logan Kellow (**Gramps**) b 1910

        m 1930 Syliva Wallace

        b 1918 d 1962

            1. William **Iain** Kellow

            b 1931

            m 1958 **Celia** b 1939

                Jenny Kellow

                b 1959

                m 1989 **Mark** Donovan

            2. Beverly Phoebe Kellow (**Bev**)

            m Hilton Barlow (**Hilt**)

Janie Fox - the 1968 researcher from Mitchell Library

    Michelle Fox - Parramatta researcher - Janie Fox's daughter.

    m 1989 **David** Donovan (double wedding with Jenny & Mark Donovan- *see above*)

Real People/Ships

Jess Hill Society of Geneology

Wilma Bond - shipping/Pottery

Charlie McGuinley - Cooper

Morley - convict ship April 1820 17 Sept 1820

Juliana, Sept 1820 to Jan 27 1821

Brixton Sept 1821

Captain Robert R Brown

Surgeon Superintendent Reed *Morley* Sailed 17 May 1820 Arrived 14 Sept 1820

Reverent Thomas and Mrs Reddall and their 7 children

Governor Lachlan & Elizabeth Macquarie

Governor Thomas Brisbane

Governor Richard and Mrs. Betsy Bourke

Dr John Harris - Ultimo dairy

Mr & Mrs Rankin, 1825 made cheeses in Bathurst

Elizabeth (Betty) Eccles

Mrs Ovens - Macquarie's cook

Bibliography

USA Cheese prices
https://babel.hathitrust.org/cgi/pt?id=hvd.32044050806330&view=1up&seq=207&q1=cheese

Life of a Cornish Miner
https://freepages.rootsweb.com/~chrissystbrewardopc/genealogy/life_of_a_cornish_miner.htm

Governor Lachlan Macquarie's Diary
https://www.mq.edu.au/macquarie-archive/lema/documents.html

Guernsey Cattle
https://en.wikipedia.org/wiki/Guernsey_cattle

Surgeons Journal From Morley 1820
https://www.femaleconvicts.org.au/docs2/ships/VoyageOfTheMorley_1820.pdf
(quoted extracts are in Italics)

Morley 1820 voyage
http://www.freesettlerorfelon.com/morley_1820.htm

Australia's cheese/Dairy industry history
https://australianfoodtimeline.com.au/first-commercial-dairy/

Cheese in Bathurst
https://www.megalongcc.com.au/Megalong%20History%20&%20Heritage/early_days_of_bathurst.htm

Australian Dairy Industry
https://www.dairy.com.au/our-industry-and-people/our-history

Reverend Thomas Reddall
https://adb.anu.edu.au/biography/reddall-thomas-2579

Australian Dictionary of Biography, Volume 2, (Melbourne University Press), 1967
https://adb.anu.edu.au/frontpages/fp2.pdf

Parramatta Government Dairy
https://en.wikipedia.org/wiki/Dairy_Cottage,_Parramatta

Elizabeth Eccles Biography
https://stjohnsonline.org/bio/elizabeth-eccles/
https://peopleaustralia.anu.edu.au/biography/eccles-elizabeth-betty-14053
Obit:- https://oa.anu.edu.au/obituary/eccles-elizabeth-betty-14053

Steps in cheese making
https://www.thespruceeats.com/important-steps-in-cheesemaking-591566

George and Janey Rankin
https://australianfoodtimeline.com.au/rankins-cheese-bathurst/

Salters Dairy Government Dairy at Parramatta
https://historyandheritage.cityofparramatta.nsw.gov.au/blog/2016/11/24/the-dairy-cottage-parramatta
NB Sunken room was added in 1823.

Cessation of Transportation - convicts arriving after 1840 in NSW
https://en.wikipedia.org/wiki/Convicts_in_Australia#cite_note-ReferenceA-28

If you loved this book, these are similar.
A prequel for all my books, and a stand-alone story.

Gentle Annie Soames is a First Fleet story with the descriptions taken directly from the Journal of Doctor Author Bowes Smith, who was on board the Lady Penrhyn.

Gentle Annie Soames
A 1788 First Fleet Convict Story
Her dreams lead to unexpected outcomes. An Australian First Fleet story.

Annie Soames is shattered by the cancellation of her debut into society, so when she hears of a position as a carer for the nearby Marchioness, she grabs it.

Oliver Quilpie, the recently married Marquess, discovers his arranged union is not to his taste; he is drawn to his wife's companion. Unfortunately, he is unable to keep his hands off her. For revenge, Annie mimics his every move while riding but is dressed as a highwayman. However, she had now fallen in love with him. This action finally leads to her arrest and transportation to a faraway land.

After some years, Oliver's wife dies, and his thoughts turn to Annie. He seeks to find her, but she has vanished. He is horrified to discover she was transported to New South Wales as a convict on the *Lady Penrhyn*. He follows with a shipload of supplies on the *Kitty*. Will Annie want to see him?

ISBN 9780645441574 ISBN ebook 9781923097063

Coming July 2024 preorder from May
The Hunter to Macquarie Trilogy
When Upon Life's Billows
Sydney 1795-1821 - Governor John Hunter

Captain John Hunter was born to a life at sea. The wind blows where no man knows, and John is caught up in the tempest. Although wrecking his ship, the *HMS Sirius*, in 1790, he became the second Governor of the rough and filthy penal settlement of New South Wales. He always seems to be in the wrong place at the wrong time, trusting the wrong people.

Helena Rosedale is not a typical female convict. She fights tooth and nail to stop the men from abusing her. She gains the name of Helena the Hellcat.

Crispin Milroy is alone in the world and one of the new Governor's security detail. Can he win the fair lady's heart? Life in 1795 in Sydney Cove is raw at best. Food is scarce, and disease often ravages the settlement. Life throws everything except death at these three, yet somehow, they survive. Why does John trust this young couple when others betray him?

What trials must Helena and Crispin endure to make their new lives in this raw town bearable? How can John ease their path?

ISBN: 9780645783339   ebook ISBN: 9780645783346

Coming 2025
Tuppence to Pass
London 1800s to Parramatta 1820s - Governor Lachlan Macquarie

Josh Callan is a London lad who makes the best of the life that has been dealt to him. Stealing from the man who killed his father gives the family a change of direction. Josh is arrested, but the judge belittles him, saying he's not worth tuppence. He is transported to the penal colony of Sydney as a convict just as **Governor Macquarie's** term starts. He proves his worth and falls on his feet, becoming the Governor's groom and confidante.

Life in the Colonial town opens opportunities they could never have dreamed about in England, but can Josh find his niche in life?

Where will this strange friendship take Josh and his family?

ISBN : 9781923097070 eISBN: 9781923097087

Coming 2025
Saddler's Song
London 1790s to Parramatta 1840s

George Ellis is a tanner's son living on the outskirts of London. When disease takes his family, he seeks to find a new life for himself. Hearing from a friend about the possibility of setting up a business in New South Wales, he sells up and leaves all he knows. His beloved violin is his most valuable item, and his talent for making beautiful music is hidden from all but a few. **Ben Parker** is a saddler and, like George, is now alone in the world as his father is dead; Ben also sells up to move to the new colony. Having booked passage on the same ship, the two meet and combine their skills to start afresh in a new world. During the journey out, George's skill as a violinist is revealed. On arrival, they find accommodation with a family with many lovely daughters. Two lovely ladies steal the hearts of the lonely lads, but how will the business survive in an animal-starved land? Access to their primary material is limited. Where will this lead them, and what is the song?

ISBN : 9780645783353   eISBN: 9780645783360

Coming 2025

Unlikely Convict Ladies - Trilogy

Dancing to her Own Tune

Co-authored by Sheila Hunter and Sara Powter

Sydney 1790s to England 1830s

Annie White is released after serving seven years as a convict in Sydney. She gets a visitor who, with his help, she can start a baking business. She is then asked to assist another sick man, **Sam** Corbett. Annie nurses him back to health, and a relationship develops. They settle into a life together, barely making ends meet; she realises she's expecting a child. Sam has his past laid bare and must adjust to the revelations. They both must face their accusers and find that the answers to their questions are not what they thought. Their life experiences seem to cling to them, and unable to shake them off, they end up back in England. They must face their ghosts and discover they are not who they think they are. How can they turn their anger and spite into love and forgiveness? The Dance of Life goes on.

ISBN 9780645110715   ISBN9780645110722

Long-listed in the Historical Fiction Company Competition 2022

https://amazon.com/dp/064511071X   https://amazon.com/dp/B09JC378YV

Amelia's Tears

Parramatta 1828 – England 1840s

Amelia Westaweller awaits her assignment in the Parramatta Female Prison. Forced to leave the relative safety of gaol, she is assigned and now faces her worst nightmare. A foul man claims her and makes her life a living hell. Then, her world goes black. A glimmer of hope arises when she hears from her brother, Jim, who has enlisted a friend to help her. She writes to Jim, pouring out her heart and telling him of the horrors of her new life. He encourages her to stay firm in her faith. All she can do is pray. When Major **Ned** Grace, her brother's friend, enters her life in Parramatta, he starts to ease her path. Things have changed, as now she has a child in tow. How can Amelia forge a new life for herself? What man could want her with her background and a child at her side? Who is the gentleman who turns her tears of sadness into tears of great joy?

ISBN: 9780645110739   eISBN: 978-0-6451107-4-6 Hard Cover ISBN 979-842061-7953

https://amazon.com/dp/0645110736   https://amazon.com/dp/B09SS855BR

A Lady in Irons

England 1800s - Parramatta 1808+

Katy Harrington is mourning the death of her husband after he died in a shooting accident. Barely coping, she awaits the birth of their child. If it's a girl, she must hand the family home to her husband's brother. The day after giving birth to a daughter, she and her daughter are left on the side of a road. She collapses and is found by someone she thought had died in a fire ten years before. **Perry White**, badly scarred himself, nurses her back to health. They marry and move in with her widowed friend, Mary.

After some years, she discovers her husband and friend in each other's arms. Now living in a love triangle, she flees. Grasping the only straw available, she intentionally gets arrested and is sent to a colony far away. By doing this, her marriage can be annulled.

What happens in the Colony is different from what she expects. Governor Macquarie comes to her rescue. But what of Perry and her children?

ISBN: 9780645110784   eISBN:9780645441505

https://amazon.com/dp/0645110787   https://amazon.com/dp/B0BCWSXB9Z

The Convict Stain Collection

(Stand-alone stories)

NO MORE, MY Love

Hunter Valley, NSW 1820s

Jess Elkin is distraught when tragedy ravages her family. She becomes the victim of a carriage accident and is nursed back to health by the driver, **Marcus Ryan**. Marcus was not expecting to fall in love. Yet, when Jess's fortunes suddenly turn for the worse, Marcus must decide how far he will go to pursue her. As time passes in Newcastle, Australia, Marcus must take a business trip and is taken by pirates. Jess is left wondering if her will keep his promise to return to her… Will she ever see him alive again?

ISBN: 9780645441536   eISBN 9780645441581

April 2023

https://amazon.com/dp/0645441538   https://amazon.com/dp/B0BSBH143Q

The Vine Weaver
Hawkesbury River area 1820s+
New Beginnings and Old Threats

In the 1820s, Australia, **Joel and Hetty Walker** live on a secluded farm on the Hawkesbury River, which becomes a healing haven for the protection of young convict women. A series of events brings **Fran Rea** to Hetty's attention, and she is taken to the farm. Fran and Hetty develop a cottage industry under the compassionate eye of farmhand **Hector Macdougal;** Hector's loving words change lives. It is to him that Fran turns when threatened.
The vines now must draw them close to survive the future revelations, and of those, there are many.

ISBN: 9780645441512   eISBN: 9780645441529
June 2023
https://amazon.com/dp/0645441511   https://amazon.com/dp/B0C6Z552Y2
The story continues in Scotch at The Rocks…

Scotch at The Rocks
Glasgow, Scotland, early 1800s to The Rocks, Sydney 1830s

Orphaned children Brodie Stewart and Heather Anderson live on Glasgow's streets. Although hungry, somehow they survive and keep out of trouble. Heather finds a job and looks to be settled; things go pear-shaped for them both. Eventually, they marry by declaration, yet even that gets messed up, and they are both arrested soon after they make their vow. In 1838, they were transported to Sydney as convicts. Heather arrives within weeks of Brodie, and they are assigned close to each other. They are now living on the docklands in Sydney, called The Rocks. They now have to forge a new life halfway across the world from their homeland.
Adventures abound, and Brodie gets press-ganged. While he's away, Heather's life changes and soon, she's officially selling Scotch Whisky at a shop in The Rocks.
You can take a Scot out of Scotland, but where did the Scotch come from?

ISBN 9780645441550   ISBN ebook 9781923097001
November 2023

Waiting at the Sliprails
The Bathurst Road 1830s
A Convict's Tale

Bea Dawes's term of conviction nears an end, and she has few options other than marriage to a stranger or going on the street.
Jack Barnes, the hired drover, wants a wife. Bea accepts his offer; then, she discovers that he could be gone for months, leaving her alone with **Billy and Netty**, part of the tribe of Aborigines who live on his secluded farm. Bea learns to love her husband and also this wonderful aboriginal couple.
Drought ravages the farm, and Jack must hit the long paddock with the flock. In his absence, a visitor arrives, threatening to destroy everything she has worked so hard for. Can Bea touch her heart? Can she cope? Will the drought ever end? And when will Jack return?

ISBN: 9780645441543   eISBN: 9781923097032
August 2023

Convict Shadows of the Past
Two Jennifers, two hundred years apart

When aged eight, **Jenny** Kellow learns of her convict family history and discovers that she was named after a convict from nearly two hundred years ago. Her grandfather's stories inspire her to dig deeper into her ancestors' convict past. From her grandfather, she hears stories of bushrangers, convicts, and life in the infant colony of Parramatta. She sets about retracing the footsteps of her convict great-great-great-grandmother to honour her. Jenny's search starts with microfiche back in the 60s, and she learns about the small tin mining town in Cornwall and the production of a cheese that sets London afire. She discovers her ancestor, **Jennifer Kellow,** has brought these cheese-making skills to Parramatta, where she taught others her craft. Echoes of the past can still be heard if you know where to listen.
Who was the first Jennifer, and what does she have to do with cheese? Why is she so elusive? Did Jenny's ancestor, Jennifer, ever see those two small crosses carved into the bricks of the Female Factory? Would Jenny ever find out her ancestor's story?

ISBN: 9780645783315   ISBN ebook 9780645783322
A NaNoWriMo 2022 book winner
January 2024

In Defence of Her Honour
London 1800s to Parramatta 1819

Bill Miller had been raised and educated with the sons of the family. The youngest, Bert, had been his best friend. However, jealousy intervenes when Bill's excellent schoolwork curtails their friendship. He wins a scholarship and enters Oxford University. When Bill's father, the old butler, dies unexpectedly, Bert insists that Bill take over the position, but it's more to oppress him. Bert's jealousy grows and festers. Now looking for a way to rid themselves of their new butler, a ruckus ensues, and Bill is arrested for assaulting Bert. The housekeeper and her daughter, **Molly Ross,** vouch for him, but it's too late; Bill has been arrested and sentenced to be transported. With Bill gone, Molly now needs to defend herself from Bert. After hitting him with a pan, she is arrested and sent to Sydney. Bill and Molly arrive with letters of introduction and compensation from Bert's father. Soon, they will be running the best inn in Parramatta with an endorsement from the governor.

ISBN 9780645441567   ISBN ebook 9781923097049

April 2024

I can't stop Tomorrow
Irish Famine 1840s to Avoca Beach, Australia

Escaping bigotry and prejudice in Ireland, the **O'Shane** family lives on a secluded farm on the west coast of Ireland. The potato blight soon decimates their farm. It's always darkest before dawn, and the two remaining girls cling to the hope of a new life. With the kindness of strangers, the eldest girls, **Clare** and **Kerry O'Shane**, head to their cousin, Sal Lockley, in Parramatta, Australia. A new, wonderful life awaits them both. **Shéamus Connor** is the annoying teenage boy who reluctantly draws Clare's affection. However, living in a convict town means ruffians abound.

John Moore is an angry and troubled Irishman, content to live alone on another secluded farm until he discovers Clare and two other lads need rescuing.

Can John protect her from the pain inflicted by an evil world?
Can Shéamus find his lost love who had fled?

ISBN: 9780645441598   ISBN ebook 9781923097056

October 2024

Madeline's Boy
England 1830s to New South Wales 1840

All is not straightforward when money and a title are involved.

Madeline Brougham is asked to care for her best friend's orphaned son when his life is in danger. **Christopher Downes** is the pawn between a greedy, unscrupulous uncle and his inheritance. Maddie must do everything she can to keep him safe, including moving halfway around the globe to take Chip to his guardian, Major Humphrey Downes, in the Australian Corps in Sydney. Humphrey's best friend, another soldier, **Major Tim Hinds**, meets Maddie, and with the support of these two men, a chase around the colony ensues. Will Maddie and Tim be able to find happiness together?

Can the three adults keep Chip safe until he's old enough to claim his inheritance?

ISBN: 9780645783308   ISBN ebook 9781923097094

Dec 2024

Jam or Marmalade for Tea
England 1820s to New South Wales 1825

Martha Hamilton is the eldest of four orphans struggling to survive on their own. She is caught stealing, tried, convicted and transported to Australia.

Guy Manning is a frustrated and injured redcoat soldier travelling to Sydney to take up a new assignment. He notices Martha trying to jump overboard and rescues her.

A convict ship is no place for romance, and she's far too young anyway, isn't she?

Can Guy save her and forge a life together for them? What connections does he have to save her siblings? And how does jam figure in their future?

A NaNoWriMo 2023 book winner
Coming October 2025

A 100-year, six-part Australian Colonial series

The Lockleys of Parramatta
Hands upon the Anvil
A blacksmith's life and love are more than work
Parramatta 1830s

Eddie Lockley's parents were transported for their crimes. Can a steadfast lad rise above his origins and guide others to succeed in a land of opportunity?
Ten-year-old Eddie longs to help his mum and dad. Living in a convict town with his family, the keen youngster has been working with the local blacksmith since his sixth birthday. But when a lieutenant doesn't stop abusing his older brother, the young boy yearns for the day when he can stand up and end the torment. Though he's thrilled when his mentor offers to send him off to learn his letters, Eddie fears he won't be around to watch his sibling's back. But as he takes on the biggest adventure of his life, the brave believer soon discovers God is looking out for everyone he loves. Does this young man in the making have what it takes to change everything for the better?
ISBN 9780994578235 Ebook ISBN 978-0-9945782-5-9 Hardcover 9798496177368
Released 2021
https://amazon.com/dp/0994578237 https://amazon.com/dp/B08TB51L19

Out Where The Brolgas Dance
Gold is found, and so is love
Parramatta 1840s
How can a question change so many people?

It's the 1840s, and discoveries across the Blue Mountains continue. Major Mitchell's new road is complete, and towns are planned and being built. Abundant land is available for those who want it.
William "Wills" Lockley, 18, has laid a solid foundation for a respectable career as a blacksmith, but the Lockley lust for adventure flows deeply within his veins. He dreads the monotony of work at the blacksmith's forge and yearns for adventure in a new frontier. Wills meets six Englishmen (*Coping with what is now known as PTSD*) who have the means to make his dreams come true. What they discover changes the Colony and their lives forever. Gold fever ensues. In the West, Wills has to deal with an uncertain romance. Does she even want him?
ISBN 9780994578242 Ebook ISBN 978-0-9945782-6-6 Hardcover ISBN 9798755445504
LP ISBN 9781923097155
Released 2021
https://amazon.com/dp/0994578245   https://amazon.com/dp/B08T6NS3XX

Diamonds in the Dirt
Diamonds, love and money… but there is much more to life.
Parramatta 1850s

Luke Lockley, the youngest Lockley son, has completed University, and his life has no direction. No job, no money, and no love. Desperately alone, he prays for guidance. How can Luke trust that God has a plan for him if he can't even find a job? He does the only thing he can … he prays. Within a week, life has changed … oh, how it has changed as his brother Wills turns up with a suggestion. Would Luke be interested in joining the expedition with John Evans? **Reverend William Clarke** needs assistance on a Government Mineral Survey. The challenge, adventure and finds are life-changing for many. However, it gives Luke meaning, purpose and direction. The condition of his heart problems also takes a turn. Can he walk away?
ISBN:9780994578273 Ebook ISBN: 978-0-9945782-8-0 Hard cover ISBN 979-8788011141
Released 2022
https://amazon.com/dp/099457827X   https://amazon.com/dp/B09NH1MLXZ

The Earl's Shadow
Who or what is the 'shadow'? How does it affect so many?
<u>Parramatta 1860s</u>

Charles Lockley is the Earl of Coxheath and spends his youth as a convict in Parramatta; he had no idea he was an Earl. He had minimal education and few social skills. His eldest son, **Charlie,** is no different.

Now faced with his own mortality, Charles has to work out how to live the remainder of his life after a near-death experience. He is called to step way out of his comfort zone in London. His action will change the world for many. The echoes from the past still haunt Charlie. London is calling the family, and they can't postpone the trip. How does the Cobb and Co. coach driver **Jim Leslie** fit in? And precisely what is *'The Earl's Shadow'* that he speaks about? What happens if the 'Shadow' is gone?

<u>ISBN</u>: 9780645110708 Ebook <u>ISBN</u> 978-0-9945782-9-7
Released June 2022
https://amazon.com/dp/0645110701 https://amazon.com/dp/B0B158SKSK

Once a Jolly Swagman
An old black Billy Can contain the secrets of an incredible life
An Australian Historical Novel
Set in 1870s Parramatta and Kent, UK

Rick Lockley, battling his family's expectations, runs away to find himself. **Jack**, a jolly swagman, takes him under his care. Even after years together, Rick knows little about the old man.

On his death, Jack leaves Rick his precious billy can; the contents reveal Jack's identity. Stunned, Rick must travel to England to finalise Jack's wishes. There, he uncovers Jack's life of love, betrayal and a link to his own family. Rick also discovers there is much more to learn about this enigmatic man.

ISBN 9780645110753   Ebook ISBN 978-0-6451107-6-0
Released Sept 2022
https://amazon.com/dp/0645110752   https://amazon.com/dp/B0B5JN1WCV

Jonty's Journey
Gems, Love, Artists and a Golden Lion
<u>Australia and South Africa 1880-1902</u>

Sydney Jeweller, **Jonty** Evans' passion for gems takes him to Africa at a volatile time. He finds the diamonds he wants and gets given a lion cub. Jonty gets all but kidnapped. His experiences in the Transvaal plunge him into questioning everything he knows of life. Soon, nightmares haunt him. (*Now known as PTSD*).

On return home, he nearly messes up his love life with **Lottie** before it even starts, and he struggles to settle. Lottie's father, **Luke** Lockley from Parramatta, takes him in hand and points him to someone who can help.

Jonty is then recalled to Africa as a liaison and reconnects with his lion, Chimbu, when he saves the life of his security detail. His life journey introduces him to the most amazing Heidelberg artists, politicians, poets, rebels, and the scapegoat soldier Harry Breaker Morant. Can Jonty bury the past and regain the peace he's lost?

ISBN 9780645110777 HC ISBN 9781923097124   Ebook ISBN: 978-0-6451107-9-1
Released Feb 2023
https://amazon.com/dp/0645110779   https://amazon.com/dp/B0BLJ7ND1Q

Convict Shadows of the Past

Australian Colonial Trilogy
By Sheila Hunter
Co-Winner of 1999 NSW Senior Citizen of the Year, In the Year of the Senior Citizen

Mattie
Coming of Age in Convict Australia

Twelve-year-old London street urchin **Mattie Paul** is convicted of petty theft and sentenced to seven years of transportation to the penal colony of Port Jackson, NSW. Peg, another female convict, takes Mattie under her wing and gives her a chance to make something of her life by teaching her to read. Mattie seizes every opportunity that comes her way. Though life is not particularly kind to her, she battles through earning her freedom, marrying and becoming a mother in her homeland. On this journey, she encounters bushrangers, is widowed, and becomes an entrepreneur in the Bathurst goldfields. She mixes with escaped convicts, but her spirit is indomitable, and she becomes a pillar and much-loved treasure of her adopted community. Mattie may be a fictional character, but her experiences are only too real and invest us in immersing ourselves in the lives of those remarkable women who helped to make Australia what it is today. *(Mattie's story continues in The Lockleys of Parramatta - bk 2+)*

ISBN 9781503252370 & ebook AISN BOOTTEDBTO
(The Story continues in The Earl's Shadow)
Released 2015
https://amazon.com/dp/150325237X   https://amazon.com/dp/B00TTEDBT0

Ricky
A boy in Colonial Australia

Ricky English and his mother immigrated from England to join his father in the new Colony of Sydney. Upon arrival, there was no sign of his father. Ricky's mum uses the tiny amount of money they brought to get lodgings in a run-down building. Things go from bad to worse when his mother dies; he is thrown out of the rooms, and the caretakers confiscate all their possessions.

Ricky lives on the streets of Sydney Town as a street waif. Ricky finds safe places to sleep and befriends freed convicts who can help him survive. One day, he encounters a lost child and helps reunite her with her family. These people try to help him, but he insists on doing things his way because of his stubbornness. However, he has found a mentor and confidante. The story follows him through his life. He survives and turns his life around, helping others along the way.   **(The Story continues in Jonty's Journey)**

Paperback ISBN 9780994578211   Kindle ASIN: B00MLYN6IG
Released 2014
https://amazon.com/dp/1500770574   https://amazon.com/dp/B00MLYN6IG

The Heather to The Hawkesbury
Four Scottish families brave a new life in a strange land.

Mary Macdonald and husband **Murd** and family; her brother **Fergus** MacKenzie; sister-in-law **Caro** MacLeod; cousin **Alex** Fraser and all their families who have had to emigrate from the Isle of Skye during the "Clearances."

The story follows the four families from Scotland on the ship out to the NSW colony in the 1850s. Mary does not cope with the changes and losses that occur in the first months in the colony. The other women in the family rely on her, and she nearly crumbles. The families struggle together through accidents, losses, trials, floods, and hard work and forge a strong bond with their new country. Trials, tribulations and triumphs see the four families make a firm mark in their new homeland. The immigrants from Scotland helped make Australia what it is today.

ISBN 978994578228   ebook AISN B01A21JYWQ   Large Print ISBN1533473641
Available on Amazon/Kindle & Large Print
Released 2016
https://amazon.com/dp/1503251438   https://amazon.com/dp/B01A21JYWQ

Author Bio

Sheila Hunter and Sara Powter were a passionate mother-and-daughter team of amateur genealogists. While working together on their family tree, Sheila and Sara made many captivating discoveries. The greatest of these was finding four convicts, and these four had very different perspectives. They were sent to Australia from 1792 to 1814 during the height of Convict transportation. Before her *passing* in 2002, Sheila adapted some of these histories into enchanting stories, her Australian Colonial Trilogy. Sara later had these published. A fourth she left unfinished, and this inspired her to finish it. However, before she did, **The Lockleys of Parramatta** were created. The first two in the series were completed before she completed 'Dancing to Her Own Tune' for her mother.

Vividly living through the Colonial Era, these books delve further into the theme of overcoming adversity in Colonial Australia and how it developed, the demise of the Convict system and the discovery of mineral wealth.

Sara intricately weaves accurate archival data and a charming narrative to create a series of tales of faith, love, loss, and redemption.

And so, two hundred years after her family arrived in Australia, Sara continues the Australian Colonial stories started in **Lockleys of Parramatta,** followed by the **Unlikely Convict Ladies** Trilogy.

No More, My Love, The Vine Weaver, Scotch at The Rocks and **Waiting at the Sliprails** are stand-alone novels, and all are part of my *"Convict Stain Collection."*

More Historical Fiction books are to follow… as more are already in the editors' queue.

See her web page to keep up to date with more stories.
With an online store available for a signed copy of Sara's books.

www.sarapowter.com.au

(Australian Postage only)

Feel free to email me at

saragpowter@gmail.com

BOOK BUB https://partners.bookbub.com/authors/6273615/edit
FACEBOOK https://www.facebook.com/profile.php?id=100063887262514

Amazon Aus QR

FREE Newsletter signup

https://preview.mailerlite.io/preview/41388/sites/77987646202184961/wCAAcK

FREE Newsletter signup

https://preview.mailerlite.io/preview/41388/
sites/77987646202184961/wCAAcK